Heart's Desire

Heart's Desire

GWYNETH CRAVENS

ALFRED A. KNOPF

NEW YORK

1986

THIS IS A BORZOI BOOK
PUBLISHED BY ALFRED A. KNOPF, INC.

A portion of this novel appeared, in somewhat different form,
in *The New Yorker* magazine.

Library of Congress Cataloging-in-Publication Data
Cravens, Gwyneth.
Heart's desire.
I. Title.
PS3553.R278H4   1986   813'.54   85-45589
ISBN 0-394-55245-8

Manufactured in the United States of America
First Edition

To my mother and father,
Sylvia Bradbury Jones and Robert Francis Jones

Heart's Desire

1

Puffs of cloud coalesced out of nothing in the enormous sky and then evaporated. The wind made a lulling roar in the wing vents and occasionally rose to a gust which hit the car and the boat trailer, shaking the bars of sunlight on the knees of the women.

"Perfect and eternal, Judy, hon. Perfect and eternal." Effie Hammond was talking and driving. Her daughter, Nancy, sat next to her, and her daughter-in-law, Judy, and Judy's baby, Maura, were in the back seat. The Hammond men rode just ahead, in a pickup truck with a teardrop-shaped camper mounted on the back. They were speeding across a sagebrush plain toward the Paradiso range. "That's what our marriages are, and let me tell you," Effie said, waving a finger at the pickup, "we have everything to be thankful for." She peered into the rearview mirror. "The trailer is fine. The boat is *not* going to fall off. Tom Senior has explained about it to me many times. We're doing just great. Right, Nance?"

"It's taking ages to get to the dam, Mom," Nancy said. On her lap was some stationery and a wooden cigar box containing a poem she had begun about a green forest pool far from the ways of men where a redheaded boy was about to dive in. She rubbed a scab on her shin where she had cut herself shaving, and as each wooden telephone pole flew past, she clicked her teeth together to make the time go faster.

"What do you think, Judy, darlin'?" Effie said. "Aren't we doing great?"

"Mmm," Judy said. She wanted to be carried along like this forever, space and light and the pleasant, rounded-off rhythms of Effie's drawl—subdued by the padded, rose-colored upholstery—pouring around her, her child on her lap. Maura sucked on an empty bottle, her eyes almost closed, her bare toes gently moving. "It's great, really great."

"I am so very glad you love this, hon," Effie said.

Judy inhaled deeply. There was more oxygen here, but she still wasn't getting enough. The air, so sharp and dry that it hurt to breathe, so transparent that the mountains in all their creviced detail were magnified, was the air in which she had grown up, but she was no longer used to it. In New York, soot fell continuously, coating the window ledges and blackening the space between Maura's nose and lips. Darkness seemed always to be descending. Judy's eyelids dropped.

"We want to show you-all just the best time," Effie said. "You know, whenever we drive up here, we think so much of you and Tommy. You are going to enjoy yourselves so much. Judy, hon?"

Judy's eyes jerked open to the diamond-shaped highway signs, the purple sagebrush plumes, the white rectangle of the back of the camper. On either side of its screen door flowed the luminous gray-green plain. Above the door was stenciled TEARDROP next to a painting of a gray teardrop. The face of Tom Senior, her father-in-law, was a pale blur in the wing mirror of the pickup.

"It's going to rain," Nancy said.

"How dare you say such a thing!" Effie said.

"Mom, you can see the thunderhead already starting up behind Paradiso Baldy." This was a barren cone that thrust above the mountain range.

"That dinky thing? That's no thunderhead. And even if it does rain, we all brought thick books, and we can also talk. We're an intelligent family. Right, Judy?" Effie glanced over her shoulder, her chin firm and held high. Two deep curves, starting at the corners of her nostrils, framed her mouth. Her cheeks were plump and smooth, her forehead was broad and fair, and her lips were a bright, pleated crimson. She wore white-framed sunglasses studded with rhinestones. "Now, Judy, how are your folks doing in Spokane?"

"They like it fine," Judy said.

"I'm so happy to hear that. What exactly is your dad up to nowadays?"

"Well, he's at this place where they make missile parts. It's like what he was doing in Cibola." Judy didn't want to say that he had failed to qualify as a welder and was still in equipment maintenance. "It's a secret, I guess."

"What isn't? I used to try and try to get out of Tom what he was doing at the Labs—in the old days they would just go off in the desert for weeks and weeks. And one time, do you know what he told me? He told me they were building a submarine base out there. You just never know. For about three days, I believed him. Now, how's your sister—the one who was your matron of honor?"

"Oh, she's staying with my folks for a while." Judy tried another deep breath. It had been a year now, but the breakup was the first in the family, and Judy's mother still didn't want anyone to know. Effie would be understanding, though. "Her husband left her."

"Well, that certainly is a shame," Effie said. "And she has some kids? I seem to remember—"

"One," Judy said. "I think it's been really rough—"

"I am certain it is, darlin'. You need to have inner resources at a time like that. You know, I have truly adored letting my mind lie fallow this summer." Last night, Effie had tried to tell Tommy, her elder son, about that on the way home from the airport, but he had laughed and said that the word "fallow" implied cultivation, which he doubted applied in her case. "Retiring early was the smartest thing I ever did," Effie went on. "I miss being at the college, but we have wonderful plans for Thanksgiving and Christmas. Tom Senior just has to make sure all our finances are okay, and then we'll take the boat and head for Baja." She pointed at a lone, squat, turquoise-colored building next to the highway. "There's Freddie's, Judy. We always stop there on the way home." They would be sweaty and hungry after the hot drive down from the mountains, and Freddie's was air-conditioned and dim, with *ranchera* music playing. The waitresses, teetering on spike heels, their black hair swept up into monumental hairdos, always giggled when they saw Tom—they knew him from the old days, when he was on the project out in the desert—and immediately brought icy mugs of Coors and bowls of delicious green chile con carne. "One of life's greatest pleasures," Effie said. "Right, Nance? Can you give me some gum out of my purse, darlin'? What are you doing there?"

"Writing a letter."

"We're only going to be gone three days. Whoever to?"

"LaDonna—"

"I swear, you just saw her this morning," Effie said.

"—except that the car keeps jiggling."

"It's only the wind. It hits the boat broadside. Don't worry." Effie glanced into the rearview mirror and then returned her gaze to the camper ahead. Tom had better not get too far ahead. "Just look at that big, golden cloud over Paradiso Baldy! Isn't that like something you'd see in a movie about heaven?"

"The Indians believe that Paradiso Baldy is the center of the universe," Judy said. "But then they say Paradiso Baldy is everywhere."

"Is that a fact?" Effie said.

They passed a red-dirt track that cut through the sage and angled toward the foothills. "The road to Callosa," Judy said. "Now, that's beautiful country. I spent a whole summer up there once."

"You have people in Callosa?" Effie had never gotten Judy's family straight. Shortly after the wedding, her folks had picked up and moved to Washington State with the four kids who were still living at home, and Judy had not seen them in five years.

"No, in college I went to Callosa on this archaeology dig. No relatives for a change. I was on my own."

"We've been blessed as a family," Effie said. "We always have so dadgummed much fun. Everybody gets along, no divorces—"

"What about Tommy's divorce?" Nancy asked.

"Well, he was so young and the marriage was so short that it doesn't count," Effie said. "Anyway, he made up for it by marrying Judy right away."

"Strange," Judy said, staring off toward the rusty folds of the foothills, thickly dotted with juniper and piñon scrub. "I'd forgotten all about that dig." She had never wanted to leave: a whole life, absorbing and crowded, and then it vanished without her even noticing. And hadn't something happened there, something important?

"That Tommy!" Effie said, chewing her gum. "When I think of him crammed into the cab of that old pickup with Dad and Bud what with all the room we have here in the Fairlane." Her voice went into a higher, more vigorous register. "You know what he said? He said he didn't trust being in a car with me driving and hauling the boat, and so I said, 'Tommy, have you ever pulled a boat, honey?' I said, 'I realize you have a very advanced mind and all and you will have your doctorate soon and I know you are a New Yorker now, and you ponder on those cosmic philosophical thoughts, et cetera, but,' I said, 'just let me ask you one simple teeny question, which is whether you have ever actually pulled a boat.' The thing about Tommy is that he's the most fascinating person you could ever talk to, and I freely admit that even though he's my own flesh and blood, but you know what he said? Judy, hon?"

"Uh, no." Judy rested her chin on the seat back. Effie was in charge, and everything was going to turn out well.

"He said, 'Those of us who are eminently capable of thinking things out need not necessarily to have experienced them directly.' The philosopher! So I said, 'Dadgummit! You listen to me, Tommy Hammond *Junior*, your daddy taught me to drive when I was seventeen years old, and now he's taught me to pull this boat, and I have pulled it many times before, for your information, and I am doing the best job I know how.' Well."

"This is a very high altitude, isn't it?" Judy said, yawning. "It feels high. Much higher than Cibola. I'm as limp as a dishrag."

Effie modulated her voice into soft, urgent tones. "The thing with Tommy is that after he gets that doctorate, he's just got to do something important and challenging. With all those brains, he could be the next Averell Harriman. He writes the *best* letters. He wrote me how you-all go to these New York parties and he picks arguments with lawyers and always wins. He ought to consider law school. He could be a Supreme Court justice. Well, he'll make a fine philosophy professor, bless his heart. With all that empathy of his."

"Sometimes I'm afraid that people don't really appreciate how promising he is," Judy said. She was hazy about what parties Tommy meant. In the four years they had been in New York, hadn't they gone to just two dinner parties and some departmental kaffeeklatsches?

"No one was more brilliant at Cibola State," Effie said. "Those highfalutin professors in the East don't recognize quality. He *is* going to be a success. A great American. He's too big for any philosophy department."

"That's just it," Judy said. He would become a person of importance in the city, in the world. Trips on jets. A large, clean apartment with big windows, more light, her feet in a pair of new brown leather pumps resting on a Persian carpet.

"Tommy and I will have our special talk together like we do," Effie said. "This camping trip is going to be as fantastic as in the old days, and I know that for a fact because I bought tons of hamburger and hot dogs and potato chips and about a million cases of beer, and we've got marshmallows and Hersheys and graham crackers, and you can bet your bootees everyone has got to have a bunch of fun when they eat that kind of food. I just want to ask you one thing, Judy, hon. Do you think the East has done something to Tommy's brain? Calling green onions 'scallions' last night! My Lord."

They had gone straight from the airport to one of Effie's fried-chicken dinners, and when Tommy asked to be passed the scallions, her eyes became hard and dark. "They're green onions," she said with fury. "Excuse my nomenclature," Tommy replied, beating his chest with his fist. Everyone laughed but Effie.

"Well, that scallion business—that was just a mistake on his part," Judy said. He had had several drinks on the plane. "He didn't mean it. He was very tired."

. . .

The camper led the way up a winding road through the foothills. A hawk hung over a ravine. "The trailer's doing fine, right, Nancy?" Effie asked. "The boat is still there."

Nancy rolled down her window and leaned out into the wind, her mouth open. Her palate immediately dried up. "Yeah, Mom," she said. She resumed writing. All her A's were in the shape of deltas, and she was cultivating a back-slant so that people would think her penmanship was the work of a left-handed person.

"Maura is a good little traveler," Effie said. "All Hammond babies are good. Although Nancy was just this little red thing that cried nonstop from the word go, and I said to the doctor, 'While I am on this table you can just go right ahead and tie my tubes. Two accidents is plenty for me.' Bud and then Nancy, you know. I was so low. And all that spring the dust blew, and Nancy cried, and I was about at my wits' end. And to think how I *prayed* to get pregnant with Tommy! I'm just telling you, Judy, hon, so you know. Anyhow, while Maura is small, she's all yours—the diapers, et cetera—but when she gets old enough to make good conversation, I'll take her to Europe with me. On the tour this summer, I saw such wonderful things—I only wished I could share them with somebody. The changing of the guard at Buckingham Palace is the most thrilling thing you ever saw. And in the hotels they give you these samples of jam and cheese. I brought back a whole purseful so everybody could have a taste. Now you know what it means to have your firstborn. It's like you never feel truly okay without your firstborn. Tommy and I went everywhere, all through the war, when Tom Senior was transferred around the country. We saw a lot of hotel rooms together, Tommy and me, and sometimes there were no rooms, and we'd have to bunk together on a couch in the lobby. And right from the start he was the most stimulating company. When he was back home after his—when he moved back home and he was sleeping on the fold-out couch, bless his heart, what a mess he kept the living room in!—when he was back with us, he'd come home at three in the morning all wound up from I don't know what and he'd drag me out of bed and we'd sit at the kitchen table, and he'd have his brandy or whatever and start telling me, oh, I don't know, the most brilliant things. About form and content. Knowledge and being. That stuff. How the purpose of human life is that we're here to gather data. We'd just talk and talk in the most exciting way. I miss that."

"Well, that certainly is one of his best qualities," Judy said. "I feel truly privileged to be his wife, plus he takes such good care of Maura and me." Around Effie, Judy always found herself talking in this way. She was already more contented than she had been in a long time. In New York, she knew almost no one. "Your hair looks great, Effie. We commented on it when we were getting off the plane. We like the bouffant idea on you." Effie's hair was golden with frosted streaks, and today it was shiny and stiff with hair spray, which gave off a strong perfume.

Dear LaDonna,
Now we're out of town about halfway towards San
Ysidro dam which is where we're camping. Big deal.
I am so bored. But I started this great new book which
Judy gave me called *The City and the Stars* by Arthur
C. Clarke about how this city is all in the mind of
this computer a billion years in the future. Really neat.
So what are you doing. Are you going to go to the
Lotaburger this afternoon as usual just to by the way run
into MR. REUBEN L. SWAPP???? Just kidding, sorry
Mrs. Swapp ooops!!! I really like babies or my niece anyway, Maura. You have to see her, she is so cute, sweet,
etc., very smart. Only one and a half and she already
talks a lot. Please excuse handwriting as the car is
jiggling in a ridiculorum way. I am going to let my hair
grow real long like Judy's. She says she wants to go to
the Lotaburger with us and see if it's still the same.
It's OK because she's really neat and all. I plan to write
poems on this trip, go into solitude and meditate in
Nature, also watch for UFOs.
                    Everyone knew her as
                              "NANCY"

They were now on the forested flank of a high plateau above the
dam. The scaly columns of ponderosa pines and the blue triangles
of fir and spruce marched away on both sides of the road for as
far as Nancy could see. The forest floor was carpeted with
bronze; the air, cool and electrified, shimmered around the glossy
crowns of the trees. My forest, she said to herself. Home at last.
This had to be her true home; the suburbs of Cibola were a
temporary mistake. She turned on the radio as a blare of saxo-
phones and guitars was dying away. "That was Tiny 'Tornado'
Montoya and the Knight Rockers," the disc jockey said. "And
this is *your* pal, Al Zamora, on this beautaceous Friday morning,
July the Fourth, nineteen hundred and sixty-nine."

The dam, only a few years old, had widened the San Ysidro River
into a big lake in the middle of a high desert interrupted here and
there by interlocking, striated buttes and rimmed to the north by
the upthrust of the Paradisos. The Hammonds rode in the boat
into a flooded canyon, past rough curves of red hills glazed by
silvery grama grass and scattered with juniper and piñon, pun-
gent in the heat, and an occasional lodgepole pine. The only
sound was the motor. The crisscross pattern of the ripples made
minute lenses that broke the light into yellow needles in the olive
depths.
    Nancy sat on a banquette next to Maura holding the child's
plump foot in one hand and the science fiction book in the other.
Far in the future, when the sun was weak and the earth was
mostly barren except for a few oases, mankind was so advanced
that, if you were in a room and wanted to leave, you only had
to think of a door and the city, attuned to your brain waves,
brought it into being. All of reality was created that way, and no
one knew it except for one boy . . .
    Maura, fascinated by what the vibrations of the motor did to
her voice, sang wordlessly to herself and waved a stuffed koala
bear. On the other banquettes, Effie, Bud, and Tommy were
hunched over, reading.
    Judy sat next to Tom Senior, who was piloting the boat, and

trailed her hand in the warm water. The bow notched precisely into the beginning of the pale green wake, which fed past the stern into the shiny expanse. Everything was huge here. Simple. Ideal. She had forgotten about that in the East, where the sky was always low, like an attic ceiling, and horizons were unavailable, and her body was always enclosed, and there were no distances toward which she could flee in an emergency. Today, she was small and free and light-headed. Beyond the purple angles and recesses of the Paradisos were more mountains, the high country, with aspen-covered slopes, cold rivers, hidden canyons. She could walk for five hundred miles straight without encountering any buildings or people: she had entered the distance that contained escape.

Effie put down her paperback, *Couples,* screwed up her eyes, and stuck her tongue out. "There is something they do in this book that I am not going to say what but it is extremely disgusting." Why was Judy wearing that little bathing suit? She was spilling out of it and didn't even seem to know. Tommy certainly didn't care for that kind of thing. Effie picked up her camera. If Judy saw a picture of herself like this, it would surely straighten her out. "Judy, darlin', don't you want to put on some kind of cover-up so you don't get burned?"

"In a while," Judy said. "The sun feels good."

"Tommy," Effie said, taking a picture of his profile, "we have to talk about the meaning of life. You know, life goals and all that good stuff."

"Mmm," Tommy said, turning a page. "Let's have an earnest colloquium. But I need more beer first."

"Would you like to take over for a while?" Tom Senior asked Judy. His voice was low and hoarse. "I'm getting tired." Biting on the stub of his cigar, he leaned forward, his forearms, thin and knotted and brown, resting on the wheel. He squinted straight ahead. His straw Stetson was pulled down on his forehead, his face in a blue mesh shadow. "It's easy."

Judy pressed her hand to her breastbone. "Me?" Her two-piece bathing suit, which she had borrowed from a neighbor in New York, made her feel overexposed and overweight. "Me drive? Tommy says my driving is a menace to society."

Tom Senior shrugged and threw the stub away. "I trust you."
They exchanged places and she took the wheel. "We'll go
slow," he said. "Keep it at about four thousand rpm." He reached
into the ice chest and brought out a sweating can of beer.

The wheel pulsed in her hands. She straightened her spine and
peered ahead. There were no obstacles—no boulders, no
drowned trees. Tommy really should have been the one to take
the wheel. She twisted around to say something, but he was
engrossed in a comic book about the Marines which belonged to
Bud. Hey, she wanted to say, here I am, driving this big, powerful
boat. Perimeters continually fell away; final ridges she thought
were dead ends turned into curves in the shoreline. She kept to
the center.

"You know what to do," Tom Senior said. "You know more
than you think."

She watched her hands and arms guiding the wheel. When she
moved it slightly, there was a lag before the boat would begin to
turn.

The river narrowed into a gorge with concave magenta rock
walls streaked with black. The engine made a hollow racket here.
The water had recently risen and then fallen, leaving half-sub-
merged bushes turning copper and gray, and muddy banks
flecked with mica where iridescent dragonflies hovered. She
heard the crisp pop and hiss of a second can of beer being opened.

"Do you feel it?" he asked her, his voice echoing.

"Feel what?"

"The illusion." He chuckled and tugged his hat down even
further, so that she could not even tell if there was a face under
it.

"The illusion?" she said, taking a quick look around. The
others remained bent over their books; Maura was asleep; the
white wake spread behind the boat; above the mountains, bellying
cumulus clouds piled up, their shadows racing across the surfaces
of the rocks and the water. Suddenly afraid that she might run
into a snag or a submerged boulder, she fixed her gaze ahead. "Is
it a hidden illusion? I don't get it. I'm very sorry." Judy and her
father-in-law seldom conversed directly, just the two of them.

"It's an illusion you have to feel," he said.

"Illusion, illusion," she murmured. The word was beginning to lose its meaning. She felt a ballooning pressure inside her head and swallowed. Illusion. The atoms of the sky and the water and the rocks and the people, all arranged into the illusion of this very second. What did he want her to feel? She became aware of her chest rising and falling, of the weight of her bones, the drapery of her flesh. She felt the presence of the other sun-heated bodies. They were all being carried smoothly along upriver: nothing but this moment had ever happened to them. "Let's see, we're in this boat, there's the sky, there's the water. Do you mean a mirage?" She looked along the edge of the water, where it met stone. There was no haze or warp in the air. "No, wait. You said it was a feeling." She swallowed again.

"In your middle ear," he said. "Don't you feel the pressure?"

"Oh, right. Are we climbing?"

"Yep. A lot. But the water keeps on looking flat. That's the illusion."

He swiveled in his seat and propped his bare feet up on the dashboard. They were blue-gray and swollen. Last night at the airport, he had worn huaraches and had walked very slowly. Effie explained to Tommy and Judy that this was just a little problem and that Tom Senior had to keep his feet elevated and take this wonderful new drug the doctor had prescribed, and watch his salt and liquor, and pretty soon the whole thing would be cleared up. Judy wanted to ask what caused the swelling, but Effie began to question Tommy about his dissertation.

When they approached their destination, the island where they picnicked every year, Tom Senior took the wheel again and brought the boat in close. They waded ashore carrying picnic things. The island was a flat sandstone outcropping, as smooth as flesh and veined with pink and maroon. It was scattered with boulders and a few trees and bushes. A crow cawed from the blackened skeleton of a pine that had been struck by lightning.

Tom Senior opened a deck chair and sat down with a beer. "Bud, set up," he said.

"Yes, sir," Bud said. He unfolded the other two chairs. He was long-bodied, with big hands and feet which moved independently, at angles, from the rest of him. He had a brush cut and a round, freckled face and round, heavy-lidded blue eyes. "Nancy has to help," he said. "Nancy, get on over here."

"Why don't you and Bud do some fishing, Dad?" Effie said. "Maura, would you like your granddaddy to show you the fish?"

"Later on, maybe," Tom Senior said.

"The bass are going to be lying real low when it gets hot, Dad," Bud said. "Maybe we should do a little fishing right now."

"I want to see my son," Tom Senior said. "Tommy, I mean."

"I am fully visible," Tommy said. He was stocky and broad-chested, shorter than Bud but taller than his father. He had wavy red hair and long sideburns, and he wore a new pair of Italian wraparound sunglasses, cutoff jeans, and an ironed and starched white shirt with the sleeves rolled up. He jerked a little black cigar out of a pack, lit it and hurled the match away, drew in a quick, audible breath, and, in a terse whistle, blew out a puff of smoke. "Perhaps a side view will help one familiarize oneself." He pivoted.

Effie handed Nancy a peach-colored bedspread with a worn satin border. "This old thing from our bed is all I could find," she said. "It's time for a new one. Chenille is what I want, white, only ten books of Green Stamps." Bud and Nancy stretched it between the dead pine and some driftwood to make a canopy. Its border vibrated in the breeze. Tommy, on his way to the ice chest, ducked underneath, caught the bedspread on his head, and stumbled. "Help! I've been blinded," he said, laughing and reeling as the canopy settled over him. "Save me!"

Judy, who was holding Maura, handed her to Nancy and helped Bud pull the canopy back into place. "Bud, I cannot get over how grown-up you've gotten," Judy said. Bud shrugged and blushed.

"You never say that to *me*," Tommy said.

"Mama gave us that spread for our twenty-fifth anniversary," Effie said to Tom Senior. "Remember, darlin'?"

"Nancy, I want you to find firewood," Bud said. "Don't bring me anything rotten or wet or green. We need tinder, which is up to a quarter inch in diameter, kindling, which is up to two inches in diameter, and any logs you can find. On the double."

Nancy ignored him. He was only showing off. She carried Maura around the island. Nancy liked to press her lips against Maura's temple; the baby's skin was pure and fair, her black, curly hair was soft, and her eyes were wide and studious. She stared at everything with the same attention. Everything was new. She had only landed on this planet recently. Someday, Nancy would have a child and a husband and they would live on Mars. Her husband would die in the test flight of a spaceship going to the outer planets. She would grow old, and become a feisty old woman honored as a pioneer in space. I knew this was my destiny from when I was very young, she would tell reporters. She had the power to see the future. "I have biplanar flammite eyes," she said to Maura, "and no one knows who I am."

Bud built a campfire and they roasted hot dogs. After lunch, Effie placed books, magazines, and a thermos of coffee next to a chair under the canopy and sat down. "Whoosh," she said. "It is so beautiful here, so picturesque. I brought *The Organization Man* —it's an important book, isn't it, Tommy? Don't you think I should read it?" He sat in the pink shade in a neighboring chair finishing off a can of beer. She gave him a secretive look, inclining her head and raising her eyebrows. "Dad, how about you and Bud going off and doing that fishing?"

"I'm too pooped to pop at the moment." Tom Senior opened a beer.

"That's okay, Pop." Tommy reached into the ice chest and brought out another beer. "We can sit and foment a serious political discussion. In New York, one never gets the opportunity to converse with someone with your, shall we say, utterly unique opinions."

"I'm ready to take you on anytime, son," Tom Senior said. "I will be happy to point out the error of your ways."

"Dad, this wonderful mountain air is going to really invigorate you and you will just love to get your hands on that fishing rod," Effie said.

"Come with me, Maura," Judy said, going down to the water. Five years ago, when she and Tommy were newlyweds and he still was in favor of the war in Vietnam, she had gotten into some big Friday-night arguments with him and Tom Senior. One time, she ran from the Hammonds' living room in tears, shouting that no child of hers would ever fight in a war. This had been shocking to the Hammonds. All Hammond men served.

Judy took Maura's hand and they waded in. The water was new to Maura, and at first she clung to her mother. She had only been walking a few months, and she still had the plump legs and protruding belly of a baby. Patting the surface, she called to the shadows under the net of light. "Come here, fish," she said softly. "Come here." The water lapped and sucked at the rock.

Judy watched Nancy climb unsteadily, a book in her hand, to the top of a boulder. She wore a green bathing suit, and around her waist was tied a yellow chiffon scarf. Its ends lifted in the breeze. Her legs and arms were long and white, her face was shiny, with mottled patches on her forehead and cheeks, and her hair was skinned back and tied into a thatch the color and texture of dried Johnson grass. She had a squarish face and torso, and her profile, with its straight nose and high slant of cheekbone, asserted an intent innocence: something within was already designing her adult beauty while she remained oblivious.

Judy wrapped Maura in a towel and put her on Tommy's lap. He kissed her cheek noisily. "This is Poppa's girl," he told his mother. Maura giggled. "Whom one loves more than life itself."

"Could you keep her out of the sun while I go swimming?" Judy asked him. "Please?"

"When is my eye not on her?" Tommy said. "Maura's a very special person. I think quite highly of her."

"Judy, I am thrilled you're going to have a swim," Effie said. "Take your time, and don't worry about Maura. You'll feel so relaxed. Dad and Bud will go fishing, and Tommy and I will stay here. We want to *talk*."

Tom Senior handed Judy a yellow life vest. "It's a rule I have," he said. "Nobody goes in the water without one."

"I'll help you with the straps, Judy," Bud said.

"She can manage just fine," Effie said.

Buoyed by the vest, Judy hung in the opaque jade water, arms and legs bent, suspended away from everything, safe, watching a dancing gleam on the surface an inch from her nose. She was at peace. For the first time since Maura's birth, she was by herself. She and Tommy had been cooped up too long, but she hadn't really registered that until the moment they stepped off the plane into the sudden expansion of light and air.

On the far shore, a pickup truck with a camper appeared. Several Indians got out. The older people seated themselves on logs facing the lake while the children played along the edge. Despite the heat, they were all heavily dressed. There was a man in a straw cowboy hat, a long-sleeved plaid shirt, jeans, and boots, and a woman in black ski pants and a sweater. An old woman wore a long dress patterned with big roses and her hair was lashed with yellow yarn into a figure-eight bun at the nape of her neck. A boy led around a dog on a leash. A little girl dandled a baby with feathery hair. Voices, nasal and halting and low, floated across the water.

Her eyes half closed, Judy allowed herself to bob and drift between the voices on the island and the voices on the shore, emptiness above, below, and all around her.

The archaeological site had been at the head of a canyon, above an Indian village. That summer after her freshman year of college was the first time Judy had been away from her family. She had also recovered at last from the loss of her high school boyfriend, who liked to race stolen cars across the mesa outside Cibola while shooting at jackrabbits with a .45; he had been ordered by a judge to enlist. In Callosa, she was completely free. She and the other students worked hard, first with picks and shovels, and then, as walls of mortared sandstone blocks began to emerge, with trowels and brushes. There was the monotonous ping of metal scraping hardpan and striking stone. Their faces were caked with red dust, and they tied bandannas around their brows to keep the sweat from stinging their eyes. At lunch, they splashed in the creek nearby. Judy would lie down and let the icy, shallow water rush over her face. When the day ended, they drove to a government

Indian school whose students were away for the summer. After dinner, she collapsed on her dormitory cot into a deep sleep. Some of the students had love affairs. She was afraid to do that, and anyway, she had a crush on the professor, a weather-beaten middle-aged man with two German shepherds and a hip flask. Everyone wanted to be like him—offhand, with an air of knowing more than he told, blunt, and able to converse casually with the Indians in the village in their tongue. They admitted him to some of their secret ceremonies. The older Indians, wearing sweet-smelling cottonwood wreathes on their heads when the sun grew too hot, came up to the site to sell their jewelry—silver inlaid with scrolling geometric designs in a substance made from melted-down 78 rpm records.

They were not the descendants of the people whose houses were being excavated—that race had abruptly abandoned its villages six hundred years earlier and disappeared. This particular nameless settlement, spread over a few acres near the stream, had been crisscrossed with string tied to stakes, and each student was assigned a section. Judy's measured about six feet by three feet. After a week or so of careful troweling and sifting, she found a few irregular turquoise and shell beads and a white pot with black geometric designs that had been ritually killed—a hole had been poked through the bottom. The professor, hinting that Judy was in for a surprise, instructed her to work very cautiously. The earth crumbled under her fingers as she went at it with a nutpick and a paintbrush. The sun burned through her shirt, her hamstrings ached, and her eyes grew dry from keeping them focused on one spot. When she stood up to take breaks, she remained in her section, absently scanning it.

She came across many potsherds, which she tossed in a pile to sort out later, and eventually, she touched a rounded object. At first she thought it must be an eroded lump of quartz, and then, as she brushed more dirt away, a pot. When she saw that it was porous bone, the parietal bone of a skull, she quickly pushed some dirt over it and went to the professor. He had warned the students that the Indians got upset whenever a burial was discovered. Judy whispered her secret to him. "Excellent," he said. He took her down by the stream, his German shepherds following. "Pay close attention now," he said. "Keep quiet. You get here as soon as it's daylight and go to work. When the others start showing up, put a tarp over the burial and work somewhere else the rest of the day." He took a pull from his flask, which was silver and stamped with Mexican morning glory designs. He offered her a drink. "Oh, no, I couldn't do that," she said, embarrassed.

They walked, and he drank. "You want to make yourself into a good anthropologist?" he said. "Want to do good fieldwork?"

"It's all I want," she said.

"Then observe at least one concrete thing every day."

The remainder of that summer term, Judy went alone every morning at dawn to the site. She tried to observe concrete things. It was chilly in the canyon at that hour, and the air held a concentrated sweetness—the exhalation of the trees and grass as the dew evaporated. The sky was streaked with orange and red, and the great wall of the Paradisos was still a dark, undifferentiated purplish brown. Every sound was crisp: the endless pouring of the creek over the rocks, the whisper of the brush against bone. The skull emerged, the delicate basket of the rib cage, the sturdy thigh and shin bones drawn up against it, the curved bones of the forearms and the wide pelvis, and as she softly swept the dust away and imagined the woman who had once connected and animated them, Judy felt her own slow breathing in and out, the reliable movements of her muscles, the growing light entering her brain. She was as happy as she had ever been.

Judy's toes scraped against a rock, and she found herself in the shallows near the far shore. She thought she heard someone calling. The old woman stood on a rock ledge that jutted over the water and sang. An iron cloud filled the sky behind her, compressing the spreading, hot gold of the sun down to the horizon. She was small and straight-spined, and she remained motionless, her arms at her sides, her fingers flexed. She wore high-topped sneakers. She crooned on. Judy pushed off from the rock. When she looked back, the woman was gone.

Judy heard the Indians' camper drive off. She swam to the shore and got out. The stone was warm under her feet. She climbed up to the ledge. Its red, pitted surface was scattered with white particles—grains of white cornmeal. She scooped up a pinch of the moist, fine stuff. Then she rubbed her hands together, and it scattered in the breeze. But some clung between her fingers, and her heart began beating in an odd way. The altitude. Taking her time, she swam back toward the island. The water seemed thick and difficult now. She thought about starting to observe one concrete thing every day; she had done it faithfully after the dig, until she met Tommy.

The Hammond family was backlit by the low sun, their long shadows merging on the rock except for Maura's; she moved in weary zigzags. Nancy sat cross-legged up on her rock. Tommy, holding a can of beer, one arm flung out in a debating posture, stood over his father, who lounged in his chair with his feet on the ice chest, his head to one side, his hand raised as if to ward off Tommy. Bud reclined on his side on a towel, his chin in his palm. Effie faced them, sitting regally, a book open in her lap, a scarf draped over her head and a big towel around her shoulders, its folds and those of her skirt and of the canopy above her head illuminated by a brassy yellow.

This tableau reminded Judy of a frieze of the gods on Mount Olympus in a Classics comic book that she had pored over as a child. A wave of happiness passed through her. What fantastic luck to have this husband, to have been taken in by this family! Tommy was a hero. And Judy was the hero's consort. He was destined to be great. "You have the profile for it," Effie liked to say. Sometimes while Tommy slept, Judy would gaze at him and feel afraid: she could lose him; he could be assassinated; another woman could grab him. She knew she was no genius, no knockout. Her thoughts and words were awkward compared with his, she came from a family that was always broke and troubled, and kept car parts in the front yard, and she was too dark, and her hips had grown heavy, and then she had gotten pregnant and slowed down Tommy's destiny a bit. But the Hammonds were nice to her anyway. Everything was right about them: Bud and Nancy were wholesome and well behaved, Tom Senior was the quiet, solid foundation of the family, and Effie was all femininity and goodwill. She always knew just what to do and how to make everyone feel composed, attractive, and brilliant. Judy hoped one day to improve herself enough to become like her—pretty, bubbly, positive, slender, able to age without wrinkling. After Judy was around Effie for a while, the world became reliably wonderful: the roasted hot dogs, the blackened pine skeleton, even the smoky campfire were all transformed into delights.

The clouds behind the Paradisos began to harden into thunderheads with steely undersides and golden, curved tops; their shadows darkened the bare, broken-off summit of Paradiso Baldy and turned the mountains violet. Judy did not want to come out of the warm water or to leave this sacred place. In a few days, she and Tommy would be returning to their narrow, poor life in the East. Winter would come. She wanted to linger on this shore forever.

Nancy looked up from her book and saw Judy coming toward the island with one arm raised, the yellow life jacket dangling by a strap from her hand. The sun momentarily caught the sheen of water on her big breasts and long torso and on her wide hips and strong thighs and gave the black ropy strands of her wet hair a chestnut halo. She was beautiful and mysterious, as if she had just stepped out of another dimension where people were perfect.

Nancy had been studying Judy since she got off the plane. When Nancy was little, Judy had been just one more adult in the living room on Friday nights talking about the same dull things as the others. But now she possessed secret information that Nancy needed to know. What that was, Nancy could not precisely say, but she was sure about it. She wanted to have Judy's small, oval-shaped hands and her full mouth with the tiny chip in her front tooth and her black eyebrows like bird wings. Actually, she wanted to be Judy—soft-spoken, happily married, and tranquil. Lately something had started restlessly pushing at Nancy from within; it made her do things like hit Bud and argue with her mother and, when no one was home, take off all her clothes in front of her bedroom mirror and cover her body with talcum powder and dance. Her mother said Nancy was losing her sweet nature, but Nancy said she didn't care.

Putting a hand on Nancy's rock, Judy pulled herself up, and with an absentminded grin, stared at the life jacket as if she couldn't remember what it was or why she had it. "Did you see the Indians over there?"

"No."

"I found white cornmeal on that rock sticking out over the water."

"They must have dropped it," Nancy said.

"No, they scattered it on purpose. An offering. It means this place is sacred."

"I think that, too," Nancy said. "I mean Nature in general, because—"

"Judy, hon," Effie called. "You have a fabulous memory. Who said, 'I am the captain of my fate, I am the master of my soul'?"

"A poet, I think—" Judy began.

"I couldn't remember. I want Tommy to find that poem. Did you-all have just a wonderful swim?"

"It was a wonderful swim," Judy said. "The best swim I ever had in my life."

"Well, I am having the best time I ever had in my life," Effie said. "It says in this article here that when you reach my age, your breasts are supposed to fall, but mine haven't done that yet."

"Moth-*er!*" Nancy said.

Judy lay on her back on the rock, straightened her legs, raised her feet in the air and lowered them. "Tommy says I'm too flabby," she said. "Ever since Maura was born, I've been seven pounds overweight." She raised her feet again.

"You look fine to me," Nancy said. "Listen, I love this book, Judy. I want to read it real slow so I don't use it up before the trip is over. I actually am a pretty fast reader. I tested the highest in my class. And I have the best vocabulary score. All I've been *doing* this summer is reading, and this is the first good book. It is so boring in Cibola, you can't believe it."

"Yeah, I was bored, too." Judy rolled onto her side and stiffly lifted her leg.

"Well, you couldn't have been as flat-out bored as LaDonna and me. When Mom was in Europe, one day we dyed our eyebrows with green food coloring and walked up to the Lotaburger and had three Cokes apiece and nobody even noticed."

"My girlfriend and I would get so bored that we used to go to the arroyo near our house and sit in the sand all day with a magnet picking up magnetite," Judy said. "By the time school started, we had this big can full of iron filings."

"What did you do with it?"

"Nothing. There's nothing you can do with magnetite except pick it up with a magnet. And one summer we built a bomb shelter in the arroyo, and we would go there and read science fiction—"

"Judy, let me ask you something. Do you think when people are born they automatically know that they're humans, or do some people know for sure and other people are only guessing how to do it? And another thing. Do you think the future already exists and we just have to get to it, or does it—"

"Judy, hon," Effie called. "I do believe Maura's diaper needs to be checked."

Judy sat up. "I never think about the future, Nance," she said. "But I used to think about it all the time. Now I'm in it, if you know what I mean." She climbed down the rock.

Nancy followed her. She wanted to discuss another kind of future, the kind which rose in a luminous vapor from the pages of *The City and the Stars*. "Judy, let me get you a Coke," she said, going to the ice chest.

"What about *my* civil rights?" Tom Senior was saying. "And what is it these kids want, anyway? Why do they want to break all the laws? How can they charge at the police with sticks and rocks and then whine about police brutality?"

"Now, wait a goddamn minute, Dad!" Tommy said. He put his beer can between his knees while he lit a little cigar. "You fail to understand the subtleties of the issue. You're just mired in rhetoric and outmoded patriotic clichés." He spoke rapidly and adamantly, breathing hard.

"Big deal," Nancy murmured to Judy. When she was small and Tommy was in high school, he and her father would not have much to say to each other for a long time and then suddenly they would have a battle. Her father got red in the face and started pacing around, and Tommy, who was on the school debate team, laughed and used big words to make him even more furious. It didn't mean anything—it was just something they did. But Judy, looking through a zippered bag for a clean diaper, frowned.

"Why do these kids think they know everything?" Tom Senior slowly lowered his feet and slid them into his huaraches. "Why do they think they can design their own damn curriculum? When I went to Texas Tech after the war—after proudly serving my country, I might add—we sure as hell did not design the engineering program." He pushed himself out of his chair, adjusted his trunks, and went over to the burned-out campfire and scuffed dirt over the embers, raising a plume of white ash. "Oh, who the hell cares?" he muttered. Treading carefully, he made his way down to the water and walked along the edge.

"Dad forms opinions like instantaneous geological formations," Tommy said. "Right, Mom?" Judy gave him a kiss on the forehead and rubbed his neck.

Someday Nancy would have a husband she loved deeply, and she would do that for him. "It's not right to fight here," she said. "And we need to be nice to Dad. Mom?"

"I don't believe I've ever seen prettier clouds," Effie said, smiling. "Although there was a similar heavenly light the day we were in Venice."

"Now she's going to tell us about Europe again," Bud said from his towel. He pressed his face against the rock and groaned.

"The thing about you that I have always cherished with the utmost in admiration, Mom, is that you're smart enough not to argue with Dad," Tommy said. He bounced on his heels. "I'm not kidding. I really admire your horse sense. You know how to manage him, how to make him feel good." He tilted his head back and drained the can of beer. "And you go along in your cheerful way and all you want is to keep everybody happy. I think that's outstanding."

"Why, thank you, darlin'. And I've always admired your sensitivity to others." She dropped her voice. "That pep talk you gave Bud about really hitting his books in summer school and trying to get into college—I've been after him about that, but he really listened to you 'cause it was a man-to-man thing."

Nancy waited for them to talk about her, too, but they started discussing courses her mother might take.

Judy pulled up a chair, spread a diaper on her lap, and called to Maura, who came weaving toward her gnawing on a raw hot dog. "How did you get so much sun, sweetheart? Tommy, did you watch her?"

"Of course, Dum-dum."

"But she was out in it just now."

"The rays are weak—it doesn't matter. The closer the sun gets to the horizon, the longer its rays. Scientific fact. It's the short rays that burn. Ergo, Maura is not burned." He drew sharply on his little cigar and exhaled with a forceful puff, grinning at Effie.

Judy pressed her fingertips against Maura's forearm and white circles appeared.

"Uh-oh," Nancy said. "She did get burned."

"A little, I guess," Judy said softly.

"I'll find that special cream of Mom's for her, okay, Judy? Is it in your bag, Mom?"

"Don't bother, Nancy, darlin'," Effie said. "That's going to turn into a lovely tan like Judy's, 'cause she and Maura have the same type complexion. I swear, Judy, you're out in the sun for five minutes and your skin instantly goes a lovely *mocha*. And here I have to sit with my snoods and scarves and skirts and long sleeves so I don't just shrivel up."

Nancy watched Judy examine her arms and then wrap them around Maura. "Here's your Coke, Judy. There's ice in it."

"Thanks, Nance. That swim wore me out." Judy picked up a women's magazine.

"Anything interesting?" Nancy asked, standing next to Judy's chair and running her fingers through Maura's damp curls. Nancy did not know where to put herself. All the deck chairs were taken except her father's and he would be back soon. She waited for Judy to tell her something.

"Dr. Spock says here that it's okay if your sixteen-month-old still wants a bottle," Judy said. "I was wondering about that."

"Don't worry, sweetie," Tommy said, taking his sunglasses off and twirling them. "Everyone knows you're a good mother. She is, Mom. Every morning, six o'clock, Judy's up stirring goo for Maura on the stove." He pantomimed this, wrinkling his forehead, sticking out his lips, and concentrating with crossed eyes on an imaginary pot and spoon.

Judy laughed, holding her hand in front of her mouth.

"I know it, Tommy, darlin'," Effie said. "Judy is so considerate. Where did you get those movie-star sunglasses?"

"He bought them at a fancy department store," Judy said.

"Now, don't start criticizing," Tommy said to her.

"Criticizing?" Judy, surprised, placed her palm on her breastbone. "How?"

"My eyes have always been very photosensitive—you know that, Mom," Tommy said. "So when you sent the plane tickets, I got these. It's dangerous to wear poor-quality sunglasses."

"I'm glad you got them, Tommy," Judy said. "Really. I mean, they look real nice."

"Yeah," Nancy said. Tommy talked about different types of sunglasses and did an imitation of the fussy salesman at the eyewear counter. The way adults went effortlessly, levelly on with their lives confounded Nancy. They were so self-contained, so satisfied. They took everything for granted. They did not speak the truth, and they assumed that was fine, even though they were always ordering *you* to tell the truth. And yet adults had certain knowledge she lacked: they knew what to do with themselves every second; they never fell into the gaps between the minutes. They never were afraid of getting permanently lost in those holes. It was a secret agreement they had, a membrane that securely enclosed them. She sighed and combed the ends of her hair with her fingers. Life, her life, as it was really meant to be lived, would surely begin soon and she would spread her arms wide and step forward and join in with all the others.

Tom Senior had walked around the island, and now he was back. His legs were an inflamed pink. "Hi," he said curtly to

Judy. He glanced over her shoulder. "What are you reading? Dr. Spock! They still have him writing for them? He should be in prison. He's the biggest dope of all—telling boys to dodge the draft. Good God Almighty!"

"I do believe I'd like to go back to the camper soon, Daddy, darlin'," Effie said. "I'd love to look at my Europe pictures some more."

"God, Mom, you brought them camping?" Tommy asked. "How many shoe boxes full?"

"I limited myself to one solitary box, hon. England."

Nancy watched her father stare at the ground and pull on his lower lip. "Next time, we'll do the hike again, Daddy," she said. "When your feet are okay."

Last year, he had led her up an old Indian trail cut into the side of the canyon. They rested on a boulder near the top, and he pointed out the forest on the opposite rim, the evergreens glistening like the tops of waves. He explained how the purplish-black slashes on Paradiso Baldy were lava flows and how the energy under the earth that had come out through the volcano was the energy that went back to the beginning of the universe, when a big bang had started everything going, including the energy in her. She examined her hands, which seemed to be tingling with that energy, and felt such elation at being alone with him—when they went camping, he usually spent most of his time with Bud —that she didn't pay much attention to what he was saying; her mind was on the journey they would make one day through the endless forest.

"Dad, remember how you told me all that stuff about the universe, and the energy and all?"

He nodded, his eye on Tommy, who was whispering with Effie as she quickly folded up the deck chairs. "I guess so, sweetheart," he said.

"Well, what is energy?"

"What? Ask your mother."

During the trip back to the camper, Nancy gazed into the umber water; in its depths were vertical striations of plum and brown. She had read about a lake somewhere, Tibet maybe, where you looked in and a vision of the future appeared. All she could see here, along the side, were shreds of reflections racing toward the stern, where the blades of the motor constantly sent up foam and folded the water over the images.

After dinner on the card table in front of the camper, Effie pinched her husband's elbow. "Let's us go for a ride in the boat," she whispered.

"Well, round everybody up," he said.

"I mean just us, darlin'. Have you ever seen a more beautiful sunset in all your life?" The disk of the sun, dropping behind the mesas, sent shafts of peach, rose, and yellow through the clear blue sky to a towering cumulus in the east. She thought of going up a stairway into a palace with vaulted halls and melting spires and arches. In the north, the clouds had melded into a single enormous thunderhead, its black underside concealing the top of Paradiso Baldy. The full moon, well up, had begun to shine and the water was a vacant, silky pink. "Let's go way out in the middle."

"It'll be night by the time we get there," he said. Picking up a can of beer, he headed toward the shore. His steps were deliberate. "I got a goddamn sunburn on top of the swelling," he said.

She followed, forcing her pace to match his. "You'll feel so much better out on the water, Dad. I know it."

"Can I come?" Bud called.

"No fair," Nancy said. "If Bud comes, I get to come, too. Only he has to help with the dishes first."

"Judy and I will take care of the dishes," Tommy said.

"This is just your daddy and me, kids," Effie said. "We're going to have a *date.*"

Effie liked to sit in the back of the boat near the engine and feel the tug of its power, but tonight she stayed next to her husband. He pulled the starter cord several times and swore. Finally the engine coughed and caught. As they swerved out into the lake, leaving a broad scallop of white, she watched as Nancy and Judy cleared the table and Tommy and Bud, their shirts off, walked away in opposite directions. It was evident to her, even from this distance, how different the two boys were. Bud seemed to be holding on to his baby fat. When Tommy was Bud's age and working as a lifeguard at the country club, he had been a Greek god—perfect build, even proportions, a finely molded face with a straight nose and a full mouth. He just took your breath away. And all that thick, wavy hair that she still had trouble keeping her hands out of. He had been a National Merit Scholar and had won a medal from the Junior Chamber of Commerce. That year may have been his pinnacle. Now there was something tired and slack about him. His face was losing its taut, handsome lines. The marriage, the baby, grad school—he was having a rough time. But carrying on, he said, bearing up, pushing ahead.

"Everything is going to turn out fine," Effie said as the figures on the shore dwindled and the expanse of water widened and became a deeper pink. "We've done the best job we could with those kids. But maybe, honey, you'll have a little talk with Tommy. I think he could use a boost."

"About what? You can't tell that kid a damned thing. He's the big expert."

"Well . . ." she began. "Well . . ." She stopped. "You know, Tom, darlin', I was talking to Bud, and there's a special new type of fantastic trailer that would be just about the most wonderful thing we could ever get. Fourteen feet long, all the extras, bathroom, shower. A gigantic water tank. We could do a trade-in with the camper and the pickup. I'm thinking of Baja at Christmas now. We could even take a baby Christmas tree with us, you know, and we'd be there on the beach, and we wouldn't have to worry about the water because we'd have our own supply—"

Tom cut the engine. "Effie, let's just look at the sunset," His voice was flat and guarded. He had been using that tone with her a lot lately.

They drifted.

"Honey, you always know everything. Why does the boat keep moving even though you shut the motor off?"

"Momentum," he said. "Actually, inertia."

She waited for him to explain further, but he said nothing. The thought for today in *Positive Wisdom*, the booklet she received every week from Positive Christianity Central in Oklahoma City, was "I am showered with God's blessings." The sky and the water were incandescent now. "I do believe that you can't tell where the water ends and the sky begins," she said. "This trip has turned out to be so much fun, hasn't it, hon? We're all having such a good time. Tommy home, all of us together. We have so much to be thankful for."

Tom Senior brought out a cigar and lit it and rested his feet on a banquette. A breeze darkened the surface of the water. They floated in silence.

I am truly blessed, Effie said to herself, gazing around.

Tom chuckled. "Effie, what in hell are you smiling at?" he asked. "There's no one here, for God's sake."

Nancy took the binoculars from their hook on the bathroom door of the camper and went to the berth above the banquette at the rear where her father lay under a blanket, his hands folded on his chest. She kissed his cheek. He was very tired. "You didn't shave today," she said. "That makes it a real vacation."

"A Benny shaved is a Benny urned," he said. It was the punch line of an involved joke he liked to tell. He had two other favorites, one ending with the line "Halt, boy-foot bear with teak of Chan!" and the other with "Hare today, goon tomorrow."

"Good night, Daddy."

He took her hand and squeezed it hard. "Be careful out there."

"Oh, Daddy! I'm just putting my cot a little ways away from the camper is all. Is everything okay? How are your feet?"

"Fine, fine. Good night, please."

She dragged an aluminum folding cot and a bedroll away from the oval of light shed by the camper, set up her bed, and lay down on her back with the binoculars. There was a valley of transparent black between two banks of cloud. The stars came toward her, as if she were lying under a fruit-laden tree. The mountains formed a serrated silhouette. The cool, dry wind brushed her face. She located Jupiter and tried to find its moons, but all she saw was

a single point of light which, because of the slight trembling of
her hand, made a figure eight over and over. She put the binoculars down and caught a glimpse of a rapidly moving spark a few
degrees below the hot blue point of Sirius. She sat up and tracked
it. It was only a satellite. She lay down again, stretching under
the ectoplasmic arm of the Milky Way, and waited. Some of the
stars had planets, and some of those had intelligent life, and if they
tried to contact her, she would be ready, face up. We have come
for you, they would say. You are one of us, your mind is bigger
than you know; it was necessary for you to forget so that you
could endure your stay among human beings. She sensed the
quietly beating energy of her body, the powdery earth, the lap-
ping of the water, the starry space, and she fell into a deep, vast
sleep.

Every hour or so during the night, Tom Senior climbed down
and made his way to the bathroom. Each time, Judy woke up and
then curled herself against Tommy's warm back to find again the
way into sleep. Their bed was where the table was during the
daytime. It made her dreams strange: they seemed to belong to
someone else. There was a crack of thunder and then Nancy
came in with her bedding and lay on the floor next to Maura.
Judy heard Tom Senior stumble over Nancy and softly swear.
She listened to the rain and to Effie's delicate, even snoring; Effie
could sleep through anything.

Judy thought about how terrible it was to age and get ailments.
Tom Senior couldn't be much more than fifty. He had never had
any problems before. Judy pressed her cheek against Tommy's
shoulder blade and touched his ribs to feel his continuing breath.
Could he ever become old and ill? It was not possible. He was so
precious to her. They would age serenely together, and watch
Maura grow up, and have more kids, and by the time they were
in their fifties, they would be like Effie and Tom Senior—youthful in their outlook, busy, happy. And Effie and Tom would
probably still be just about the way they were now. . . .

Judy dozed. She opened a door in the kitchen of her new

white-and-pink house and started down to the basement. Something was decomposing down there. In fact, the basement itself was decomposing. She rushed outside. A scream filled her body and then contracted and rolled into her throat, where it locked into the web of tightening muscles and woke her up.

2

I remember everything very well. I remember the day we took Tommy to the airport. I went early in the morning to Sonia's and got my hair done, and came back and dolled myself up in my best fiesta dress, the yellow with the silver rickrack, and put on about a gallon of Chanel No. 5. I always loved going to the airport so much. You feel connected there, you feel in touch with the important part of the world, the places where things really happen. Cities where people rush along crowded sidewalks and through millions of glass revolving doors into tall buildings, and glamorous women bring their little poodle dogs along when they go to ritzy beauty salons to have massages and manicures. Of course, there are all those effeminate, stuck-up men who talk too fast and think they know everything, and there's all the dirt, crime, Communism, and so on, but I don't mind any of that. The mark of an educated person is to be broad-minded.

Anyway, thanks to Judy, we were late getting to the airport, so Tommy and I ran ahead to the gate while everybody else lumped along behind, and I was so glad we had a chance to be alone for a minute, because I wanted to give him a huge last-minute booster shot of confidence. He needed that from time to time. When he came home after the Army, for instance, after we so hoped he would be a career officer—that LuAnn just did not work out in Germany as an officer's wife and it was a terrible trial for him, and he was disillusioned about public relations, which is what he did in the Army, and then sad about the divorce and all

—I basically had to give him the Life Talk. You know, where you say: This is my life and what I want is to take charge and go back to college and get that degree because my life won't be worth a plugged nickel without it, and I'll knock myself out to do my very best because that's what counts and everyone is pulling for me and there is nothing that would make my parents prouder, and the world is desperate for people of my caliber. Well, my advice and Tommy being back in the bosom of the family sleeping in the living room and working nights at the Ramada Inn and going to school and me typing his papers certainly worked, because he did just spectacularly and won all the good scholarships. He really needed to come home for a *transfusion* sometimes, and so when we were in the airport, I said, "Now, remember our special talk, darlin'. The fireside chat."

Up at the dam, after the others had gone to bed, Tommy and I sat in the dark and drank coffee and Kahlúa, and we just *communed.* He had to have that. He had to talk and think, no matter what the hour. Although I am not one to go around telling other people what they should do and only wanted to pour all my energy and willpower into Tommy, I was firm with him, and I said in no way whatsoever was I about to criticize anything he was doing, and in no way was he a disappointment, but as he was now getting a little old to be considered "promising," he had to make the big push and not just hope to slide by on his sheer charm and gift of gab, as wonderful as all that was, that this was graduate school now, and I knew all about that. Six years ago I did my master's in counseling. And so now in the airport I told him, "You get yourself back to New York in one piece, and you use that time without family"—I was keeping Judy and Maura with me for a week, to help him out—"and you get yourself up every morning at the crack of dawn and hit that typewriter first thing, and you shut your eyes and you say to yourself, 'Dadgummit, I can write this dissertation, the Lord is helping me to write this dissertation, I see myself accomplishing and achieving this task with His blessing.' And you will have nothing to interrupt you or distract you, and you will practically be finished by the time Judy and Maura come back, and Judy can just type the thing up for you and that will be *that.* You are going to make the plane, we have six minutes. I know she will do everything in her power to help you, 'cause I'm sure she must love you, and I'll have a talk with her so she really understands that what with all the competition you require a slam-bang type of dissertation, one you can publish, *you will publish,* and make us all so proud, and once you do that you can start truly earning a living and put these days of being broke behind you, and there is nothing stopping you from doing the world's best possible masterpiece, and with your empathy you can be greater than those Bertrand Russells and all of them. Right, Tommy, hon?"

We went into the new departure area where they have all these murals of the mountains and Indians and so forth, and one whole wall is glass so you can see the runway, and there was Tommy's plane, and people climbing up the stairway to it, and seeing that always made me catch my breath. Sometimes Tom and I came to the lounge here for a drink just to watch the planes. Tommy told me how glad he was I had said all that. He said, "I feel so turned on about it now, Mom. I had a great idea, I mean a once-in-a-millennium idea, up at the dam, which I will write you a letter about, and I'm restructuring the whole concept. Those bastards at the department are so prejudiced against original concepts, so touchy about anything that threatens their way of thinking, but I am going to show them."

I told him, "You just say to yourself, 'I am the very best, I am the very best. I am destined for greatness.' And hon, you can't expect that people are going to understand your unique talents right off the bat. When they criticize you, you have to tell yourself that you are absolutely special." We had to stop because we had run smack into the glass wall.

The others finally caught up. Judy was carrying Maura and poking along with Tom Senior, who was barely moving in those old loose huaraches he insisted on wearing. Tommy put out his little cigar in one of those urns filled with sand and he gave his big smile—the best set of teeth in the family, perfect and white and not a single filling—and he said, "This is my last one, everybody. I hereby quit."

Then Nancy had to pipe up with "You said that before we went up to the dam. I remember. That morning, you said, 'I hereby—' "

Tommy got a bit huffy then. He said, "That is a female thing, always reminding one—"

Nancy's eyes filled with tears, and I quickly said, "I just love it when Tommy makes one of his dramatic announcements." I raised my hand over his hair. I wanted to put my fingers in it— he'd stopped using hair oil; I guess everybody had except Tom —but I was worried that Tommy might not like that. When you have a grown son that you have held and changed and cuddled and now you're only allowed to shake his hand, it feels very funny.

Now, here's why it was always interesting to be around Tommy. He made goodbyes more than goodbyes. An average person would have chitchatted away until it was time to get on the plane, but Tommy lifted up his arms and made fists and said that forthwith he was going to place himself on a strict physical-fitness regimen. Well, I was so thrilled I clapped my hands. He'd always been devoted to keeping in shape—he used to be on the high school swim team, and when he came home from the Army he joined a gym, but when I saw him this time at the dam in his swimming trunks, it was obvious that he'd let himself go. He said, "It's essential to buy a set of weights. Hemingway always got himself into fighting condition when he was working on a novel. That's what I'll do."

Judy, who'd been pretty quiet, said "Weights?" in a kind of surprised way. "Can we afford them?" Then she lifted her eyebrows nervously and smiled at me, probably because the other night at the backyard barbecue we had, Tommy had told her that he wasn't correcting her or anything and so she shouldn't get offended but that she had better be careful about her nagging and try to be more like me. It had come out that she hadn't had a new pair of shoes since the wedding and was keeping the soles on her flats with adhesive tape because they couldn't afford to have them repaired, and the tape fell off when she was playing Ping-Pong instead of keeping an eye on Maura, who went in my bedroom and messed with my clock radio, so that it went off in the middle of the night. Tom was upset to think that any son of his could not buy his wife a pair of shoes but he didn't say anything except to me, later—the usual thing with him. And I told him that Judy didn't apply herself and if she did, she could earn the money for some shoes, and anyway Tom certainly knew the kids were strapped—that was why I sent them the plane tickets in the first place. Plus I hoped a visit from Tommy would get his father out of the dumps. There was no one more fun to be with than Tom when he was in a good mood—on Friday nights, for instance, when we went to the Crystal Birdcage Lounge—and I wanted him to go back to being that way, and I was sure I could ride out this gloom and doom he was in at the moment, but I thought Tommy could really cheer him up, or at least distract him with one of their famous debates. Argue, that boy loved to argue. He had this mysterious power. He could get everybody going at the same time, I mean I do not know how he did it—for instance, one minute he was talking about the fallacy of the marketplace at the Ping-Pong barbecue and the next minute Tom Senior was pacing around, burned up at me for no reason, which never happened, and Nancy was bawling and Bud was doing his sullen-teenager act, and even Judy got upset enough to speak up and say I forget what, and Tommy told me that, by the way, he had suffered horribly as a child, he was raised like one of the underprivileged, only scuffed sneakers to wear, and I said, "But Tommy, you scuffed them *unnecessarily!*" And he just laughed, which only made me mad, and I went in the house to my bedroom and started to write a rebuttal. He was probably the most incredible orator since William Jennings Bryan as far as getting people stirred up.

Judy kept smiling in that strange closemouthed way of hers and then she giggled and said, "Last year Tommy was going to study judo, and he enrolled at this place, and he bought this very special white shortie bathrobe they wear, and then he decided to try sculpture classes instead."

Tommy said to Judy, "That was last year, Dum-dum, when I had a lot on my mind." To me he said, "I'm sure Leonardo da Vinci never had to put up with this. Judy possesses many similarities to an elephant. One of them is that she never forgets. But God knows one loves her."

Well, we all cracked up. Judy put her hand over her mouth like she always did when she laughed. "We love her, Tommy, honey," I said. "And we're going to take good care of her and put her in a pretty little box with a bow around it and make sure nothing happens to her." Actually, one of my plans was to take her out to lunch and drive her around, because I do feel if you can get to know a person thoroughly, without prejudice—and I used to teach this to my civics classes and to the girls I advised when I was assistant dean of women—you find out they're basically like you, and what with Tommy around I had never really gotten to know her, but he had chosen her and so she had to have some fine qualities, and since she didn't talk much, it was not easy to figure out what they were, although she certainly floored me when Bud was doing a crossword puzzle and she knew that the Amazon was the largest river in the world, at least by volume. Tommy said it wasn't, and she said maybe he was right and that she had it all wrong, maybe the puzzle meant by length, and in that case, the longest river was the Nile, followed by the Amazon, the Missouri-Mississippi, the Yangtze, and the Ob. On the other hand—nothing against Judy—she couldn't even get Tommy up that morning. She kept coming out of the den, where they were sleeping on the new couch that folds out into a bed, and saying that he insisted on just a few more minutes of rest. Finally, an hour before takeoff, I lost my patience with her and went in and had Tommy on his feet in no time.

Judy held Maura up for Tommy to kiss and said, "Daddy is going bye-bye up in the airplane."

Tommy told Nancy, "Stay as sweet as you are. It's very womanly. You're about due for your first bottle of Chanel. For Christmas, I'm going to give you a makeup kit and teach you how to use it, and you'd better pluck your eyebrows where they grow together." That was a beautiful thing about Tommy: he had taste and standards. He didn't want his women to get fat, and he wanted us all to wear Chanel No. 5 and be feminine.

Nancy turned red, which was her way of handling just about

everything. Her hair was in her eyes and she was standing with her stomach and her chin sticking out. I said, "My Lord, at least stand up straight." Sometimes I wanted to just put my hands on her like you do on bread dough and go to work: pull her hair off her face, push in her gut, haul up her shoulders, straighten her clothing.

Tommy punched his brother on the shoulder. He said, "Try to stay awake, Buddy."

Bud said, "No way, man."

Tommy said, "Seriously, senior year is the best of all."

Bud hit Tommy above the elbow, that boy-thing of hitting each other all the time. Bud said, "Hey-hey-hey. Me and some friends, at homecoming, we're going to get all these old tires from the dump and take them up to Mount Goodnight and set them on fire, and everyone will think the volcano is going to erupt. A regular riot!"

I said, "Bud, please: 'Some friends and *I*.' "

"Fascinating," Nancy said through her teeth.

I said, "Nancy, that kind of smart-aleck behavior gets you nowhere. And you better remember in case you ever want to get married that honey catches more flies than vinegar." I said to Tommy, "You are happy and content and you have had a peaceful vacation, and you want to work like the dickens now."

" 'Let it not be forgot that for one brief shining moment, there was Camelot,' " Tommy sang.

I shook his hand while giving him a half embrace with my other arm, and I accidentally banged his upper thigh with my big wicker handbag. I said, "We have a handshake relationship."

Tommy lowered his voice and said to me, "Remember what I told you, Mom. Take the toughest courses you can. Read the hardest books. Challenge your mind." That made me feel so thrilled. I started thinking about how I would visit him in New York, and he could show me the campus and the philosophy department. At the campfire, he'd told me that the unexamined life is not worth living and that man is a thinking reed, or something to that effect. But best of all, he told me that no one would ever believe I was forty-nine—I looked ten years younger. He also confided in me that, while he loved Judy with all his heart and soul and every fiber of his being, sometimes when she asked him to take the garbage downstairs or to watch Maura when what he needed to do was think about his concepts, it was difficult to bear. That was when I decided to keep Judy with me for a week.

Everyone started to look a little droopy, after the race to the gate and all, so I wanted to get a cheerful mood going. I said to Maura, "Isn't this fun at the airport, hon?" She just stared at me. She was still a little mixed up about who I was. I said to Judy, "You know, hon," I said, "when Tommy went away to the Army, he had this big picture taken of himself. It was so handsome. You were really handsome then, Tommy. He gave us this huge gigantic picture. I guess he thought we would forget about him, huh, honey?"

He put his teeth together and made his lips tense—when he did that it always made him sound somewhat prissy—and he said, "I thought one might appreciate a visual memento of one's eldest, who is, after all, the scion of the family." He bounced from one foot to the other like a boxer.

Bud said, "Way to go, Tommy."

I said, "Your visit was too dadgummed short."

He said, "Well, *c'est la vie.*"

I said, "Please excuse me for saying it again, please excuse me for being the Mother, but I can't wait for you to finish up so you can come back here and bowl everyone over with your fancy New York credentials and get your career totally revved up."

He gave his ticket to the woman at the counter and winked at her and rubbed his hands together. He waved to us. He said, out of the side of his mouth, like a nightclub comedian, "Off to achieve and accomplish. When you see me again, please address me as Dr. Hammond. But when you'll see me again, one never knows."

Suddenly, Tom stepped forward and gave Tommy a quick hug.

I could almost not believe this. I had to look away and blink: I watched a little truck pulling a wobbly baggage trailer away from the airplane. I had not seen my husband embrace my eldest since he was twelve. Just after Nancy was born, Tom had disappeared for six and a half days. He left a note saying he loved this woman—she was horrible and fat, by the way—and had to be with her. Tommy became the little man of the house; he scrubbed the floors and babysat and kept me company while I tried to think what to do. When Tom finally showed up, he hugged Tommy hard, and Tommy just stood there, his arms at his sides, his face white. Since that day, on rare occasions, like Tommy's graduations and weddings, they only gripped hands or clapped each other on the back.

Maura kept singing, "Bye-bye, bye-bye." Except for her, everyone was pretty near to being weepy, including Judy, who had Tommy all to herself ninety-nine percent of the time and would be with him again in a few days. Tommy was always able to make everyone feel tragic. Maybe it was his hair—it was exactly like President John F. Kennedy's.

On the way home, no one spoke. I was doing the driving because of Tom's feet. He had not been able to drive since we came back from the dam. I said, "This is hardly a funeral." Tom put his chin down and he looked very tired. I said, "Cheer up, darlin'—it's not like this is the last time we're ever going to see Tommy. I know he's going to do great. He's in the forefront of America's new generation. We can be real proud. He is going to finish that dissertation and get that doctorate and land a great job. I know it. He's going to wind up here. Meanwhile, we can visit him in New York."

Tom didn't say one word. He puffed his cigar so hard that the air inside of the car turned blue and I had to roll down the window even though the wind coming in messed up my hair. Now, I am a quiet person, never one to push, but I felt I had to speak up. I said, "If you would just break your vow never to go east of the Mississippi." He refused all plans to visit New York or Europe. He didn't like Easterners. He didn't like cities. He didn't like foreigners. He said all that, but he didn't really mean it. Same with his constant complaining about being worn out. He needed to think in a more positive manner, and then he would have felt a lot better. I said, "I have the most terrific, wonderful plan! Tonight, let's have us another big barbecue, with steaks and corn on the cob, and we'll play some more Ping-Pong on your wonderful table." Tom had built the table before the kids came. "That table is the greatest Ping-Pong table in the world. Won't that be fun? Kids?"

Bud said he'd get to work on the backyard.

Judy said, "I love the way Tom Senior broils steak."

Tom rolled his window down and then rolled it up.

I said, "You hear that, Dad? Judy said she loves the way you broil that steak. Mmm."

He said something soft like "Thank you kindly, Judy."

Nancy said, "What does 'saila-vee' mean?"

"It's a boating term you wouldn't know beans about," Bud said. "Right, Judy?"

Judy said, "It's French for 'That's life.' "

I said, "Why, I didn't know you knew French, Judy!" I wanted to keep the good mood going. I said to Tom, "Won't that be fun, darlin'? A nice barbecue? And how about a giant batch of ice-cold margaritas?"

Tom didn't answer. When we turned onto the freeway, he pointed at the sky, above the Cibola Peaks. He said, "There goes Tommy." His voice was hoarse, which meant he was getting another one of those summer colds he had trouble shaking.

3

I put Maura down for a nap. I remember feeling very alone afterward. The house was quiet: Effie, Nancy, and Bud were at the store, and Tom Senior was asleep on the couch in the den. I went outside to the patio, sat down at the end of the picnic table shaded by a cottonwood tree, and began to read a news magazine someone had left there. The cicadas made a late-afternoon whickering. Tom Senior's new little black cat from the animal shelter prowled around the legs of the Ping-Pong table and reared up to sniff at the metal barbecue, a sort of a kettle on a tripod. Bud, under Tom Senior's supervision, had weeded and raked and watered the dusty earth beyond the brick patio and mowed the patch of lawn by the tool shed; the moisture made the dry air sweet. Against a rear cinder-block wall, next to a pile of lumber covered with a tarp, was Tom's garden—rows of tomatoes, marigolds, cosmos, and hollyhocks—and a clothesline hung with a white bedsheet.

Beyond the cinder-block walls were other backyards enclosed by identical walls, and other houses identical to the Hammonds': flat-roofed boxes in bleached-out shades of pastel stucco with rounded corners to give the appearance of adobe. When I was growing up, on the edge of town, my family lived in the only frame house—it had once been the bunkhouse of Rancho de Cibola—and it had stuck up like a gawky sail in the sea of boxes. I'd always longed for a regular, new home like the ones my friends had, like the Hammonds'. Tommy had promised that if and when we moved back here—after he got his doctorate and was appointed head of the department at Cibola College—he would build a place up in the foothills with five bedrooms, servants' quarters, and stables. He'd even drawn some plans on notebook paper. But I would have been just as happy in a house like this one, in this neighborhood. Maura would have a yard to play in, I'd be able to drive to Piggly Wiggly for groceries, we'd go to the mountains on weekend camping trips, and there was always the Sagebrush Drive-in, and the new Monte Vista Shopping Plaza going up out on the mesa. And there was the Lotaburger —but when I went there with Nancy the other night, it was no longer the warm, familiar place smelling of hot grease where I used to meet my friends. It was a cube of glass and stainless steel and white plastic that people kept going in and out of, strangers, and I wondered how they could appear in the town I remembered and fill it up.

I put down the magazine, which had a cover photo of Allen Ginsberg in long hair and a full beard at a peace rally, his hands raised, the fingers parted into V signals. Four fighter jets in formation painted vapor trails high overhead and vanished just as their sonic booms shook the house and rattled the barbecue. I hoped that the jets would not crash into Tommy's plane. I hoped that there were no burglars with butcher knives waiting for him in the apartment. He was going to phone as soon as he got home. This was the first time I had ever really been separated from him, and everything I did and thought and felt was now covered with a cloudy film. When I was alone with Maura and he happened to come home late from the photo lab where he was working part-time, or he stopped for a beer with people from the department, I couldn't stand it. I tried to avoid going out without him whenever possible. Lately, when I woke up in the night, I found myself making sure he was still breathing.

Tom Senior came out of the house. In the gray shadow of the doorway, he looked for a second like Tommy's double. They resembled each other so much that I was worried that someday I'd come up behind my father-in-law and mistakenly put my arms around him. But Tommy had the handsomer profile—sometimes when he went past I thought of gods, kings, presidents—and Tom Senior's features were blunter and more rugged. His lips were not as finely shaped, the bridge of his nose was broader, and his expressions had none of Tommy's easy charm. His sharply focused eyes, his squint lines, and his thin, firm mouth gave him a directness and strength that made me shy.

"Hi," he said. "I didn't know you were out here." He kept his voice down, maybe because he knew Maura was napping. But then he usually spoke quietly to me, as if he wanted to be careful. He held a glass of translucent orange liquid with a maraschino cherry floating in it. "Would you care for a manhattan?"

"No, thanks, that's all right," I said. He was supposed to avoid alcohol.

"Ever had a manhattan?"

"Gosh, no. I don't think so."

"I'd be happy to make you one," he said. "You only live once."

"That's okay, really," I said. "But thank you very much."

"It would be very easy for me to make you one, and then you could say you'd had a manhattan in your lifetime." He waited. He had aged considerably in the years we had been away, but he had also become more interesting-looking, more defined.

"Well, okay," I said. "If it's not too much trouble."

"I'm making myself another one anyways." He finished his drink and shuffled away in his huaraches, and I tried to think of how to remind him not to drink. Effie kept saying that he hadn't relaxed enough to let the medication work; she was going to take matters into her own hands and watch his salt and liquor and get him and his poor feet back to normal.

Tommy and I were going to get everything back to normal, too, which was to say, to bliss. Walking, just the two of us, along the high dirt embankment that had been bulldozed up to block the river, we had worked out a perfect plan. It started when I told him how happy I was to be there and that I'd just realized how sad I'd been in New York. He said I hadn't been feeling sad in New York, I'd been feeling guilty about not pulling my weight.

I was surprised about that, but Tommy had a way of knowing things about me that I didn't know myself—I didn't have his sensitivity, and he often had to point out what I was doing to people, how I was not being appreciative enough, or sincerely interested in their problems. And he said that I had failed to help him to focus all his time and energy completely on the dissertation. He was right. I kept waiting for the day when we would be together, alone, without the terrible pressure he was under, without any interruptions, when he wouldn't have to study or go to school or to work and I wouldn't have to do anything and we could lie in an embrace and gaze into one another's eyes. There had never been time for that.

He explained to me that it was important to have life goals, to say: This is my life and here's what I'm going to do with it. He said that once he finished his dissertation and got a good job, we would have money, a big house, babysitters and a housekeeper, and he would be able to concentrate on what I should do. He said I would make a good nursery-school teacher. (I was flattered, although I secretly saw myself as an anthropologist, studying strange peoples. I didn't know if I had the ability to get a degree —I had always read a lot, but I never did very well in school. People with degrees had mastered something so difficult and mysterious that it seemed impossible that someone like me could ever reach a level like that.) But right now, he said, it was up to me to provide an atmosphere for him of complete calm and order and I had been feeling bad because I hadn't been doing that. As usual, it bothered me that I was doing something wrong and didn't even know it, but on the other hand, I was fortunate that I had a husband who loved me enough to help me with these things.

We made a plan. He would get up at six every morning and write the dissertation until nine-thirty, when he left for the photo lab. He would also write all day Saturdays at home while I took Maura to the playground or to museums, and he'd spend Sundays in the library and evenings reading and rewriting. By Christmas, if I did what was necessary, there would be a version for me to type. He was going to draft a notice that said "Highly Talented

Typist" for me to post in the laundromat near the campus to get more work. I would earn enough so that he could cut down on his hours at the photo lab. And I was going to keep the apartment scrubbed and neat, stay caught up with the laundry and the grocery shopping, and always have dinner ready when he came home. And I'd have to budget the weekly allowance he gave me so that he wouldn't be forced to go to the store on Saturdays, which he hated, because I'd run out of cash and he was the only one who could sign the checks. (On our first date, he told me that Hammond men didn't permit their women to get involved in finance and so his mother, who was smarter than his father but never let his father know it, turned over her endorsed paychecks and received an allowance. He said his parents were still as much in love as they had been on their wedding day. I'd been earning my way through college and had my own bank account, but I was relieved to surrender to the Hammond way of doing things.) I wanted to write this plan down, but Tommy said he could easily remember it.

I told him all I wanted in life was for him to be happy. If he was happy, then I would be happy. We walked along, Tommy kicking red clods into the green water, where they slowly dissolved, and I took his hand and kissed the backs of his fingers. I felt very loving toward him, more so than in a long time, since maybe before Maura's birth. We used to stay up late drinking wine and he would tell me his philosophical thoughts, but after I got pregnant, I kept dozing off, and then after Maura was born, I never got enough sleep. But now Tommy told me that he felt loving, too. I asked him if we could take a bedroll and sneak away from everyone that night. The two of us merging under the stars is what I had in mind. I said, "Just for a half an hour?" He said that it would look very untoward. At the far end of the dam, in the opposite wall of the canyon, was a dark oval. I thought it might be a cave, and I wanted to go see it. But as he turned to walk back, he said it was nothing, just a discoloration or a shadow, and, anyway, he was exhausted, and he wanted to have a nap and a beer and talk to his mother. On the way to the camper, he reminded me to help out with the chores and to remember to thank his parents for their hospitality. I think that was the night, at dinner, that he promised to buy me a new pair of shoes.

Tom Senior returned with our manhattans.

"Thank you so much," I said. "We're so grateful for your kind hospitality."

"Who's 'we'?" he said. "I don't see anyone else but the little guy." He snapped his fingers and the cat came to him. Sitting down across the table from me, he propped his feet up on a deck chair. His ankles as well as his feet were now swollen and smooth. They looked womanly. "Here's how." He lifted his glass and I lifted mine.

I had always imagined a manhattan as a cocktail sophisticated people in elegant dress would hold high while fox-trotting to the music of Glenn Miller. But this was cloying, and it had a bitter aftertaste. I wished Effie would come back soon and tell him not to drink. Besides, she'd help the conversation along. So far, I'd managed to avoid spending any time alone with Tom Senior, and I wasn't going to fall into an argument now by blurting out the wrong thing. I wanted to say something effortless and positive, to charge the atmosphere with enthusiasm the way Effie did.

Tom Senior was watching me. "Do you like it?"

"Oh, it's great, it's very different. Absolutely delicious. It tastes just great. But I thought you only drank bourbon and 7-Up, and a margarita once in a while."

"Yeah, that's all I drank for years. Now I like manhattans." He pulled a cigar from his shirt pocket, lit up, and tapped Allen Ginsberg's face with his knuckle. "Now, there's a real, genuine, honest-to-God phony." He laughed softly.

"Allen Ginsberg?" I wanted to be very cautious: this could be a trap. I'd run crying from the living room five years ago; now the war was much worse. I had piloted the boat so carefully up the river. He had trusted me. It now seemed to me that he and I had been alone in the boat. Illusion, he had said. "Yeah, I guess so," I said. "I guess he—"

"Allen Ginsberg is a real dyed-in-the-wool phony," he said,

leaning back. In the harsh sunlight, his expression collapsed, as if his original face had melted. "Yep, a one hundred percent phony."

"Yeah, I guess so, kind of," I said.

"No 'kind of.' He really is a phony. You know how I know? And I really do know."

"How is that?" I tried to sound pleasant.

"I know because I am a real, genuine phony, too."

I thought he was kidding. I smiled, but he remained grim. My face burned. I shifted in my chair. "Oh, that can't be—"

"Please, don't *you* start the Pollyanna stuff."

We were silent.

"I am a bigger phony than any Allen Ginsberg ever was," he said in a trembling voice.

I felt a faint pang, a beam of piercing light arriving from an enormous distance. "Oh, no," I said. "Oh, no, please, really." My voice went thin. "You're not a phony." I meant it. He had never struck me as pretending to be something he was not. He usually stayed in the background. I pushed out a laugh, hoping to take the conversation back into shallow waters.

"I've been a goddamn phony all my life."

I couldn't bear his face, so I watched his hands: they were broad, with thick fingers, and they shook. Until now, it had been such an ideal visit.

"I mean, I've led a phony life," he went on. "It's all been an act. Even the arguments with Tommy—as if I gave a goddamn. I've never done anything real. I wanted to be a painter or—I don't know—even a cartoonist. Nothing fancy. I had encouragement from my art teachers when I was a kid. Even won this contest. But my folks wanted me to be an engineer. Same old story. I started college, then everybody thought there was going to be a war, so I enlisted. Married Effie. There I was, flying a plane, and then Tommy came along. After the war, we weren't going to get by if I fiddled with painting. So I did what everyone else wanted and went to engineering school. Never did much care for my job. Now, when I think of the things I've helped to build at Cibola Labs—well, I could cry in my beer." He was silent for a while. He pinched his lower lip and tugged on it.

I rubbed my bare toe along the sand in the cracks between the bricks of the patio.

"Sometimes I don't even know what I'm doing here," he said. "After the war, after I was discharged, I was riding the train back to Cibola. But I got off one stop before, in Mesita. In those days it was nothing but a water tank, a windmill, a couple of cotton-woods. And then brush and sand in all directions until you reached the mountains. Effie was in Cibola, and she'd already picked out this place—this was all just vacant lots and the house hadn't been built yet. Anyways, I got off the train. The train left."

Another silence. I waited.

"I walked away from the tracks and out onto the mesa, and I just stood there," he said. "I can remember everything about that day—the sun, the shadows, the way they moved, the sound the breeze made, the smell of the sage and creosote, the birds. My own shadow. I was just one more thing on the mesa. Around dark, another train came. Someone came and got me, hauled me by the arm. Said, 'Here you go, sailor,' and put me on it. All the way to Cibola, I kept thinking: This is the truth, I've found the truth. But then I saw Effie, and she had Tommy along, and they'd been at the station all day, and I forgot the whole thing."

"What about the painting?" I asked. "Didn't you take a course at the college last year?"

"What? Oh, yeah. Did pretty good at it, if I do say so. The professor had some nice things to say—but they don't mean anything to me. Nothing does. There's no sense to anything. Now here I am, I'll never see fifty again, I feel like hell, and I'm a goddamn phony. Excuse my French, but I feel like someone else lived my goddamned life instead of *me*. I'm so goddamned mad at myself I could spit."

He threw his cigar into the barbecue and slowly got up and shuffled around the patio squeezing his hands together, his back to me. I held my drink against my forehead, rolling the glassy coolness against the skin. It was wrong for him to carry on like this. He was being a—a what? A bad sport. Where did Effie ever find her words? "Well, Dad," I said. "You're a wonderful, terrific artist. We think you're just great. We have your carving of that desert hawk right up over the mantel in our apartment. Tommy hung it from the ceiling with some fishline so it looks like it's flying. It's really nice. You really are great, you're a wonderful father, and you're really—"

He turned and made a cutting motion with the flat of his hand. "Bushwa," he said.

I flinched. I was getting confused. "No, really, it's true—"

"This patio, this yard, this house—they're all nothing. Can't you see that? The people in this house—nothing! In one second, everything could be gone. You go along thinking everything is a certain way, and in one instant, it all can change."

"Now that you're only working part-time, you could do more painting—" I began. I wanted to get his mind off this strange track. I wanted to help him, to talk to him about how to be a success. But I had no idea how someone became a painter or a cartoonist, an artist good enough to sell paintings or to get cartoons into the newspaper.

He sat down, kicked his shoes off, put his feet up, and lit a fresh cigar. "Too late. I've lived a phony life, Judy. I want you to know that I've lived a phony life. There's an invisible glue holding the world together, glueing everybody into set patterns while they prance around pretending they're in charge. You can be in the service or a student riot or a grad school and it's the same stupid thing. No one tells you to pay attention to your own life. You don't believe you're going to get old and die and that there's no prize at the end. No one talks about it. They talk about 'hope.' And then you're old. Do you understand what I mean? Probably not. How old are you? Twenty-four, twenty-five?"

I swallowed. I glanced at the doorway and listened for the slamming of car doors, but there was only silence. Tommy had told me to be helpful, and I should have gone shopping with Effie. "It's not too late!" I said. Even if it was, why was he telling me all this? Maybe he was drunk. "You're still young," I said.

"When I was your age, I thought I was going to live forever."

No one in the family had ever said anything like this before. It was Tommy who had planned to try to have a serious talk with his father—Tommy was always saying that was what he wanted —and yet the whole vacation, the two of them had never been alone.

Tom lowered his legs. They were still sunburned and peeling: the skin was shiny and taut over the shin bones. He bent over his feet, which were steel gray. The leather huarache straps had left deep imprints in his flesh. "Want to see my stuff?"

"Oh, yes," I said. "That would be really nice."

He stepped into his shoes and led me into his workroom off the patio; he had built it after converting the garage into a den. It was close in here and dark except for the rectangular glare from the single window. Everything was clean and orderly. He went over to some metal shelves where power tools were arranged along with jars of bolts, nails, and other hardware and pulled out several big, flat packages wrapped in black plastic. "I'll just take off the body bags," he said, chuckling. As he lifted them onto a trestle table, the vein under his earlobe bulged. For a second, he leaned forward, gripping the table, his eyes closed.

"Are you okay?"

He shrugged. He unwrapped the plastic to reveal a painting of the Cibola Peaks, lavender splayed with yellow slopes of aspen.

"Very nice. You did it?"

"A few years back," he said.

"It's just perfect." It resembled many paintings I'd seen in local restaurants and in art shows at the college.

"No," he said. "It's pretty poor. There's nothing real about it."

"Oh, don't say that," I exclaimed. Again, my voice sounded tinny in my ears.

The next painting was a swirl of deep reds and purples around an empty oval of indigo mingled with gray and black. I couldn't tell whether the colors were supposed to be emanating from the center or if they were being drawn into a deep whirlpool. It was a weird picture.

"I painted that one a while back—there was about three months when I couldn't sleep at all," he said. "Something would get me out of bed, night after night. Anyways, I gave up trying to sleep and came out here and started painting. I painted all night, night after night, and then I'd go to the Labs in the morning, and then after dinner I'd come out here and paint some more. That's when I did this one." He held up a canvas of a greatly enlarged and detailed cottonwood leaf, heart-shaped, the midrib and branching veins outlined with a pulsing, silvery white. "And this." An identical leaf, partially withered, half glowing, half dull brown. "And here's a sunset from when I was flying over the Gulf during the war. Best goddamn sunset I ever saw. I wake up sometimes with it in my mind." Another whirlpool, also empty in the center, with colors streaming outward in softly blurred concentric circles of gold, orange, red, and violet.

"These are very beautiful," I told him. "I like them."

"I thought you would," he said.

The colors vibrated in the dim room. I had no idea if the paintings were any good—that was for someone with taste, like Tommy, to judge. I only knew that I'd never seen anything similar before and yet they had an eerie familiarity. "Have you showed these—to anyone?"

"Nope. Here's the last one. Not finished. Haven't felt up to it lately." It was a nude, done in loose, soft brushstrokes. She was seated, her back turned, gazing over her shoulder, her skin coolly radiant, a detailed, straggling coil of brown hair at the base of her neck. Her face was not painted: a few pencil marks indicated a chin, jawline, nose, and a somber, staring eye. The mouth, slightly open, was tender.

"This is . . . ?" I thought he would say it was the model from the art class. He was silent. "Effie?" I asked, and immediately felt naughty. This woman was voluptuous, composed, and still.

He laughed with genuine pleasure and gave me an open glance. I realized that until this moment he'd always been making an effort. With me, with everyone. He dropped the black plastic over the painting. "That's not Effie, and don't ever mention it."

"She's beautiful," I mumbled. My face was hot. My upper lip was wet. The air in the room was thick.

"The damnedest thing—I can't remember her face. I remember everything else. I have dreams about her, but not about her face." He smiled at me, and a sheen came over his eyes. I busied myself wrapping up the paintings.

"Here we go," I said cheerfully. I helped him lift them and slide them back into their hiding place behind the shelves. "There!" I said. "There we are."

A jar of bolts skidded off a shelf and smashed on the concrete floor. I started to pick up the broken glass. "Don't bother about that," he said.

"No, I'll get a broom."

"I told you, *forget* it."

We went back out to the patio and sat down again. The leaves of the cottonwood gave off a sugary fragrance. The altitude made the air, lit by the slant of the late-afternoon sun, deep and alive and intelligent. The sky overhead was a clear gold, and the peaks, the foothills, and the houses were all swept by this brilliance, which washed the cinder-block walls with gold and dimpled the sheet on the clothesline with golden shadows like an angel's robe in an old holy painting. A lawn mower whirred next door. Muffled voices came from inside the house. A mild wind stirred the ashes in the barbecue, releasing the tarry odor of burned-out briquets.

The light touched Tom's heavy, lined features. The relief that he had shown a few minutes earlier was gone, and now his eyes, hollow and fixed, rested on me in a weary yet urgent way. I had the fleeting sensation that we had been transported here from a very distant place where we had been partners and were now compelled to communicate with each other using only the local language. He gave me the desperate grimace of a charades partner under the rule of silence.

Effie appeared, a basket of potato chips in one hand and a bowl of dip in the other. She was wearing a ruffled yellow blouse with a scoop neck, and her hair, newly lacquered, gleamed. "Dad, I have your favorite dip. It's sour cream blended with that dried onion soup, Judy, hon—you can make it for Tommy in one second. He just loves it. Can I refresh your drinks any? Manhattans! I tell you, Judy, you live with a man a million years and you think you know him inside and out, every single day you can count on the fact that he is going to have at least one bourbon and 7-Up, and all of a sudden he starts drinking manhattans and never has another bourbon and seven! So exciting! Well." She beamed. "Have you two been having a wonderful daughter-in-law–father-in-law talk?" Tom and I were silent. Laughing, she pulled up a chair and sat down. "After all this time, your husband suddenly starts drinking *manhattans*, takes up the *guitar*, adopts a *kittycat*. I swear! What's next, Dad?"

Tom Senior finished his drink and picked up a handful of potato chips.

Effie smiled at him. "Well, darlin'?"

"Nothing," he said.

4

Dear Judy,
This is the free time in typing class which means you
get to type anything you want so I am writting writing
you this letter. How are you? How is Tommy? How is
Maura? We miss you. How is the disertation going? Are
you taking Maura to the playground alot, when you're
not typing things, that is. Maybe I could be your assistant
(ha ha). We are fine. Mom is fine. Dad is fine. Bud is
fine. The cat is fine. I am fine. I am doing really great.
I am having a lot of fun at school. I guess that is all for
now so goodbye. I don't know what else to say so I will
tell you where I am.

Here is where I am. This room has no windows. They
built the new part of the school without windows in case
of nuclear attack. Isn't that great. It is more or less white
but with hand prints already on the walls. It has a ceiling
with squares and millions of little holes in them. There
are two blue doors both shut even tho it is very hot and
the fans arent working yet but the principal says they
will. There is the blackboard which is really greena dn
has today's assignment on it, Pages 43–58, All the A
Exercises. We never do the B or C Exercises and that
is fine with me. There is also a big yellow and red chart
which is a picture of a typewriter keyboard and your

supposed to look at that not at the keys. But you know
what, Judy. I am looking at the keys. The girl in front
of me is Ruthi Garcia who is very popular. She is sweet.
She always says hi to me in the halls, which is very nice
of her. She is wearing a bouffant which really sticks out
and a white blouse with the collar turned up and a full
red skirt that looks really nice. She always looks really
nice. I can see in her purse under her desk she has a can
of hairspray and maybe that is how she does it. I would
never think of bringing hairspray to school but it is a
neat idea. She goes with Orlando Ethelbaugh who is
a big track star. Well, thats about it for Ruthi.

Mom got the pictures back from the vacation and I look
so bad that I can't believe it. We had to put the boat
om tje bacluard becaise we wpm't be using it until we go
to Mexico in Dec. Except Mom is trying to get Daddy
to take us up to the dam one more weekend while the
weather is still nice. But football has started (ugh) so I
don't know what we will do. The weather has been very
hot hardly like fall. Guesw what? We might get this
trailer which has ten times more room than the good ole
camper. But it just depends because Daddy loves the
camper. It has been vey boring here. School started (ho
hum, big yawn, if you know what I mean.) I am taking
American History, English, Geometry II, Typing and
Steno, P.E., and Sociology. Bud is on the bowling team.
He wanted to be captain but he's not. Actually I never
speak to him because he thinks he is God's gift to the
universe just because he is now a senior (BIG DEAL)
and he has these stupid friends that usc a lot of swear
words, that is the sign of a weak mind if you ask me.
And he is always with these certain people who shall
remain nameless and they have to talk loud and say
things and I think they do other things which I will tell
you about sometime. But youhave to promise you won't
tell my mother. My mother made me take typing instead
of French like I wanted or Latin II because no matter

what you can always get a job if you have your typing
and shorthand. Shorthand is kind of neat because it looks
like Martian and you can write stuff really fast. I will put
some shorthand at the bottom of this letter so you can see
how good I am (brag,brag). I have so much studying 6to
do this year its a crying shame, geom. II especially, and
I never even figured out Geo. I, just made up the things
and I passed, who knows how. But already I am way
behind. So I have not read the Arthur C. Clarke books
you sent but thank you very much, I will read them
when we go to Mex. at Xmas. I like to have my birthday
presents early, this way I don't have to wait until March.
I don't mind if they are used at all, I like seeing your
maiden name in the front. My friend LaDonna does not
believe yhou should write an X in Xmas because it is
taking Christ out, but it doesn't matter to me as I am not
a Christian (don't tell my mother) but Pantheist, you
believe in Nature, which I think maybe you do or maybe
you are still Catholic?? My mother says you are not real
Catholic because you married Tommy and you only have
one kid. At the dam you remember I asked you if you
loved Nature, the sky, etc. and you said you certainly
did so I think you might be a panthest but you probably
wondered why I didn't say a word. I did not want to
talk about that as Bud was listening and once I told him
about my creed and he still makes fun of me even thou
gh you are not supposed to be prejudiced against any one
becauwe of race, color or creed. My friend LaDonna has
this big crush on this boy. Here is the thing about this
boy.

FACTS ABOUT REUBEN LEROY SWAPP

!. HE has red hair, green eyes that some times look
gray or even brown. He combs it straight back and he
has a widows peak, also freckles.

2. He is about as tall as me but very thin.

3. He wears his watch backwards on his wrist which is
really neat.

3a. He has little golden hairs on the backs of his hands.

4. He always sits in the rear of th e blass, he is in hstory with me and Ldonna. He never takes off his jacket, which says BYU on the back because that's where his brother used to go but he quit and then got drafted to Vietnam.

5. He doesn't talk very much and he never raises his hand in class.

6. He lives six and a half blocks from us, 2801 Herrera Drive South.

7. He is a sacker at Piggly Wiggly. He was in the Junior Rodeo once, barrel-racing.

8. I forget what else but LaDonna talks about him all the time and I have to hear, she evenpasses me notes in class about him. Which could get us both into real trouble of a deleterious nature. However, we do not use our real names. I don't think he loves LaDonna no matter how much she loves him, hje just ignores her or if she goes up to him and says something, like she says, "I vould beat you up if I wanted, I am veryu strong" he just looks disgustedly away. So you tell me Judy if you think he loves her. I am telling you that everythime she speaks to him he just looks disgustedly away. She is just so conceited you can't be;ieve it. I need to know your opinion on this. LaDonna just is so sure he does and she wants to give this Hallowween party and invite him and then uninvite all the other people so it's just him andher and she is going to say, I just don'g know what happened, maybe they got the date wrong. Can you BELIEVE that???? I can't!!!

How do you like this letter so far? Pretty neat, no? (Ahem) I prefer this type of letter to business letters because you have to put the address, etc on the letter then on the envelope. You have todo everything twice, I don't see why. It is very boring. Did you know I am a xanthocroid? Daddy has learned some new songs on his guitar. The one that sounds the best is the theme from

the Pink Panther which is his favorite movie anyway.
Mother says after he practices he couldget a job plaing
at a nightclub, so WHO KNOWS? OOOPPS Mistake
meep meep meep forgot to release the shift key. we saw
a movie today about Ft. Ticonderoga, ERPY Productions
and we call it that because frankly you just want to barf
it is so dumb. Reuben and the other boys inthe back of
the room made this ball out of tinfoil and they were
passing it around and biting on it. Very intelligent.
This girl Zoe Simms in Hiastory read my palm. I have a
very long life line but my love line is a mess!! This girl
(Zoe I mean) goes to this church and they believe
in reincarnation. There was tthios little girl who
remembered where she had lived and took the
peoplethere. If you love someone in this life, its because
you were married to them before or whatever. This
question interests me greatly and I would be interested
in what you think about it. I told her about how you
dreamed about the tablecloth before my mother sent it
to you and how you dreamed you were going to have
Maura before you got PG. Zoe said that meant you were
psychic. Are you psychic Judy? Do you know all about
that? If you tell me Iwould not tell a soul.

asdfasdfadfjkl;jkl;jkl;asdfjkl;asdfjkl;asdfjkl;

This letter is certainly getting very long! I like to write
letters actually. Good thing I don't have to turn it in
because it has to many mistakes and I would just literally
die if I did not get an A in typing, I mean how dumb
can you get? Do you think that everyone on the earth is
truly human or do you think it is possible aliens from
another falactic civilization could inhait human bodies? I
know this sounds like SF but it is on my mind b3cause
of a dream I had that these aliens in human form had
landed and were chasing me and I ran home and hid in
my mother's bedroom and they were there also. But they

looked exactly like people, you could only tell from
a feeling you would get which I can't describe (that
feeling) but it tasted like metal and was unbelievably
scary. And thenall the aliens were at Cibola Labs and
they were getting the bombs. I went to the mountains
to hide. I know it was just a dream and I think I saw
a movie like that at the drive-in when I was little but
anyway the next day I am telling you that everyone
seemed like an alien to me. Judy I feel very lonely
sometimes. I know you know what I mean because you
said when you were my age you felt that too even
though you had three sisters. With me I think it is
because I was born idfferent from everyone else and there
is no one but you I can tell about this to, it is so weird.
Please don't think I am insane. Maybe I am. There is
absolutely no one to talk to in this place, I'm not kidding.
All people want to talk about is the cheerleaders, who's
going out for homecoming queen, clothes, who is with
what boy, who went all the way, all of that crap (ezcusa
my FRench), and we'll be walking down the hall and
LaDonna is talking about Reuvben L. Swapp that boy
I told you about and I am saying LET ME OUT OF
HERE!!!! IT IS pure D h--- for me. My mother says
Ishould just be real sweet, friendly etc. and join a bunch
of clubs, that'swhat Tommyu did and look at Bud on the
bowling team. Well, I just feel like crying. Because no
wonder Tommy was so great in high school, just look
at him. He is a genius. And Bud just goes along with
everybody. That boy does not have a mind of his own.
But just because he's a boy and a senior to boot he thinks
he can get away with literal murder. He doesn't dp tjhe
dosjes wotj ,e amu,pre. O jave tp dp tje wjp;e lotcjem
,use;f. amd je kist (ignore booboo) He doesn't do the
dishes with me anymore, I have to do the whole kitchen
myself, and he just gets smart about it and Mom thinks
its cute!! Daddy was going to speak to him about keeping
the car out late and then just got tired and went and alid

down. It made me so mad, I can't even be at LaDonna's down the street for five minutes without getting yelled at. I think he even smokes MJ if you kjnow what I mean by that. At the beginning of the summer you know how that blouse you gave me was too big? Well not it fits just perfectly and looks good on me if I do say so myself (boy is that Nancy Hammond stuck up and conceited is what you must be thinking). My mother got me a blue sweater and a yellow plaid skirt with blue lines in it for school. I am not insane about it but its okay. We were spupposed to go to a movie Sat. nite to see James Bond and then we didn't because my father said he didn't feel like it. So Bud gets the car, what else? I am so depressed you wouldn't believe it. Reasons: 1. I don't have a boyfriend. 2. I don't even know a single boy who doesn'tgross me out, I mean they are so stupid in this so-called school. 3. I could just lie down and die.

asdfasdfasdfjkl;jkl;jkl;asdfjkl;asdfjklk

The group I like best now is Crosby, Stills, Nash & Young. What do you think of them? Do you get them on the radio in NY? You know what, this letter is so dumb I am not going to send it.

5

Dear Tommy, Judy, and Maura,
Your last letter was so magnificent that I had to show it
to Dean Easterling when I went over to the college for
the freshman women's orientation luncheon at the dorm
which he so very kindly invited me to as I am now
emerita—I mean it was a real masterpiece and also witty
& creative as usual. — His son Goren from your class in
high school has just gotten tenure and his dissertation is
going to be published by the U. of Michigan Press and
his other son has started an architecture firm in Chicago.
They had those little tiny corn muffins and you can eat
a couple hundred of them before you know it, and as an
appetizer *pomegranate juice!*— I am enclosing the menu.
It made me so pleased to see all the fine young women,
some of them just off the ranch but smart as a whip you
can be sure and so eager to learn and get acquainted—
I got my hair fixed in a new way at Sonia's, the beehive
concept, but Tom said it looked too much like Madame
La Pompadour so it's back to the drawing board—I am
giving serious thought to what you told me when we
were watching *Peyton Place*, that hairdo of Dorothy
Malone's.— Bud and I are trying to talk Dad into buying
this new kind of outboard motor, a Bearcat, absolutely
the finest, more horsepower, and we told him that we
need a Bearcat desperately, Nancy needs a Bearcat,

Maura needs a Bearcat, and if we don't get a Bearcat there is no way life can go on—so keep that in mind when you write home, because I know your father would be thrilled not to have to spend ten minutes starting the motor every time he wants to take the boat out and then it chugs for two seconds and dies on him and he gets so furious. — The weather has been beautiful and warm and we are planning to drive up to San Ysidro, one final trip with the camper plus a detour up into the national forest to see the aspen turning, which has got to be one of the most beautiful sights God has given us to witness on this earth, and it always makes your father feel so good—and on the way back we will stop for green chile con carne and Coors on tap at Freddie's and think of you. — Then when we come back we're going to clean up the camper until it gleams and try to do some kind of trade-in, probably involving this fantastic 14-ft. trailer so that on your next visit you won't have to sleep on the kitchen table because there will be real berths for everyone. And then I am getting a professional manicure and that is *it* for outdoor living for a while.

Bud and Dad have had the College Talk, and Bud will apply to Cibola College in the spring—it was really empathic of you to write him that letter about trying for Harvard, but with those gentleman's C's, and all the talks I had to have with the principal, Cibola is going to be great for Bud, it's what Dad wants, although I don't know what he's going to do about the military obligation and it would be a shame if he had to interrupt his studies. Next year we will have to have the Secretarial School Talk with Nancy, which is a two-year course and then she can get a job at the Labs and help pay Bud's way— and then the year after that the Kittycat School Talk with the little guy, which Dad still hasn't named. Here is something we can't get over—Dad joined a *classical* record club and now he listens to that disaster music all the time. He is absolutely doing great, mad at the Pres., mad at the Republicans, mad at the Democrats, mad at the governor, and I am trying to talk him into driving to California next summer, pulling our new trailer and the boat with the Bearcat—I see no reason why the boat trailer can't be hooked up to the trailer trailer. He says we better see Calif. before the N. Vietnamese capture it.

Friday night we are going to take Bud to dinner at La Posada for his birthday—sure wish you could be with us for La Atmospherea, and we will definitely toast you and send you all our love. We are giving him swim fins and a snorkeling mask for Baja at Christmas. He is really flourishing and will be teaching a swimming class on Saturdays to the Cub Scouts in the spring and also wants Dad to teach him whittling.

Nancy is just *blooming,* she loves her teachers and everything she's taking—has made a lot of friends and I think this year she is going to be in the popular crowd. With that attitude of hers, she didn't want to make the effort to fit in—but I told her that if she wanted to have more friends she would have to *be* a friend, start being more outgoing, not just say whatever smart thing she thinks, stop reading that horror space junk and start to read the sports page if she wants to talk to boys, and get involved in things like the homecoming float. I still remember when you kept having to run to the super-market to buy more boxes of tissues to stuff in the chicken wire—in fact, I think I still have your crown up in the closet in case you need it. (Joke.)

Here are some books I just bought at the bookstore opening sale at our proud new Monte Vista Shopping Plaza—*The Age of Reason. Early Greek Philosophy. The Philosophical Dictionary. The Queen's Paramour,* which is a wonderful historical novel about Queen Elizabeth which gives you a real *feel* for the times and has lots of useful information so that when I go to read *The Age of Reason* I will already have a certain amount of background.

Now I have to fix dinner. Hamburger is the most

wonderful thing in the world—one night you have
hamburgers, then the next night you have sloppy joes,
and then the next night chili, and then the next night
meat loaf. —We are all so happy and healthy and busy —
things could not be better. Anyway, we send you love
and we know you are all doing so beautifully in your
wonderful apartment (doesn't Tommy do an amazing job
of scrubbing, Judy? He likes to keep it a secret, but he
also knows how to wax floors) — and New York in the
fall must be the most inspiring fantastic place for you to
achieve every possible success in every way, and let each
moment be rich and full for you.— We are so proud.
Hi to Maura & Judy.—

Love you,
Mom-Effie

6

Early in the morning, when the radiator began to clank and hiss, my night self, knowing its time was up, tried to exert a force on my waking life. My dreams took on weight and solidity. The shadowy diagonal plane leaning over me became a dark-haired, passionate man, a figure who often appeared to me and then slid away just as we were about to make love. I shot through winding canyons with porous sandstone slabs pocked with black openings and across sage plains, the little purple flowers rising toward me, magnified. Tommy and I sat in Effie's kitchen. She was putting dishes away and telling us in her even, cheerful voice about how Tom Senior had died. I was stricken. I spread my fingers on the gray-and-white Formica of the table. When did he die? October, Effie said. She was nicely dressed, and she moved efficiently around in high heels, as if she had just come home from someplace special. She chattered on, describing symptoms and treatments, and I saw his skin turning gray.

The medical facts she gave were so specific that I was sure I could find them in a reference book, but they shriveled in the band of light that was forcing open my eyelids, and I was left with Tom's gray face and Effie sliding a plate into a cupboard and smiling. I lay there next to Tommy looking at the soft panels of shadow on the low, slanted ceiling and the dull bar of overcast sky between the curtains. The air was humid and cold. The grinding of heavy machinery began, followed by the rattle of bricks and other debris tumbling down a wooden chute: some tenements at the end of the block were being torn down. Was there any reason to think Tom Senior might die? He was young. He was healthy. The problem with his feet was surely taken care of by now.

I put my hand on Tommy's cheek. His mouth, stained purple from last night's wine, was open, and his hair made a halo of curls on the pillow. For the first time, I noticed a net of fine lines puckering the pale, concave crescents under his eyes. I watched his collarbone rise and fall. If anything were to happen to him, I would die. Maura came thumping into the bedroom in her sleepers. "It's a *beautiful* day!" she said. Effie had greeted Maura that way every morning while we were in Cibola. I picked her up and tickled her and took in her morning smell of stale milk and baby powder. Everything was okay. It had just been a dream. I decided not to tell it to Tommy.

I liked telling Tommy everything—my dreams, my thoughts as they arose, what I had been doing while he was away during the day. "We two are as one," he had said when he proposed to me. To be included in his being was a gift, an unexpected gift. We were in the Crystal Birdcage Lounge at the time, drinking maitais, and he was telling me about his parents, what a great marriage they had. It was our first date, and I couldn't believe that he would even want to see me again once he found out how ignorant I was, and so when he proposed, I accepted with both a peaceful feeling that destiny was leading me along and the fear that he couldn't really mean it. He would certainly change his mind once he found out what I was really like. I saw myself in a play, telling myself the story of my life: And then Thomas R. Hammond proposed to you, and you married and had handsome, articulate, blue-eyed children and a very happy life. He said he was an excellent judge of people. "One would have to class you in the Earth Goddess category of females," he said. "Oh, thank you," I said, trying to make out what he meant. I assumed he would eventually drop me—other, better women would naturally want him. But at least I'd have a decent boyfriend for a

while, just about the nicest, smartest man I'd ever met, someone
without a police record, someone to go to the movies with. I was
no longer as afraid as I once had been about being an old maid
—I'd only been back from the dig a month and was still ex-
hilarated about finding the burial and about observing one concrete thing every day. Even though Tommy assured me that
night that he was planning to propose to me in a year, after he
graduated, I didn't quite believe him. He just seemed to like to
talk. But he was very tender, and very emotional. He said he
wanted me to be pure on our wedding night; it wasn't going to
be like his first marriage. A few weeks later, he took me to meet
his family, and the next day, he said there was no reason to wait,
and before I knew it, there was a wedding and we had moved into
a little apartment near the campus. Tommy had to teach me what
it meant for two to become one. When I unpacked my things, I
got out a pot from my great-grandmother. It was squat and
wide-mouthed, off-center, and had a smooth reddish-brown surface flecked with shiny mica. She had made it with clay from the
bed of the San Ysidro, which flowed near her house, and given
it to me when I was small because we had the same name. The
pot was the one thing that I didn't have to share with my sisters;
I used to put my face to its mouth and smell mud, and think of
the pitcher in the fairy tale that was always brimming, no matter
how much wine was poured out of it, and when the light caught
the bits of mica in the bottom, I pretended they were stars. When
I grew older, I forgot about the pot, and stored it away in a carton
along with my little collection of fairy tales and science fiction
and some pillowcases I'd once embroidered with the idea of
putting them in a hope chest. "I think my pot will look nice on
top of the bookcase," I told Tommy.

"*Our* pot," Tommy said. "The correct phraseology is: 'We're
going to put *our* pot on the bookcase.' Except we're not—it
belongs in the cupboard, preferably on a high shelf in the back.
I'm going to have to give you lessons in good taste." And he held
me and kissed me. I thought: Now I'm not alone anymore, and
I'm going to become a better person. And he did tell me a lot of
things, like not to wear black shoes with a brown dress and to
stand up straight. He was older. He already knew how to be

married. He told me that his first wife had been too bossy and too
nosy—she wasn't feminine like me. Almost every day he said that
he loved me, and he often held hands with me when we went out.
Sometimes, after a couple of bottles of wine, he talked about how
my goodness was his salvation. I didn't quite follow that. I trained
myself to say "we" instead of "I." It was easy. The "I" had been
new anyway—acquired only recently, in the presence of the
skeleton of a woman who had died six hundred years earlier.

The only person I'd ever been able to confide all my thoughts
to was Tommy. But since I'd come back from Cibola, I hadn't
gotten around to mentioning the strange conversation with his
father on the patio, or the paintings. I don't know why. And I
concealed the envelope of birthday money Tom Senior had
slipped me the day before I left. "If Tommy knows about it,
you'll never see it again," he told me. He chuckled, and I figured
he must be kidding; at the right moment, when we really needed
some money, I'd surprise Tommy. Tom Senior suggested buying
some shoes. "Tommy promised to do that," I said, and Tom
Senior just shrugged. "Tommy always says about you that you
are a very fine person," I said. "And it's true." I used part of the
cash to buy a present for Tommy, an Indian wedding pot. It was
patterned with cream and red-ocher bird figures and had two
throats and two intertwined handles. The rest of the money,
wrapped in an embroidered Mexican shawl Effie had given me
for my birthday, remained in a trunk, and often came to my
thoughts, a kind of compelling, crackling electricity around it.

Tommy didn't want to wake up. Maura patted his eyes. "Poppa?"
she said. "Poppa?"

"Poppa's sleeping," Tommy murmured.

"Maura wants to say good morning," I said. I kissed his forehead. "So do I."

"Well, sometimes I just want to feel like a separate person,"
Tommy said. He turned on his stomach and pushed his face into
the pillow. Then he stretched out an arm. "Wait. One hug for
Maura."

He slept, as usual, until the last possible minute and then left in a rush, kissing me while knotting his tie. As he ran down the stairs, he told me to phone the photo lab and tell Meyer, the manager, he had been delayed. "Love you," he said.

"Love you," I said.

Meyer answered the phone by saying, "Yeah, Judy, I know."

The force of the dream stayed with me. I dressed Maura and carried her toys into the living room, cleared last night's dishes from the dining table and put them in the oven in case Tommy came home before I had time to clean up, and went to the manual typewriter on the dining table. I resumed a big typing job—a geology student's dissertation about lunar tidal influences on the earth's crust.

I learned many things typing dissertations. I knew, for instance, that the twenty-four-hour day was invented by the Babylonians and contained 86,400 seconds—each second corresponding to the length of time of one heartbeat of a healthy human body at rest. (I'd mentioned this to a man seated next to me at a dinner party given by Tommy's departmental adviser, and he said, "I would like to get better acquainted." He started asking me lots of questions and I was embarrassed and changed the subject to my husband's scholarships.) I knew that bodies fall at the rate of thirty-two feet per second squared, becoming steadily heavier as they approach the ground. I knew that farmers in Kiangsu plant cotton in wheat fields before the wheat is quite ready to harvest. I knew that women dream in color much more frequently than men do; I also knew that dreams were supposed to be connected to something hidden and didn't mean what you thought they did. The dream about Tom Senior probably symbolized something. I'd typed one dissertation about how all the people in a dream can be interpreted as parts of the person's mind. But in my dream everyone was completely real. Effie was Effie. Tommy was Tommy. Tom Senior was Tom Senior. I was me.

Sometimes I dreamed about things that pushed at the surface of the world until they happened. When we were still in Cibola and Tommy hadn't decided yet where to apply to graduate school, I dreamed that we lived in a dark city and sat in a little apartment at a table with a red-and-white-checked cloth. Then Tommy decided to go to school in New York and for Christmas Effie sent us a red-and-white-checked tablecloth. Another time, I dreamed I was holding a baby girl. This baby is yours, a voice said. Then I accidentally got pregnant with Maura. Sometimes my premonitions didn't even bother to pass through dreams. Once, when I was five, I was sure I was going to find something special as I walked to school across the mesa. I kicked aside a gourd vine and there, sticking out of the dirt, was a white quartz spearhead. Another time, I was in the kitchen with my mother making enchiladas when I suddenly had a vision of the wind blowing through the bedroom I shared with my sisters; I saw the turquoise-and-gold ceramic lamp on the bureau smashed open, revealing a dull gray interior. I hurried into the bedroom just as a gust of wind lifted the curtain so that it knocked the lamp to the floor. The base broke open, and I saw its dull gray interior. When I met Tommy, in the student union cafeteria where I was working, I immediately disliked him. He slid his tray along until he came to where I ladled out soup, stared at me in that cocky way of men who are sure of their good looks, brushed a lock of red hair away from his eyes, said, "Split pea, please," and then winked at me when I handed him his bowl. Out of nowhere the thought came to me that he was cute, very cute, cute enough to be a television star, but there was something I didn't like about him, and that was funny, because he was going to be my husband. A couple of times a week he'd come into the cafeteria and wink at me, and I always turned away. Then we got together at a party, and while other men there poured beer over one another's head, he spent the whole evening sitting by my side chain-smoking, his attention fastened on me, speaking rapidly and with certainty, telling me his life goals, telling me I was the most wonderful woman he had ever met in his life. I simply didn't believe him; he didn't know a thing about me. The next day, he came to the cafeteria with a copy of his favorite book, *The Rubaiyat of Omar Khayyam,* and read me a verse about wine from it while the other people in the line stood there staring. In two months, we were married.

The noise of machinery and demolition stopped. I looked up from my typing. The diffuse light coming in the window, which faced an airshaft, had dimmed. It was cold. Maura, up from her nap, dragged in a bedsheet she had wrapped around her middle. Toys and newspapers and cornflakes littered the floor. A terrible emptiness came over me. This sometimes happened. It was always at the end of the afternoon, when the light started to fade and the definite black of night had not yet arrived, and it was always when Tommy was away. I wanted to cry but I couldn't, I became very thirsty and sick to my stomach, thought stopped, time stopped, the world contracted to a narrow gray tunnel, the clutter around me scratched at my skin, and I got a terrible headache; I felt as if I were breathing poisonous gas. When Tommy arrived, he would bring me a glass of water, he would hold me, he would tell me that a lucky, strong girl like me could not possibly be sad, and he would describe all the fantastic things that were going to happen to us after he got his doctorate, how Maura and I would have lots of beautiful clothes, and a cleaning lady would come, and I would no longer have to haul the laundry to the laundromat, and we would buy a car and take trips. We would go to the mountains, whatever mountains they had around here. As he talked, I would doze in his arms for a few minutes. When I awoke, I would be fine. I wouldn't remember the constriction until the next time it happened to me, and then it was as if I had never escaped it at all.

On this particular November evening, I pushed toys, books, and Tommy's guitar from the couch onto the floor and lay down in the darkening room with my palms over my eyes and waited for him to come home. Maura put her face next to mine. "Are you sick, Mommy?" she asked.

"Just tired, sweetheart," I said. "Why don't you go get some crackers?"

She ate from a box of saltines while she arranged her stuffed animals around my head and feet. Tommy was very late tonight.

He had probably stopped at the library after work. I tried some deep inhalations. The back of my head throbbed. The window became black.

"Mommy, I'm hungry," Maura said.

"Get yourself some cereal out of the bottom cupboard."

"Don't want to."

I made myself get up and turn on some lights. I drank a glass of water. There was nothing to fix for dinner, and I had no money to go to the store. I was able to turn up a third of a cellophane bag of dried noodles, a can of tuna fish, and a can of mushroom soup. Maura stood on a chair next to me by the stove and was dropping tubes of macaroni into boiling water when Tommy came home.

"It's so wonderful to see you," I said. "You are the light of my life."

He carried a big paper bag. "Hurray, we're having dinner before midnight," he said, kissing me. His face was red and his skin was cold. He smelled of beer and tobacco.

"I'm sorry," I said. "I don't know where the day went." I put my head on his chest.

He patted my back. The water bubbled and blossoms of steam rose around the three of us. Tears came to my eyes. I felt restored. "I am so glad you're home. I started feeling really awful. I was trying to finish up this typing job but I didn't make it. I've got another one coming tomorrow."

"Work was absolutely harrowing today," he said. "*I* am totally bushed. I wore myself out trying to convince them to set up the billing procedures more efficiently. I had to stay and have a few beers with Meyer in an attempt to persuade him. He needs my brains, my energy. But I fail to comprehend how I can continue working there much longer. I give it my all, and it completely saps me." He pulled a jug of wine out of the bag. "Only two-ninety-nine a gallon," he said.

Just then I bumped the hot pan and burned my hand. I had to run cold water on it. "Tommy, honey," I said, "if you have a premonition—a dream—and then it comes true, how does that help you? What's the point?"

"Well, first you have to define 'premonition.' Is it premonition

qua premonition, is it a conclusion you have arrived at uncon-
sciously because of an agglomerate of subliminal facts, or is it
actually a metaphysical event? Get your definitions straight, and
then we can discuss the value of said matter. Maura, you are
amazing, cooking like that. You'll be a chef, a chef-ess, at the
Waldorf-Astoria in a few years. God, I am beat." He drank a
tumbler of wine and refilled his glass.

"If only the department had room for another instructor, you
wouldn't have to put up with that dumb job," I said. "And you
could get started—"

"Please don't say another word, Judy," he said. "I am well
aware of the parameters of the situation."

"I'm sorry. It's not your fault." I had decided never to mention
the dissertation again, and then I had gone and done it. Last
month, on my twenty-sixth birthday, I had taken a blank index
card and written out my goals: Do not talk about dissertation. Be
sweet and helpful. Keep house in order. Meditate—develop center of calm. Observe one concrete thing every day.

When I put Maura to bed after her bath, I called Tommy in
to say good night. She stood up on her pillow and Tommy and
I kissed her warm, damp cheeks at the same time, and she
laughed. This is all I want, I said to myself. I am so fortunate.

We ate on the couch with our plates on our laps. "One doesn't
touch one's face while eating, sweetie," Tommy said. "It's
frowned upon."

"You mean me? Why?" When he gave me advice about how
to act, I didn't always get the reasoning behind it. "I was just
thinking about something."

"A lady never touches her face in public." When Tommy
corrected me like this, his voice went into a higher pitch and sped
up. "Suppose I'm the head of a department and we give an elegant
dinner party, and you're munching away with your hand on your
jaw like this." I had to laugh. "Ridiculous," he went on. "And
what are people going to think of my truck-driver wife?"

When we were first married, he gave me a lot of advice about grooming and manners. I was very ignorant. My family had never used table napkins, for instance, and when he took me to meet his parents and his mother served me a plate of cake with a paper napkin, I folded it up and put it in my purse to save and use as a handkerchief. Tommy wanted me to be a lady. He was the only person who ever told me the truth about my appearance. When we were getting dressed for that dinner party his adviser gave, I tried to look as nice as possible, mascara and the works, and just as we were starting out, Tommy happened to notice that I had a faint mustache. I had had no idea. I was horrified. But he promised that after we were rich he'd send me to a place where they removed unwanted facial hair. He also taught me not to look at other people in public, and to keep my hand over my mouth when I laughed to hide my chipped tooth, and never to grin, only to smile. And he said that the less I talked, the more feminine I was.

He put his plate on the floor and lit a little cigar and made a face at me. "What's on your mind, sweetie? I divine that you're preoccupied."

"I was thinking we ought to call your folks."

"Why?"

"I don't know—it's been a while since we talked to them, and your mother hasn't written for at least a month. But I'm sure everything is fine. They're probably busy."

"Well, we could phone," he said. "But what excuse could we use? They'll wonder why we're spending the money."

"You could ask them whether they went up to see the aspen," I said. "Whether they got the trailer. How Effie likes her course. What Bud is doing about college."

"Mom was talking him into enlisting," Tommy said.

"Really? I thought your dad was against that. I thought he wanted Bud in college and ROTC. Anyway, you always have the right words to say. They'll be thrilled to hear from you."

"One can never be sure," Tommy said.

I went in the bedroom to the illegal extension left behind by the previous tenant and waited while Tommy made the call.

"Hi, hi, hi-dey," Effie said. "We are all doing really great.

Bud's bowling team is fantastic and will probably go to the state tournament, and he is having so much fun, and Nancy has to make the Globe Theatre out of cardboard and Dad's got his guitar out, and I tell you, he ought to make a record. He sounds exactly like Chet Atkins. And I'm doing my 'Totalitarianism and the West' midterm paper, and we've got a fire going in the new fireplace in the den. You should see it—some kind of black metal and it looks just like a pointy witch's cap. Dad and Bud just finished installing it and we got all these piñon logs, and the entire house is just *perfumed* with them. So we're having a high old time."

"I'm so glad," I said.

"And how's the dissertation going, Tommy, honey?"

"The deadline was extended. The whole concept is being restructured and at the moment I'm reorganizing the whole photo lab. That place would collapse without me. Meyer says that your son is manager material par excellence."

"Tommy is so wonderful," I put in.

"Well, darlin'," Effie said to him, "there is no question that whatsoever you set your mind to you do better than anybody else. Now, let me see if I understand. Are you restructuring the concept which you had already started restructuring up at the dam, or is this a new restructuring? Which reminds me, I was in Dean Easterling's office just to say hi and he showed me this brochure that sounded like the most wonderful thing on earth and you should do it. It's a program for Americans who want to broaden their cultural horizons. You go to Oxford, England, for a summer session and you actually attend Oxford University, and you know that's got to be the best university there is. Plus you get to go to Stratford-on-Avon, which I saw, and Stonehenge and things like that. So when you have your doctorate and get some money saved up, that's definitely what you should do. I'll send the brochure."

"Sounds ideal," Tommy said. "I'm getting really fed up with New York. You have no idea of how hard it is just surviving an average day here. I'm worn out all the time trying to scrape together a living, one never has a minute to think, then there's the dirty laundry, et cetera, so some kind of program abroad would not be out of the question."

"Well, after you finish your dissertation, you just go to Oxford and think a blue streak, and they could even hire you to be a *don* or whatever. And then you get yourself back here to Cibola. Everyone will be so impressed if you've been to Oxford. Listen, darlin', it sure has been nice talking to you, but it's your nickel, so—"

"Are you going to get the trailer you wanted?" I asked. "Are you still going to Baja or someplace for the holidays?"

"I believe so, hon, but we have to wait and see," she said. Her voice softened. "You know that trouble Dad was having with his circulation, with his feet? Well, next week, he has to have this catheter thing. Everything is probably going to test out fine, we're totally sure of it, I know it, and Dad knows it, too, because he's in wonderful shape."

"Oh, no," I said, but they didn't hear. I sank down on the bed. In the cracks in the plaster above the headboard were threads of soot. I felt sick.

"So it's a minor procedure," Tommy was saying. "Nothing serious."

"Well, it's what the doctors think is best, darlin'. Here's Dad to say hello."

"How are you?" I asked brightly.

"Not too good." His voice was faint. Maybe the connection had gone bad. He said something else.

"What, Dad?" Tommy said. "Can't hear you."

"The doc thinks I'll have to have major surgery. To remove the scar tissue and strengthen the walls of my heart."

There was a silence.

"Then you'll be a new man, you can count on that," Tommy said. "You'll be back in the saddle in no—"

"Six weeks of total rest after the operation. If I make it—"

"The medical expertise today is so advanced, so incredibly sophisticated," Tommy said.

"There's not a thing to worry about," Effie called into the receiver as Tommy was saying, "You are going to do just fine, Dad! It's going to be great! You'll be feeling so much better."

"The doctor says Dad is young and strong," Effie added. "Which we always knew!"

"You know we're thinking of you," I said, barely able to make my voice work. I couldn't force myself to say he was going to be all right, and anyway, he hated that kind of talk.

"Tell them, Dad, honey," Effie said. "Tell them this Dr. Kaufman we're going to has a fine medical background. He has diplomas from every place you can think of."

Tom Senior muttered something I didn't catch, except for the word "miserable."

"Well, good luck with the catheter thing," Tommy said.

Effie took the phone. "We're all pulling for him and we know you are, too. This is no huge thing, it's just routine, and we're going to get it out of the way as fast as possible, and get Dad rested up, and it will be all over before you know it, and that will be *it,* and then we're going to trade the camper in on that really fine trailer and go *everywhere.* So, are you-all having a good time? What's the weather like there? Any snow yet?"

After we said our goodbyes, I went to the typewriter.

Tommy poured himself a glass of apricot brandy. "He sure sounded morbid," he said. "He seems to have decided to create a major issue out of a routine procedure. He does that sometimes."

"Do you know what the catheter does?" I asked. "How it works?"

"Oh yes. It has to do with the bladder. All that fluid buildup that was bothering Dad."

"But he was talking about his heart."

Tommy opened his mouth so that his jaw was slack and shook his head. For an instant, he seemed frightened. Then he turned away and rubbed his hand back and forth across his lips. "Do *you* know what's happening?"

"No," I said, surprised. "And I don't understand how you can get scar tissue on your heart. What in the hell is going on?"

"You don't have to get mad about it. You don't have to talk like a sailor. Maybe it has something to do with those heart attacks."

"Heart attacks? What heart attacks? Your father had heart attacks?" I cranked a piece of paper into the typewriter, listening to each tick of the ratchet. Why hadn't I known? Maybe I could have done something—paid more attention when he was trying to talk to me. Why all this pretending?

"Oh, they were just small ones, about ten years ago. Well, Mom sounded really up, so I think everything is fundamentally okay."

From the street came the noise of a bus with a rattling engine. Tommy picked up his guitar, stretched out on the couch with it on his stomach, and started playing. " 'Black girl, black girl, don't you lie to me,' " he sang. He had once considered becoming a folk singer, but he got married to his first wife and went in the Army instead.

I began to type very rapidly. "Every point on the earth rises and falls twice a day," I typed.

7

About five in the morning, I woke up from a sound sleep and went into the kitchen and plugged in the coffeepot and opened the refrigerator and got out the turkey carcass. There wasn't much meat left on it—the poor thing was two weeks old; we'd celebrated Christmas on the thirteenth, before Tom went into the hospital—but nothing in this world gives me more pleasure than stripping bones. It's like peeling a sunburn, or peeling the lint off the screen in the dryer. The ribs are just like paper, and you have to use your nails to get those tiny bits of flesh out, and then the legs come off with a pop. The cat came swaying in, complaining and dragging her belly—she was going to have kittens any minute, and since Tom had gone into the hospital, she hadn't been right. She howled sometimes for no reason, and she was always trying to get into his workroom. The coffeepot made that low, choked gurgle, and the house was so quiet that I began softly singing "My Adobe Hacienda." Lately I couldn't get that song out of my head. I wrapped the little pile of meat in foil and put it in the freezer compartment and threw away the carcass and went into the chilly den.

According to *Positive Wisdom*, the booklet I got in the mail every week—Mama started me on that subscription when I left home to marry Tom—today's thought was "God is in all things." I sat down on the sleek new sofa next to the fireplace. Our new den! I kept telling people how I just couldn't get over it. It was a place of beauty and calm. After being crammed into three small bedrooms and the scrunchy living room and kitchen for so long, seeing the den every morning when I got up made me feel like I was living in a palace. I faced the Sears home entertainment center—this year's big family Christmas present; TV, radio, and phonograph all in one gigantic walnut-veneer console—and a pair of elegant wrought-iron wall lamps I had bought with twelve books of Green Stamps, and I meditated.

I belonged to the Positive Christianity Fellowship, based in Oklahoma City, and it was definitely my kind of church: no preacher, no services, no building fund. You just subscribed to *Positive Wisdom* and prayed or meditated every morning for a few minutes. You avoided negative thoughts and tried to put everything in a positive light and you lined up with God's goodness, and by keeping that up, well, then you became good. And it worked. I was famous at the college for my power to boost anyone out of the dumps. In an emergency, you were entitled to call the Positive Power Hot Line and put the name of someone in need on the Positive Prayer list, and people at the center prayed for that person around the clock. I put Tom's name on the list on the day of his surgery. He came out of there so cold, and he kept clutching my hand. I have never seen a human being so frightened. I was smiling with joy. He asked me what in the hell I had to smile about, and I said, "Because you made it, 'cause you came through the surgery just fine, darlin'." It turned out he thought he hadn't gone in yet; the drugs had confused him. Well, then the biggest grin you ever saw came over his face. He said, "I am so thankful." It was the most religious thing I'd ever heard from him. I put his name on the list again, ten days later, when the cardiac team said he wouldn't be out of intensive care by Christmas.

I'd concentrated on having him home by Christmas Day, even though we'd decided to celebrate early, but maybe I hadn't worked hard enough. Usually, I pictured myself full of the power of God's grace—that had kept me together lately—but now I closed my eyes and visualized Tom sitting in his Barcalounger, plucking his guitar, his face tan and healthy, his heartbeat regular and strong, and I squeezed my eyelids tightly together and pushed into that picture the feeling that all was good and right.

It was hard work. Tom was still in intensive care, still limited to five minutes' visiting time every hour. It was good and right that he had had the surgery, of course. The doctor had given us the odds beforehand, but I couldn't recall now what they were, and, anyway, it didn't matter: I knew Tom had to survive. I felt so grown-up in the doctor's office that day. Tom and I were just a pair of kids, really, ready to shoot off on some new adventure at any minute—people still mistook Tom for forty sometimes— and there Dr. Kaufman had been, talking to us about life and the alternative. And Tom and I had nodded thoughtfully, just like adults do in the movies, but then Tom had gotten scared and down-in-the-mouth after that, and I had had a lot of trouble convincing him that everything was going to be all right.

Yesterday, he had actually sat up in a chair. That was so wonderful. He *had* to come home soon, that was all there was to it. He belonged home. It was true that sometimes he got restless— but then I always had a fantastic plan ready, like buying the camper and touring the national parks, or building the workroom on the back of the house so he had a place to putter at all hours of the night, or turning the garage into a den. He and Bud had broken through from the living room to the garage, put in the picture window, nailed up the pine paneling, and installed the fireplace, and I picked out the orange vinyl sofa and the avocado shag carpeting. And, for Tom's Christmas present, the Barca-lounger so he could keep his feet up. He belonged here, strum-ming his guitar along with the TV tunes, his cigar and manhattan handy.

The den was filled with Tom's presence—the cigar smoke was already permanently in the curtains—and when I took a deep breath and I smelled the ashes from a burned log, warmth went all through my body. For the past several weeks a tight steel cable strung through my spine and neck had thrummed and twanged constantly, and now it just stopped and went slack, and I sighed and folded forward. Something inside me surrendered. Every-thing was going to be fine. My husband, the man I had loved for most of my life, was coming home, and what God wanted me to do in preparation was to clean house.

I rapped on Nancy's door hard. I said, "Nancy, hon, giddy-up! We have to clean house for Dad."

Well, she was out of that bed immediately, looking almost like she did when she was small, her face bright pink and plumped out, her nightie wrinkled up around her knees. She stared at me. She said, "He's coming home?"

I said, "I know absolutely and finally for sure that everything is going to be all right now," and these words just leaped out of my chest, where my new strong feeling, my conviction, had been born, and they sounded very forceful in the little hallway between the bedrooms and the bathroom. I said, "It came to me that Dad is going to be fine, that he's coming home soon, and what we have to do is clean this place up real good."

She said, "Bud has to help, too."

I said, "When Bud gets up, he'll pitch in—don't you worry. But let's let him get his sleep right now."

She said, "But *Mom!*" and I said, "He is a growing boy and needs his rest, and anyway he was out late last night with his pals. When you're a senior, you'll get to have fun and sleep late, too."

She just sniffed and said, "I bet."

I went into the kitchen and phoned New York. Judy answered, and she started talking about how they'd been trying and trying to call. She told me they had phoned after the surgery and Bud had said things went okay. She said, "But we couldn't get any details from him, and we tried to call you on Christmas but I guess you all were at the hospital." And on she went like that. Judy tended to talk too much on expensive long-distance calls, so I just said I had some wonderful news for Tommy, and she said she would go wake him up.

He got on, and his voice was thick, and he said, "This is a phlegmatic holdover." He had always done that. If you got him up out of deep sleep, he made a weird statement of some kind.

Later he never remembered it, so you couldn't ever find out what he meant.

I said, "Wake up, honey. Dad is coming home real soon. We just all know it for a fact."

He said something like "Huh? No, wait, what's the—?" Then he said, "Let me get this straight. I had assumed that he was already home." I'd only let Tommy in on the best parts all along —I never told him that his father was still in the intensive-care unit, and I ordered Bud and Nancy not to say anything, because the thing was, Tommy tended to get very dramatic, and I hadn't wanted to get involved in calming him down when I needed to concentrate on Tom.

I said, "Darlin', he's about to come home, and he is doing just fine."

And he said, "That's the best news in the world."

Nancy and I took down the Christmas tree and swept up the needles and then sprayed carpet shampoo on the carpeting and vacuumed it, and then we took down the kitchen curtains and put them in the wash. I went running from room to room, just incredibly invigorated by the excitement in my rib cage, and I had on these springy high-heeled mules that sort of bounced me forward. I changed the sheets on my bed and on top I put the white nylon quilted spread the kids had given me for Christmas. I had hinted for chenille, but no soap. I dusted the bureau and wiped the glass on my wedding picture and put on some Chanel No. 5 from the giant bottle Tommy had given me on my twenty-fifth wedding anniversary. I only used it on special occasions, and so it was still nine-tenths full. I scrubbed the stove, the refrigerator, and the sink. Nancy cleaned the cat box without arguing that it was Bud's turn.

When Bud woke up, I put him to work washing windows on the inside—it was too cold to do the outsides—and I told him, "We'll get this house just perfect and then you can go out with your pals if you want, because when Dad comes home, you'll have to stick around." Bud had a cough and his hair looked like he had combed it with an eggbeater. He was letting his crew cut grow out, and it stuck up in tufts. "That's cool, Mom," he said.

Without a doubt, the sweetest of my children. Not a lightning intellect, but really, really sweet, and popular, too.

I pressed forward. I had the feeling I was pushing with all my might against some gigantic solid thing. At one point, I went into the bathroom and found Nancy scouring the bathtub so furiously that I was a little alarmed. Her elbow was going up and down like a piston, her hair was hanging in her eyes, and I said, "Nancy, hon! I do believe you are the best scrubber I ever saw. And look at that gorgeous sink! Do you know, I honestly believe that deodorant soap is one of the great inventions, one of the best things that ever came along."

Nancy said something I didn't catch into the tub. I had to run and change my clothes. Later, when I came back in and started to brush my teeth before I left for the hospital, she was sitting on the edge of the tub and her eyes were red. I was furious, and I whispered to her very firmly, "Nancy! No crying! You stop that. You are not going to shed a single tear. Not one. You are happy, not sad, and I do not want to see one more tear. Your daddy is going to make it, and he's coming home to this house, and we're going to do everything in the world to make him happy, and crying isn't going to help. So cut it out."

That burst of energy propelled me right into the new fluffy white wool coat that I'd given myself for Christmas. I loved every single thing I got for Christmas—Tom's nightie for me every year, for instance, and the bedspread, but no one ever gave me what I really wanted no matter how much I hinted.

As I drove to the hospital, I put on my reddest lipstick, using the rearview mirror. I was in the habit of doing all my makeup on the freeway on the way to teach my 8 a.m. civics class at the college. If I do say so myself, the red set off my skin and my hair —I had just started wearing the same hairdo Dorothy Malone wore on *Peyton Place* and it looked pretty good. Tommy's idea.

Kitty, the intensive-care unit nurse, was laughing with another nurse when I arrived. When Kitty saw me, she said, "Oh, Mrs. Hammond," her voice dropping. "You look real nice today."

I said, "Thank you, Kitty. You've had enough fun with my husband. I'm going to take him home."

She said, "He is such a dear man." Kitty was in her early twenties, way too pretty to be a nurse, with those red spit curls. In the hospital, Tom was surrounded by lovely females. After his surgery, the people from Tom's division at the Labs had sent over a cute little girl to report back by phone on how he was doing. And then she brought a very attractive friend. And other women from work came by. Just to see how he was. There were more good-looking little girls at the Labs than I had ever seen at the New Year's parties.

Tom seemed very small in his bed. The neatly folded sheet and the smooth blanket pressed him down into nothing, just flat. He had never been a big man, and today he was like a ten-year-old. Tubes came out of the crook of his elbow, from the back of one hand, and from a nostril. His skin was gray—almost a blue-gray. But I could see some definite improvements: his eyes, for instance. When he was well, and in a good mood, his eyes looked like he was ready to make a joke. Today they weren't like that, but at least they were rested, like a baby's, and bright. And his face. It was still a bit puffy and marked with the strain of the ordeal—he looked the way he had the time he and Bud had to push the camper out of the mud at the dam—but the hollows under his eyes were definitely going away. His heart had to be pumping more blood.

I said, "Sweetheart, darlin', you feel much better and you are coming home." I spoke with every ounce of my strength, putting my whole being into each word. "Everything is going to be all right."

He started to say something. He said, "Just promise me . . . " I couldn't hear the rest because his chin was down and that machinery he was hooked up to made a rushing sound, or maybe it was the ventilation system, because whenever I stood by his bed I had the impression that a window was open and wind was blowing in.

I said, "What is it, hon?"

He mumbled, "Promise—"

I said, "I promise. Anything. Now, what are you saying?" I put my head next to his.

He said, talking in a light way so that he didn't put any pressure on his chest, "If there's a lot of pain, morphine. If there's more of this pain, morphine. Morphine."

I said, "Yes, darlin', but you won't need any of that stuff. You are coming home. I just know it." I didn't want to tell him how I knew, because he'd always been so skeptical of Positive Christianity. "I've got Bud washing windows, and Nancy is doing I don't know what all, and that house is going to be spick-and-span when you set foot in it, and we'll have a piñon log burning in your fireplace, and your guitar all plugged in—Tom? All right?"

He said, "The morphine—don't forget."

He had had his first heart attack eleven years ago, out on the golf course. He said he never wanted to experience pain like that again. He had the second and third attacks just after that, in the hospital, and they'd given him morphine. In the past few years, he had had some tiny attacks at home, and we didn't tell anybody. I believed it only made you sicker if you went on and on about your illness, and Tom just hated hospitals, and anyway, after a while he was always fine again. When the swelling in his feet wouldn't go down, and he kept coming home earlier and earlier from the Labs, and he said he didn't care whether we went to Mexico for Christmas or not, I made him go to Dr. Kaufman.

Dr. Kaufman had a suite on the top floor of the hospital, the sixth, with Navajo rugs on the walls, and Indian pots on a shelf, and big picture windows facing the mesa, the freeway interchange, the airport and air base, and the peaks. I thought about how fantastic it would be to have a place with a view. A house is fine if you're tied down with family and all, but I've always felt there's nothing like an apartment with a view. Until a few years ago, Cibola didn't have any buildings over four stories high, but now some really nice six-story apartment complexes were going up around the new shopping plaza. Sometimes when we made plans about our retirement, I talked about an apartment, but Tom would say, "Where do I grow my tomatoes? And where do I park the boat and the camper? And how about the little guy?" Meaning his cat.

I waited in the doorway. I am not one to impose. I said, "You asked to see me?"

Dr. Kaufman said, "Hi, Evelyn." He took my hand and pressed it softly, as if I was the person who was ill and he had to measure my strength.

Well, I squeezed his hand real hard and I beamed at him. This doctor was a mere kid. He looked like some proud Mrs. Kaufman's boy—tanned, broad-chested, long sideburns like Tommy's. Now, why hadn't Tommy ever considered medical school? He got good grades in biology. The doctor seated me the way a waiter would at a fancy restaurant and then he returned to the other side of his desk and sorted through papers.

I said, "Tom looks lots better today."

The doctor didn't say a word. And then: "Ah, this is what I was looking for." He came around the desk with a pen and a piece of paper with a drawing on it and began talking.

It was a sketch of Tom's heart, and how the surgery had been done, how the veins taken from his legs had bypassed the obstructed blood vessels in his heart—these were shaded in with red ink. The scar tissue on the heart wall—that was figure-eight scribbles in black. In first grade, Tommy drew every Christmas angel on the class mural with their little bodily parts in great detail. The doctor spoke so quickly—these Easterners, how did they learn to talk so fast?—that I couldn't follow him. He'd made me this drawing the day after the operation. Even then I couldn't keep track of the terminology, and now it was hard to listen all over again to something I hadn't wanted to learn about in the first place.

I said, "We went over that picture already, Dr. Kaufman." I was very cheerful, to let him know I didn't really mind all that much. He nodded and kept on talking. Something about weak walls and too much scar tissue. I still didn't care to think about that surgery. The doctors had actually lifted Tom's heart right out of his body. And so where had Tom been? If his blood was in a machine, and his heart was over here, and his body was packed in ice, where was Tom?

Now Dr. Kaufman was sliding his pen sideways, using it as a pointer (it said "J&B Auto Supply" on the barrel), and he was talking, but all I heard was the blood in my ears, like a roaring wind, and the room was gray and freezing, as if it might start snowing inside. I was fascinated by his hands, the dots of pores on the backs of his long fingers and his fingernails, so absolutely clean, the cuticles pushed back, the nails clipped straight: how did he get them so clean? In the movies, surgeons stood at the sink, scrubbing. I felt heat in my face, and my hands went cold, and my breathing didn't go in and out right—somehow I was doing it backwards. I frowned and nodded and shook my head to show that I was following everything.

On our first date, Tom and I had gone to a Randolph Scott movie—you could say that Tom resembled Randolph Scott, a smaller version—and when he walked me home, we stopped in the schoolyard and sat in the swings. And then he kissed me. After that, he used to pick me up after school in his Hudson and drive to a cornfield. I would take off his shirt, and he would always have on an undershirt—I could never get over that; I hadn't known a thing about men's underwear, since my father had lit out for California when I was four. I would lean my head against the center of Tom's chest, place my palm on the under-shirt-seam binding, and feel his heart begin to beat fast. His heart was very precious to me then, and I was happy to have that power over it. How I loved Tom! How I had cried and pined when he went away to join the service! And Mama finally said, "Well, honey, *go* to him, then." I'd told the story of our marriage, over the years, to different listeners, and everyone always said, "Effie, you were right to go after him." I wore a suit with a peplum that pinched in at the waist—my waist was so tiny then!—and Tom was so handsome in his uniform. The picture was in the silver frame on my bureau, and in all modesty I have to say that it showed a beautiful, happy couple. My face in that picture expressed total satisfaction: what I'd willed most in all my life had happened. At that moment, I thought I'd always be pretty much as happy as I was then, but now I went back to thinking about Tom on the operating table packed in ice, his blood over there in some machine, his heart lifted out—

I said, "What are you saying to me, Doctor?"

He said, "There is nothing more we can do." His face sagged, and his gaze cut past me and out the window, and he said, "There will be no pain." Snow covered the peaks, but the mesa was brown. Dr. Kaufman no longer looked like someone's son; he seemed old, and very disappointed in the way things were turning out for him. He spoke to the silver ashtray on his desk. He said, "He's not going to make it."

8

Effie sat in the cold car in the parking lot. People arrived, people pulled out. Shadows became thin and flat, but she had no sense that time was passing. Everything stayed still. The broken dashboard clock. The steering wheel. She rested her forehead and arms against it. She was freezing. The white coat did her no good at all. The cold lay in her mouth and soaked into her body. She could taste the frozen asphalt and the winter earth below.

Finally, she checked her watch. She had to go back, in great shape, smiling, to be with Tom. She went to a pay phone in the lobby and called Tommy. "The words," she said. "You have to say the right words when the time comes." He kept saying, "What went wrong?"

She drove home to get Nancy and Bud. Nancy said Bud was out on the mesa with Teddy Roybal, the boy across the street. He had gotten a motor scooter for Christmas.

"How dare he?" Effie said.

"You told him when the house was done he could run along and have a good time," Nancy said. Her voice was shaking.

When Nancy and Effie went into Tom's room, he lifted his head, and the monitor showed his heart beating irregularly. "Mr. Hammond, don't *do* that!" Kitty said. She patted Effie on the arm and went out.

Effie walked toward the bed. She was thinking that there was something she wanted very much, a present she had always wished for: one of those crystal balls with a winter scene inside, a little house and a fir tree, and when you turned the ball upside down, snow fell. It almost never snowed right in Cibola—just on the peaks.

She took Tom's hand, and he whispered something. "What is it, darlin'?" she said.

"What I have seen!" he said. His expression was joyous. The strain had left his face, and his skin seemed to radiate a light of its own, under the hospital fluorescent light, in the pale green room. "Don't tell!"

The machinery, except for the hissing and bubbling of the oxygen, was quiet. He had only one tube left, and that was in his nostril.

"We won't tell, hon," Effie said.

"Don't tell anyone—they'll think I'm nuts. Effie—what I have seen! Not like anything I've ever seen before! I can't describe it."

She stood still, holding her breath. She felt as if she had no feet, as if her body were starting to dissolve. The room was filled with an intensity. It was like a strong perfume, or a low hum, or a cool light. She glanced at Nancy. She was aware of it, too. What he had seen!

"We won't tell," Effie said.

Nancy picked up his other hand. It had blue puncture marks on the back where the tubes had gone in. She held her lips tightly together. Her shoulders were shaking. But she was not crying.

"Effie, you can't imagine! Nancy—listen—"

"It's okay, hon," Effie said. "You're going to get out of here real quick. I've got a brand-new plan. We're going to trade in that old teardrop camper and the pickup and get that gorgeous fourteen-foot trailer at RV-Land. And we're going to go to California, just take our time. I'll drive while you relax, and that trailer has a real shower and a bathroom, and all the extras, and we'll go back to that beach—what's its name, where we sat and counted the waves? You know, looking for the ninth wave? And you can just play your guitar, and paint all day, and I'll read and study—oh, philosophy—and we'll just go along like that, with me driving. I can pull a trailer okay. I pulled the boat trailer with no problem."

"Effie, *don't* buy that trailer," he said. "Don't buy *any* trailer.

Promise. Did you ask about the morphine? I just can't take any more pain. I had it again, and they didn't give me a shot."

"Darlin'," Effie said, "I do believe your voice is the strongest it's been since the operation." She knew the doctor was wrong. "Look, Nance, how wonderful he looks!" she said. "You're doing fine, hon. You don't need those machines." Effie beamed at Nancy to get her to agree, but she just stood staring with her mouth set. "And guess what!" Effie said. "Tommy is coming for a surprise visit. I talked to him a bit ago and he said he happened to get some time off."

"What I have seen!" Tom said. He tried to hoist his head and shoulders off the pillow. The nurse came swishing in on her crepe soles. "Mr. Hammond," she said. "Please."

Nancy and Effie had to go back to the intensive-care waiting room. A man in a plaid parka was in the phone booth crying noisily over the receiver.

"People should go somewhere else to cry," Effie whispered. "Nancy, Dad was just *glowing.*" She could not help smiling. "Did you *see?*" What he had seen! Maybe it had to do with her morning meditation. From now on, he would take her religion more seriously.

"But didn't Dr. Kaufman say . . ." Nancy began.

"God knows more than any doctor, Nancy," Effie said. "Your father has *seen* something."

Nancy closed her eyes. Something very big was happening just beyond the limits of her perception. When she opened her eyes, her mother's face was close; her skin, too, glowed. It was like the glaze on pottery.

"What about the morphine, Mom?" Nancy said. "Hadn't we better ask the doctor, just in case?"

Two nurses went racing toward Tom's room. After several minutes, Kitty came out. She said, in a very quiet voice, "Mrs. Hammond."

By the time Effie and Nancy got to his bed, he was gone. He just wasn't there anymore.

.   .   .

Everything stopped for a while. It was like that moment after the rodeo fireworks go off and before their colored sparks disappear into the dark air. In the center of the world, nothing was happening. Out toward the rim, actions were taken, decisions were made, papers were signed. Effie looked down, as from a great height, and saw a hand, hers, write "Mrs. Thomas R. Hammond." She was now the chief priestess in a ritual she had been preparing for all her life. The worst had happened, and yet she was continuing. She had always thought of God as a personage giving orders. Now she knew different: no one had told her about the splendor of everything being ripped away, and there you were at the heart of the empty world, where nothing happened —all events turned like spokes from where she stood, her arms extended, writing the name.

Judy squatted in front of a suitcase with a broken clasp and a tear in the lid mended with black electrician's tape. She held a folded sweater of Tommy's. It will be cold there, she was thinking. She closed her eyes and saw a tunnel of swirling yellows and oranges, and a little airplane flying through the tunnel. Tom Senior was the pilot, and he was yelling, "I'm free!" She had been hoping as hard as she could until that moment that he would survive, that Effie, with her broken voice on the phone saying they didn't think he was going to make it, was wrong. But now Judy sat back on her haunches and gazed upward. She saw the foot of the bed, a pair of jeans hanging on a doorknob, and a poster Tommy had recently put up. It was a picture of an earnest, sloe-eyed brown boy of about twelve with the caption *Viva la Huelga*.

She went into the living room. Tommy was on the couch, a big tumbler of brandy in his hands, watching loose wet snow tumble down the airshaft. The ashy light from the window was reflected on his face. "He's all right," Judy said, touching his shoulder. He didn't move. "Whatever happens, he's going to be fine. I just know that."

"How are we going to get there?" Tommy said. "I don't know how we're going to get there."

"I made the reservations," Judy said. "We'll have to go to the bank to get the money out. You'll have to write the check. Listen, the pain is over for him."

"Mom said there was no pain," Tommy said.

Nancy watched the radiance emanating from her mother's face. After they left the hospital, Effie had a million things to do. They went home and Effie told Bud, and she gave him a list and some money and sent him out to the supermarket. She got her biggest purse out—it was of white wicker—and, driving fast, went to the bank. "Act normal," she whispered to Nancy. "Nothing has happened, everything is fine." She talked for a few minutes with the bank officer about whether it was going to snow, and then went to the safe-deposit box and emptied its contents into her purse. She told Nancy to remember that these were very important documents and Nancy was not to let her lose track of them. From the bank, Effie phoned the beauty salon and made an appointment. She kept telling Nancy things to remember. "Remember that we have to pick out a casket, even though he's going to be cremated," Effie said. "Remember to call his office and tell his boss." She was busy the way she was before they left on a trip.

"Shouldn't we call Tommy?" Nancy said in the car when they stopped to get gas.

"I believe we'll wait, darlin', until he gets here," Effie said. "I need to run into the 7-Eleven and get a couple of packs of gum. Shoes—we all need new shoes."

When Tommy got off the plane that night, he was no longer a winsome young man. He had become middle-aged and haggard. His hair blew over his forehead. Effie and Nancy exchanged glances. The same thought struck both of them: It was Tom. He had come home. The whole thing at the hospital hadn't even happened.

Effie went alone across the floodlit tarmac in her white coat. She walked slowly. It seemed right. She stopped a yard away from her son. She smiled at him. "Your daddy's gone," she said.

Tommy's face was so terrible that she was worried that he would start crying and carrying on and interfere with what she and Nancy were experiencing, and Bud, too, since they had told him *What I have seen!* She had given Tommy the main fact. There was nothing else to put into words.

Judy was behind Tommy, carrying Maura bundled in a blanket. Her face was composed. She took a step toward Effie. They smiled at one another. Judy had never seen Effie looking so young or so lovely.

They walked in silence to the parking lot. They walked and breathed in the cold air exactly as they should, and around them settled the crystalline night, just as it should, and snow started falling. Bud, sniffling, drove.

"Here's Main, Judy," Effie said as they passed motels and neon. "Isn't it great?"

"Sure is," Judy said.

"At least the house is really spick-and-span," Effie said. "I tell you, nothing happens in this family until the house is clean. People are going to start coming. The Roybals already brought over enchiladas. And I want to tell you, Tommy, hon, Bud and Nancy scrubbed and scoured, and every corner in our little adobe hacienda just gleams like it never has before. The last time we had such a clean house was when you cleaned before Nancy was born. We only clean when big things happen."

"It's all those years in between that it gets so bad," Bud said. His voice was thick.

The house had a festive air, and that was correct, too. The old woman next door had already dropped off a flowering poinsettia, and next to the casserole of enchiladas on the kitchen table was a silver paper plate piled with cookies in the shape of Christmas trees, along with a card from Tom's boss.

"We must take nourishment," Effie said, almost to herself. "Right away, before it's too late."

"I'll just put Maura in bed and then come and help," Judy said.

"I think a round of bourbon and sevens would be appropriate," Tommy said. "I'll make them."

Effie watched herself get out six plates. But that was too many. She counted them again and put back two. But that didn't leave enough. She shoved all the plates back in the cupboard and closed the door. She turned and saw Judy watching her. They both were floating, floating together, rising and falling on invisible waves.

Everyone took chairs around the kitchen table and sat forking up small bites from the casserole and eating cookies and drinking. No one mentioned the death or any further details. They talked about the snow, the new shopping mall, and what Bud ought to take at college in the fall.

"Driver's ed.," Tommy said. He was on his second bourbon and 7-Up. His face was not so heavy now.

"Drag racing," Nancy said. She tasted her drink: her first alcohol. The acrid taste hidden in the sweetness made her lips curl back. She forced herself to take a gulp.

"Boating," Judy said. Her eyes filled with tears. Then she swallowed, straightened her back, and smiled. "These cookies are fantastic."

Effie looked at Tommy and Bud. They seemed to be someone else's children. Nancy, though, had kept the glow. All the tiny muscles around her eyes and mouth had become smooth: she appeared newborn. And Judy. Judy sat very still, absorbed, her eyes wide, her black hair gathered into a bun at the nape of her long neck.

Effie hated for the day to end: her every gesture had been unique and exact and perfect. She was afraid if she fell asleep the joy would stop and all the noise and disorder on the edge of the world would rush in. Last summer, at the dam, she and Tom had gone off in the boat, just the two of them. Tom was in a bad mood. But there they were, just the two of them, and you couldn't tell the difference between the rose-gold sky and the rose-gold water, and Tom had asked her why in the world she was smiling.

She did not want to go to bed, but she had never in her life missed a night of sleep. "You-all can stay up, but I'm hitting the hay," she said. She went to her bedroom door. In the dim room, the silver frame of her wedding picture gleamed dully.

Tommy got up and followed her. "Mommy," he said. "Mommy, are you all right? Are you going to be all right?"

She couldn't help glaring at him. "Tommy, hon, your daddy always says—always said—that I fall asleep before my head hits the pillow."

She closed the door and got into the yellow nightgown Tom had given her for Christmas this year and lay on the bed. Everything had turned out so differently from what she had planned. She had intended that she and Tom would grow old together, and die instantly in a crash, and be cremated and scattered—over the San Ysidro dam, maybe, or someplace nice like that. He had been so frightened before the operation, and then afterward, too, when he thought it hadn't happened yet, and they both had been angry about being told the odds. But then his death had turned out so differently from what either of them had expected. Maybe it hadn't even happened yet. She lay with her legs together and her palms crossed over her chest—this was part of the ritual, too —and as her attention began to ebb and her breathing to slow, she knew that in some way she would never be this complete again, and that the poinsettia would wither, and the white bedspread would darken, and Nancy would grow up, and the picture in the silver frame would fade.

9

When I saw the man in the black suit go past the picture window, I was lying on the couch in the den watching *Star Trek*—the one where the crew of the starship *Enterprise* beams down to a hostile desert planet and everyone gets separated and then captured by this evil underground civilization.

I opened the front door and the cold wind blew in. The man was holding a white box. He asked me to sign something and then he handed it to me. I said thank you and so did he. Then I didn't know what to do. Maybe there was some special thing that was expected of me at this moment. He didn't seem to have a clue either. "Well, bye," I said after a while. "Thanks a lot."

I closed the door and just stood there for a while holding the box. It was about ten inches on a side. It was made of thick, shiny cardboard, like a box from Boutique Julian. On the lid was a label that said "Eagle Funeral Home." It had an eagle and an outline of the Cibola Peaks and someone had typed in: THE REMAINS OF THOMAS R. HAMMOND, SR. The box was very heavy —it had its own field of gravity.

There was no one to ask what to do. My mother had taken Tommy and Judy for TGIF at the Birdcage, Bud was out driving around with his friends, and Maura was in my room taking a nap. Until today, we'd all stayed close together. My mother treated us to lunches and dinners at nice restaurants, we went to the movies and on a drive in the mountains, and we showed Tommy and Judy the Monte Vista Shopping Plaza. This new life was like an all-day, all-night party. I was constantly changing clothes, and I stayed up as late as I wanted. My mother was always sending me out to the 7-Eleven to get things like chocolate-covered dough-nuts and orange juice for breakfast. So it was strange to be home alone. This afternoon, I'd tried to keep Maura awake by doing her hair and polishing her nails, and I got out all my dolls, but Maura put herself to bed while I was dressing Barbie in a ski outfit.

The kitchen table didn't seem like the right place for the box, although that was where we usually put the mail. The coffee table in the den and the end tables and my mother's writing desk in the living room were jammed with flowering plants. Their pots were wrapped in pink, lavender, or mint-green foil. Each time a new one was delivered, my mother would say, "I hate pot plants." She refused to water them. I started to take the box to Dad's workroom, but then I remembered how cold and dark it was there. So finally I carried it into the den and put it on the carpet between the fireplace and the TV. "Warp Five, Mr. Sulu," Cap-tain Kirk was saying. The ashes were going to be scattered. My mother had talked about taking them next summer to Big Sur, or to Bryce Canyon, or maybe just up to the San Ysidro dam.

I didn't mind where the ashes were scattered, as long as they became one with Nature. I'd told Tommy this, and he was very sweet. He complimented me on my maturity. He said something about how I'd kept from getting mired in outdated religious concepts. Then he explained a lot of things I forget now, but what it came to was that the ashes were already part of Nature because Nature is everything. "Nature *qua* Nature" is what he said. "Nature *qua* Nature?" I said. "Right," he said. I was flat-tered that he was talking to me in this way. I pictured a cloud of particles, hardly matter at all, blending with the reflections on mountain streams and the shine on pine needles. My plan was to go into the forest and feel my father's presence. I'd opened the door of his workroom a couple of times and stepped inside, but I came right out again. When I held his hand the last time, when he was saying not to tell what he had seen—and I didn't, but my mother did—I felt his presence more than I ever had in my life, but his hand almost wasn't there, and that was weird after all the times it had been hard and strong, pulling me across streets and in and out of boats and up mountain paths. Afterward, my mother's face was exactly the same as when you brush loaves of bread with egg whites and then bake them, and the shine doesn't look like it's on the crust but in the air around it. And her eyes got dark in the way they used to the second before she would raise her hand to hit me, and she ordered me not to cry no matter what. So far, I hadn't, but when I looked at the box, a big bubble swelled inside my chest.

Let me see what I remember. The funeral. There's a lot I've forgotten. It was sunny and warm for January. I wanted there to be huge storms—rain, snow, hail, thunder, lightning. But no. Not one cloud. I hated the sky. LaDonna babysat Maura. Bud drove. When my mother got in the car she said, "Why do I keep having to do this? First it was Mama, then Cora." Cora, her best friend, had died of cancer the year before and willed Mom all her clothes, but she sent them to the Salvation Army, except for an embroidered Mexican shawl that she gave to Judy. "And now Tom. I have *had* it." Everyone was quiet. That was the only sad thing she ever said; until then, I'd sort of thought she knew something the rest of us didn't, something that made her peaceful and content about what had happened. Then she talked about the nice weather and about the lunch reservations at La Posada.

We went into the funeral home walking very carefully. We all had on new shoes and the soles clicked on the stone steps. I tried to walk as lightly as possible. I kept my elbows close to my sides and my teeth clamped together; I was afraid I'd bump into something or trip. I was wearing a navy-blue sheath of my mother's. It was too small for her and so she gave it to me. It was kind of small for me, too, but she'd paid good money for it at Boutique Julian. There was a horrible yellow window that was supposed to be stained glass and had crosses in it, and crucifixes, and Stars of David. Judy and I stopped for a second to look at a map, a copy of one, actually, showing the old-fashioned idea of the universe, with the earth in the center and the sun, the moon, seven of the planets, and the fixed stars going around it. Rings within rings. I'd seen this map before, in the dentist's office. And there was one of those hard black leather sofas with metal studs like you see in doctor's offices. There's probably a store where dentists and doctors and funeral directors get their stuff, or maybe they order it from the same catalogue. Maybe the idea is that you sit on the uncomfortable couch and you look at the fake map of the ancient universe, and then you forget your troubles. You forget that you have to have your teeth drilled or you have to get a shot or that your dog just died, and you think: Oh, how interesting, in the Middle Ages they believed that there were only seven planets, but now we know better. This is only my idea about this, and I don't know if it's true. The terrible thing was this: since Tommy and Judy had arrived, I kept forgetting what had happened. It was fun to have them visit, just the way it had been last summer. Tommy would start making jokes or Mom would talk about how we might move into a new house in La Golondrina Park up by the foothills for more gracious living, and I'd forget how bad I felt. I could only keep the real situation in my mind for about a minute every now and then. And each time I went over that day in the hospital, I kept hoping maybe it had turned out different and I'd made a mistake in remembering, the way I always think six times seven is fifty-six. Because he was so happy.

In the chapel there were about forty people, mostly from the Labs, I guess, and Mr. and Mrs. Roybal and the Moras and Mrs. McCory and some other neighbors, and at the front was a huge black coffin covered with an American flag. I tried to sense whether my father was there. But nothing. I wanted to leave. The size of the coffin was all wrong, and anyway, he would never have visited a place like this. He hated getting dressed up and going out—he hadn't worn his suit since Tommy and Judy's wedding.

I kept waiting for my mother and Tommy to do something about the situation. To put a stop to the organ music, for instance, which was the kind you hear in that gloomy, air-conditioned steak house near the Interstate. The Red Flame. But my mother went on smiling a little and walking up the aisle in her usual bouncing way, only more slowly, and Tommy bounced along next to her. I thought, as if I didn't know who they were: Oh, of course, they walk the same way because they're mother and son. I counted the rows of pews by clicking my teeth. I tried to think of words to recite in my mind to prove that I was doing all right, but all I could come up with was "Mary had a little lamb." When we reached the front pew, I heard someone behind us whisper, "What a tower of strength that woman is!"

Judy sat next to me. My mother had taken her to Sonia's and now Judy's hair was teased and smoothed and wrapped into a high dome around her head. Crescents of light reflected off it when she moved. I don't think she'd noticed the coffin before. When she did, she started sobbing. My mother turned and glared, her eyes so hard and dark I thought she was going to hit Judy.

Tommy got up and read from a piece of notebook paper he'd been folding and refolding. He looked awful, even in the expensive new suit Mom had bought him. The skin on his face had gotten loose from the bones. His hands were shaking. He said what a fine person our father was. He said he was a man for all seasons, a Renaissance man. After a while, Tommy calmed down. He said our father was a scientist, an outdoorsman, a friend to all, a good American, a great human being who had led the good life as defined by the Greek philosophers. And then he read the words from the Bible about how there is a time to sow and a time to reap.

Afterward, we had to stand around while people greeted us. That was the worst part, because if you were in a moment of forgetting the whole reason you were there and thinking about something else, then someone you didn't even know would come up and pat you and tell you how sorry they were. And if you remembered why you were there, then you wanted more than anything in the world to be somewhere else, thinking about something else, and someone would come up and prevent you from doing that. Several people congratulated Tommy on his speech. Finally we made it to the parking lot. My mother had the flag folded into a triangle under her arm. She said, "I sure could use a margarita and an enchilada."

. . .

On the starship *Enterprise,* five men in collarless uniforms stood in formation and allowed beams of light to disintegrate them into shining dots. A second later they were reconstituted on the hostile desert planet next to some red rocks. There are two things I know for certain about the future. One, nobody will ever have to open doors by hand. Two, no one will wear collars.

I don't think it was Judy's fault that she'd started bawling at the funeral. When we got home from the airport, she took me in my room and told me that at about the time my father went, she'd had a kind of a daydream of him flying in a little plane with rounded-off wings through beautiful clouds and he was very happy. She asked me not to mention this. She was probably right not to tell my mother, because why would Judy get to have a vision about Dad when the people who were really his relatives didn't?

It was always my job to get things ready for TGIF. Fridays after school, I used to straighten up the house, put out clean ashtrays and bowls of potato chips, and maybe I'd make some kind of dip, and take the highball glasses down from the cupboard. My parents would come home from the Birdcage talking a lot, louder than usual, and their faces would be pink. In the old days, Judy and Tommy were usually with them. After my father bought his guitar, he'd sometimes sit strumming softly while everyone talked. Just background music. After a while, my mother would fix fried chicken and french fries, usually, and maybe I'd bake biscuits. Dinner was always late, but nobody cared because we were full of potato chips and dip. And then all the good TV programs came on.

After *Star Trek,* I set out pretzels and some carrot cake from the McCorys, and I tried making a dip with a can of tuna fish and some cream cheese, but it wasn't too good, and so I added catsup, which at least took the brown away.

When my mother came in the front door with Tommy, and Judy behind them, and everyone laughing and talking, I figured for a second that my father was locking the car and would be right in. My mother threw her purse on the couch by the door like she always does. *Whap!* And then her quick footsteps. The sounds of my mother coming home. "Did you-all have a wonderful time with little Maura?" she asked me.

"It was really fun," I said. "I painted each of her nails a different color, and I did her hair in three ponytails, and then she fell asleep and I played with my dolls."

"Thanks so much, Nance," Judy said. She was preserving her hair in that dome, which my mother thought was a big improvement. More adult. "That was really sweet of you."

"Anyone who can spend more than an hour with Maura when she's awake has won my deepest gratitude, not to speak of awe," Tommy said. One thing about this new, partying life was that everyone was so appreciative of everyone else.

My mother wanted to know if there had been any phone calls. "I swear, I've got so many things going on," she said, heading for the den. "I feel like a corporate executrix. The insurance man didn't call? Or the lawyer?" Then she started telling Tommy about probate and some deposit certificate or something. How it had been Grandpa Hammond's and how Dad had gotten it after Grandpa's death because they had the same name, and then she'd borrowed it from the safe-deposit box before anyone found out.

I really meant to point out the other box, but she was busy talking, and I happened to get a little sick to my stomach. So I just took drink orders. As I was leaving the den, Judy said, "Oh, lookee—a late Christmas present! How nice—who's it for?"

The box stayed where I'd put it. I vacuumed around it. Judy watered the plants on the end table next to it. No one mentioned it.

One day Tommy said the time had come to go back to New York. My mother asked him to stay a little longer. "We're having so dadgummed much fun," she said. "And you know there's nothing but snow and slush back there." Tommy phoned his work and got his leave of absence extended. He said he was paid by the hour and didn't have vacation time. Never in my life will

I talk or think about all the boring things like certificates from the bank, or deposits, probates, leaves of absence, politics, the war, etc. Most of the time, that's what they talked about. Just the *sound* of those words made me want to pass out. I'd have preferred to discuss whether telekinesis is possible, or what happens after you die, or where everybody really comes from. I mean, one day you're not here, and then you are, and you don't remember how you got here. It seems to me that's a very crucial subject, but everyone ignores it. I used to think that old people just got smaller and smaller and became babies and then the whole thing began again. This girl at school believed in reincarnation, which is very interesting, but where do you start? If you go back through all your past lives, etc., then you still don't know where you came from. At least this girl had no idea what her church said about that. But I can tell you one thing about church. I used to go with LaDonna to her church quite a lot, First Methodist, and nobody there believed a thing: they had to be faking it. So what you're left with is Nature, in my humble opinion, because there it is. People should just shut up about all the other stuff.

Two days before Tommy and Judy really had to leave, my mother took us to La Posada again. She said she had an important announcement. She was dressed up and had on all her silver jewelry. "I've been thinking on this," she said. "And I want to say it here, in this beautiful restaurant, because, kids, your daddy loved this place. He wasn't too big on dining out, but he loved La Posada; he loved the flowers painted around that adobe fire-place in the corner. And so what I want to say to you at this moment is that you-all have to go to the airport and for fifty dollars, which I will pay, you have to charter a little plane. Tommy, I already found out all about how you do it. And it is your duty as the firstborn son to go up and scatter the ashes. That's what Dad would want. Bud and Nancy can help. Some over the river and the valley, some over the mesa, especially over Princess Darla Heights and the house, and a little over the foot-hills and the peaks. It will be a wonderful treat for you-all, going up in a plane like that. Maura, honey, would you like to go up in an airplane? Wouldn't that be fun?"

"My first time," I said. Flying in a plane—fantastic! "LaDonna will just die."

"Maybe the pilot will let *me* fly it," Bud said. "There's nothing to it. That's what Dad said."

"I'm sure you'd be a good pilot, Bud," Judy said. She patted his arm. He blushed and laughed through his nose.

Tommy was wearing Dad's navy blue blazer. He just smoked his little cigar and frowned, and we watched him. He cleared his throat. "Well, Mommy, after due consideration, I have to say that if that's your supreme desire, I think it is a memorable and fitting tribute to our father."

"Oh, darlin', you always put things so *eloquently,*" Mom said.

"Tom Senior always did say how much he loved flying," Judy said.

"But you come too, Mom," Tommy said.

My mother shook her head, making her dangling earrings clink. "No, no. I want you-all to do this. For Dad. You know what I adore about this place? Those Mexican blouses the little waitresses wear. Dad always thought those girls were so cute. They're a little plump, though, don't you think?"

I looked up at the ceiling, at the old, blackened log beams. For a moment, I felt the clear, deep feeling I'd had in the hospital room come back.

"I've never done anything like this before," the pilot said. He wore a baseball cap, mirror sunglasses, and a faded leather jacket that was peeling. We stood around him in the bright sunshine. A cold wind was blowing. Tumbleweeds rolled from the mesa across the runway.

"I would assume one simply opens the window and scatters," Tommy said. He was fairly nervous. He made jerky gestures while he talked and he was smoking hard. Whenever he sucked on his little cigar, the skin around his mouth went white.

"Don't have windows that open," the pilot said. He had a drawl, and didn't move his jaws or any other part of his body when he spoke. "But I reckon we can open the door a crack. It'll be okay." He turned to me. "Young lady, let me give you a hand."

He helped me up into the plane. I was wearing my new wheat-colored jeans, the black turtleneck LaDonna gave me for Christmas, and my same old car coat. I'd tried to figure out whether to dress up or not, and then there wasn't enough time, so I just wore what I had on. I climbed into the back and strapped myself in. It was like a narrow cave. There were only four seats. Through a little round window, I watched Judy speaking to Tommy, and Maura sitting on her hip waving at me. That hairdo didn't really suit Judy all that well, frankly.

Bud climbed inside and bumped his head on the ceiling. When he sat down, the whole plane jiggled. "Judy and Maura can't go up—not enough room," he said. He was pale today. His eyes were red. He had combed his hair over his forehead and it looked really stupid. "Oh, shit, this is great!" he said, examining the instrument panel. "Jesus Christ, how can he read all these things? How can he tell what's going on?"

"Maybe Maura could ride on my lap," I said. "We've been promising her nonstop she could go up in the sky."

"She'll get to go when they fly back to New York," Bud said. "That little skunk has been up in a plane more times than we have, which is easy since we've only been in one zero times."

Tommy ripped open the top of the cardboard box and took out a dark brown can the size of a sugar canister. He handed Judy the empty box and she and Maura walked toward the edge of the runway. A gust of wind flattened the yellow grass on the mesa. Goodbye, I thought, goodbye forever. I don't know why I thought that.

I already knew that the box contained a can. The night before, Bud and I had been in the den while the others were out and he'd carefully slit the tape sealing the box and pried off the lid of the can. When he looked inside, he smiled in a very weird way that I wish I could forget: the corners of his mouth turned up and his lips pulled away from his teeth. That was the way he was now, especially around his friends. The big tough guy, able to take anything. Everything always a laugh.

.   .   .

The plane made a loud racket and I was pressed back in the seat as we taxied along the runway. Suddenly the ground dropped away. Judy and Maura became tiny, waving figures. For the first time in my life, I could see all of Cibola at once. The airport and the air base. The freeway and the Interstate and all their loops and cloverleafs. The roofs of the houses like Chiclets laid in rows along the streets. The gray foothills where the new subdivisions were, with circular drives and empty swimming pools. The town seemed so important when you were on the ground. Now it was just not that big a deal. The pilot pointed at some low, windowless buildings behind a fence on the far side of the base and beyond them to several big metal towers. There were strange shapes cut in the earth out there: they looked like geometry problems. Every now and then something would catch the light, something metal, or a windshield, and there would be a flash.

"Security installations," he said in a loud voice. "You're not permitted to fly anywhere near them or the Labs."

"Right," Tommy said. He sat next to the pilot. "Our father was an engineer at Cibola Labs."

"See that mountain?" The pilot waved toward one of the larger foothills. It was shaped like a pyramid and had a perfectly smooth whitish face with a railroad track in a zigzag. On the top was a tower made of girders. "That mountain is filled with the stuff they make at the Labs. That mountain is filled with nuke-uler weaponry."

"I wasn't aware of that fact," Tommy said. "But I'm not surprised."

"Heck, yes. It's classified—that's why you didn't know."

That didn't sound right. My father would have told me if the Labs made bombs. A long time ago, I'd asked him what he did at work. He said he dug holes and other guys filled them up. When I got older, I realized that he was an engineer, but I'd never thought about exactly what that was or what he did. He had to make calculations, and he had this slide rule, and he wasn't supposed to talk about his job because the Russians might find out. "They don't make bombs at the Labs," I said.

Bud and Tommy turned to me. "Sure they do," Bud said. He laughed.

"What did you think they made?" Tommy asked me.

"Something to do with guided missiles?" I said. When I was small, sometimes my father would be away for long stretches. Once he brought me back a hula skirt from some island. Tests, my mother said. Dad is at the tests. But for quite a while, he hadn't gone anywhere, and last year he said he didn't like his job anymore, and he came home early most of the time. "Dad never worked on bombs," I said. "Did he, Tommy?"

The pilot shifted himself around to look at me. I was two big-headed, round-faced dolls in the mirrors of his lenses. "You kids can be proud of your daddy," he said. "He helped keep this country safe and strong. If it wasn't for your daddy, we'd probably be speakin' Jay-pan-eese."

Flying was so easy. It was like nothing. We went toward the river. It made a deep, red cut in the mesa. The fields on either side were yellow, and the trees and scrub on the banks were leafless. They looked like the gray tufts you find under the bed. When you saw the Cibola River from the ground, it was hardly there at all—it was disappointing, just a muddy brown trickle most of the time, with islands of red-brown clay. But from the plane, I saw that it was a wide blue ribbon, just like a river in a geography book. Somewhere north, the San Ysidro flowed into the Cibola, and so if some of the ashes fell into the Cibola, my father would sort of become a part of the river he liked the best.

Tommy tried to open the door next to his seat a crack. The pilot reached over to help. The door tore all the way open. My insides dropped: Tommy was going to fall out and lose the can. I started forward but I was stopped by my seat belt. "Are you strapped in okay, Tommy?" I shouted. But the wind was so loud he couldn't hear me.

The peaks were snowy, with black shadows cutting down their faces. Above them was the half-moon. It was almost transparent in the clear blue. The peaks kept changing shape as we flew, and I saw that there were all kinds of hidden canyons and other, smaller mountains that I hadn't even known about. I clicked my teeth together to mark them in my mind. In the car on the way to the airport, Tommy had said that this was a solemn, special ceremony and that each of us would take turns doing the scattering. I was going to be last—I was supposed to do the foothills and the peaks, or Mount Goodnight, anyway, the closest one. But there was no way I was going to be able to scatter anything, because we couldn't move around in that tiny cabin and change places, especially with the door open. Think of opening the front door and instead of a yard, there is endless sky.

Tommy let go of a handful of light gray ash and it came right back inside. I remembered last summer by the campfire when we had a discussion about what you should do with your body after death, whether it was better to have it buried in the deep woods, where it would blend in with the soil and provide food for the trees, or to have it cremated. My mother would always say, whenever we camped at a beautiful spot, "Scatter your daddy and me right here." Tommy laughed and said he wanted to be scattered very high up, so his ashes would get caught in the jet stream and be blown around the world, and maybe blot out a little bit of sunshine going to the people below, and eventually come back down to earth and get in people's eyes.

He let some more ashes go and they blew into his face. He shook his head. He rubbed his face with his forearm and took another handful and leaned out still farther.

My eyes were stinging and watering. I watched the particles disappearing from his palm in the sunlight. They swirled away until only some bits of splintered bone were left. Then those went, too.

"You really got to get yourself out much more," the pilot said. "It's all coming back inside."

"Better stick your ass out there," Bud said. He laughed. "Come on, Tommy! Let me do it! I'm bigger than you. I can do it. I'm not scared."

"I'll handle this," Tommy yelled, his eyes and cheeks squeezed up.

I reached out to grip his shoulders. But that didn't help—when he leaned out as far as he had to in order to get the ashes to stay outside the plane, I couldn't do anything to hold him.

Then we were over Princess Darla Heights. I never knew that

all those flat roofs were just gray asphalt. They moved underneath us, and so did the brown lawns, and the backyards and the patios. The way scenery passed under the plane made me think of *2001*, the last part, when the astronaut is gliding over some weird planet.

"Hey," Bud said, "there's Lincoln Avenue, there's Chamisa, there's Cagua. Try to hit Cagua, Tommy."

Tommy's upper body was completely out of the plane now. I clapped my hands over my ears, which is what I always do when I think something bad is about to happen. I would not dream of covering my eyes. Below was the Monte Vista Shopping Plaza parking lot.

Tommy held the can out and turned it upside down, and the ashes made a sideways plume and that was it.

"Way to go!" Bud said.

"Did you all have a beautiful time?" Judy wanted to know. "It must have been gorgeous up there. Such a clear day." She held Maura, who was looking at a new little book, *Sleeping Beauty*.

I couldn't talk. Tommy and Bud shook hands with the pilot. They all were covered with gray. It powdered their messed-up hair, their eyebrows, the creases around their mouths and eyes, the folds of their coats. Tommy had a dark smear running from under one eye down to his chin. He looked like he was wearing makeup for the role of a sick old man in a school play. Then I saw that I was all covered, too. I brushed the sleeve of my coat and a puff of gray came out. I pressed my lips together and tasted grit. I wanted to stay close to the others, but when I started to walk, my legs trembled.

"Tommy nearly fell out of the plane," Bud told Judy. He was still talking in a loud voice the way he had in the plane. "It was a riot."

"But you had your seat belt on, didn't you, honey?" Judy said. She had her free hand on the back of Tommy's neck.

"The presence of a seat belt was scarcely enough to provide consolation," Tommy said. "I need a drink."

I felt light, almost as if I didn't exist. My legs had practically disappeared. I had been up in the sky and seen everything, and now I was down on the ground, where I had to go one step at a time. Everyone had become very far away and small: I thought if I reached out to them I'd discover that they were standing on the horizon.

As we were getting into the car, I asked Judy about the box. I wanted to keep it. Maybe I would preserve something very precious in it.

"Oh, boy," Judy said. "That dadgummed box. Tommy said to get rid of it, and so I went walking all over the place looking for a trash can, and I couldn't find one near the runway, and then I went into the terminal, and they just had those big ashtrays with sand in them, and wastebaskets with teeny slots, and in the ladies' room there was another one with a slot just a little too small. So I tried to tear the box up, but the cardboard was too thick, and there was Maura saying, 'Mommy, why are you doing that?' I wound up leaving it next to a wastebasket near the phone booths, and I scratched out the name on the label so your mom doesn't get a call from some janitor. And then I bought Maura a book at the newsstand—the very same book I had when I was a kid, believe it or not—and then we came out and watched you land. It was perfect. Such a wonderful thing for Effie to think of."

It was strange. Judy was no longer Judy. Was she just trying to cheer everyone up and she considered that was the best way? I asked Tommy what he did with the can.

"I don't know. I think I left it in that poor bastard's plane."

I asked him if we could go get it. I really wanted it. But Tommy just rolled up into himself and said there was no way we were going back to that plane. Bud kept tilting his head back and pulling his upper lip over his teeth as if he had to sneeze. You went up in the sky, and when you came down, everyone was different. Except Maura. She was humming to herself and turning the pages of the book, and she seemed the same.

My mother was waiting for us in the doorway. When I was little, I used to think sometimes she was a queen, the queen in the movie of *Snow White*. Now she was all dressed up, and she'd had her hair done. She seemed very peaceful. "Why don't we all go out to dinner?" she said.

Tommy pushed past her and went into the kitchen. "A drink first," he said.

"If it hadn't have been for Dad, we'd all be speakin' Jay-pan-eese," Bud said. He went into the den and turned on the television. A football game.

"Where are we going?" Judy asked. "Should I get dressed up, and Maura, too?"

"I think we should go to the Red Coach Inn," Effie said. "It's this old-English-type place that just opened in Monte Vista Plaza and they have this gigantic stone fireplace, and their specialty is spit roasting. I'm just dying to go there."

Judy took Maura into the bedroom. I stood there. I couldn't think what to do. What made my mother so collected? I wanted to tell her that the airplane plan hadn't worked out very well. I wanted to cry and beg her to make things so that the whole business could be done over, the right way. But she was looking at me expectantly.

"Nancy, darlin'—just tell me one thing and then that's *it* and I don't ever want to talk about it again. Was it just what your daddy would have wanted?" She had put that pale makeup on that hid the freckles and made her face look perfectly smooth, and she was wearing her best fiesta dress, the full-skirted yellow one with the silver rickrack.

"Yes, Mom," I said.

10

It was the day of the solar eclipse. Tommy was going to bring home some black transparencies from the photo lab for us to look through, but then he forgot about it. I hadn't reminded him. After I tried to ask him what I was doing wrong that he had not wanted to make love to me since Christmas and he said I had too many needs, I'd decided not to ask him for anything ever again. I don't know if he noticed. He got up late that morning and took a shower and shaved, even though it was his day off, and he put on a starched and ironed shirt and went out. He said he had some things to do. I didn't ask what. I'd hoped he would watch the eclipse with Maura and me and explain it to her.

I went to the hall closet to look for some old pieces of film. The shelves were full of stuff. Molded plastic toy parts, a Raggedy Ann doll with her cotton batting oozing out, one little bedroom slipper in the shape of a duck (its mate had fallen apart, but Maura loved the slippers so much I couldn't throw this one away), a tangle of yellow yarn from a sweater I'd started to knit for Tommy after he proposed, some pages of a Tiffany's catalogue I had found at the laundromat, an unopened pediatrician's bill, some Christmas-tree ornaments missing their hooks, a nearly empty bottle of cough medicine with a ball of cotton stuck to the side, newspapers Tommy was saving—the top one had an enormous headline saying MEN WALK ON MOON—mixed in with his school papers, a box of sculptor's clay, his floor plan of the house we were going to have built in the Cibola foothills, a dried-up mascara wand, a little bar of perfumed soap in the shape of a rose that I'd been given as a high school graduation present, torn nylons that I could wear in an emergency, blank income-tax forms, a mitten . . . Finally, I found a shoe box full of photographs. In a packet of pictures Effie had sent us in the fall were a few negatives that seemed black enough.

I brushed Maura's hair and pushed her arms into a jacket that was getting too small, and we went downstairs to the stoop. From there we had a clear view over the tenement roofs of the part of the sky where the eclipse was supposed to take place. A group had gathered. It was nearly spring, and everyone was in a good mood, the way people are when they're waiting for a parade. I decided to observe a man with thin blond hair and a little mustache who sat on the top step reading a journal titled *The Administration of Lower Extremity Amputations.* He had on a white jacket; I'd often seen him in the supermarket but hadn't realized he was a medical student. I didn't always remember to observe one real thing every day, but the fact that there was going to be an eclipse made me more alert. I watched the way he slid out of the shade as it came toward him so that he stayed in the warm sunlight. He ignored the other people, but he gave a little smile to the man who came up the steps and stood beside him. This man, who had a long black ponytail and a drooping mustache and wore black leather pants and a black leather sleeveless shirt, sat most of the time in the window of his basement apartment across the street reading comics and guarding his motorcycle, which he kept chained to a sapling. Maura greeted him happily; how did she know him? I pulled her close to me. Sometimes he shouted at passersby for looking too long at his motor-cycle.

"Just a few more minutes," someone said.

I gave Maura a negative. It was of Tommy in front of the camper last summer at the dam: his lips were white, and his swimming suit, face, and chest were black, and so was the band of sky behind him.

She studied the negative, her eyebrows, which were clearly defined half-circles, drawing together.

"Who's that?" she asked.

"The sun is going to be covered up by the moon," I told her, pointing at the sky.

The sun was a bright disk. A cool wind blew. A shining flock of pigeons wheeled overhead, passing in and out of the shadows of the buildings. Two explosions came from nearby, their claps levitating everything for an instant. No one paid any attention.

The explosions had started a week ago. I was in the playground with Maura at the time, and I grabbed her to my chest and ran all the way home. I thought the park was being bombed. Students making explosives had recently blown up a townhouse, and snipers were shooting at people in parks on behalf of some liberation cause. Tommy said the liberationists had good reason to shoot and destroy. I said, "Do you think the people in charge are going to say, 'Great! We've been misguided, but now that we see what you're doing, killing people and blowing up buildings, we're in complete sympathy with your cause and we will do all we can to help you!'?" He said my grasp of the issues was feeble. Anyway, the blasts turned out to be from the site down the street where the tenements had been demolished. The clerk at the supermarket told me that the rock under them had to be dynamited in order to make the excavation deep enough for the foundation of a new high-rise apartment building. I took Maura over to see the bulldozers grinding around in the bottom of the pit that had appeared. There was a lot of muddy water down there, and I overheard someone say that it was because of an underground creek that ran right along our street. Before I fell asleep at night, I would think about the creek flowing below and feel very happy. The explosions were now routine, but they still made me imagine the city in ruins, the revolution Tommy talked about coming to pass, our own building a shell, Tommy gone . . . I would climb through the wreckage of our apartment, wondering what to keep and then deciding to take nothing. I'd pick up Maura and leave with only what I wore—shorts and a tank top and sandals. I would be sad, but I would escape, make my way West somehow, crossing the George Washington Bridge on foot, alone and brave.

"That negative won't protect you enough," a new voice said. The man looked familiar. He handed me two squares of black film. "Use these—I brought many."

"Oh, thank you," I said. "Thank you very much." I'd never gotten used to the unfriendliness of the city—I still came home from the store or the subway hurt by the rudeness of the people who pushed ahead of me or didn't say "You're welcome" when I thanked them. When someone happened to be kind, I wanted to lay my head on his chest and cry.

He had dark brown eyes that went slightly upward at the outer corners and a heart-shaped face. His hair was dark and fell in flat curves over his ears. He was tall and straight-spined. I kept thanking him, and he watched me. His gaze came straight to me, moving through a vacuum, no air between us. I couldn't stand it. I bent over and gave Maura a transparency, taking in his sheepskin coat, his red-and-yellow silk muffler, his old Levi's, and his polished brown boots. "Don't stare at the sun directly," I told Maura.

"Here it comes," the man in black leather said.

"Right you are, man," the medical student said.

"Here it comes," said the man at my side. He had a husky voice I had heard before.

"Here it comes," Maura said, looking down at the gutter, which was filled with dirty clumps of ice embedded with bits of tinsel. People stood with their heads back, holding pieces of black film in front of their eyes and commenting on the progress of the invisible moon. I didn't use my piece because I didn't want to miss anything. The shadows softened and their edges blurred. The sun began to disappear. It shrank to a thin crescent and the air became still.

Someone in the building put on a record—unbearably loud, peculiar music. "*Death and Transfiguration,*" the man next to me said.

"What?" I said.

"Strauss. Richard, that is."

"It's getting closer," the medical student said to the man in black leather.

The pigeons flew to windowsills and under pediments and roosted.

"Maura, it's the eclipse," I said. "The birds think it's time to go to bed." I wanted her to remember today. It would be fifteen years before there was another eclipse like this. "Look up in the sky, sweetheart."

But Maura insisted on examining the ground through the black square. She aped the comments she overheard. "It's getting bigger now," she repeated. "Closer and closer." She walked up and down the steps. "Here it comes! Here it comes!"

A darkening fluid poured around us. I was excited and a little afraid. "Amazing," the man murmured, and I felt his breath against my temple. A deep blue twilight fell, and the air became very cold. Talking stopped.

As the sun emerged, the opening bars of "Here Comes the Sun" came out of an upper window, drowning out the brassy roar of the other music. Maura was gone. I found her in the well of the building next to the stoop playing around some freshly painted garbage cans, her hands blotted with green.

The half-eaten ball of the sun traveled through a net of cloud, and I wanted to make a wish, the way I did in Cibola when I saw a falling star. This occasion had to be put to use. It couldn't just pass without something being made to happen. But I didn't know what to wish for. Except for the month in Cibola, which Effie had made very pleasant for us in spite of the funeral, we'd had a hard winter. We were broke at Christmas—I gave Tommy the wedding pot, and made a yarn doll for Maura, and Tommy couldn't afford any gifts at all—and then after we came back from Cibola, we were worse than broke, having lost a whole month of work. On top of all that, Tommy said the world had launched a Stop Hammond movement: there were difficulties at the photo lab and in the philosophy department. He had used up his scholarship, his stipend wasn't renewed, he still had to pay full tuition because he hadn't handed in his dissertation, and the manager of the photo lab had decided to stay on and so Tommy was no longer in line for that job, although he continued working extra hours without pay. The happiest he had ever been, he told me, was last summer at the dam—he just hadn't known it then. He wanted one big happiness to descend, and he said he was getting tired of waiting. I was more of a ragpicker, finding happy moments here and there, but I couldn't figure out how to give any of them to Tommy so that he wouldn't get so fed up.

As I carried Maura up the steps to the double doors of the building, I decided to spend the day cleaning house and then take some of my secret birthday money and go buy steak, and after Maura was in bed, I'd light candles, fix drinks and a nice dinner, wash my hair and brush it until it was very shiny—I'd been keeping it in braids so that I didn't have to bother with it when I got up—and put on my wedding-night negligee, and when Tommy came home, I'd gaze into his eyes and tell him about the eclipse while "Here Comes the Sun" played on the stereo. He'd borrowed that Beatles album from some guy. I would get him interested in me again the way he had been when we were first married—after three months of going without, that shouldn't be too difficult—and we'd get organized and plan our life. I'd bought a yellow legal-sized pad for just this purpose when we returned from Cibola and all it had been used for so far was for Maura to draw on. For a long time, I'd been meaning to create a special evening, which I'd read about in a magazine in the laundromat as a surefire way to get your man in the mood, but when he got home at ten or eleven like he did most nights lately, I was just too tired. But today I'd drink a lot of hot, strong tea and keep awake.

"You're leaving?" the man asked. "It's not over yet."

"I have to." I held Maura's wrists to keep the paint from getting smeared on our coats. "I have to get this mess off her before it dries. Thanks for the film."

"Still interested in archaeology?" he asked.

"Excuse me?"

"The burial at Callosa and all of that sort of thing."

I pulled open the heavy doors and the glass rattled. "Callosa?" I said. He held them open for me, and, touching me briefly between the shoulder blades as if he were helping me through some difficult passage, urged me to go through. In the dim, fluorescent-lit foyer, I stared down at the dirty brown linoleum.

"When we met, we talked about Callosa—the excavation you were on there. Remember? I said to myself, 'Not only is she interested in Indian ruins, she probably is an Indian herself also.' Later, I wished I had asked you. I've seen you sometimes pushing a stroller around, but you were so preoccupied I didn't want to bother you." He followed me to the staircase, his hand going into his pants pocket as if he were searching for a key.

It bothered me that without my knowing it someone could observe me and think about me and remember things I spoke about. Why would anyone see me? What could there possibly be to see? "I know I didn't do any typing for you," I said. I would have remembered his interesting appearance. The only places I went, in my discrete, opaque sphere, were the supermarket, the laundromat, and the library. Maybe he'd been in line at the librarian's desk.

"Are you?" He put one foot on the stair step and it creaked.

"Am I what?"

"Indian." He smiled—uncertainly at first. His mouth was trying to figure out what to do. One corner of it came up and then the other and at last a sweet, balanced curve was formed.

I was frightened. "Aren't you in the philosophy department?" I now had an image of him standing, very erect, heels together, in the department's basement lounge, with its sprung sofas and scratched coffee table. I used to meet Tommy there on Friday afternoons, after the graduate-student kaffeeklatsches, and we'd walk home together. Once, while I was waiting outside the lounge with Maura, I overheard someone say "Hammond's beautiful wife." I figured it was some kind of joke, and I thought about it for weeks afterward. Tommy didn't go to the department anymore. He was always at the photo lab, or sometimes he'd see friends, and he stayed up most nights now drinking wine and singing folk songs to himself in the living room. "In the graduate program?"

"Not really," the man said. "I have friends there whom you know. Ed Biederman—"

"Oh, yes, my husband's adviser." I took a breath. I was doing all right. He wasn't a murderer. I shifted Maura on my hip and tightened my grip on her wrists.

She kept pulling away. "Mommy," she said. "Let me down."

"My husband is Tom Hammond—" It was important to say his name, to let this man know.

"Tip Scarborough introduced us."

"Oh, a good friend of ours!" I said. Tip wasn't all that good a friend, really. He'd invited us to a dinner party last fall, the second one since our move to New York, and Tommy had said that night, as we left, "Our place next—Judy will make her enchiladas." But the idea of having someone to dinner was too much for me, and then Tip criticized some theories of Tommy's and so we never had him over. In fact, except for the neighbor lady across the hall who loaned me things and babysat Maura once or twice, we had never had any guests.

"We were in Morocco together, Tip and I," the man said. "I'm Viktor Kassell—Vik."

"You were the one who went over on the freighter with him? And you lived in Fez?"

"I am that person," he said. He gestured upward.

I continued up the stairs. "I guess I should tell you I'm Judy Hammond."

"I know," he said.

When we reached the third-floor landing, I stopped by the door, which I'd left ajar.

"Now, tell me the truth—are you?" he asked. He pushed the door open and remained with his hand against it, his arm curved protectively over my head. It was like the moment at the end of a first date when I used to be baffled about whether a kiss would occur, and in fact, as he looked down at me, his lips moved slightly. I was afraid again. I hugged Maura to me. And then his eyes flicked away.

"Am I what?" I asked.

"Hey, is that a pot you found at your excavation?" He was looking at the two-throated wedding jar. It was on the mantelpiece under Tom Senior's carving of the desert hawk, which stirred on its fishline.

"I didn't dig that up, I bought it," I said.

"Yes, I should have realized that—it's new. But the design is —it's beautiful." He spoke in a low voice. He had, not an accent exactly, but a sort of hesitation. "But I prefer the pot next to it, actually."

"Really?" I had set my great-grandmother's pot out after I came back from Cibola because the color reminded me of the canyon walls at the San Ysidro dam. Tommy never objected; maybe he didn't notice. I carried Maura to the kitchen sink, lifted her up over a pile of dirty dishes, and put her hands under the running water and rubbed at them with a bar of soap. He remained in the doorway, watching. I didn't know what to do. I felt as if I had blacked out for an instant and revived with everything slightly rearranged. Here I was, rubbing soap on these little hands: how did I get here?

Maura kept squirming and saying "No!" I put her down and she ran into her room.

I became aware of the newspapers and toys spread around, the stacks of overdue library books, the dusty brick-and-board bookcases, my hair hanging in my eyes and the tips of my braids wet from the sink, my sweatshirt stained with cherry cough syrup, the pictures scattered on the couch. In the gray light from the airshaft window, they seemed unbearably bright and false: the water of the San Ysidro was a brilliant turquoise, the earth a burnt red, the trees and scrub a brownish green. The Paradisos were bleak, Paradiso Baldy was ashy and sterile, and the sky was the color of a heavily chlorinated swimming pool. "I'm sorry everything is such a mess," I said. "Would you like a cup of tea?" I didn't have anything else to offer, and in fact there were only two tea bags. I didn't want to be impolite, but I hoped he would say no.

We sat by the window talking, the teapot between us on the red-and-white-checked tablecloth. Maura sang, "Oh, no, don't let the rain fall down, my roof's got a hole in it and I might drown," and put her stuffed animals to bed on the couch under his coat.

"Where did I tell you about Callosa, the dig and all?" I asked him. "When was it?"

He laughed, turning his head to one side while keeping his eyes on mine. "You must guess."

That made me uncomfortable. "I think I remember," I said. This wasn't true. "Where are you from?"

"All over," he said. His parents had come from Rumania, but for some reason they weren't really Rumanian, and during the war they went to a place called Kazakhstan and Vik had been born there. "I am a displaced person," he said, and his mouth turned down for a second. His father was a businessman who now lived in Mexico City and his mother was a decorator who had wanted to come to America and live in a city whose name had always given her beautiful dreams, Buffalo, but once she saw Buffalo she chose New York. She had a place downtown where Vik was staying at the moment.

I held Maura and rocked her to sleep.

"I just came back from a year in India," Vik said.

"My husband would be so interested in that," I said. "He would love to talk to you. We want to travel, too." I told him we might move to Guyana, Chad, or Liberia. "We're waiting to hear which one." I explained about the international teaching program Tommy had recently applied to. Actually, I wondered if anything would come of it—Tommy had also asked for various grants and none of them had come through—but being with this man made me think it was entirely possible that I'd soon find myself in an exotic land.

"And I'll be going to Mexico and hitchhiking through South America in a few weeks—if it's right for that to happen."

"Well, if you happen to come to Guyana, please look us up," I said.

"You can count on it. I may even make a detour." There was a silence. He seemed to be concentrating on something. A single line appeared between his wide-set eyes. It was the sort of line I could imagine appearing when he was taken by passion. His sweater smelled of camphor. He watched me. Startled, I returned his gaze. Maybe we had met in a former life.

I looked away. "I hope my husband comes home soon, so he can see you," I said. I wanted to declare: My husband and I married for eternity, and now, five years later, we are more perfectly in love than ever; you would have no idea about the magic of that, since you are a wandering bachelor with, no doubt, many women, but you can see from my calm, fulfilled aura the truth of what I'm saying. I will permit you a glimpse into a life of happiness you know nothing about. But that's all—just a glimpse. Because I am really very content.

I carried Maura to her room and put her in bed. I stopped in the bathroom and undid my braids and brushed my hair. I straightened my eyebrows with a moistened fingertip. When I returned to the table, I was horribly aware of what Vik must be seeing: a dowdy mother, a bad housekeeper, a needy female. I asked him what India was like.

"Well." He allowed himself a private smile. "Not easy to answer that. I became very exhausted. Moved around a lot. Third-class railway carriages, sleeping in temples—the whole bit. I was in Goa, freaks everywhere. This one guy—he went up in a tree. Stoned on *charas*. He didn't want to hear it anymore. He just didn't want to hear. India is overwhelmingly complex, you know. The smells alone . . ." He shook his head. "The cheap pastry that is India," he said. "People go there searching. They think: Well! Mysterious India! And it is—but not in the way you expect. You go all through that, then you get beyond it. It becomes *de trop*. I missed my Wheaties. I wanted to come home."

"And home is—?"

"No place. The mind has no place to rest."

"Oh," I said. The sun was low enough now to send a shaft of light between the buildings. It struck the brick wall opposite the window and made the dust particles in the airshaft golden, as if a tomb had been opened and a light shone inside. Then it was gone. "The mind has no place to rest?" I said. "What a strange thing." I got up and switched on a lamp and made a second pot of tea with the old tea bag and the last fresh one. I hoped for more from him: he had arranged his concentration, his secretiveness, his tilted eyes, his faint accent, his bearing to dam up some tremendous force. What he said didn't matter very much. It was the way he moved that fascinated me, the way he carefully grasped his mug and lifted it and looked at it before taking a sip. And it was the way he didn't move, holding alertly still while I spoke.

At the end of the day, I realized I hadn't shopped for dinner. But I never knew anymore when to start cooking. At first I worried about Tommy out there with the gangs with baseball bats, the muggers, the speeding cars, but not so much since my decision never to ask for anything. What if I invited Vik to stay and eat with us? What if Tommy came through the door this very minute? It was really all right: they had friends in common; Tommy had met Vik already; it would be something new for a change, having a friend here, and anyway, Tommy said he was tired of the people in the department.

I came back to the table with the teapot and immediately bumped into the strong field of Vik's presence. Even keeping my eyes down, I knew I was being seen. I didn't want to think about him reaching for me in his deliberate way—his hand on the small of my back—and putting his mouth on mine, but there it was, the image had planted itself in my brain, its roots radiated into the pit of my abdomen. "I just have to check on my daughter," I said, afraid, and went into her room and stood there breathing. She was okay. She was sleeping hard, her cheeks chafed, her hands in tight fists. I wondered if Tommy would get home safely, without an air conditioner falling out of a high window onto his head. "It was really nice meeting you," I whispered, "but you will have to leave now."

I went back to the living room, dropped into my chair, and refilled his mug.

He was silent for a while, alone with the intense energy that he kept almost hidden. He described how his cameras were stolen in Bombay, how he had to make the journey across Afghanistan and Turkey without taking a single picture. Was he a photographer, then? He said that Turkey was a giant kindergarten, with men pushing and shoving like nasty little boys, not a sign of a woman's influence anywhere. I stroked the side of my warm mug upward with my fingertips.

He said that after he returned to New York he'd met a man in Chock Full O'Nuts who told him everything he had been looking for in India.

"And what was that?" I asked.

" 'Nothing lasts.' " He stood up. He had a long, flat torso and perfect posture. "Including this surprisingly beautiful day. Strange—the eclipse, seeing you."

I went to the couch and picked up his coat. A giraffe, a rabbit, and a squirrel fell to the floor. The coat had curlicues of red embroidery on the softly tanned hide. "I never saw a coat like this before—where did you get it?"

"Kabul," he said.

I held it up to the light and ran my hand through the long strands of the fleece lining. It smelled faintly of sandalwood.

"Judy," he said. "You don't look like a Judy."

"I'm actually not," I said, and—I don't know why—for the first time, I was proud of that fact. "My real name is Rosario. After my great-grandmother. But I've always been called Judy. My mother loved *The Wizard of Oz*."

"She should have called you Dorothy."

"She'd already named one of my sisters Dorothy."

"*Rosario.*" He gave it the Spanish pronunciation, thoughtfully rolling the *r*'s. "Why don't you try it on? The coat."

"Oh, no," I said.

He took the coat and held it open for me. He had big hands. "*Das Ewig-Weibliche zieht uns hinan,*" he murmured.

"What did you say?" I slid my arms into the sleeves and pulled the coat around my waist. I felt exactly and gently embraced.

After I gave Maura her dinner and read to her from a book of rhymes a poem that went "He never came back, he never came back, he never came back to me, to me, he never came back to me," I put her to bed, and I sat in the chair where Vik had been sitting. The camphor smell, very faint, remained. Across the table was the chair, the empty chair, I'd occupied for several hours. He'd seen me sitting there, in my dirty sweatshirt, my hair all over the place. What had we talked about all that time? I couldn't remember. He'd used foreign phrases. When I cleared away the mugs, my eye caught his muffler on the couch. It was weightless yellow silk with a repeated red flowing symbol. I folded it into a square smaller than my palm and hid it in the shoe box with the photographs and placed the box in the back of the hall closet behind the Christmas-tree stand. According to Tommy's desk encyclopedia, Kazakhstan was known for its melons. In the phone book, I found a Tatiana Kassell downtown. I thought it was time I started teaching myself a foreign language.

When Tommy got home, I wrapped my arms around him tightly and kissed him hard. "I'm so happy to see you," I said. "It's been an interesting day."

"Please," he said. He detached himself and took a bottle of vodka out of the freezer. I didn't even know he had put one there. "I am so tired. No dinner?"

"How about some eggs? I could scramble some."

"I just need a drink. Any mail? Anything from Mom?"

Tommy got up three times in the night, each time turning on the bedroom light and pacing back and forth from the living room.

"What's wrong?" I asked, forgetting my vow.

"Working it all out, thinking," he said. He went into the living room and tuned his guitar and sang, "I am a man of constant sorrow."

Maura had a bad dream and cried. I got out of bed and went into her room and picked her up. After a while, she dozed off, and her head lolled against my breast, and I remembered how I had met Vik. It must have been over a year ago. He had been at that dinner party of Tip's, but he was very different then. He wore a gray checked suit with a red handkerchief in the breast pocket, and all he wanted to talk about was Johnny Carson. He had a Johnny Carson haircut and did Johnny Carson double takes. His face appeared flat and his eyes round. He was twitchy. He said the people he was living with drank Jim Beam whiskey every night and watched Johnny—it was the high point of the day. At the table, he was seated next to me. He interviewed me. He asked me what my major had been before I dropped out. I told him about the Callosa dig, and he cocked an eyebrow or rolled his eyes when I made my replies. After a few glasses of wine, I told him how a second is the same duration as the heartbeat of a healthy human body at rest, and he said he wanted to get to know me better. I made a big point of mentioning my husband and his scholarships. Then, Vik had seemed to be such a jerk that I couldn't stand even to look at him. Now I couldn't stop thinking about him.

11

I am not one to get excited and overwrought, and so I calmly
stood on the threshold and pushed at the thin air over the sofa,
and then I crossed the living room, which I'd just had recarpeted
in a gold-and-white tweed three weeks ago when I believed I was
going to be getting the money, and I went into my bedroom,
opened the top drawer of the bureau, and went through it for the
third time. It's funny how there are things you come across every
day but don't pay them any mind and then all of a sudden when
you're hunting for something else, there they are. I found plenty
of things—the curly hairpiece I'd worn to the Bowlarama New
Year's party five years ago, the shocking-pink gloves I'd bought
at that department store in Paris, the yellow satin lingerie case
Judy made last year for my birthday. So sweet and thoughtful,
but who in the world would ever have enough time to remember
to put their underwear in a dinky little bag? I took the mortgage
deed for the house out of the lingerie case, shook the pages hard,
and then put it away again, snagging my thumbnail on the satin.
I reached all the way into the back of the drawer with both hands
and patted around in circles. Then I stuffed everything back in
the drawer and shut it and went again to the front door and
meditated for a second and then pretended I was dropping my
purse on the sofa. I went back to the bedroom, opened the
drawer, and searched through it again.

Then I went and sat down in the den and prayed. There was
a big March dust storm going on. The wind rattled the windows

and hit them with showers of gravel. You couldn't see a thing outside but a wall of brown cloud. Inside, it was stuffy and hot. Talk about wanting to climb the walls. Even though the doors and windows were shut tight, and last year Tom had weather-stripped everything, the dust still got in. It just materialized. There were layers of brown on the windowsills and little dunes inside the thresholds.

I had definitely put that envelope in that drawer. I remembered it very clearly. Last week I brought it home from the lawyer's office, all the documents were in it, and when I got to the front door, I had to clamp it between my teeth so the wind wouldn't rip it away while I was putting the key in the lock. I don't know how many scarves and school papers and things I've lost in dust storms. One minute you have the thing in your hand, and then it's gone, it just vanishes. I know I had that envelope in between my teeth because I worried about getting lipstick on it and so I kept my lips pulled back and I was thankful no one was watching. I came inside, dumped my purse on the sofa, and I still had my coat on, and I was thinking how quiet and soft the new carpeting was and how it made the house seem twice as big, and I thought: I won't take off my coat, I will go straight to the bureau drawer with this envelope and hide it before I do anything else. Because my life was in that envelope. I knew, I knew for sure I hid it way in the back of that drawer, where no one would ever look. There was absolutely no question that I put it there.

It's a well-known fact that burglars read the obituary column, wait a few months, and then rob the widows. I'd already hidden some silver bracelets and earrings in a teapot on a high shelf in the kitchen cupboard, and I'd stuck a hundred dollars in small bills into *The Good in Existential Metaphysics*, this fat book Tommy had left behind last summer, and I was also careful not to tell people I was widowed. Even Mr. Dee at RV-Land didn't know. He still asked how Mr. Hammond was doing when I showed up sometimes to sit in the beautiful fourteen-foot trailer, and I'd say my husband was just fine and that I was hoping he'd change his mind and trade in the camper so we could buy the trailer.

I had a few more minutes to pray, and then I had an appointment with the probate judge to go over the documents in that envelope. I had taken a shower and dressed up, and I'd gone to Sonia's to get my hair done, and when I came back to pick up the envelope, it was gone. It was just not there. Dear God, I prayed, give me back my envelope, it's *mine*. I was married over three decades and I *earned* what was in that envelope. I had the babies, I was the helpmeet, I did all the right things.

I called Sonia's, but there was no envelope there, and I knew that, but you have to do all you can. I calmly went through all the motions one more time, starting at the front door, and then when I got to the bureau, something made me yank the drawer out and turn it over on the bed and shake it. A box of face powder spilled, but I didn't have time to think about that. I combed through all the junk on the bedspread, and I accidentally jabbed myself with an ivory elephant brooch that had belonged to Mama. Nothing. There was no way an envelope could just disappear under gloves and scarves and jewelry boxes. There was no way on God's earth it could just vanish into thin air. I suddenly felt very energetic and muscular. That sometimes happened: I'd be peacefully sweeping the kitchen floor, say, and then something would come over me, and pretty soon I would be rearranging the living-room furniture, running around with a couch on my back, and I was like one of those mothers you read about who has the strength to pick up a car to rescue her son from underneath it and I would not be able to stop until the whole house was cleaned and changed around. I pulled out the second drawer and threw it on the bed, and the third and fourth drawers, too. Nothing. No envelope. But nothing.

A blast of wind came through the house and the front door slammed. I rushed into the living room. Nancy was there, wiping her eyes. Her hair had turned stiff and brown, and her face was coated with dust. She said, "My skin is permanently pitted, Mom. Just look! And on my birthday."

I said to her, "Nancy! The most awful thing has happened. The worst thing in my life has happened. You had better tell me where that envelope is and you had better tell me fast, because I have to be at the judge's in twenty minutes and I *cannot* find it anywhere."

She said, with her coat half off, "Envelope?"

I said, "Don't be stupid. You know what envelope. The envelope I showed you when we went to the bank on *the day* and I got it out of the safe-deposit box and I told you that you always had to remember about it and guard it with your life because it was the envelope with everything in it. The envelope that I hid in the top bureau drawer. You must have seen it. You had to be the one who took it out. You're the only person who goes into my bureau." She would always go into my drawers and borrow I don't know what all and then lose everything.

She said, "I wasn't in your bureau, Mom. Honest. I don't know about that envelope. I swear."

I said, "Nancy, I could just wring your neck! The envelope with the deeds to your daddy's property in Oklahoma, the bonds, the certificate of deposit, the will your daddy and I wrote out together." Tom had read a book about how you could have a will without using a lawyer and save a lot of money if you followed this certain legal form. "To my beloved wife, Evelyn Garnet Hammond," it began, in Tom's Palmer method script, "I give and bequeath . . ."

Nancy looked like she was going to cry, or maybe it was just the dust, but I would have gone insane if she had shed one tear, so I lifted my hand and said "Nancy!" and she jumped back. I made my voice soft. I said, "Where's Bud?"

"Who knows? He's with his friends. He never tells me anything. I think he has the five o'clock shift today."

A terrible thought came into my brain. "You don't suppose his friends that come over sometimes—maybe they were in my bedroom? No. They're nice boys. Well, dadgummit, we are just going to have to tear this house apart."

She said, "Can I wash my face first? I don't want dust in my pores. My skin just cleared up, and I want to look nice tonight at La Posada."

I said, "Nancy, listen, there's no time," and while I was talking I went over to my little writing desk, which I bought after I visited Monticello and I saw what kind of desk Jefferson wrote at and said, That's for me, and then I found one kind of like it at Patriot Furniture. I tried to explain the situation to Nancy. "That's every cent we have coming to us, and if we don't find it, we are going to be in big trouble, believe you me. We won't even be able to buy a hot dog. Maybe we can replace some of the documents, but the most important one, that certificate of deposit, your daddy took from his father's safe-deposit box when *he* passed on, and just kept it because he and his father had the same name and we never told a soul or paid taxes on it. So how can I ever get that replaced? The answer is I can't. *You* may do all right, you're young and maybe you can catch a man, but that was supposed to take me through my old age, which is still a long way off." I was practically panting. I pulled the drawers out of the desk and turned them over. Canceled checks, every one of them filled out in Tom's hand, made blue fans on the carpet. Years of bank statements, THOMAS R. HAMMOND, accordioned out, along with a bunch of tax returns in pale green, pink, and blue. Tom would say, "You sign here, Effie," and I signed. And he protected me. I didn't ever have to even so much as glance at a water bill. For the first time in my life, I was now going to be making out my own tax return. I'd been kind of looking forward to that, but not anymore. Nancy was just standing there, staring off. I said, "Whatever are you gawking at?" I thought maybe she saw the envelope.

She said, "The den picture window is moving." The wind was heaving it in its frame. "The reflections make the room look like it's jumping around."

I said, trying to keep my voice under control, "Nancy. Please. I don't care if it blows to smithereens. I don't care if the house burns down. I want you to go into my closet and pull every last thing out. Check behind the shoe rack and under that little piece of carpeting on the closet floor. You don't suppose the carpet men took that envelope, do you? No, I was with them every minute. They didn't go near my room and I told them Mr. Hammond was coming home soon in case they had in mind to try anything."

I got down on all fours and sorted through the papers. I knew all along I hadn't put the envelope there—the desk was the first place burglars would head for—but if I didn't go through the routine of looking in the wrong place, then the envelope wouldn't be where I was supposed to find it when God decided I could have it back. I made different piles of the papers, and I found the expensive stationery I'd bought to write thank-yous in January, and I thought about how many hours of Tom's life had gone into all these documents. He was so careful about things.

I went into the bedroom. Nancy was lifting shoe boxes out of the closet. I said, "Nancy, you know the envelope is not going to be there. Help me move the bureau. Fast, because I'm due at the judge's."

The bureau was a heavy, almost black, claw-footed monster that had belonged to Tom's grandmother and had come all the way from St. Louis by covered wagon. Not my favorite piece of furniture, as I am a blond-oak sort of person, and even with the drawers taken out, it weighed a million tons. We pushed and strained. The wedding picture and the Chanel No. 5 fell over. Finally the bureau came away from the wall. I reached behind and ran my hands along the backboard. It was thin and warped, and I got a splinter in the heel of my hand. I said, "Nancy, I do not understand this. Now, think. T-h-i-n-k. Are you absolutely sure you didn't get into my drawer to borrow a pin or something? Really think. Last Thursday at three p.m., I know I put that envelope right in the drawer, and now it's gone."

She said, "I didn't go anywhere near that drawer, Mom."

I said, "You obviously do not grasp the importance of this." I repeated what the envelope contained. I explained the consequences. "No college for Bud—he'll have to enlist or be drafted. I'll have to go back to work. You'll have to get a part-time job until you finish high school and then full-time. I don't know how you can go to secretarial school unless you send yourself. Clear out the top shelf of the closet. Look behind those boxes. Look behind that box the slide projector is in."

I went to the front door and pretended again that I was bringing the envelope home and putting it in the bureau, which now was against the bed and showed shadowy rectangles where its drawers had been. I started to say something to Nancy. I started to say, "Do you think your daddy . . . ?" I stopped myself. I'd had some very crazy feelings in the past three months, but I had enough sense to keep them to myself. A few weeks back, I was hanging up some sheets in the backyard when a wind came out of nowhere and ripped the tarp off the boat. One morning I had been alone in the house, in the kitchen, and I thought I heard him clear his throat in the den and say my name. But he couldn't have made the envelope disappear: it contained everything he had built up over the years and set aside for me. Turned out he had put everything in order last summer after we came back from the dam —made lists of the assets and dated them and put them in the safe-deposit box. And he had bank accounts I hadn't even heard about. I always thought we were not particularly well off. I made room on a corner of the bed and sat down. Black came over my eyes, red-black, and then gray foam that finally slid down so I could see again. I said, "I didn't imagine it. I had that envelope."

Nancy said, "Maybe you could call the judge's office and just ask? Could I borrow these gold high heels sometime? I mean, in case lightning strikes and I ever get invited to a dance or something?"

I said, "They would have phoned me, hon. But I'll call them anyway. I am not leaving this house until I find that envelope."

That night, for the first time in my life, I didn't sleep. I went like a cyclone through every drawer and closet in the house. The wind was still blowing to beat the band, but every now and then it would stop and the house would be completely silent. I found a lot of things that I'd thought were lost for good, like my honor society pin, and I came across a bunch of Army underwear of Tommy's. And more stuff of Tom's. I had sent his clothes to the Salvation Army except for a perfectly good blue blazer which Tommy could wear when he came back to Cibola to be a professor. I don't know how I'd overlooked Tom's old dented aluminum suitcase, which was packed with wide neckties and an aloha shirt he bought when he went to the tests in the Pacific. I just couldn't picture him in an aloha shirt to save my life. And I found his Masonic ring in one of his old wooden cigar boxes along with the letters I had written him during the war. I started to read one, telling about how I hadn't written because I was in the middle of *Gone With the Wind*, but then I just couldn't go on. I took out the books from the bookcase headboard of the bed, and that's when I found the pocket pad. A little spiral pad.

I sat on the edge of the bed, with all the drawers and all the nylons and brassieres and girdles and face powder and books, and I held that pad in my hand. I said: I don't want to open this. You hear about widows finding the notebooks, the address books. I put it back in the bookcase, and set *The Organization Man* in front of it.

I went into the kitchen and fixed a cup of instant coffee—it was too much trouble to brew coffee anymore—then I climbed up on a chair and went through the top shelves of the cupboards. I took down the Windsor Rose wedding china, the cut-glass punch bowl, the waffle iron, and the silverware box. The whole time the wind made a sound around the kitchen door like someone humming through a comb and tissue paper. I figured the notebook was probably nothing. But it could contain Tom's last statement about things, something of that nature. He was pretty deep, really. Tommy always said his father was an anti-intellectual, but actually he sometimes had very interesting thoughts. One time when we were driving up to the dam, he told me how there was energy everywhere—in the sunlight, even the wind against the car was energy. I said, "We're talking about God here." But he said it was physics. He almost never told his feelings. I began to wonder whether the pad had his thoughts about me. His love for me. I'm sure it just got stronger and stronger with every passing year.

I climbed down and went back in the bedroom. The inside of my head pounded, so that all the junk on the bed seemed to shake. On the first page he'd written his name and address. On the second page:

Rose Madder
Carmine Madder
Parma Violet

Funny names. I let out a long breath. On the third page were figures:

4 $2\times8\times8$
2 $4\times4\times6$
2 sheets ¾ A-D ply

ht - 2½
w - 5
l - 9

1 qt. green
1 pt. white

The rest of the pages were blank.

When it grew light, the wind stopped for a while and I went out to the car and looked in the glove compartment, under the seats, and under the floor mats. I found a matchbook from Adelaido's Bar. That was in Mesita, but it wasn't the place we stopped at when we went through. We always went to Freddie's. What had he been doing at Adelaido's?

When Nancy woke up, I asked her to help me move the bed away from the wall. I discovered a notebook with a yellow flowered cover that I bought last summer when Tommy said I needed to organize my thoughts. On the first page I'd written some quotes for inspiration: " 'Do the thing and you will have the power.'—Emerson. 'You are the resource in communist society for the society to use up.'—William Tyler Page, 'The American Creed.' 'I saw all the people coming towards me, and all the people were me.'—Zen." On the next page was something I started last summer, I don't remember why.

I understood the boy whose shirts I ironed too well,
and that's when I began praying that his charm and

empathy for other people, their happiness and hurt,
his wit, his intelligence would never cross the hairline
between a youthful honesty and a knowledgeable
maturity when he might someday use people, gullible
and trusting, where he might use God's gift to maneuver
others—I understood him so well—that I never
questioned him—I still pray.

Nancy waited by the bed. "Mom? Can I go get ready for school
now? You want me to make you some fresh coffee?"
I said, "Darlin', I only want you to remember that you can have
all the brains in the world but if you use people, if you don't care,
it's no good."
"I don't get what you mean. Did I use somebody?"
"No, honey."
Bud came to the doorway in his pajama bottoms and stood
there scratching his belly. He was trying to grow a beard, which
I considered a danger signal, and I'd already told him a number
of times that it looked like pubic hair.
I said, "Whatever happened to your butterfly collection, hon?"
He said, "I think you made me throw it out when we cleaned
out the garage to build the den. Or maybe I gave it to Teddy
Roybal."
I said to him, "One thing about you, darlin', is you never mean
anyone any harm, and you don't manipulate people, and I want
you to know how much I appreciate that. I would never say one
word against Tommy, but the whole time Dad was in the hospital, they never called and I do not understand that. Maybe Judy
didn't want him to run up the phone bill. Nancy, before you get
ready for school, you go through all the wastebaskets in the house
and the garbage cans out in back." After she left, I got out the
spiral pad and showed Bud the page with the numbers. He started
smiling like a baby with that cupid's-bow mouth of his. It was so
sweet I could have taken a picture. He said, "This is from last
summer when Dad built the Ping-Pong table—it's the measure-
ments and the plywood he needed."
I said, "Well, then, I guess we can throw it out." It was just
no good having reminders around.

But he asked if he could keep it, and I couldn't say no to him.

After the kids left, I went and sat in the den, which was now the only room—except for Tom's workroom—still in order, and I tried to focus on today's thought from *Positive Wisdom:* "The ground where I stand is holy." Someone had come into the house in the past week and stolen that envelope. Nothing else had been taken: Mama's ivory brooch was still in the bureau drawer and the grocery money for Nancy was on the kitchen table. Dean Easterling had told me that the Mafia was starting to come into Cibola and take over the nightclubs and restaurants. Maybe they were sneaking into people's homes, too. All that Tom and I had built up was gone. All those years came to nothing. I would never get my job back at the college—I'd been replaced by a twenty-four-year-old former homecoming queen with a master's from Texas A&M. I'd have to beg for work at the 7-Eleven on Lincoln and get shot in the head at two in the morning by a drifter.

When I saw the mailman's little three-wheeled white-and-blue car, I ran to the door. Someone might have found the envelope and put it in the mail. The mailbox, an old black tin thing I never liked, was screwed into the cinder-block wall under the porch light and the screws were beginning to work loose. I told myself to remind Tom to fix them when he came home. I was sitting at the table with the mail in my hand before I realized that Tom wouldn't be coming home, and then I thought how silly it was to be thinking up orders to give him when he wasn't even going to be here, and then I thought: When he gets home tonight, I'll have to tell him how silly I was. That kind of thing happened to me every day. There were some hospital and laboratory bills— after two and a half months they still kept coming, a flyer from Piggly Wiggly saying liver was on sale, sixty-five cents a pound, and a letter from Tommy.

The great thing about Tommy was that he was such a fantastic letter writer. He should have lived in another century. When he was stationed in Germany, he wrote me the most wonderful

descriptions of the base, and the Germans, and his thoughts on
European politics and economics and all that kind of thing. I used
to take his letters to show people at the college. Tommy hadn't
written all that much since he moved to New York—where
would he find the time what with Judy and the baby and the
dissertation?—but here was a real letter, typewritten. I had to
smile to myself as I unfolded it. He'd been such a help to me the
whole month he was here, staying up nights and talking and
talking, and now he was probably sitting in New York feeling
what I was going through and wanting to cheer me up.

Dear Mom, Bud, Nancy, Cat and kittens, Camper,
Pickup, Boat, Car, etc.,
I am writing this during the second blizzard of the week.
This has been the year for infinite amounts of snow.
Result: Judy is right now hanging over the bathtub doing
the laundry because it's impossible to get through the icy
streets with a hundred pounds of dirty diapers, sheets,
Judy's old torn underpants, etc., loaded on the stroller. I
went over my reorganization of the dissertation structure
with Biederman and I must say he was quite impressed
with the expanded concept, which I have been giving my
very all since I decided that the schema I had come up
with last fall would not be an adequate framework for
my new original concepts. I will discuss this with you
at length over brandy at some point in the future. I have
not had the time I need to pull everything together
because the photo lab has been very hectic, with total
reorganization afoot. The upshot of all this is flattering
to your firstborn, as I was promoted to assistant manager,
which basically means a considerable degree of greater
responsibility and longer hours. No raise but if I can
prove myself I think that will happen. I feel I have a
great deal to contribute to the place and have already
evolved some managerial procedures which significantly
impressed the owners. I think if I so desired I could
become quite the corporate manager but I have more

important things on my mind at the moment and have
been making some exciting plans for the future due
to a program I just heard about. It is an international
placement program for doctoral candidates—good pay
and excellent fringe benefits at great universities around
the world. It sounds ideal. I see myself on a tropical
isle penning my dissertation and holding seminars on
Aristotle with the dusky-skinned local intellectuals, piña
colada in hand. Meanwhile, there is a matter I would
like to bring to your attention, a small item but at the
moment extremely urgent. Staying in Cibola in January
for so long meant we didn't earn any money. I am
considering requesting a raise, and Judy has taken on
extra typing, but we are still a month behind on our rent
and have been getting our sole nourishment from a third
world diet Frantz Fanon would approve of. Thank God
Judy knows how to make those frijoles. I can hold off
on the various bills, but the rent is a problem, having
to duck the super whenever possible, etc. All of this
financial oppression is certainly character-building, but
makes it problematic for me to pull the dissertation
together in a cohesive fashion. One has to consider the
fact that Judy and Maura have their needs which are
unusually pressing at this time. So I am wondering
if it would not be too much trouble for you to be kind
enough to think about possibly co-signing a bank loan
for $250 just to tide us over. As you know, I would
never ask for myself. If it were only me, I could live at
the Y. Anyway, as if it isn't abundantly clear by now,
your help would be greatly appreciated in this temporary
matter at this time.

Like all of Tommy's letters, this one just ended. Maybe he'd
cut school the day they taught complimentary closes and signa-
tures. My hands were shaking so badly that I could barely fish my
address book out of my purse and turn the pages to find his
number. The reddish-black wave hit me again. When it fell away,
I dialed.

Judy answered in that very friendly, very cheerful way, which I did not believe for one minute. It set my teeth on edge. She said, "Effie, hi! Well, how are you? What a nice surprise."

I said, "Get me Tommy."

She said he was waking up. "He's running a little late for work this morning. He'll be right here. Is everything just fantastic? Bet the weather is warm there—"

I said, "I want to speak to Tommy."

When he picked up the phone, he sounded half asleep.

Talk about crawling through a wire. I said, "Wake up and die right, Tommy Hammond Junior. I have only one single thing to say to you and what I want to say to you and your wife is *No.* I have had enough of your needs. I am tired of you feeling sorry for yourself all the time. Your father and I raised you the best way we knew how and paid for everything, even bought you that expensive saxophone you never touched and supported you when you came back after your divorce and paid for your divorce and paid for your college and paid for your wedding and paid for your vacation last summer so you could insult me with your dadgummed 'scallions' this and 'scallions' that, and I paid for you to come out in January and took you to one fancy restaurant after another and bought all your food and even Maura's diapers and now you have some kind of gall trying to pry money out of me at this very trying time in my life. For your information there is no money for anything and there never will be. I am a widow left alone with two children to support, I have house and car payments and I'm still getting hospital bills I don't know whether the insurance is going to cover, and you have the unbelievable nerve to ask me for money when you're supposed to be a grown man and after the way you acted when your poor father was in the hospital sick and having such a hard time and you didn't so much as write or call to see how I was managing, and here you expect me to drop everything and shell out every time I turn around when I've just lost every single thing I own on this earth. I have one thing to say to you and that is all, which is—It is time to stand on your own two feet and stop using people and looking for a free ride." And I hung up.

I wanted to go get in the car and just drive and drive, straight west, and never look back and never tell a soul where I was going, but what I did was go in the kitchen and haul the refrigerator away from the wall. That's what I was doing when Mrs. Roybal from across the street knocked.

She was thin and had blue-black hair and light brown skin, and she wore a starched housedress and a starched white apron, and she was carrying a covered dish. She always talked like she was asking questions. She said, "My sister and me, we've been making tamales all morning? My niece, my little goddaughter, it's her birthday tomorrow? And I know it was Nancy's birthday yesterday? So I thought I would bring you some? They're pretty mild?"

The wind had died down. I stood up and pushed my hair out of my eyes—my hairdo was completely shot—and I told her what a nice person she was. I said, "Why, thank you so much for your consideration. Bud really loves those tamales. We all do. There is nothing in this world we like more than your tamales. And that's so sweet of you to remember Nancy's birthday."

"I always remember because little Teddy has his birthday the day before? And we did their parties together that time." She just stood there for a while, and then she said, in that little voice of hers, "Are you okay, Mrs. Hammond? Is everything all right?"

I said, "Everything couldn't be better." I was thinking about poor Nancy. I would have to make it up to her.

She said, "We have the Holy Family statue at our house this month, and I put a candle for Mr. Hammond?"

I said, "Why, thank you so much. Bless your heart."

She said, "You know the Moras? Down the street? They had the Holy Family statue last month, and they put a candle also. Mr. Hammond helped them do that sliding glass door."

I said, "You haven't by any chance seen a big brown manila envelope blowing around outside, have you?"

She shook her head. She said, "You didn't lose something important I hope?"

I said, "Don't worry about it, it's nothing."

12

Dear Judy,
How are you? I am fine. We are all fine. It is really hot
today. I am on my mother's bed; it's the only cool place
in the house because nobody knows how to hook up the
air coolers. My retarded bro. only remembers how Dad
took them down. I am supposed to be doing Geom.; but
I tell you I do not understand one thing about it and I
have been in that class all year and even though I was
good at algebra (all A's). I don't get how you prove
something in geom., like two triangles and whether they
can fit into one big one. The best way in my humble
opinion is to look at them; and see if they can fit. But no.
Mom wants to go to California; also England. What
bothers me is that the other kids in the class; Indians in
the back included and they don't speak English; get this
and I don't. So anyway, I am using my graph paper to
write you this letter and also draw this beautiful flower
with my friendly handy-dandy compass. Pretty neat, no?
Mom says, LaDonna on the phone. Probably a trick to
get me in the kitchen to do dishes. More later.

More later. LaDonna wanted me to do this thing that
is so gross I do not believe it. I am utterly grossed out.
Here is the thing. At the bus stop today after school this
boy I think I told you about, Reuben L. Swapp was

there with Teddy Roybal and some other boys and all of a sudden Reuben comes up and grabs LaDonna's binder and won't give it back, and they go off on Teddy's motor scooter. Then LaDonna went berserk, pixilated, and corybantic because there were some notes in the binder from me, one about how in study hall Reuben was doing an imitation of Ray Charles trying to slap hands with Stevie Wonder and Mr. Petersen threw an eraser at his head. But I said to LaDonna that note is signed with our made-up names, not our real ones (she is Sweet Little 16 and I am Stella Police; which is a name I saw in an Indian newspaper when we went to that trading post last summer and you bought the pot—). And I told her don't worry. Then she THINKS he might see the little calendar she keeps in there with the days of her periods marked off. CATACLYSM & CATASTROPHE!!!
Oh God, she is dying on the bus I tell you; so then she phoned me just now and said I have to call Reuben and ask for the binder back. She can't do it because she will just lose her mind so good ole Nancy to the rescue.
I can not believe I said I would do this. I told LaDonna; he is just a little retarded bowlegged guy, a you-know-what-kicker right off the ranch, what is the big deal here??? Because LaDonna found out by being real sweet to Reuben's sister that a few years ago Reuben's father tragically died and they had to move into town. He also has two brothers, one went to BYU until he dropped out and then got drafted. Really I don't think Reuben is dumb because I saw him reading The Last of the Plainsmen probably for a book report but I think he just wants to act dumb like the other guys. I am so hungry and there is nothing in the refrigerator but some liverwurst and half of an old Arby's roast beef sandwich, we could literally die of starvation and etiolation in this house and I mean it. And here is Mom about LaDonna on the phone again. Back to the kitchen.

. . .

Later

LaDonna wanted to know if I had done it yet and I told
her I was resting up for it. She wants me also to find out
if he *likes* her so I said; well come on LaD, you want me
to say "Excuse me Reuben, but LaDonna Vance is madly
in love with you and by the way could you drop
everything and bring her binder over tonight and also
give her a big kiss." But all she could think about was
whether to wear the blue halter top with her blue
checked shorts when he comes over and if I don't call
him how she will have to lay down and personally die.
So I said I would do it. I dial his number.

His mother: Hello.

Yours truly: Hello; may I please speak to Reuben.

R's mother: Reuben it's a girl!!

A deep voice (bro.): A girl calling you Rube. Ha ha ha.

Reuben answers the phone like he's being strangled:
Hello.

Me: Hi Reuben; it's Nancy Hammond.

R: Hi Nancy.

Me: How are you doing?

R: I'm doing fine.

Me: That's good.

R: How's your cow?

Me: How's my cow?

R: I don't know, I just said that.

Well this letter is getting too long. I asked him if he
could please take the binder to LaDonna, it was an
emergency, he asked his mother and she said he couldn't
go out on a school night; which is hardly a surprise
because they are Mormon. So I said; "Saila Vee" and
then I was so mad I hit myself on the head with the sink
loofah because I could not believe I had said that. He
wanted to know what I said and I told him, Well,
nothing; the French say that. It means that is life. Now
he is going to think I am some kind of Brain. When
I told LaDonna he wasn't coming she just screamed;

because she had already washed and set her hair and she said she was going to tell the principal what he had done and that ought to make him think twice.

I am telling you, Judy, love is just not worth it except if it is like you and Tommy I mean. It is so retardedly gross. What else can I tell you about. Bud is lying on the rug in the den with his head under the home entertainment center listening to the Woodstock Album as loud as it will go and torturing the cats. Do you like Suite: Judy Blue Eyes on that album? I know you don't have blue eyes but I thought you would like it anyway. Here is Mom. Going to the closet. Getting out pink cowboy pants and cowboy shirt with the pearl snaps. "Fascinating" as Spock would say. She says a big hidey-hello and when are you guys coming out and she misses you. Hi hi hi hello. Oh what a thrill; we get to eat. She is taking us to Arthur Treachers to celebrate about the envelope. Relief!! It was stuck between the drawer and the bureau back the whole time. She wants you guys to come out for Bud's graduation and etc., etc. Now she is telling me all this stuff to say but she will just have to write you herself; my hand is tired.

Your letter about the eclipse was very interesting. Are there a lot of eclipses in New York; or was this a special one? I hope Maura is fine. Ask her if she wants a kittycat.

                    Love ya,
                        Stella Police

P.S. I just ate all the liverwurst (ugh.) I don't know why Mom gets it; nobody likes it.

13

"Lots and lots of outside," Maura said when Judy carried her out the front door into the cool morning air. The sky was an infinite, cloudless blue. The jagged ridge of the Cibola Peaks threw a violet shadow across the housing developments, the brown mesa, and the freeway.

She placed Maura on the back seat of the car and, kneeling in the sharp, rust-colored volcanic cinders that covered the front yard, slid Maura's sandals onto her feet and squeezed her toes. "Where did those long legs come from?" Judy asked. "What happened to my little baby? Did the elephants take her away?" Maura laughed and pushed her soles against Judy's hands.

The sensations of the dream from which Judy had been awakened were still with her: the delight of being rescued, securely held, and swept up into the air. The dream had been about some elephants who lay on their sides asleep, their chests gently heaving, while others milled around. She and Tommy wandered among them. Something bad was going to happen. A big trunk reached down, gently embraced her, and lifted her out of the path of invisible harm.

"You ready to go to California, Maura, hon?" Effie said, putting a stick of gum in her mouth as she came toward the car. She carried a stack of books under one arm, and she felt as if she were a carefree girl, that nothing bad had ever happened to her, and that she was setting out for school, eager to learn, her stomach full of oatmeal, her behavior and attitude good. "Let's go, go, go!"

Maura's eyes widened as she stared up at her grandmother, who wore turquoise pants, a yellow blouse with stiff ruffles down the front, sunglasses with glittering frames, and a pink see-through scarf over her hair. Her hair was uniformly golden and glistening, high and rounded like the crown of a hat.

"Maura, Effie asked you a question," Judy said. Effie did not want to be called Grandma. "No Granny or Nana stuff either," Effie had said when Maura was born.

"Where we going for our vacation, hon?" Effie asked. "Nancy!" she called toward the house. "Let's get this show on the road!"

Maura was silent. "To the *beach*," Judy said to her. "Come on, tell Effie: 'We're going to the . . . ' "

"We'll have lots of talks when you can have an intellectual conversation, Maura, darlin'. I'll take you to Oxford, England, or someplace like that."

"Oh, how nice, Maura!" Judy said. She saw Effie and Maura hand in hand on a broad lawn rimmed by ancient gray buildings, Maura a lovely young woman, an intellectual.

"Ocean," Maura said.

"Why, darlin', you are so intelligent," Effie said. "Just like your daddy. You're going to get your doctorate for sure."

"Maura, tell Effie where we are right now," Judy said. "Maura has a big vocabulary, Effie." Maura was watching Effie's shiny red lips move as she chewed her gum. Judy touched Maura's knee. "Sweetheart, listen. Tell Effie where we are right now."

Maura frowned and looked away, at the house, a faded pink, flat-roofed box. She picked at a loose thread on her sundress.

"Come on, you can say it. Where are we—right now?"

"We're right *here*, Mommy!" Maura said, about to cry.

But Effie had already turned her back and was walking away. "What a gorgeous trailer—just look, Judy!" An incandescent happiness hummed in her chest and made her want to jump in the car and press her foot down on the accelerator. The trailer took up a quarter of the front yard, which was where Bud had left it after their trailer-pulling lesson on the mesa last night. "What a perfect day for driving! Judy, hon, how does that poem go? 'I sing of the open road' or words to that effect? You have such a fabulous memory."

"Gosh, I can't remember," Judy said. She had also forgotten that her fabulous memory was her special trait. Effie had special traits for everyone. Tommy—genius. Bud—sweet. Nancy—practical. "Sophomore lit. 'I sing of the open—' Who was that? Walt Whitman!" Judy was surprised at herself. "The Brooklyn *Eagle.* Gosh, I haven't thought about him for years. 'I sing of a live oak—' No, wait—"

"Don't worry about it, hon. All those years, I truly hoped that some of my students would get what it meant to be an American, but I still didn't count on any of them remembering for two seconds after graduation one single item from the Bill of Rights. And here you are, two years of a fine education at Cibola State, but now you are a New York City person and you have plenty of other, more important things to think about, probably. Where did you get that little teeny skirt?"

"Greenwich Village." Judy, who had recently learned she had beautiful breasts, crossed her arms over her chest. She didn't want Effie to notice that she was not wearing a bra under her tank top.

"Judy, hon, I just have to tell you, because if there's one thing I've learned, it's that you have to say the good things to the person while they are around to hear them, and what I want to say to you is that you are certainly smart about hiding your brains so no one would imagine, and I admire how you make Tommy proud of *his* brains and take care of him and make him feel like a man, and that's what he needs. Lord knows. The perfect thing about you two is that you can talk to each other. That's what Tom Senior and I had."

"Why, thanks for saying that," Judy said. She wanted to be reminded of all the good things about Tommy and of why she needed him. He was employed, for instance, and he had not taken a vow of poverty. He was not floating until the moment was right to hitchhike from Mexico City through South America. He had plans. He had wanted to marry Judy. He loved Maura. He had a wonderful family. Effie would come up with other things. Judy had not thought about him much at all lately except to wish that he had never existed and that somehow from birth on her life had followed a different path. But when that thought came to her now, standing in the Hammonds' front yard under the benevolent sky, she knew she deserved a beating. "We do have this terrific rapport," she said to Effie.

"It's that empathy of Tommy's," Effie said. "My, my, look at how long your hair is now—isn't it a lot of trouble? Well, anyway, girls, we're hitting that open road, free as anything. Let's get going." She inspected the tubing coming out of the big silver propane tank that rested above the trailer hitch. She was glad to be out of that house, and if she could have had it her way, she never would set foot inside it again. Little things had started to go wrong. Water oozed from the base of the kitchen tap. The bathroom doorknob was coming loose. The new carpeting was already getting tracked up and clawed by the cats. She wanted to live in peace in the trailer and study the great books and go to work on the basic questions: Who am I? What should I do about it? What survives the body? "Let's see," she said. "That Mr. Dee at RV-Land said to make sure the tubing doesn't come loose and to check the hitch. It's fine. The drive will be a snap."

"Of course," Judy said. "We are in good hands."

"Tom Senior, bless his heart—he always used to take full responsibility for all this stuff. He'd have to go into reverse on some muddy mountain road and nothing but a ten-million-foot drop under the rear tires, and I'd have my hands over my eyes and I'd be saying the Lord's Prayer and sending out the mental message to Tommy that the will was in the silverware box on top of the kitchen cupboard. But Tom was always so careful and responsible. Now I know. No wonder he got to looking so tired. I tell you, when I reached way to the back of that drawer, and I touched that envelope—I'll never in my life understand how it could have slid behind like that—I just felt his pure, sweet love. I felt he was watching over me, and that envelope had all his love for me in it."

"What envelope was that?" Judy asked. "Nancy wrote me something—"

But Effie had hurried away to examine the tires of the trailer.

Tom always checked the tires before a trip. "Maybe I should get Bud out of bed to look at the hitch one more time and wangle the trailer out onto the street," she said, returning to the car and opening the door. "But he had to work until one in the morning, poor thing. And anyway, he already showed me what he learned. Mr. Dee told him everything while I was doing the trade-in on the camper. It will be fine." Her smooth forehead wrinkled as she squinted westward, toward the freeway, which curved across the surface of the mesa beyond the housing developments and ran parallel to the valley. She was still not perfect when it came to turning or backing up. "I don't foresee any problems." She made her voice low and confiding. " 'Cause we're going to get right on the freeway and that takes us to the Interstate, and it just whooshes you straight to California and directly to the beach campground, and Tom Senior and I were there before, and I know there's plenty of parking lot to turn around in when we're ready to head back, and probably some nice man will be glad to help us. I won't have to use reverse at all."

"Oh, you'll be great, I know it," Judy said.

"What did you say? Can you stick my purse in the back seat?" She turned to the house and cupped her hands around her mouth. "Nancy, right this minute!"

Nancy came out lugging a shoulder bag. She was dressed in orange shorts and a black sleeveless blouse with a black scarf tied around her waist. Her hair was pulled up into a tightly bound ponytail, and she wore whitish-pink lipstick and blue eyeshadow. "I slept wrong on my hair when it was wet and I got a crimp," she told Judy. "It made me look just like Jeanette Montmollen, the school library assistant—ugh. So I couldn't do my hair loose like you did. What do you think of this new look?"

Judy nodded.

"Oh no!" Nancy said. "Cherry nail polish—clashes with the orange shorts."

"You just get right on in, Nance," Effie said. "I swear."

"I brought Hot Tangerine and polish remover," Nancy said. "I can redo them in the car. My legs are so white. I hate it. I should have worn jeans. Where did you get that headband?"

"A friend," Judy said. "It's from India."

Effie cautiously nosed the car into the street.

"It looks like that Indian writing," Nancy said, taking her wooden cigar box out of her bag.

"It's Sanskrit. 'Om.' The sound of the universe."

"I didn't know the universe made a sound," Nancy said. "Dear Sweet Little 16," she wrote on a piece of lined notebook paper.

"Such a darling trailer," Effie said. Dear Lord, please protect us, she prayed. The thought for the day was "I walk in a shower of divine blessings." She stopped at the corner of Cagua Boulevard. It had not even been paved when she and Tommy picked out the lot for their little adobe hacienda. Just surveyor's stakes, dirt, and tumbleweeds. Tom was out of the Navy and on his way, but because of the housing shortage, she hadn't dared wait for him. She and Tommy visited the model home and she made the down payment with some war bonds she cashed the very same day. For Tom's homecoming, she got her hair done and put on her wedding suit, and she and Tommy wound up waiting all day at the station for some reason, and when they saw Tom get off the train and look around, blinking in the late-afternoon sun, they went running up to him, and she drove him in the old Hudson straight to their lot. He didn't say much—he never was a talker —but she could tell he really loved it. After the house was built, he used to say that he liked the place better the way he first saw it—but he didn't mean that. " 'Oh, dear, departed days that are no more,' " she said. "Who said that? Never mind. It's onward! The open road and adventure, et cetera." She waited a long time at the intersection, even though there was no traffic, and kept her signal going, and finally turned past the 7-Eleven, Hair Facts, Rainbow Bowlarama, Rancho de Cibola Realty, and Taco Bell. "You know, girls, I see myself going everywhere now, nothing to stop me."

Maura's hair was long now, thick and easily tangled. "Where's my brush?" Judy said. "Has anyone seen my purse?" No one answered. She repeated the question, louder.

"It was on the kitchen table," Nancy said. "I thought you'd decided not to take it."

"Oh, well," Judy said. One more thing disappearing into chaos. When she packed up the household last week in New York, it was as if she let go of objects and they threw themselves willy-nilly into the boxes: the wedding album, Tommy's papers, cracked mugs, torn magazines, single socks, empty prescription bottles, shrunken sweaters, photographs (but not Maura's baby pictures; she put those in her suitcase for Cibola, along with her favorite books and her great-grandmother's pot). Tommy interrupted her work—he wanted to leave the Indian twin-throated wedding pot on the mantel a little longer, and he didn't want to take down Tom Senior's desert hawk yet, and he removed the fondue set, a wedding present still in its cellophane wrapping, from a carton. "We never did make fondue, did we?" she said. "Maybe I'll make some before I go," he said. She laughed, because he had never cooked, and he grinned, and she saw him for an instant the way she used to: boyish and cheerful, a freckled American bound to succeed, prepared to be cherished by grateful foreigners far away. The night before she flew to Cibola for Bud's graduation, there was a crash in the living room. In the morning, she found the desert hawk resting on the pieces of the pot. It was just one more omen. And so obvious. All that month, songs on the radio had been telling her what was happening to her, and she had been warned by the American Bible Society poster on the subway walls ("GOD IS NOT MOCKED. WHAT YE SOW YE SHALL ALSO REAP"), and now by this message. She cried, and Tommy explained that the detonations down the block all spring had loosened the hook in the ceiling, that was all, and he promised to spend his spare time before he left glueing the pot back together, and they both pretended that would happen.

"Honestly, now," Effie said, "don't you think the trailer is just the place to improve the mind, girls?"

"Absolutely," Judy said.

"We'll sit around the Coleman lantern at night and read aloud from *The Dialogues of Plato*."

"Right, Mom," Nancy said. "Our IQs will go up a hundred points. We'll be the smartest people on the beach—until the tidal wave hits." She raised one eyebrow, made her eyes go dull, and gave Effie a deadpan grimace that was new to Judy.

"Nancy!" Effie said. "No negative—"

"Just kidding, Mom."

"You are a nice person—that talk doesn't suit you," Effie said. "I do feel so liberated, Judy, hon. Let's see, left here. There's the old Piggly Wiggly. We do all our major shopping at K-Mart now."

"But Piggly Wiggly is a fantastic store," Nancy said. "We don't go there enough."

"At K-Mart, you can get a huge gigantic box of Tide for peanuts," Effie said.

Judy began to cry silently. This is how it will be, she said to herself. This is how it will be for the rest of my life.

"Turn signal. I'm doing just fine here, and the only hard part will be this dadgummed cloverleaf. You could just get stuck going around forever. Girls, look both ways. Anyway, I feel really liberated. Not like I want to go and burn my brassiere or anything—I can't understand why it's supposed to be so great to go flopping around without one. But having this trailer! All those insurance policies, bless his heart—is it clear? His last— Can I go? Okay. Can I change lanes? I can't see behind me in this one—"

"Outside mirror, Mom." Nancy leaned over the seat back to squeeze Maura's arm and caught a faint aroma of something subtle and spicy. "Judy, is that a new perfume?"

"Oil of sandalwood," Judy said, pressing a tissue to her face.

Maura delicately rested her hand, her fingers together, on Judy's thigh. "Can I have a cookie?" she asked.

"Later," Judy said.

"Tom Senior, bless his heart—just about his last words were —okay, now I'll go. Now. No, wait. Wait. Girls, I believe I'll just stay where I am. Then we're ready to exit. I do always like the right-hand lane the best. You just go along, minding your own —there's a truck. Let him go around me. I don't mind. We're in no rush. Right, girls? Anyway, we made it, we're on the freeway. Yay!"

"Yay!" Maura said, clapping her hands.

"McDonald's, five billion sold," Effie said. "You wonder how they could sell five billion hamburgers, but when you realize you've eaten about a million of them yourself, then you *know*. Nancy and I go once a week, Judy, now that they have this wonderful Filet-o-Fish, and you get this tartar sauce along with it. I was kind of hoping Bud would get a job there so he could wear one of those hats. But I think Minnie Pearl's suits him fine, and he'll have some money saved up before boot camp. At first he was bringing home one bucket of fried chicken after another —so considerate—and the best slaw, but I believe we all got a little tired of it. Anyway, we'll each lose ten pounds on the beach. Right? You know what Tommy says about flab on his nearest and dearest."

"Judy is as skinny as a rail," Nancy said. "I never saw you so thin, Judy."

"Nevertheless," Effie said. The trailer cabinets were packed with Fritos, marshmallows, giant Hershey bars, graham crackers, and hot dog and hamburger buns. The refrigerator contained sour-cream dip, chile-con-queso dip, hot dogs, hamburger, frozen french fries, Coors beer, Cokes, an onion, a tomato, and a small head of iceberg lettuce. "I sure do wish Tommy could be here," she went on. "He could be the commentator. You know, he could be on the TV news. But he's kind of doing what Albert Schweitzer did, right? And Schweitzer won the Nobel Prize. What I can't figure out is this: when he gets his doctorate, where do we go for the ceremony? I mean, if you-all are living in *Africa* while he finishes his dissertation."

"I'm not sure," Judy said. Effie didn't know that Tommy still had not started his dissertation. He had joined an antiwar group. Sometimes he didn't get back until dawn. When he was at home, he often stayed up all night by himself drinking and singing, and after the time Effie had screamed at him on the phone, he spent hours writing her letters which he never sent. One morning after several days without sleep, he announced that he was on the verge of a major breakthrough: he paced the living room spilling red wine from a tumbler and said he was about to understand everything, and already he saw that his destiny was being warped.

Maura and Judy had too many needs. One had to lead one's life, stand on one's own feet, not ask for anything. He talked rapidly about things Judy did not follow. He had seen a picture of a red Lotus sports car in *Playboy* and it made him weep. If she wanted other men, he understood. The world was in complete revolution. Everything was going to change. He wanted to go to the best men's store and buy a white suit and a wide, bright tie. She went out to the laundromat, and, staring at the wavering pink screen of a television there, she made a decision. When she returned, he said he had lost his clarity. Effie called a few weeks later and said that her worries were over and she was sending plane tickets so that they could go to Bud's graduation. But Tommy had too many commitments. Before Judy and Maura boarded the plane, they sat on molded white plastic seats in the terminal, and Judy tried to keep Maura from playing with Tommy's little cigar stubs in an ashtray. "I've thought and thought and what's coming out about this is that I've made the supreme effort and I'm worn out," he said. "There is a plateau of estrangement. You don't care about one's needs. You don't need me anymore." "I really do," she said, afraid. "Everything will be better in Africa." Ever since the international program had accepted him, they had been saying that to each other.

Judy tried to think of something nice to say to Effie. "Did I tell you he's grown a beard?"

"Now can I have a cookie, please?"

"I believe Maura wants something," Effie said. "Judy?"

Judy looked through the bag of distractions she had prepared for Maura for the long trip. "I forgot the animal crackers, sweetheart," Judy said. "Here's a book."

A flatbed truck passed by with a nose cone clamped in a metal frame. "Lookee there, Maura," Effie said. "There goes a big *rocket*. Your granddaddy, bless his heart—he helped engineer those."

"Is that really true?" Nancy asked. "I thought he worked on the bomb."

"Honey, your father did many important things because uppermost in his mind at every moment was how to take care of his family and to serve his country. And he was so good that the Labs would have him do one thing, and then they'd send him off to do something else. There was nothing he didn't do."

"I thought it was all classified," Nancy said. "How do you know what he did?"

"Darlin'," Effie said, "when—if—you have a husband, you'll understand. You always know what your man is doing. I mean, I don't know exactly what all he did, but I know it was important, and his boss and lots of other people from the Labs made a big point of telling me that. After."

Nancy turned on the radio. Three Dog Night blared out "Mama Told Me Not to Come."

"Nancy, darlin', please. I have to concentrate. On the Interstate you can turn it on." Effie had a surprising tolerance for rock 'n' roll played loud. She could just shut it out. "This new Olds, this power steering, it's like honey—you can drive with one pinkie. It's so much better than that old Fairlane. It's even better than the Lincoln, which I honestly never liked much." A few years ago, Effie had been driving because Tom Senior had had a few too many TGIF drinks and somehow the Lincoln was destroyed in a collision at an intersection. No one was hurt.

"They all lived in a house in the woods," Maura murmured to herself, tracing with her fingertip a picture of Sleeping Beauty pricking herself with a spindle, her mouth an O. "From the curtains of Israel."

"Sure is a lot of traffic in Cibola these days," Judy said. "It's gotten so built-up." Cibola was never the way she expected to find it. It was never just empty mesa, sharp peaks, and wide sky: the landscape in which she had first realized, riding on a bus next to her mother, that the hands pressed against the window glass were her hands, that this was where her body lived, and that there was no escaping. "What a mess it's turned into."

"What, hon?" Effie's window was open, and now that the car was going faster, the wind made a buffeting racket.

"Nothing," Judy said.

The freeway mounted the edge of the mesa, where Judy used to go horseback riding. They passed a go-cart lot, Krazy Karlos the HubKap King, J&B Auto Supply, and the Cibola County Hospital. Its windows flashed in the sun. "People love this place because of all the beauty," Effie shouted. "Movie stars buying land all over the place." She was suddenly overwhelmed by fatigue. She did not want to be doing this, or anything else. Transporting these people, protecting them, cheering them up, getting them to live right. Her arms grew very heavy. The windshield was dirty—Bud had promised to clean it and had failed. "Don't you just love being back here, Judy? Be it ever so humble, there's no place, et cetera."

Judy wished that Effie would roll up her window, but it was evident from the way she hunched over the steering wheel, her head swiveling so she could monitor the outside mirror as well as the rearview, that she already had a full quota of tasks. Judy started to ask Nancy to reach across and close the window but then had a picture of Effie getting confused, Nancy blocking her vision or even nudging the steering wheel, and the trailer going astray.

"The beauty of this place is special," Effie continued. "You can have your New York, your Africa. Seems to me Tommy with all his genius could get the philosophical perspective to finish that dissertation right here."

"Look, Maura," Nancy said. " 'Cowboy Car Parts—Prices You Can Hang Your Hat On'—see the cowboy on the sign?"

"Well, we're really thrilled about Africa," Judy said. "I really mean it. It's going to be so wonderful. And we won't be so broke for a change." Soon, as Judy listened to Effie, Tommy would become able, stalwart, loving. Judy looked down at a fifty-foot-deep, concrete-lined ditch. It was empty. There were several of these where arroyos had once meandered from the foothills across the mesa and down into the valley; their purpose was to channel flash floods. "I played up toward the foothills in that arroyo," she said. "We would tunnel into the banks and make bomb shelters."

"Don't you agree that this is the most beautiful spot in the world, Judy?" Effie shouted. "Here's downtown."

Judy used to ride the bus downtown to the library, a cool adobe building with a musty smell; it was near the railroad station, and so she got to see whores, syphilitics, Indians, bowlegged cowboys, and Negroes wandering in and out of the pawnshops, the smoky pool halls, and the dark bars where ranchero music played. Now a yellow cloud hung over craters and heaps of rubble where bulldozers and cranes were at work. "This looks like it's been bombed," she said. "And is that smog? In Cibola?"

"What, hon? This is going to be beautiful. Concrete terraces on different levels, planters, the Hanging Gardens of Babylon idea. Plenty of parking lots. Here's the interchange. I'm sure glad we stayed in this lane. Here we go, making a figure eight. Isn't this fun? Hang on!"

The heat of the Interstate blew in. It had four lanes going west, and beyond a ribbon of corrugated metal railing and the concrete-lined ditch, four lanes going east.

Maura leafed through Judy's old Mother Goose. " 'Hickety-pickety, my black hen, she lays eggs for gentlemen,' " she recited, pretending to read as she patted a picture of a big speckled black hen and astonished men in frock coats.

Dear Sweet Little 16,
Well, we made it out of the driveway so I'm writing
you this letter. So far the trip is not very exciting because
my eyes are still glued shut (Mom made me get up at
2 billion AM in the morning!!!). Started this fantastic
new SF book Judy brought me (her favorite) called
Childhood's End by Arthur C. Clarke about so far this
mysterious space ship in orbit around the earth and these
aliens are the Overlords so Mankind can evolve to the
next stage. So, what are you doing? Besides kissing
REUBEN L. SWAPP'S picture in your yearbook??
(Sigh, swoon.) Tonight I will try the telepathy
experiment. Hope you remember.

Nancy put the letter back in the cigar box and got out some pink stationery with deckled edges and pressed it to her face. The sweet taste of apple blossoms struck the back of her mouth. "My dearest darling Reuben," she wrote in purple ink.

> My heart is so full that I do not know where to begin to tell you my true feelings which are very serious about this love I feel for you. I am not going to reveal my true identity as it may cause others pain and you may not like me even, but if you do I would like to know as soon as possible. I am going to put one rose petal in this letter and if you think you know who this is and if your feeling the same as me, that is love, or even really liking me a little or somewhat, wear this petal or put it

She tore the second letter into little pieces and let them rain into her open bag.

"Nancy, darlin', whatever are you doing?" Effie said. "You watch the traffic for me. It's pretty heavy."

The day was huge and filled with light. The peaks were a ridge of chipped blue glass. A brown haze spread over the valley. "That *is* smog," Judy said. "I don't believe it."

"What, hon?"

Judy leaned forward. She could smell Effie's powerful hair spray. The wind, stronger now, was making dents in the taut pink chiffon stretched over her coiffure. "Is that smog?"

"Cibola is one of the top twenty cities for population now," Nancy said. "We're so very proud."

"We do not need your sarcasm, Nancy," Effie said. "This is a *fun* trip."

"But the air was always so good here—people with TB came here to get cured," Judy said.

"You see, hon, it's the cars. You have to understand. People need to get around, they have to get to work. And it's the same old dust, plus you have extra from all the construction . . ." She did not want to go on.

"Did you hear about the starve boys, Mommy?" Maura asked.

"What?" Judy said. " 'Starve boys'?"

"Mom, could you roll up your window?" Nancy said. "The wind is making my eyes water."

"Sure thing, darlin'." Effie lifted her left hand from the steering wheel and started to roll up the window.

Don't do that, Judy said silently.

Effie's right hand mimicked the back-and-forth motion of her left as she turned the window crank. The steering wheel began to wobble. Effie grabbed it with both hands, but the wheel kept moving one way and then the other. "Nancy," Effie said. "I can't—"

As the gyrating steering wheel continued to slip through Effie's hands, the car swerved from side to side. The trailer began to sway and weave. It went to the right when the car went to the left, and then the car was jerked to the right and the trailer went to the left. Great waves of momentum, S-shaped waves, whipped through the car and tossed the passengers from side to side. They could feel their insides going one way while their limbs went another.

Judy encircled Maura tightly with one arm and held the other out stiffly against the seat. Nancy pressed her hands against the glove compartment and began a thin scream. It made it more like a scary ride at the state fair than an accident. Judy didn't really feel like screaming, but she decided to join in. The duet was refined and high-pitched, without much air behind it.

Effie thought their voices sounded like a choir she had heard in a church in England. Sweet and medieval. No matter how much she fought, the steering wheel continued to spin through her hands: it was the wild momentum of the trailer that was guiding the car, and *where was Tom?*

Judy pushed Maura down on the floor and arched over her, bracing herself against the seat back with her elbows and knees. This way, Judy reasoned in the very slowly congealing flow of time, in which thoughts were like bricks falling from a lazily toppling building, my body will shield hers when the trailer crashes through the back of the car.

The car rammed into the metal guardrail, then tipped forward. It was pounded over and over as the trailer bounced and hit, bounced and hit. The guardrail shrieked as the fender ground against it.

There was a lengthy hesitation. And then the car rocked abruptly forward and began to nose downward, pushing at the railing. We are going to go over, Judy observed, feeling the languid avalanche of thought. Effie clutched the steering wheel, her arms rigid. Below was the deep concrete canyon.

Maybe we will just be very badly injured, Nancy thought. I was just starting to live. This isn't at all the way I thought it would turn out.

Judy gauged the drop: about fifty feet. Metal creaked against metal, and the trailer would not stop banging the car. The trailer was very heavy, she thought, and the fall was a long one; it would increase the weight of the trailer. The impact would be severe. But maybe Maura could be saved. Judy's body might somehow lessen the crushing impact and protect Maura from the pieces of glass and metal. There would be a hard blow, and then nothing.

The sounds of metal grinding against metal continued. Then there was the click-by-click ratcheting of the emergency brake. A red wave came toward Effie. It washed over her eyes and then became a foaming black. Her head dropped forward against the steering wheel.

Everything stopped. They hung there, at the edge, in the sunlight, in a great silence.

14

"The car was bumping!" Maura said. She began to cry. I kissed her damp forehead and squeezed her. My arms were shaking. Since Effie had started to roll up her window, everything had passed across my awareness like reflections sliding over a mirror. I held Maura tightly and stared into the ditch below and then at the lanes of traffic moving slowly on the other side, and then at the empty dome of the sky. "Everything is okay, Maura," I said.

"Mom?" Nancy said. "Are we safe?" Her voice trembled.

Effie, slumped over the steering wheel, jerked herself upright. "We can still make Needles for dinner," she said. She kept her hand on the emergency brake.

A large, sunburned head came through her window. "Excuse me, ma'am. Kin I hep you?"

"Oh, bless your heart, you surely can." Effie smiled. It was not her biggest smile, but it was close. "Could you help us straighten this thing out and get it back on the road?"

"I sure as heck thought you were goin' over the edge into that culvert," the man said. "You were fishtailin' all over the place." His tone was flat. He was thin, with knotted forearms. He had a steady, mild expression. "Matter of fact, I strongly urge you ladies to get out while I back this up."

"We do need a man," Effie said. "We're on our way to California, we want to get there by tonight, this is a brand-new trailer—"

"Well, it's jackknifed across two lanes now, and we don't want it getting hit again."

I stood with Maura in my arms in the breakdown lane next to where the man had parked his truck. On the side it said "Navaho Freight—Line of the Blue-Eyed Indian." There was a portrait of a handsome Indian. "See that, Maura?" I said. But she kept her face pressed against my breast. I was weak and nauseatingly alert. I had to protect her. At any moment a car could swerve over and hit us.

A month ago, Tommy had sat at the typewriter with a bottle of brandy, still trying after two weeks to think of a reply to his mother's phone call. I didn't see any reason to reply; all I thought was: Good, now we can be completely together, free, we don't have to depend on anybody. I stood at the medicine-cabinet mirror trying to figure out how I looked with my hair pulled back into a tight chignon. I wetted and flattened the frizzy curls along the temples.

Tommy breathed hard and typed, stopped, breathed hard and typed. He bit his fingernails, one at a time. "Women have the terrible power to destroy," he said.

In case he was speaking about my power—as if I had any—I said, "I try to be good." And that was true. When I'd phoned Vik that morning, twenty-four hours after I had made my decision in the laundromat, he said he would come over and pick up his scarf, but I told him to meet me someplace else. I was afraid to have him in the apartment. He suggested a coffeehouse downtown. I couldn't talk to him on the phone and also see him on the same day, because that would be wrong, so I said I would meet him the following day. The neighbor lady was going to babysit Maura. I planned to wear the shawl Effie had given me, black, embroidered with red and yellow poppies, and smelling sweetly of mildew from the trunk, and a yellow minidress I'd secretly bought with my birthday money from Tom Senior.

"I'm going to tell her that my boss *gave* me the rent money out of his own pocket," Tommy said. His boss had made him a long-term loan. "I'm going to tell her she's always been a bad mother. She would send me alone to the movies when she and Dad went out, and I would have to wait alone for them to pick me up on the corner downtown with all kinds of strangers around. And I was only six years old. She put me in incredible danger. And left me alone."

As I moved through the dark amber light in which Italian landscapes and marble busts and vacant tables were suspended, my body hung like a piece of trembling cloth from my shoulders. I hadn't been eating much lately, and Tommy's constant rearrangements of sleeping and waking, along with Maura's steady rhythms, had enclosed me in one endless day shadowed by busy dreams. As I came to the table where Vik sat—at first I didn't recognize him—I bumped into the pointed spindle of a chair back. Later, I found a big bruise on my thigh. Violin music was playing. I asked him what it was. I was sure something bad was going to happen. "Bach partita," he said. His eyes were a translucent brown—I'd forgotten that—and he fixed them on me, and spoke quietly, with his faint hesitation of an accent. I pulled his scarf out of my purse and shoved it at him, the ends fluttering. He started talking about the scarf, his good old "om" scarf from Benares, and how the design meant "om," the sound of the universe. I felt a flash of annoyance: in my daydreams, we never talked; our communion was wordless. He handed the scarf back and said he wanted me to have it. He was giving up everything. I carefully asked him what he meant, what his plans were. He said you couldn't force anything, you just had to let things happen, and that if it was right, he'd soon be in Mexico City, and then, when it was right, he'd be in South America, and meanwhile, he was floating. I saw myself in the yellow life vest in the thick green waters of the San Ysidro. I told him about the dam in the middle of the mountain desert, the old woman on the ledge, the sacred cornmeal. He was fascinated. I didn't mention Tommy and the family. Already it seemed to me that they had never existed.

The man backed the car and trailer away from the battered, distended railing. "Nothing happened," Effie said. "Everything is fine."

After a lot of maneuvering, he managed to align the car and the trailer and point them westward. Effie spoke to him, smiling frequently as they examined the hitch. "Okeydokey," she said, getting into the car. Nancy followed.

I held Maura on my hip. We were alone on a cliff at the edge of the world. Everything was plain and hard and hot. Cars slowed down and then sped up. Others remained motionless. I was just one more object in the landscape. Heat rose through the soles of my sandals, and harsh, tarry fumes clung to the back of my throat. I couldn't make myself go toward the car. I looked around for a way to walk off the freeway. Maura and I would just go. Toward the mountains. I closed my eyes and saw the web of shining threads tying me to Vik, to Tommy, to everyone, stretched thinner and thinner by air and mountains and plains and deserts. The earth's curvature would snap the threads and I would be free.

Voices saying my name hung in the shimmering air. On the last day with Vik, before I went underground to take the subway train home, I told him that I hadn't expected to fall in love with him, that I hadn't intended to suffer. "I thought I could get away with something," I said. He leaned over me and put his mouth against my temple. The sky went dark. "Everyone suffers, Rosario," he whispered. There was no way to walk off the freeway. Images were glassy and curved near the black rim of my vision. Holding Maura, I piloted my weightless body through space to the car.

Effie took her time entering the stream of traffic, and Nancy stuck her head out to make sure the lane was clear.

"There's just a little problem with that propane tank," Effie said. "So we'll get off at the next exit for a second and find a service station. I'm going to drive pretty slow so that the tank doesn't fall off. Let 'em honk all they want. I'm not worried—we'll be able to make time on the Interstate. And wasn't that man wonderful? So *courtly!* Y'all okay? Maura? Judy, I do believe I could use a fresh stick of gum. In my purse back there, honey."

Maura remained tightly curled against my chest. I twisted around to keep an eye on the trailer. The propane tank and its tubes jiggled but they seemed to be staying in place. What was the little problem? Didn't propane blow up sometimes? I handed Nancy the pack of gum.

"You want some?" she asked me.

I shook my head. I had no spit available to chew gum.

A police car appeared, the red light on top rotating and the siren going. "I guess he wants to get by me," Effie said. "I'll pull over a little bit."

He veered in front of us and stopped. "Lady!" he shouted, getting out and coming toward us. "Lady!" He left the light flashing and the police-band radio talking. "Lady! Where do you think you're going?" He sounded like a movie cop and looked like one, too—tanned, extremely handsome, mirrored sunglasses. He carried a clipboard and a pen. I wondered if I could fall in love with him. He was probably married. And a cop, to boot.

"We're going to California, Officer," Effie said, smiling.

"Don't you know what you did? Don't you know what *happened?*" he shouted. While he lectured her loudly, and she slowly shook her head, I shut my eyes. *Dearest Vik, Today I was in an accident and I thought of you.* Effie explained how she had to get the propane tank off the road. She said it was no fault of his that he didn't realize that she was the retired assistant dean of women at Cibola College.

He walked around to the other side of the car. I leaned out of my window. In a quiet voice, he asked me my name and age. I could only think of the name I was given at birth and I could not remember my age. "Rosario," I said. "Rosario Springer."

"Address?"

"None. I'm sorry. I don't know."

"You're a little shook up," he said. He had fans of fine white squint lines in his tan. "Look, I can't enforce anything because I don't know what happened."

I wanted to fall on his shoulder and cry, and tell him how from now on I would be good, how I was alone and how, for the first time, I realized I was going to die.

When I got out of the car, the dry heat rising from the cinders in the front yard made my sinuses ache. The midday high-altitude purplish glare bleached out the sidewalks and the houses: everything was ashen. Cicadas whirred in the Chinese elms, and traffic hummed in the distance. I looked at the trailer hitch and at the battered rear end of the car. I tried to put Maura down but she wouldn't let go of my neck. Effie patted the hitch and blotted her lips together.

"Can I do anything for you?" I asked.

"Oh, no, hon . . . I kind of think I'll just have Bud unhook this. He must be up by now. And then I'll—"

"Are you all right, Effie? I mean really?"

"I certainly am, hon. And then I'll call the nice insurance man, and we'll call Tommy, and then I have the most wonderful plan. We can jump in the car and go for stuffed sopaipillas at Chico Rico. They do the lettuce there so nice, it's all shredded really fine. I don't know how they manage it. What do you think, hon? I know you love that food. Doesn't that sound like lots of fun? Maura?"

Maura turned her face away.

"No," I said. "No, thank you." My voice seemed to come from outside of me, from the air. I barely recognized it. "It would not be fun to jump in the car," I said loudly. "It's over." I did not know what I was saying. I was shaking. "*This is it, this is it.*"

Effie's mouth opened and her eyebrows lifted. Then she set her jaw and went toward the house, her footsteps crunching on the cinders.

Nancy sat in the trailer on a banquette next to the open door eating potato chips. "Dad," she said. "Dad should have ordered more cinders when he had these put down last fall. These don't cover enough. Weeds are starting to come up."

I lifted Maura into the trailer. In Vik's mother's apartment, when I got up to leave, hoisting myself out of a cocoon of pillows on a divan, I'd pushed myself into his arms instead. A month passed, and everything changed in me. In the dim coolness of the subway, Vik had said something as we embraced at the turnstile. It was our last minute together. A train roared on the level beneath us, making the concrete platform shudder. What? I asked. What did you say? He held me and said it again: *This is the closest I've ever come to love.*

The cabinets of the trailer were flung open and the floor was littered with dishes, pillows, canned goods, clothing. I put Maura down and sat across from Nancy. Her eyes were red. "Dad told her not to buy a trailer," Nancy said. She stared out the door.

"Well, we're not going anywhere now," I said.

"You think Mom doesn't want to go to California?"

"I don't know. I'm not going. I know that."

We looked at each other. I could sense the fear in her chest. She pulled at her lower lip just the way her father used to do. "But Mom said everything was fine."

"You remember in *2001* when things are falling apart on the Jupiter ship and the astronauts who are still alive go sit in the pod to talk about HAL?" I said. "And they think that the insane computer, which is trying to kill them, won't know what they're saying? Remember?"

"Yeah," Nancy said. She shifted her haunches on the sticky vinyl and reached down and picked up a first-aid kit and the book of Plato's dialogues. "They made a big mistake."

"Did you think we were going to go over?" I whispered.

She nodded. "Well, I don't know. Mom says she was in control the whole time."

"I want to sit on your lap, Mommy," Maura said.

"It's too hot, sweetheart," I said. "Sit next to me. Here's a potato chip."

"No," Maura said.

I started to remember what had happened and then stopped. Nothing was going to be right again. I said to Nancy, "I wasn't scared when I thought we were going to die. I only got scared afterward, when everything was okay."

"I know what you mean." She pressed her knuckles hard against her upper lip, making the space under her nose go white.

The trailer doorway framed the red cinders, the dusty elms along the street, the peaks. For an instant, I saw a corner of the sky rip open, revealing dazzling light. Then it was just sky again.

15

I pulled the curtains in my mother's room together at the bottom to block out the McCorys' TV antenna and left a crack open at the top so I could look at the peaks. In the heat, they were exactly the color of Schaeffer's Washable Blue ink. I would never get to the mountains again unless I found a boy who had a motor scooter or a car and wanted to take me. Bud had gone to boot camp, I still didn't even have my learner's permit (my mother said I wasn't the type to drive), and ever since last week, when my mother had had the *little* accident—she ran into the back of a pickup on her way to philosophy class—she'd been talking about getting rid of the car and taking the bus. Judy—Judy could drive, but she was hopeless. I spread my school things out on the bed and lay down next to *Adventures in American Literature.* Two of the cats jumped up on the pillows and watched me. I started memorizing "Thanatopsis." I said aloud the beginning:

> *"To him who in the love of Nature holds*
> *Communion with her visible forms, she . . ."*

When my mother decided to enroll in the college summer session, she made me sign up for summer school at Cibola High, junior English, and now I had to memorize one hundred lines of poetry in six weeks. About two lines a day. Most people were doing "The Raven" by Edgar Allan Poe—exactly a hundred lines, but then they were repeating the class, and anyway, if you thought about it, the poem didn't mean anything. Just a lot of noise, in my humble opinion. But "Thanatopsis," by William Cullen Bryant, had old ocean's gray and melancholy waste poured round all, and the golden sun, the planets, and all the infinite hosts of heaven shining on the sad abodes of death. Only eighty-one lines, though, so I also had to memorize "Goodbye, My Fancy" by Walt Whitman to make up the difference.

There's something so great about lying in a quiet, dark room telling yourself poetry. I could have done it the rest of my life. I would have preferred being in my own room. But usually my mother's was in better shape than anyplace else—we'd never gotten around to getting things organized after the great envelope hunt—and it was always cooler, being on the north side of the house, and even though she'd gotten rid of everything of my father's, sometimes I could still catch his odor: cigar smoke and Wildroot Cream Oil. And it was nice to stretch out on the big bed instead of a twin. Sometimes I had strange thoughts on my mother's bed. That one day she would be old, with white hair, lying under the white bedspread in that room, breathing like the old man lying in that glowing room at the end of *2001*, and then that I'd be in that bed, old and white-haired and breathing. Waiting. And on the ceiling would still be the elephant shape in the stucco, a sort of an elephant, only with the legs of a buffalo. And my great-grandmother's claw-footed chest of drawers would still be towering against the wall like a black bear. " 'She speaks a various language; for his gayer,' " I said aloud. I could probably do more than five lines a day and finish the job early.

The door opened with a bang and my mother poked her head in. She was in her orange-striped bathrobe and had cold cream on her face and her hair in big pink sponge rollers. "Honey, we're going to go look at model apartments in a bit." In a whisper, she said, "Judy may be coming with us. I told Maura to ask her." Judy hadn't left the house since the trailer accident, but we didn't say anything about that. We'd phoned Tommy and we each told him how the car suddenly went totally out of control for no reason at all and how Mom saved our lives by putting on the emergency brake at the last minute, and Tommy said, "The secret of the universe is adaptability." My mother and Tommy talked some

more, and then she wound up yelling at him, "I *am* being philosophical! Don't you get philosophical with *me*, Thomas Hammond Junior." And then she said that was *that* and we weren't
going to talk any more about what had happened. So we didn't,
and most of the time Judy stayed in her room with the curtains
closed. I thought maybe she was mad at me about something.

"What about that kitty-box mess?" my mother said, jerking the
rollers out of her hair as fast as she could.

"Mother," I said. "I am studying." Her movements left colored
streaks in the air that pained my eyes.

"Well," she said, "make it snappy."

"I'd just like to very politely point out that Dad used to pay
us to do it," I said. But she was already gone. " 'Into his darker
musings, with a mild,' " I said.

LaDonna was in Uvalde for the summer, and I got a letter from
her every day. She mostly wanted to know whether I'd call up
Reuben and find out if he *liked* her. We hadn't seen him since
school let out, and he hadn't spoken to her since he gave her back
the binder. But what else did she have to think about in Texas?
"Dear Sweet Little 16," I wrote on a piece of notebook paper.

> You can't believe how boring it is and I do not have a
> guitar lesson until (thrill) Fri. Now what do you want
> me to ask Reuben. Be more clear. Am I supposed to say
> do you like LaD. or do you really like LaD. a lot a lot.
> I don't want to blow it so let me know. No news.
> We've been going around doing stuff (going for stuffed
> sopaipillas, etc.). It is one billion degrees F. and this aft.
> we have to go look at apartments, Mom's idea. Big deal.
> Bud actually wrote a letter. He says food is outstanding,
> men outstanding, etc., they promised him 1st Air Calvary,
> that's outstanding also. Judy is fine, Maura is fine. They
> still have my room so I am in with my Mom (Gaaahh!!!)
> until Judy goes to Africa, except now she says she might
> go to Mexico with Maura first. (????) I want to move into
> Bud's room but Mom says I have to stay with her and
> anyway his room is to hot. The cats are panting, that's

how hot it is. Judy is acting like a real zombie, she used
to be so great. But probably without Tommy

I crossed out the zombie part, and then I got bored. I took the
special pink stationery out of my binder and tried a new way of
writing, with the letters round and almost lying on their sides:
"My dearest darling Reuben Leroy," I wrote, because I was
thinking that someday if I really got to know Reuben, I wouldn't
call him Rube like his friends or Reuben like LaDonna did, I'd
have a particular way of speaking to him, and when we were
together on a cliff in the forest at night viewing the lake below
in the moonlight, I'd say very softly "Reuben Leroy," and tears
might even come to his eyes when he heard that, after his long
loneliness in his mountain cabin. I wrote:

I cannot go on this way hiding what I feel for you in
my heart of hearts. I have loved you since 9th grade
(Mrs. Apodaca's class) and will always go on loving you
my darling forever, I am yours no matter what happens
or even if you go with someone else or get married.
If you feel this way too then come to my house,
3524 Cagua Blvd., I'm always here except when I'm not

All of a sudden I got dizzy and crumpled up the letter and
stuffed it in my binder. I came across *Childhood's End*, and I lay
down and read until my mother charged in and said, "Nancy, I
am telling you. And you shouldn't be reading in the dark. You'll
ruin your eyes." She yanked the curtain open and the sun reflecting off the aluminum siding on the McCorys' garage blinded me.
I pressed the book into the bedspread so she couldn't see the
cover, which had teardrop-shaped spacecraft on it. "I have this
test coming up," I said. My head began to pound.
"I mean *now.*"
"All right." I started to get up and she left. I read for a few more
minutes and then put the book down and sat there staring until
the bureau, the doily, the big bottle of Chanel No. 5, and the
pictures went radioactive. If you're in a certain mood, you only

have to stare at something for as long as you can without blinking and that happens. The edges of things get wavy and a glow jumps along them. One time LaDonna and I tried staring into each other's eyes and what happens is the other person's eyes get huge and you never want to see them again. The other thing you can do is stare at the back of someone's neck. Pretty soon they'll turn around. I put my feet on the floor. I felt tired and weak. What was the point of everything in the world? My bones even hurt a little. I sprinkled some Chanel between my breasts. Tommy said I was ready for Chanel but he never gave me any, and I wondered if he would send me some from Africa. Probably not. I went down the hall toward the bathroom. The shower was on and Maura was chattering to Judy in the rush of water, and steam came out from under the door.

One of my beds was covered with stuffed animals and picture books, and a pink sundress had been laid out along with a little undershirt, a pair of ruffled panties, and two tiny socks. On the other bed was a pair of lacy bikini panties and the yellow mini-dress. When Judy got off the plane in that dress, my mother said, "New York." On the night table were some books Judy hadn't told me about yet. But then she hadn't been talking much. The top one was called *The Diamond Sutra.* I opened it to a dog-eared page with a lot of underlining: "If the mind depends on anything it has no sure haven." I sat down on the bed. The title of one chapter was: "*It Is Erroneous to Affirm That All Things Are Ever Extinguished.*" A sheet of paper fell out. It was covered with Judy's tiny, slanted writing. "Dearest Vik," it said at the top. "You haven't written and I don't understand—"

My head seemed to swell and my face got hot. I felt sick to my stomach. I had to close my eyes for a while. I quickly shut the letter inside the book and put it back exactly where it had been, next to a candle I'd made in fourth grade for my father by melting blue and purple crayons in a milk carton full of hot wax. One of the cats came in with a big grasshopper in his mouth and batted it around for a while. Then he crunched it between his teeth.

I went to the closet to figure out what the correct thing was to wear to look at model apartments. I really wanted to stay home by myself. I hadn't been alone for months, and ever since we'd seen Bud off at the bus station (many jokes, etc.), my mother hardly ever let me out of her sight. She drove me to school every morning and picked me up afterward, whereas I used to have to beg her for a ride if there was a dust storm; she'd say going on shank's mare in bad weather was character-building. And now she was always taking me to McDonald's or Taco Bell after she got back from the college, and that was fine with me because the house was hot and didn't smell very good, and there was never anything to eat. But I preferred the old days, when I could do whatever I wanted without anyone paying attention. " 'Into his darker musings, with a mild,' " I said. I stepped into my red cotton skirt and rolled it up around the elastic waistband to make it into a miniskirt, and I put on a blue sleeveless blouse. It was too small, and it separated between the buttons, but it was my favorite.

There was a gagging noise in the corner of the room. The cat vomited up the grasshopper. My mother came in wearing her pink slip. She got into the rest of her clothes while she walked.

My head was gigantic, and a sharp pain was beginning to spread across my forehead. " 'Of the last bitter hour come like a blight,' " I said.

"I am not asking you about that cat box again, Nancy," she said. "It has been three weeks."

"Mom, Judy is in the bathroom." I wasn't about to cross Judy's path.

"You-all had better darn well take care of it when she gets out." She pulled her yellow fiesta dress over her head.

"I just put on clean clothes, Mom," I said.

She tugged down hard on her dress and came toward me while she was zipping it. I stepped back because her eyes were dark and she had them screwed up. "My Lord," she said. "Pull that skirt straight. And your blouse has gaposis."

"I'll tuck it in better."

"Best throw it out."

"Mom," I said. "I adore this blouse."

Just then, the bathroom door opened, and my mother disap-

peared into her room. Judy came down the hallway wrapped in
a towel. She was carrying my hairbrush. Maura ran ahead of her,
naked, her chubby legs pumping up and down, her hands
clamped on her scalp. "Just one quick brush, Maura," Judy was
saying. But Maura wouldn't let Judy near her hair. Judy dropped
the brush on the bed. She smelled of that new perfume, the
sandalwood. She undid her towel, and I turned around and went
in the den. Didn't she have one ounce of modesty?

My headache was getting worse. The Woodstock album was
on the stereo. It was the only record I played now. The side with
"Suite: Judy Blue Eyes." I switched it on and tried to remember
the feeling of *Childhood's End*. The starry realms, the wise Overlords from an advanced intergalactic civilization who ended all
war and took care of everyone on earth so the children could
evolve. Last summer, when I slept outdoors at the dam, there had
been a cool, dry wind, the black, infinite sky, the stars icy and
close. Yes, that was the feeling. Cold emptiness. Keeping myself
surrounded with that, I went slowly into my mother's bedroom
and got *Childhood's End*.

My mother was at the chest of drawers. "Dadgummit, this
right-hand knob is loose," she said. "I swear, I do not know what
to do."

I went back in the den and lay on the couch with the book. The
warm vinyl made my arms and legs sweat. "Dearest Vik." A few
years ago, LaDonna found a marriage manual in her mother's
drawer. I couldn't believe the things in that book, but a terrible
ringing inside me told me they were true. For a long time afterward, I tried to forget, but every night those pictures came into
my mind. After a while, it didn't matter so much anymore, I
stopped feeling horror when I looked at grown-ups, and then all
I remembered was that I remembered something; and then I
forgot, more or less. "Dearest Vik." I put down *Childhood's End*
and picked up the guitar, which stayed propped against the end
of the couch where my father had left it except for when I
practiced or went to my lesson. I strummed the three chords I had
learned so far—C, F, and G; I don't know if they were the ones
Crosby, Stills, Nash, and Young were using—and I sang with

them, "Sometimes it hurts so badly I must cry out loud, I am sorr-y." And I tried to think about the future evolution of the human race, its end in its present form except for the one who survived, the one the Overlords protected.

" 'To him who in the love of Nature holds,' " I said to Maura. I held her on my lap in the front seat so Judy could lie down in the back. She couldn't ride in the car now unless she stayed down below the level of the windows and covered her eyes. That really annoyed my mother, but she kept quiet about it. "Come on, Maura," I said. "Say, 'To him—' "

"Don't want to," Maura said. "One, two, three, fighting four. Let's sing that." So we sang the Country Joe and the Fish song: "And it's one, two, three, what are we fighting for? Don't ask me, I don't give a damn . . ."

We got off the freeway just before the east-west, north-south interchange, right across from the Monte Vista Shopping Plaza. It was the first place we took Judy after she arrived because we wanted to show her the graduation gift we'd picked out for Bud —a rifle at the sporting-goods store. But she couldn't have cared less, in my humble opinion. She'd stepped off the plane looking like a foreigner—very slender, her cheekbones sticking out, her eyes outlined in black, her hair in a flat, tight coil on her neck, her elbows close to her sides. Her face had gotten tight and small. And lately, she hardly said a word, and when she did, you had to ask her to repeat herself because her voice was so low. During conversations she'd just stare, and most of the time she didn't seem to know anyone was talking to her. My mother said it had to be the altitude, that your blood goes and gets thin or whatever.

"Bud is going to rise through the ranks so fast it will make your head spin," my mother said. "It's just as well he didn't go the college-and-ROTC route, because if he qualifies for helicopter-pilot school, and gets through okay, he'll *be* an officer—a warrant officer, that is, which is just as good. And besides, this way he'll get to know the *men* and you have to have that. Because I know eventually he'll get a very high rank. Bud has that calm you need, grace under pressure, it's called. And he's going to be so happy following in his father's footsteps, and then later, they promised he can come right back here and he'll get his college in—they'll pay for it. He'll be right back in the bosom of the family. Your daddy can advise him all about the college stuff—right, Maura?"

"Right," Maura said. "Right-ee-oh. Felix, the wonderful cat."

A muffled noise came from the back seat. Judy was lying down with her forearms crossed over her face.

Mom kept on talking. "Your poor daddy, Maura, alone in New York having to do all the packing and cleaning up. I can just picture him scrubbing the apartment. I remember when Nancy was a baby, we were by ourselves or something, and your daddy just got down on his hands and knees and scrubbed all the floors and waxed them very nicely. He was quite the little man of the house. He's going to be completely worn out when he gets to Liberia."

"I packed and scrubbed before I left," Judy murmured.

"What, hon? I didn't understand that part he said on the phone about a possible postponement. Did you get that?"

"Uh-uhh," Judy said, shaking her head under her arms.

"It's probably red tape," my mother said. "But you're sure it's all right with him if you take off for Mexico all by yourself without the slightest idea where you are going to stay or how you'll manage?"

"Mmmm," Judy said.

"You know we just really love having you-all with us, and you can stay here till the cows come home," my mother said. "It's just a whole bunch of fun, you and little Maura. Right, Nancy, darlin'?"

I rolled my eyes. Oh, please, Mom, I said silently.

We drove into the Marina del Mar Luxury Townhouse Park. "I don't get why it's called Marina del Mar," I said. "We are at least five hundred miles from anything even faintly resembling an ocean."

"But look at that beautiful pool," my mother said.

There were three buildings two stories high, red brick with black X's in planks around the first story. The roofs were rounded and gray like toadstools. We parked in front of the rental office next to a yellow-brick planter with little dried-up bushes in it. "This Tudor styling really reminds me of England," she said. "Half-timbering is what that is. It's Elizabethan." Except for a couple of saplings, the entire area was paved. "No yard to take care of, Nancy, darlin'. Not that anyone at our house has pulled up a weed in a year."

The rental agent took us across the parking lot. He wore a big gold class ring with the initials CC.

"You're a Cibola College boy," my mother said. "I'm Effie Hammond—assistant dean of women. That is, until last year."

"Oh, Mrs. Hammond!" he said. "I thought I recognized you. You are the greatest civics teacher who ever lived."

"Oh, well, the teaching—that was just extra." My mother beamed at him.

"No, really, I was amazingly inspired by your class. Hal Washburn?"

This happened to my mother all the time. They stopped on the asphalt and talked. In the glare, this man, standing and swaying a little in his white loafers with pinpoint airholes, bulged toward me. Heat rolled off of him. He had blond curly hair with wide sideburns, and droplets of sweat in the sideburns. He wore a bolo tie with a clasp made from a big slice of polished agate. In it you could see what looked like brown mountains and a blue lake.

Finally he started the tour. "Our luxury complex has a complete sauna system and we feature a fully equipped modern laundry center," he said. I figured he had memorized this speech. " 'She speaks a various language; for his gayer,' " I said under my breath. I liked the easy, expert way he spoke, like those national park rangers who give the same talk twenty times a day.

The model apartment had an upstairs—ten steps, which I counted by touching my tongue to the back of my front teeth—and low, whorled ceilings. I thought I was going to love the place, but I didn't. It smelled rubbery, like the carpeting department at Sears. All the furniture was shrunken. Even the double bed was less than double. I felt very bulky, as if I might go to scratch my nose and knock over the little floor lamp, or turn around and accidentally crush Judy against the wall, and the wall would break open and we would go sailing through the hole.

"Flocked wallpaper!" my mother said. It was red with a raised, velvety, looping design of intertwined initials you couldn't quite make out. "My dream."

"Yes, ma'am," Mr. Washburn said. "And this here is what we call a galley kitchen, Mrs. Hammond. With your top-of-the-line appliances, dishwasher included."

"I never did like a huge kitchen myself," my mother said. "You're just cleaning it all the time. What does your mama think about that, Maura, hon?"

Judy didn't seem to hear. She was holding Maura on her hip and gazing around.

To keep myself from passing out from boredom, and to get that "Dearest Vik" out of my brain, I pretended that this was the apartment where Reuben and I would live. When he came home after work, I'd have drinks and a bowl of pretzels ready. Mr. Washburn invited us to step out on the balcony. It was a narrow concrete ledge with a black metal railing, and we couldn't all fit. Judy stayed just inside with Maura.

"There's the pool down there," my mother said. "Oh, boy!"

Judy cleared her throat. "Can children, uh, ever come and use the pool?" she whispered.

"Excuse me, ma'am?"

Judy stepped out onto the balcony and repeated the question. She had a grip on Maura so tight that the skin on her thighs was stretched and pale.

"Uh, actually, ma'am, I am truly sorry, but I don't believe the management allows children in the pool. This is what is known as an exclusive adult community."

"Oh," Judy said. "Thank you." She blushed and turned away.

"Just look at that spectacular view!" my mother said.

I thought about standing here with Reuben under the stars. Arcturus, Betelgeuse, Altair, Vega. Then I thought: What if I lived here alone, a career girl, and Reuben was my steady boyfriend and just came over to visit, and I would have a lot of cute clothes? I could take him out on the balcony and show him the sky. But if we were married and this was his home, he would probably want to lie on the couch and watch TV.

"You can see Cambridge Heights and La Golondrina Park— the really quality developments," my mother said.

"We think of Marina del Mar as a quality development, Mrs. Hammond, without the homeowner's burden of upkeep," Mr. Washburn said.

"Burden is right," my mother said.

"You can even see what movie is on at the Sagebrush Drive-in," I said.

"How soon are these apartments going to be available?" my mother asked. "What are the terms?"

I went inside. Judy was looking at a miniature coffee table with a leaf-shaped candy dish on it filled with colored marbles. I felt strange being alone with her. "They have porno now," I said in a low voice.

"Excuse me?"

"The Sagebrush has porno movies now," I said.

"Porno," Judy said. She lifted Maura's hand away from the marbles. "Porno," she said again.

Judy lay down in the back seat and I got in front with Maura.

My mother fanned herself with the shiny brochures. "It is so hot, but you can bet your bootees it's hotter in Mexico," she said. "I remember during the war, I left Tommy with my mama, and a lady friend and I took a bus down into Mexico and wouldn't you know it, my period started and it was a hundred and twenty degrees on that bus, and I was dying, and then we got off the bus in some town, I forget where, and we went to a restaurant, and I just want to tell you that it was the worst meal I ever ate in my life, I was sicker than a dog, and I said to my lady friend, 'I am going home this minute,' which I did. And the men in Mexico. I mean you are not safe and you're worried every second. But you don't have to go to Mexico to worry about that. I've had so many little girls at the college come to me and say they wanted to move out of the dorm and live off campus, and I would sit each and every one of them down and say, 'Honey, us women are *vulnera-ble.*' And those girls were so grateful for my advice." She opened a brochure. "It's luxury but it's actually pretty reasonable when you consider all the extras," she said. There were pictures. People drinking cocktails by the pool, but it was some other pool, long and deep blue, surrounded by palm trees. A couple having dinner at a table with flowers and candles in a big living room with red carpeting and pink drapes. Another couple, all in white, holding tennis rackets. "Flocked wallpaper—I cannot get over that. And think, Nance, no more washing dishes. We can be ladies of leisure and sit out on that balcony in the mornings and drink our coffee and read and look at the peaks."

"You really serious about this, Mom?" Until now I hadn't believed we would leave the house. It was the only place I'd ever lived. I knew everything about it: The caved-in panel of the bathroom door from the time when Bud was chasing me and I locked myself in and he tried to kick down the door. The zigzag crack in my bedroom wall that looked like a lightning bolt. The secret way the living room was when I would go in there in the morning before anyone was awake and it would be dark and all the big blocks of furniture sat there like gods. I couldn't imagine home being anywhere else, and, anyway, my mother's plans kept changing. Some days, she had the idea of living in a trailer court, and other days, she said she was going to leave the trailer in the yard and use it as a study. But she never went near it. Other times, she said we would go to England and enroll in college there together, Oxford maybe. None of those ideas seemed real to me, though. I didn't know if I could be the same person if I lived in another place. I asked her about the house.

"First I have to work out your daddy's insurance and so forth, see what it comes to after they're through doing everything, and when the check comes, I want to put down a deposit first thing. Bless his heart. He would have wanted me to rent a luxury townhouse apartment, although he wasn't much of an apartment person himself, not a city man, really. Maura, tell your mama that what I mean is that I think that everything really does happen for the best, and what I am sure is going to happen is that you-all will move back here and you want to start out in style, and the house has the new carpeting plus very fine furniture, antiques and all, and the den furniture is brand-new, and you'll be every bit as happy living in the house as we were, 'cause your mama and daddy have that same special something Tom and I had. 'Cause it's a family-style home. The family-style thing is over for me, and at heart I've always basically been a city-apartment-type person. Don't you think these here townhouses just *feel* like New York City? What does your mama think, Maura, hon?"

Maura looked at my mother. The car was stuffy and smelled of hot metal. I wanted to get going, roll the windows down, let some cool air blow in.

"It's funny," Judy said to the ceiling. I thought maybe she was talking to herself. "In New York, when they say 'townhouse,' they mean like a five-story brownstone. They have them in rows along nice streets. I don't get what they mean by townhouse here. This is more like—I don't know—like a motel, maybe?"

My mother pressed her lips together. She put on her dark glasses and pulled out of the parking lot so fast that the wheels squealed and Maura grabbed my blouse with both hands and tried to hide her head between my breasts. When we reached an intersection, my mother said, "I believe it comes from history." She used her soft voice—the one for when she was being polite and not saying what she really thought. "The lord of the manor would have his country estate, and then when he would go into town, he would naturally have his townhouse. That's what Marina del Mar kind of reminds me of—Merrie Oldey England and all that. If I lived here I would take a more historical perspective about things."

Judy sat up. "I think I forgot my purse back there," she said.

If I just let myself go blank, I could get into the mood of *Childhood's End:* I was there in the hot car on the freeway with my eyes open, but really I was surrounded by endless, cold, black space.

"We'll leave most of the furniture in the house, and I believe we'll get one of those hidey-bed sofas for the apartment for when

Bud comes home on leave. What do you think, Nance? New furniture?"

"Great, Mom."

"You can decorate your new bedroom in a grown-up style. My idea is that we would have to have quality things. Right, Nance?"

I saw myself in fashionable clothes from Boutique Julian. My waist would get small, my legs would get tan, and my freckles would disappear. Reuben would visit me at the pool.

Maura started singing. "One, two, three, fighting four. Be the first one on your block to have your boy come home in a bock."

"Box," I said.

"Nancy, hon, you don't sound thrilled. Are you thrilled? I am honestly thrilled by this apartment."

"I'm thrilled, too, Mom," I said. "But what about the cats?"

"They don't allow pets, but Maura loves those kittycats, don't you, darlin'? We'll come to the house and visit the cats lots. Are you thrilled, Nance? I mean, really?"

"*Yes*. I said I was thrilled." I was wondering what would happen to the cats while Judy and Tommy and Maura were in Africa.

"Well, you don't sound thrilled, Nancy Hammond," my mother said.

"I really am. It's just that I'm practicing to be a zombie."

Judy happened to hear this, and she laughed. "Practicing to be a zombie!" she said. She laughed for a long time, very hard, her mouth open wide, showing her chipped front tooth. "Far out," she said, wiping her eyes.

Maura laughed, too, and reached over the back seat and patted Judy's head. "Far out," she said. "Far out, Mommy."

"Far out?" I said. I got the sick feeling in my head and stomach again. "Where did you pick up that expression?" I couldn't look at Judy. I focused on a billboard for Krazy Karlos the HubKap King—a cartoon figure of Krazy Karlos wearing a giant crown made of hubcaps.

"I guess it's going around now," Judy said. "In New York."

"New York," my mother said. "I bet those Marina del Mar townhouses are every bit as luxurious as anything you could find in New York City, and you sure aren't going to find a pool like that outside your balcony, and a view of the Cibola Peaks."

"Jackie Onassis would give anything to live in Marina del Mar," I said.

"Nancy, don't get smart," my mother said.

Judy started to laugh again. "Practicing to be a zombie," she said, keeping her arm across her eyes.

To him who in the love of Nature holds. We turned on Lincoln past the 7-Eleven, Hair Facts, Rainbow Bowlarama, and Rancho de Cibola Realty and onto Cagua. I thought about how Princess Darla Heights would look after the bomb fell—just rows of scorched foundations with pipes sticking up. *Communion with, communion with.*

16

It was one of those red-orange summer dusks when everything in Cibola looks like it's on fire, and Nancy was in the den with Maura listening to a record of some boys with high voices saying over and over again "four dead in oh-my-oh." The kids loved that junk and went around singing it and you didn't have a clue as to what they were talking about. The radio never even played *my* music anymore. Judy was shut up in her bedroom as usual. Talk about *immured*.

I said to Nancy, "Let's you and me just slip off to the Dairy Queen," but she was fixing Maura's hair in little ponytails and they were waiting for *Star Trek* to come on.

I said, "I can remember when you would have given your *life* for a chance for me to take you to the Dairy Queen," and I went in my room and closed the door and shooed the cats off of my bed and pushed the unfolded laundry to one side. There was an old pink smudge on the spread from face powder, and the cats had left dusty brown circles wherever they decided to lie down, and they clawed at the tuftings or whatever you call them. I threw myself down.

I honestly thought that if I let go at that moment I could expire. Life was too much for me. Not one thing was working out the way I wanted and I had to do everything alone. And I mean everything. All the insurance problems from the big accident *and* the little accident, the washing and ironing, never mind keeping the house clean—it had been a mess since Judy and Maura came

—plus the visits to the income-tax man, plus philosophy class, which was very hard. And I was also trying to make myself stay alert and keep everyone's spirits high.

I got up and started folding the laundry. The energy I needed just to get the kids under control and headed in the right direction was ten times more than I had these days. I was thinking about going to visit Bud at Fort Polk before advanced infantry training started just to keep him, you know, *honed*, and I had to work on how to get Tommy fixed. I just had that awful mother's intuition that he was in trouble, although certainly what he did was his own business—after all, he was a grown man—but the Africa thing didn't sound so hot, it had never seemed quite real to me, and he seemed to have other things on his mind, although I couldn't say what, and I knew I could help him, but Judy wouldn't say boo about a thing. Judy herself really needed straightening out. All she did was lie on her bed in a daze while Maura got into everything. I don't know how Tommy tolerated that, but now I saw why he'd dumped her on me when in fact all I had done was phone and very generously invite them *all* out for Bud's graduation. At the time, I was so happy about finding that envelope that I didn't think. He said, "Great, we'll be there," and then pretty soon he had arranged things so it was just Judy and Maura because he couldn't get away, he was at a crucial point in his dissertation, and then he worked it so that they would stay with me for most of the summer until he was settled in Africa, but his trip kept getting postponed, and each time I thought: Well, he needs my help here, so I went along with it. And now I was paying the price. Not only was I feeding Judy because she didn't have a dime, she never wanted to do anything fun and she would die before she would wash a dish or say a cheerful word. I told her I would only be too happy to lend her any of my books, but all she mumbled was "Oh, that's nice." The way she acted, you'd think *she* was the one who had lost her man. I remember how happy and enthusiastic she was when they got married, and even last summer she was pretty bouncy. But there's something about her I just never figured out. Still water is supposed to run deep, but in her case I'm not so sure. Tommy once said she just wasn't *verbal* but she had astounding *comprehension*. So who knows? But I don't think anyone would contradict me if I made the tiny observation that she was not realizing her God-given personal capacities to the fullest.

I needed to work on Nancy, too. She used to go along with me so sweetly about everything, but now she'd started showing her stubborn streak. She was already saying something about not wanting to go to secretarial school, but I didn't feature her going to college—what if she upped and got married like Judy? All that money just wasted and no secretarial skills to speak of.

I was exhausted. I could see why in India wives just jumped on the funeral pyre. I was completely alone. And the little accident had been the last straw. You have to wonder why fate singles you out. I was reviewing my notes for a quiz in logical positivism, which I am against, by the way, and I just bumped into the back of that pickup truck lightly, hardly did a thing. "Just kissed it," as I told the man. And *I'm* the one who got the sore neck, which was already aching from the other accident, but the man was so mad at me, and my insurance agent was, too, and the police suspended my license, which is hardly fair because these things were certainly not my fault. I kept telling everybody that. With the big accident, the mistake was hooking a car with power steering up to a trailer, and how was I to know that would cause it to lose control? No one ever had the consideration to inform me of that possibility. How could I have possibly known that? And nobody—not me, not Nancy, not Judy—even *saw* any of the other vehicles involved in the big accident. We had no idea. Judy and Nancy still didn't know, and I never told Tommy or Bud, either. And the pickup at the stoplight took its own sweet time when the light turned green. You have to say it's fate, and I was trying to study what fate was. You've got your *will,* and you do all you can with that, but then there's *fate.* All I know is that none of these things would have happened if Tom was still with me, and try as I might, I could not get it out of my head that he had deliberately done all this to me when I was not in the least ready. He went so fast. What ever happened to those lingering illnesses with the whole family gathered around to get love and final instructions and wisdom? And furthermore, Tom was hardly even Tom those last months.

When he left after Nancy was born and he phoned after a week, I said, "I don't care. *Just come home.*" I didn't ask any questions because I had complete love and forgiveness for him, and he didn't mention anything ever again except once at TGIF when he got pretty lit and he was looking around and smiling and all of a sudden he said, "Now, why in the hell did I run off with her?" Judy and the kids, and probably Tommy, too, thought he was talking about me and it was a big joke. For six months now, in the back of my mind, I'd been saying *Just come home.* I was worn out from that and from trying to keep everyone happy. I didn't feel like a human being, I went on doing every single thing I was supposed to do, but what made me Effie was gone. I hadn't even finished growing when I married Tom. I grew another half inch. I've always considered myself a youthful person, but maybe that was over now; I was feeling my age. I should have had myself cremated along with him and our ashes would have mingled. When I thought about that, I really wanted to die.

I lay down again and crossed my arms on my chest. If I passed on right now, the first thing would be that I would not move anymore. I would be completely still. And then the cold. Cold, like rocks in the winter, like the ground, but I wouldn't feel it. It would be like fainting—when you revive, you don't remember. Like that moment when the car was about to go over the edge. I just blacked out. I needed to ask Dr. Desai, my philosophy professor, about this, about what it is that you're present and then you're not. Like anesthetic. Tom didn't even know the operation had taken place. And he was happy in those last moments, so it can't be all bad. Anyway, there I would be, my body cooling, and I remember clearly the cooling closet upstairs in my grand-mother's old house: the people used to be stored there until the parlor was ready, and then they were brought down and laid out. There I'd be, no consciousness, no desire, no more feeling low. Absolute rest. Cremated and scattered. The kids knew I wanted cremation, but I thought I'd better leave a note to remind them.

They would cry. Tommy would cry the most. He once told

me I was the only woman he really loved, and I believed him. The others were more or less extra. All right. The kids would go out to dinner at La Posada while I went into the place where they cremate you. My body is burned, my very own body not mine anymore but just a *thing*, like a log. I always liked to burn the Christmas wrapping paper after the gifts were opened. It was so depressing to see it in the garbage with eggshells and blobs of gravy dumped on it. Okay. So I am burned and scattered. Tommy would do it from that plane. Over the mountains, over the town. Maybe some of Tom's ashes were still floating up there.

I sat up. My heart was pounding. I wanted to scream. He was not anywhere. There was no place I could go and find Tom! Tommy never should have insisted on the scattering. Now there was no place to go, no stone, no family plot—he was *nowhere.* He had been somewhere, and now he was *nowhere.* I can't remember who came up with the idea of cremation. It seemed beautiful at the time.

I lay back down. Tom did not exist. This man who was everything to me, a part of me, most of me, and now he did not exist. No one knew what I had suffered.

Okay, back to the original line of thought. I was burned, scattered, I could feel myself leaving Tommy by the handful, and there I was in the air over Cibola, the pure air, with the sun, the clouds, the peaks, the moon, the stars. Did I just hang there in the air? Was that the story? Was Tom just hanging there? Would I still feel like myself? Or like some other being? If I lost an arm or a leg, that would change who I was, but I would still feel like myself. Now I was talking about losing my entire body. Transparent, in the air over Cibola, but what was going to keep me there? Your body kept you glued to one spot on the map at a time: now there was nothing binding me together. I chased around the sky trying to collect my ashes so that I would be in one place. But I kept expanding and disintegrating, filling the sky. I was everywhere. And freed from all the busywork of life. I was plenty fed up with having to start over every morning, meditate, make the instant coffee, get my girdle and nylons on, comb my hair, wash the dishes so they could get dirty again, go to class, afterward sit in one office or another while some man behind a desk told me about minimum deductible, pick up Nancy and drive around making cheerful conversation. No wonder I was so tired. No wonder I had gotten wrinkles on my *neck* in the past few months. Death would be an extra-long vacation.

I lay with my arms at my sides and waited. All right, I was ready. Let death come. My breath was shallow. My heart was thumping in an uneven way, or was it that I just noticed it for the first time? I lay there barely breathing, witnessing myself die.

A jet broke the sound barrier and made the windows rattle. Nancy was playing that song again. "Four dead, four dead in—" It was "Ohio" they were singing, that was it. "Four dead in *Ohio*." I heard Maura singing along. She didn't know what "Ohio" meant, let alone "dead."

I got up and put on my lilac cowboy pants with the matching ruffled blouse, the outfit Tommy said last summer was a little too colorful, and I slipped on my mules and went into the kitchen. I was dying, but now I had to make dinner. You never die when you want to.

I slit open the hamburger buns and phoned Tommy and said, "I no longer want to be the matriarch."

He said, "You mean matriarch *qua* matriarch or in some other sense?"

I said, "I don't know. I just don't see why I have to carry the whole family on my back. I don't see why you-all have to go away to Africa. But I am not one to interfere: my children are old enough to know right from wrong and to live their own lives, and you should just do whatever you want."

He said, "All our stuff has been shipped. I'm basically camping out here with my toothbrush. Friends are feeding me, et cetera." And he said, "It's been so harrowing that one is utterly exhausted."

I said, "And just how is that dissertation? You must have had a lot of time to work on it since you quit the photo lab. But I suppose there's all kinds of important business you have to take care of before you go, and I know Judy said there was some money coming for her or something, from her little typing jobs?"

I unwrapped the package of hamburger, and I said, "I just don't know what to do, I've tried to tell her in the nicest possible way —what I mean is, do you know that when you send that money Judy is planning to take off for *Mexico City* until you get settled in Africa? Did she tell you all about that?"

He said, "This whole Africa thing is taking longer than anticipated, and the city is no place for her and Maura now that everything has been sent." While he was talking, I started thinking about taking Nancy to the movies. He said, "The money I intend to send her will go further in Mexico—"

I said, "She doesn't need one red cent *here*. She has everything she could possibly want and we are having the best time. Tonight I'm cooking a beautiful dinner just for her and Maura because Nancy and I will probably go out to a drive-in, and you know how that is. You're sitting there and they show a picture of a hot dog on the screen, and then you have to go to the snack bar. Judy never wants to go to the drive-in anymore or anyplace else, but she has our wonderful adobe hacienda to make herself at home in, and I've shown her the books I am studying for my course and she could borrow them anytime she likes and improve her mind, and I even found out that there are free courses she could take at the college, and I gave her that notebook from last summer when you said I should organize my thoughts, but my thoughts are organized to beat the band—and just the other day we had the best fun looking at model apartments that were so gorgeous you could die. Luxury. And Tommy, flocked wallpaper! Was this Mexico idea something you decided?" I pulled the ground meat apart into little chunks, ate a few bites, and dropped the rest in the skillet.

He said the plan was Judy's. And of course I would never say a word because I don't believe in interfering, but I don't see how Judy would dream that one up by herself. I pushed the hamburger around with a spatula and I said, "Mexico—Mexico City —alone in the summer? Just where is she going to stay? And then somehow she has to get a plane to Africa. And taking poor little Maura where there are all those diseases, Maura who loves her Effie and Nancy so much." I opened the sloppy-joe mix and poured it over the hamburger in the skillet. The meat turned dark red. It didn't taste too bad. "Well, Nancy and I can manage, and I'm going to try to see Bud when he finishes boot camp. We have to think of how to make absolutely sure he gets into helicopter-pilot school."

He said, "Helicopter school? How would he qualify? They're not taking high school kids, unless the Army is getting desperate."

I got annoyed. I was trying to concentrate on spooning the sloppy-joe mix over the hamburger buns. I said, "Tommy, your brother happens to be highly qualified."

"But there happens to be a war on. It's suicidal."

That was Tommy—high drama. I said, "Don't get yourself all worked up over nothing. I told Bud he had to dream the impossible dream and be the best he could possibly be and do our family honor in the service, and he said so sweetly to me, 'I know that, Mom,' and you know he was dying to be a pilot like his father, but the Air Force wants you to be a college graduate, and anyway helicopter is what everybody does now, and he is going to do very well at it, and he is going to dedicate himself to helping our country, which certainly needs all the help we can give it to stop those Communists from killing our boys, and he is going to learn a useful, practical skill, and I will not listen to you on this subject because you are in New York City with your intellectual know-it-all friends and you don't have a blessed idea what's truly going on and what can happen to a great nation if it fails to be eternally vigilant, and I only called to tell you that I don't want to be the matriarch anymore. I am through."

He said, "What does this mean, substantively?"

I said, "Why don't you just *come home?*"

17

I tapped on Judy's door. "Is it all right to come in?" I said. I heard her blow her nose.

"Sure," she said.

When I opened the door, I saw a piece of my pink stationery disappearing into a book she had on her lap. I'd given her the stationery when she lost the notebook from my mother. Even though it was afternoon, Judy was still in her blue baby-doll nightie. Her face was thinner than ever, yellowish, and her eyelids were puffy. There were two lines between her eyebrows that used to show when she frowned or seemed confused. Now, they never went away. Maura was asleep on the other bed, surrounded by stuffed animals, her legs and arms spread wide, her mouth open.

I had in mind to tell Judy that I didn't want her to be mad at me anymore, or at least to ask her what I had done wrong. I knew I had put that letter back exactly where I found it. "You still reading?" I whispered. "You like that book? Is it any good?" I tried to read the title. "*The Upani*—what?"

"*Upanishads,*" she said.

"You sure do a lot of reading." I waited for her to tell me something, but she didn't speak. "Certainly is hot," I said. "No rain for three weeks now." I couldn't look at her. "Well, so, anyway. My hair. I don't know what to do about it and I have my guitar lesson this afternoon."

Judy thought for a while. "You want me to fix it?"

"I'd really appreciate that," I said. "I can't make it anything but awful." I suddenly had an urge to cry.

Her eye was on the corner of the room, where a cat was stretching from a carton of my father's books into an open suitcase. Judy had brought all kinds of stuff with her and never had gotten around to unpacking. There were toys and books and record albums and crumpled clothing, and there was the pot from her great-grandmother that she hadn't wanted to leave with the movers. "You have a brush?" she asked. "I don't know where mine's gone."

She sat on the den sofa and I sat on the floor between her knees. There was a soap opera on television. "You used to do my hair a lot," I said.

There was a silence. "The mailman will be coming soon," she said.

"You hear from Tommy lately? Does he know what day he's leaving yet?"

"Nope," she said.

My mother had talked to Tommy the other night, but I wasn't sure if Judy knew that. I decided not to mention it. "You really going to Mexico?"

Sad organ music came from the television. "I'd like to," she said. "I always did want to travel."

The soft tugging on the ends of my hair made me dreamy. I looked out the picture window at the yellow grass stalks poking up through the cinders and at the trailer, the sidewalk, the street, and the Roybals' house on the other side. I was hoping to see something different for a change—an ocean maybe. I remembered how Judy and I had sat in the trailer together after the big accident. She said something so odd then that it didn't fit with anything else and so I couldn't think now what it was. But I remember saying to myself afterward something like: This is the only person I have. But that didn't make sense. I had my mother, and Tommy, and—I hated to admit it—even Bud. "You won't believe this, but I actually miss Bud," I said. "I hope he's all right."

"Mmm," she said.

Another silence, so long that it made me want to talk and talk. "I worry about him," I said. "I mean, he *is* in the Army, and there *is* a war. . . . Mom says everything is fine and he won't necessarily be sent to Vietnam. But the night before he left, I was up watching TV when he came home so late, and he told me that he never wanted to enlist, he did it because Mom thought he had more choices than if he was drafted, and he said he hated the idea of boot camp, and he didn't even want to try out for the pilot training. I don't know why he said that. That's not true. I do know why. He'd been tripping on mescaline all day and he was starting to come down. Please don't tell Mom or Tommy, Judy. Please promise me you won't, because he made me promise."

"I promise," Judy said.

"The really strange thing that was so bizarre was that I liked the way he was, drugged. He was really sweet, like he used to be, and he was scared and he talked about that. I felt so sorry for him, and we tried to figure out how he could get out of the Army or go to Canada or something. I was going to give him my hundred-dollar savings bond from Grandfather Hammond. But I guess now he likes it. I mean, if you believe his letters."

"Mescaline," Judy said. "Boy."

I wanted to tell her that Bud had actually cried and said he missed Dad, but I felt uncomfortable about that. "Remember last summer, when we played Ping-Pong?" I said. "And Tommy kept making all those jokes about you and you were laughing so hard you kept missing the ball?"

" 'A pirate's delight—a sunken chest and a pot of gold' is what he said." Judy's voice was dull.

"Well, anybody can see that he was really kidding about that," I said.

"Whatever happened to the Ping-Pong table? Did Effie give it to the Salvation Army?"

"Oh, no," I said. "She had Bud take it apart, and they put it in the workroom."

"Be right back," Judy said. She went in her room and returned with some record albums I hadn't seen before. She put one on the turntable. Violin music. She didn't bother to turn off the television.

"What is that?"

"Bach—a violin partita."

"Dad got interested in that kind of music," I said. "Disaster music. I never heard classical before he started playing it last fall." The music seemed to divide up the air into precise blocks, and it made me think in a strange way. "Could I ask you something? Do you think there are parallel universes? I mean, in another universe, there's another Nancy and another Judy except that everything is slightly different—maybe we live inside a giant crystal and, say, the cats are dogs? Sometimes I think that—it's like I can feel this other life of mine going on somewhere else. I just hope the other one is more exciting."

"I know what you mean," she said. She actually sounded interested. "There could be another life where we were in total contact and we could see through walls. And we wouldn't have to lug these bodies around. The bodies are what get us in all the trouble." She started talking about the body as a garment and about fear and desire, but I didn't follow her. I followed the music, which was changing the shape of the room. I could feel clear air going to infinity right overhead.

"I know what you mean," I said. "But do you think in that other universe the you and the me could know about us here? And what if they're sitting like we are wondering what it's like that we live in this thing called a 'house' and there's this something called 'hairbrush' and these things called 'hands' and 'carpet' and 'trailer'? I mean, it's so weird that we think everything we do in this world is so important, that it's the most important thing in the universe and here we are in this nothing place. It's just one place, it's nothing."

"Nothing is right," she said. "We're so far away from everything."

"Yeah," I said. "The sun is this nothing star. If anything big happens, it's not going to be in this little solar system—we'd be the last to know. We're on the edge of the galaxy. You can figure that the most advanced civilizations are in the center of the galaxy —and anyway, the Milky Way is this nothing little galaxy." I thought about galactic headquarters and pictured a metallic tarmac that went all the way to the horizon, and big silver spaceships landing and taking off, and all the serious, important beings coming and going. "I mean, the things they have to deal with in the center must be huge. Like, 'Should we rearrange the Pleiades or are they okay where they are?'"

"We could just as well be in these bodies as someplace else," Judy said. I could tell she had stopped listening to me. She piled my hair on top of my head and let it fall, piled it up and let it fall.

"Could I ask you a personal question?"

"If you want help with birth control, the answer is yes," Judy said.

My face got hot. What kind of girl did she think I had turned into? Was she talking to me like this because I was more adult or because she had changed? "*No,*" I said. "I was just wondering if you and Tommy have joke names for each other. It's not any of my business, and if it's too personal we can skip the whole thing."

"Joke names," she said.

LaDonna's and my joke names suddenly seemed incredibly embarrassing and childish. "You know, made-up names. Like Stella Police."

"Dum-dum," she said. "Tommy sometimes calls me Dum-dum."

"Why?"

"I guess he thinks I'm dumb," she said.

"Oh, he's just kidding," I said. I went over the new lines: *Of morning, pierce the Barcan wilderness. / Or lose thyself in the continuous woods / Where rolls the Oregon, and hears no sound, / Save his own dashings—and yet the dead are there.*

On the television, two women sat at opposite ends of a white sofa and held cups and saucers and argued politely. They had on a lot of makeup for women who stayed home all day, and they wore high heels. "Keep away from Whitney," one woman said coldly.

"Is your guitar teacher cute?" Judy asked.

"Really cute. He wears his hair in a little ponytail. But he's nineteen. And he's taken."

"Do you flirt with him?"

"Oh, sort of," I said. "I don't know." The truth was, I did not know what flirting was. It was a secret some girls had, and I was not one of them.

"You could just look at him and then lower your eyes. You know, give him the message that you're interested. But don't be too eager."

This was what I longed for someone to teach me. But suddenly I thought of "Dearest Vik" and felt awful.

"Oh, you are so goddamned free and you don't even know it," Judy said.

I tried to turn around and see her face, but she had a tight grip on all of my hair.

"You should just go out and have *fun*." I could tell that she meant something specific, but I was afraid to ask what. "You should find out what's really going on in life," she went on. "So you don't make any dumb mistakes." She gently lifted my hair and twisted it, and my neck tingled. "I was about the only girl in the senior class at Cibola High who didn't get married the week after graduation, and it was only because my boyfriend was arrested and the judge told him to join the service or go to prison. I felt like an old maid. That's why I went to college."

I had no idea Judy had even dated anyone but Tommy. "What did your boyfriend do?"

"Grand auto theft. He joined the Navy. I went around thinking no one would ever want me. Don't go around thinking that, Nancy."

"I won't." Actually, I thought that all the time.

"Remember when Tommy started bringing me over for TGIF and you'd come waltzing out with a tray full of drinks in those Flintstones glasses the gas stations were giving away?"

"I figured those were the fanciest ones," I said. "They're all broken now." The first time Judy came to the house, my mother fixed her famous cherry pound cake, which is frozen cake from the supermarket and you top it with cherries in syrup and squirt it with a can of whipped cream, and she made tea because Tommy said Judy drank nothing but tea, and she told Bud and me to behave. Mom wanted to get Tommy back on his own. It was hard on the weekends when he would sleep until two in the afternoon in the living room and we would have to tiptoe around. We were surprised that Judy turned out to be so dark, but Tommy explained that she had been out in the sun all summer studying archaeology. My mother liked Judy a lot. "After the first time you came over," I told her, "Mom sat Tommy down at the kitchen table and told him he had better marry you, and Tommy said he had already proposed, and Mom said, 'Talk is one thing. You better just go ahead and tie the knot right away.' "

Judy was surprised, which surprised me. "Really?" she said. "I always wondered what the rush was."

"Mom said she would personally help out with his finances if he got going on it," I said. Judy stopped brushing. Maybe I hadn't put it right. "I mean, it's great the way everything worked out," I said. I'm sure my mother loved Judy. She loved everyone. But some things had happened. Judy and Tommy asked for money in the spring at the worst possible moment, and then my mother decided to forgive them, but I don't think her heart was in it. And there was another thing that had made her mad and that had bothered me, too. "Judy, when Dad was in the hospital, why didn't you and Tommy ever call?"

"We tried," she said. "No one was home. And then one time Bud answered, and he was drunk or something and we couldn't get a word of sense out of him. I wanted Tommy to keep trying every day. But he figured Effie would let us know if anything big happened. All we heard was that everything was fine. Except secretly I was worried. I had had this dream." She started brushing again.

"Which was?"

"We were sitting in the kitchen and Effie was telling us how your father had—how he was gone. That was last November."

"Have you dreamed about him, you know, since . . . ?" I hadn't dreamed about him at all.

"Only once, in March. Effie was cleaning house. She was busy racing around, and she wanted me to take his books down to the basement. In the dream, this house had a basement. I did, and there he was, in his bathrobe, under the house. He looked great —his color was good, and he was strong. The bookcase was turned to the wall, and we pushed it around. It was pink and white. And then I looked at him again and he was very weak and tired and old. I said, 'You're dead, aren't you?' And he nodded."

It seemed impolite that she had talked to my father that way, even if it was only in a dream. "Mom wanted to get rid of his books, but I kept them," I said. "His college textbooks. He took Portuguese. Isn't that weird?"

"Your father was a mysterious person," Judy said. She went to the stereo and turned over the record. "Is your guitar teacher sexy?"

"I'm really in love with someone else," I said. I described the Reuben situation while she pinned my hair up in a complicated braid. When she finished, she rested her hand on my head and spoke in a tough way that was new to me. "Well, kid, when you're in love, you're helpless. I wouldn't worry about LaDonna too much."

"She says this boy, this senior in Uvalde, is crazy about her."

I went in the bedroom, to the mirror. Maybe the music had something to do with how I felt. I had become someone else. I was sleek, like an adult who led an elegant, intelligent life. I came back with my cigar box and took out a sheet of blue paper and gave it to Judy. In the center, in tiny letters, was:

> god
> it's all done with mirrors.
> there's less than meets the eye.

"Very good, Nance," she said.

"Oh, thank you!" I had never shown anyone my poetry before.

"There's the mailman." She got up quickly and went to the den window. I could see her shoulder blades through her nightie.

"You sure have lost a lot of weight. Tommy will like that."

She shrugged. The mailman parked his car by the curb and crossed the cinders, but he passed our mailbox without delivering anything. I handed Judy another poem, "Existence."

> is it a fragrance?
> is it a chance?
> is it a fence?
> o tell me, what is existence?

Judy drew in a sharp breath and put her fists to her eyes and rubbed hard. She sniffed.

"You okay? Judy?"

"Not feeling too good all of a sudden," she said. "But the poetry is great." She went into her bedroom and closed the door.

I turned off the record player and went to her door. "Listen," I said. "I hope you feel better. And I'm really glad you fixed my hair and all. And I liked the music." I didn't know how to thank her for speaking to me for longer than she had in weeks.

That night it stayed very hot. My mother went to the air-conditioned library at the college to work on her big mind-body paper. Judy must have felt better: she actually left the house. She decided to walk with Maura up to the Lotaburger for an ice-cream soda. I saw a pink envelope sticking out of the pocket of her miniskirt.

I didn't have much time to myself, and I wanted to make the best of it. I put on my new flamenco record. My guitar teacher sometimes played a few runs of flamenco, showing off after he demonstrated a chord. He never played anything through. Neither had my father; he sat watching TV and strumming a few bars of this and that. Now the *soleares* filled the den and made me shiver. All the doors and windows were open, and a breeze came through the screen door. The house was dark except for the yellow lamp on my mother's desk.

I was alone. I could smoke a cigarette if I had one, or even a cigar. But when my father went in the hospital, my mother threw away all his cigars. I could drink a bourbon and 7-Up or take off my clothes and dance—with the curtains tightly closed, of course. I wandered around. I looked into the bathroom mirror. I curled my lips back and checked my front teeth. Too big. I turned my face from side to side, trying to catch a glimpse of how others saw me. I kissed my mouth, wondering what Reuben would see and feel, and left a whitish imprint on the glass.

I opened the refrigerator and then closed it and went into Judy's room, my room, to the carton in the corner. My father's books had dull red and dark green covers, most of them. *The*

Calculus. Principles of Atomic Engineering. Introduction to Modern Literature. Table of Logarithms. They had a medicinal smell. I got a queasy feeling. I picked up my father's Christmas candle, took it in the kitchen, and lit it at the stove. Moving carefully so that the flame stayed lit, I crossed the living room—at the screen door, the flame bent over on its side for a second—and went into the den and put the candle on the end table. The flamenco kept going. I half closed my eyes and stared at the candle and tried to make myself feel weird, but nothing happened.

In the junk on top of my mother's desk, I found a sheet of the heavy notepaper she had bought for writing thank-yous after the funeral, and I went and sat on the floor next to the candle and wrote:

waiting . . .
o life, what are you in your visible forms
that I in communion seek

The chug of Teddy Roybal's motor scooter came from across the street and I went to the window. The Roybal garage door was open, and inside, in a cube of yellow light, were Teddy, the motor scooter, and Reuben. The boys had their shirts off, and Reuben was holding a wrench.

I hurried into the bathroom and dabbed some blue shadow on my eyelids. I changed out of my old T-shirt into a tank top of Judy's, rolled up the legs of my cutoffs another notch, and I was out the front door before I knew it. I checked my hair: the braids still pulled tightly against my scalp. I felt my knees brushing together. What excuse could I use? I never spoke to Teddy. But then a new power in me pulled me across the pavement, which was still warm from the heat of the sun.

"Hey, guys," I said.

"Hey," Teddy said. He was short, thin, and dark, and a lock of wavy black hair hung in his eyes.

"Nancy," Reuben said. "Say."

"Fixing the motor?" I think they were really looking at me, and I pretended to ignore that.

"Yeah," Teddy said.

Reuben started throwing the wrench in the air and catching it. His torso was slender. He was freckled and sunburned.

"What's up, Nancy?"

"Oh, nothin'," I said.

"Let me test her, Teddy." Reuben clanged the wrench down on the floor, got on the motor scooter, and revved it loudly. He concentrated on the handlebars and then roared out on the street and made several fast circles. ·

"Hey, man, what are you *doing*?" Teddy yelled. "Rube! *Hijo!*"

Reuben slowed down, dragging his cowboy boot on the pavement. "Sorry about that, chief. Nancy, you want a ride?"

I was afraid for a second, but I found myself getting on the back. I held on to the springs under the seat and we took off. When we got to the corner, I thought I saw my mother's car coming down Lincoln. "Oh, no!" I said.

"What's the problem?" he shouted.

"I forgot something. I have to go back to the house."

"No sweat," he said, wheeling around. When we pulled up in front of the Roybals', I saw that the car wasn't my mother's after all. "Listen," Reuben said. "What are you doing with yourself?" He grinned at me.

I was thinking that LaDonna and I had invented him, and that he turned out not to be the person we had invented at all. He was short. His upper teeth really stuck out a lot. His face was narrower than I remembered, with high cheekbones. He had the ranch-kid look—stringy and squint-eyed. I probably should have mentioned LaDonna, but he'd said "*yourself.*" What was I doing with my *self*? What a personal question. I stood there. He turned the handlebar grips and the motor scooter growled and jumped. He looked up at me and all the blood left my heart. "Oh, you know. Goin' to school, goin' to summer school with all the hoods who flunked out."

"I ain't seen you at the street dances."

"Street dances?"

"Oh, man, every Saturday night there's this outstanding street dance in the Monte Vista Plaza parking lot. They got live bands and everything. Tiny 'Tornado' Montoya and the Knight Rockers. Candy Lopez and the Midnight Auto Supply."

"Oh, well. Far out." What was the right thing to say? What did the popular girls say? "I've been kind of busy."

"I figured, 'cause I ain't seen you at the Lotaburger either."

"Well, LaDonna went to Uvalde, and I've been taking guitar, and my sister-in-law and her kid are living with us—they're really sweet—and there was this accident we were in on the freeway with that trailer there in our yard, but nobody got hurt—"

"What happened?"

"Oh, it was nothing. All of a sudden the car went out of control and the trailer started fishtailing, and my mother saved our lives by putting on the emergency brake before we went over into the culvert."

"Oh, man. The steering cable snapped?"

"Nope," I said.

"Why did the car go out of control? All by itself? That don't sound right. Sounds like the driver—"

"Well, it just did." For a second, he irritated me. "Anyway, we're probably going to move—"

"Out of town?"

"Nope. To the Marina del Mar."

"That new thing."

"Yeah," I said. "Well, I guess I better be gettin' back."

"Listen, Nancy, maybe you'll get your buns to the street dance sometime. Seriously."

"Okay!" I sprinted across the street. The asphalt was smooth and warm under my bare soles.

"Good night, Stella Police!" Reuben shouted.

I rushed into the house and went into the den and took off the flamenco record, and put on my new Steppenwolf album as loud as it would go, "Born to Be Wild." I turned on the lights and started dancing, and then I noticed that the candle was still burning. I blew it out, and I took the poem into the kitchen and shoved it way down in the garbage, under a pizza carton. Judy and Maura came home, and on her way into the bedroom, Judy, without a word, handed me a double-dip chocolate ice-cream cone, and it was the best thing I ever tasted in my life.

18

I got up from my bed and went into the den. Tom Senior was sitting on the couch looking through a stack of recent family photographs. They were brightly colored, and everyone was smiling and having a good time. I was so happy to see him. I sat down and kissed him—his cheek was still warm—and he began to cry. "So that's what Effie is doing—she's trying to keep you alive," I said, crying, too, out of pity for him.

The clock radio in Effie's room went off full blast. Six a.m., the Pal Al Zamora show. It was so loud that the sound was distorted, as if the microphone were inside his mouth and the music, too. I'd tried to keep Maura out of Effie's room, but she must have gotten in and fiddled with the dials. Now Effie was leaving it on loud to punish me. She probably knew that I was never able to fall asleep until dawn. I got up to close the door, which I'd left open in the hope of a cross-breeze, and stepped on a half-digested cicada one of the cats had brought in.

I went back to bed and lay there crying and went through all the thoughts I went through every day when I woke up. They were like gymnastics. I was trying to get in shape to do something, but I didn't know what it was.

I thought about Vik and how he and I had never talked about the future, never made a single plan. It was all in the moment, in the narrow bed in his orange-and-brown room in his mother's apartment. I didn't know my body was capable of such ecstasy. I could barely stand it. Each moment was a mountain to be climbed; I'd never lived like that before. "We have no raison d'être," Vik said. And we had no future, so time spread out sideways when we were together. "You're so innocent!" he kept saying. Now I was not.

I thought about my financial situation, something I had never done before. I still had no money, except for about fifteen dollars from the fifty Tommy had given me when I left New York and thirty-five dollars left from the secret birthday money from Tom Senior. But I needed that just to buy food for Maura until Tommy sent money or tickets to get to Africa.

I thought about whether I wanted to go to Africa. From the beginning of our marriage, I'd dreamed of how we'd travel to some wonderful place where we would be left alone to concentrate on each other without any pressures or interference. Now I had no interest at all in that.

And I tried to think about Tommy, but I wasn't able to for very long. Vik always took over. His hands, his mouth. But last week, during an attack of loneliness, I'd phoned Tommy. He was drunk. I couldn't understand him very well. I think he said, "One tends to build liaisons." Or was it "One needs to build liaisons"? But I didn't know who he meant; sometimes when he meant me, he'd use "one." "One keeps one's elbows off the table." "One does not end a sentence with a preposition." But other times he meant himself: "One hardly gets a moment to sleep." Maybe it had to do with the international teaching program. Or his activist group. Or maybe some other thing. He said he'd gone motorcycle riding with the black-leather guy from across the street. "It was a trip," he said. I had never heard him use that expression before. Gullible and trusting, that was me. Effie had written it all in that notebook she gave to me. My thoughts went back to Vik. His hands, his mouth.

These gymnastics always ended with a terrible pain in my chest and me crying and picturing myself leaving, Maura in my arms, heading on foot toward the mountains. Pal Al Zamora said that it was the thirty-ninth day without rain and that the temperature was going to hit one hundred again today.

I waited until Effie and Nancy had left for school and then I got up, turned off the radio in the middle of Hank Williams singing "Weary Blues," found a doughnut in the kitchen and gave it to Maura, and watched TV with her until the mail came. Nothing but windowed envelopes for Mrs. Thomas Hammond from insurance companies. I walked around the house in the suffocating heat with tears running down my face, and then when my sobs got out of control, I went out to the patio so that Maura wouldn't hear me.

The bricks were hot under my bare feet. I sat in the strong sun at the picnic table. It was splintering and gritty. No one had bothered to bring it inside for the winter. The tarp thrown over the boat had slipped halfway off: the vinyl banquettes were already yellowed where they had been exposed. Effie had given the boat to Bud. A few days after his graduation, while she was making dinner, I came into the kitchen and found him at the table with a pencil and a long printed form. He was writing very, very slowly. I asked him what he was doing. "I am *so* stoned!" he whispered. "I am so *wrecked*. I am so *wasted*." He told me he was applying for assignment to the First Air Cavalry. "I am so *bombed*," he said. I quietly said that if he ever changed his mind and wanted out, I'd do all I could to help him. He seemed shocked at my suggestion. Then he started laughing, and Effie asked him what was so funny. "The butter dish," he said.

Two air conditioners sat in the dirt, along with the framework of the Ping-Pong table and some slivering pieces of lumber. The barbecue lay on its side and burned briquets spilled out of its black basin. Grama grass and Russian thistles and goat's-head thorns had sprung up everywhere. A few ragged cosmos were all that remained of Tom's garden. The mesa was coming back: another year and sagebrush would take root.

I opened the door to the workroom. In the window was a spiderweb weighted with flies. On the trestle table, sitting in a layer of brown dust littered with moth wings, were a dozen or so foil-wrapped flowerpots with black spikes sticking out of them. There was a smell of turpentine. I stepped inside, and immediately the arch of my foot found a piece of broken glass. I jumped backwards, and as I did, a shadow came tilting diagonally down on me and hit me on the head, hard.

Staggering, I pushed the weight aside and held my head until the blackness drained away. The Ping-Pong table top. It had been propped up right next to the door. The blow was hard and angry. Effie might as well have hidden behind the door and hit me over the head with a two-by-four and shouted, "That's for what you've done to my son!"

I was afraid to stay in the house. "Let's go mail a letter," I told Maura.

"Why?" she said. I got her dressed and I put on a tank top and some shorts and sandals, and we walked in small steps down the street. I couldn't put too much weight on my cut foot.

"Where are the people?" Maura asked. The street was flooded with purposeless sunlight which was so harsh it made everything black through my nearly closed eyes. The sidewalks were gray, clean, hot, and vacant except for tufts of dried grass between the slabs. The houses were all alike, the yards were all alike, with their campers and pickups parked in the driveways. There was not a soul anywhere. Above were the peaks, as familiar to me as my own body, and an empty sky.

"Oh, inside," I said. "In their houses, in their cars, in their cans of soup."

"Why?" she asked. "Can we go to the park?"

"There's no park here—the park is in New York."

"Why?"

"I guess because everyone has a yard." I pointed out a square of stiff brown grass in front of a sun-bleached turquoise house. Two car seats were placed at right angles in the black shade by the front door.

At the corner, I gave Maura the letter and hoisted her up so she could open the mailbox. "Hey, in there!" she called into the ringing darkness, smiling at the power of her own voice. "Hey, you guys!"

As soon as she dropped the envelope inside, I couldn't remember whether the envelope was addressed to Vik or to Tommy. The letter inside was to Vik. I was pretty sure of that. Because I had spelled out his name in Sanskrit. "Either one," I said aloud. "It doesn't matter."

"Why, Mommy?"

At the 7-Eleven, I bought a box of cereal, and then we went home and ate it in front of the television. We watched a program about a pretty young career girl living in a huge, beautiful apartment in Manhattan and suffering from a ghastly dilemma—two men had proposed to her and were sending her chocolates and bouquets, and she didn't know how to tell her steady boyfriend. Maura loved this show and giggled along with the canned laughter. I couldn't imagine what she understood of it.

Once I had just come into the apartment from an afternoon with Vik when the phone rang. I was sure it was Tommy calling to tell me he knew what I was doing and that he had taken Maura away from the neighbor lady and was never coming home again. When I answered, a man said, "Well, who is *this?*" I said, "Mrs. Thomas Hammond." He said, "Tommy's mother?" I said, "Wife." And he said, "I *don't* believe it!" and hung up. Lately, I kept hearing that voice. If I said to myself, I am Tommy's wife, I heard that man's surprised "I *don't* believe it!"

I tried to telephone Vik at his mother's. I would explain to Effie when she got the bill that Tommy had asked me to reach him at that number. The white phone rang in that cool, ordered apartment, with its Persian carpets, silk divans piled with embroidered velvet cushions, and windowpanes covered with filmy blue-green fabric so that the whole place seemed to be underwater. "My head aches and I want you, I will do anything, anything" was what I planned to say. "I forgive you for not answering my letters." Ever since I'd written him my plan of meeting him in Mexico City I hadn't heard from him. The phone rang and rang. I telephoned Tommy. I didn't really expect the phone to be connected, and when he answered, I started to cry.

"What's the matter, sweetie?" he asked.

"I don't know," I said. "What I mean is . . ." I thought of how, lying day after day in the dim bedroom smelling of cat urine, I'd been traveling away from him. And then it seemed to me I had been doing that for much longer; from before the eclipse. I just hadn't known about it. When I got pregnant, my body started leaving the body I was used to; it happened immediately. I learned then that everything could change overnight. One morning I awoke and I was tired and sick and I didn't care about anything except the baby growing within me. Although I began to feel better after a while, I had never gone back to being what I was. My body had left Tommy before I had. I wanted to ask him if he thought I was right about this. I could see my cells changing, forming another body at a distance. I didn't know how to explain this to him.

"It's probably, you know, that time of the month," he said. "It's incomprehensible what's going on anywhere and of course everything has its ramifications. But cheer is a prerequisite. Willpower, also, and you are a lucky girl and you have a fine daughter and you're surrounded by a loving family, and everything is fine, and you're a happy, peaceful person, and things are just getting better and better, and you know I love you every minute of the day."

"I want to come back to New York," I said. "I don't want to be in this place." That was true.

"Well, of course one would love that more than life itself but you know that it's a stark impossibility." His voice sped up. "You're helping Mom by being there with her. You and Maura. She adores playing with Maura, you know that." Where had he gotten that idea? "Has she signed the lease on that apartment? It sounds fantastic. Sure wish we had some place like that. How is she, by the way? I hope you're being a good guest. She seemed extremely burdened the other—"

"If you send my check, I'll leave." This was five hundred dollars I'd earned typing a huge dissertation on the Mayan long-count calendrical system. The graduate student had mailed the check after I left for Cibola. "I'll go—I'll go to Mexico. Or someplace."

"Well, about the check. That had to get deposited. There were some unexpected expenses and funds are of necessity going to be limited for a while. Shifts are taking place here in regard to the whole Africa thing."

"What do you mean?" Maybe he had a girlfriend.

"Well, it's too complicated—many ramifications, a multitude of various factors."

He went on talking, but I stopped listening, except at the end, when he said he'd bought a wide necktie in psychedelic colors and a Steppenwolf album. It was only after he hung up that I wondered how he could play the record, since our phonograph was now in Liberia.

Effie and Nancy didn't come home. Sometimes that happened— they would eat out and go to the movies, or Effie would take Nancy over to the college library to study. I read Maura *Sleeping Beauty,* the only book she wanted to hear anymore, and then I lay in my bed, my foot throbbing, copying the Sanskrit alphabet out of the Sanskrit grammar Vik had given me. So far I'd learned all the characters up to VR and could write TAT TUAM ASI, which means "That thou art" or "Thou art that" or "This is this," and CITTA-VRTTA, which means the mindless, noisy whirling of the world. Meanwhile, the cats batted around some shiny black beetles that had started coming into the house and Maura played "wedding" with her stuffed animals and a box of tissues. She made bridal veils and trains of tissue, and sang, "You are special, this wedding, the two three four, of the starve-boys, you are special."

Just as I was trying to fall asleep, I heard the screen door bang and then the refrigerator door open. After a while, I got out of bed and put on my nightgown and went into the kitchen with the hope that Effie had gone to bed and Nancy was still up. I wanted to warn her about the Ping-Pong table and explain why the workroom was open.

The round fluorescent ceiling light, shaped like a coiled serpent, cast a greenish, shadowless glare. Effie was talking to Nancy and walking around with a butcher knife and a cantaloupe. She put the cantaloupe on the counter, raised the knife, and brought it down hard. Plunging her fingers into each half, she pulled out the dripping seeds and slapped them into the garbage. She opened the ice cream and scraped rapidly at the hard white surface with a scoop. Her eyes were glittery. She flipped balls of ice cream into the cantaloupes and then slammed two spoons down on the table. "Why, Judy, what ever are you doing up?" she said when she saw me in the doorway. "I surely hope we didn't wake you."

"Oh, I was awake," I said.

"What, hon?"

"We went to see *Easy Rider,*" Nancy said, frowning and brushing at her skirt. "God, there were so many bugs on the front porch. Ugh. You already saw it, right?"

"In New York," I said. Vik had taken me, and when I saw the mountains and the open plains in the movie, I cried, and all night I dreamed of rushing with complete freedom through that landscape. I was hurt that Effie and Nancy hadn't invited me along, although I knew the reason. I'd tried going one night to the movies just after the accident. I thought I would be all right with Bud driving. I made the mistake of sitting up while we were on the freeway. The car was racing along—too fast—but all motion had stopped. The traffic in the opposite lane was frozen. Soft crosses of shadow were fixed between the blue-green circles of glare cast by the streetlamps. The red taillights ahead were still and so were the fans of white the headlights made on the asphalt. The words people were saying made jagged pieces in the air. I lay down and waited for the fishtailing to begin.

"It was so very interesting," Effie said. "We enjoyed that movie just so much, right, Nancy?"

I sat at the table and rubbed my scalp. My skull still ached. My fingers were hot. I spread them on the cool gray Formica in front of me. When I looked up, my gaze scratched against Effie's, making my eyes hurt. I realized she was talking to me. I closed my eyes. "And the scenery in that movie is just breathtaking," she was saying. "I am sure some of it must have been filmed up near the dam. And they go to this commune. Judy, hon?" I opened my eyes to the mask of her face, which kept on talking. She had hated the movie.

"LaDonna told me about that commune," Nancy said. "There are fifty-six members and they're all married to each other and they're all supposed to be really in love."

"That's not love, that's just s-e-x," Effie said. "You know that deal at the end, Judy, where they go in the cemetery and take the LSD," Effie said. "Is that what it's like? Is that a 'trip'?"

"I don't know," I said.

"But don't people in New York take that LSD? I read about that in *Life*. You must have tried it. What's it like?"

"I don't know," I said. I had no air in my lungs.

"What, hon?" She went on talking, and I thought about what Vik must be doing. Sitting in the patio of his father's house, a beautiful girl in white serving him a margarita. "Well, it was so fascinating to see that, and those poor boys." She came close and her whole face contracted around a tiny black point of rage as she continued to talk and smile. I kept my fingers flattened on the table. "We only have the one cantaloupe, but we could give you a piece," she said.

"You can have mine," Nancy said. She pressed her lips together, and I thought she must be making an effort to keep from crying. In fact, this is what she had been doing for months, but she'd forgotten, so that the extra work of getting from minute to minute now seemed normal to her.

"No thanks, it's okay, really," I said. "I think just an aspirin."

"What, hon?" Effie said.

"No, thanks," I said loudly. I felt dizzy.

I went back to bed. I tried mentally relaxing my body. Toes, feet, legs, hands, arms . . . Then I did what I'd been doing every night for weeks. It had become so real to me that I would wake up in the morning with my legs aching. I imagined how I would pick up Maura and walk out of the house, down Cagua to Lincoln, up Lincoln past the new housing developments to the open mesa—I used to ride around there, first on horseback, then, when I was older, in a car with my high school fiancé while he shot at jackrabbits—and across the mesa and up over the ridge and onto the huge sagebrush plain that was completely empty, except for the little town of Mesita, and stretched all the way to the foothills of the Paradisos, and I walked along a cold mountain stream, stopping to wash my dusty feet and to give Maura tuna fish sandwiches, and I followed the stream to the San Ysidro River, where there was an adobe house on the red clay bank, and I tapped at the screen door, and a withered old woman came to the door, brown as a tree, and asked me my name, and I said "Rosario," and her name was Rosario, too, and she thought she had died and that I was her young self, holding a child, reuniting with her, and she let me in to sleep on a narrow iron cot with Maura, and we stayed with her until she took her last breath, and then I walked with Maura to the dam, and along the embankment where the green water met the red earth. Usually by the time I reached the adobe house and lay down on the cot, I was asleep, but tonight it was too hot, and I was stabbed by a peculiar alertness. Maura moved restlessly on her bed, throwing her arms and legs this way and that. The cats pounced and coughed in the darkness. I imagined swimming in the cool water of the dam, held up by the yellow life vest, the bowl of the sky overhead.

"Bugs!" Maura screamed. "Bugs, Mommy!"

"Shh," I whispered. "It's just a bad dream. Quiet." I was afraid she'd wake up Effie, who would murder us.

"They're all over!"

"No, Maura," I whispered. "I'll show you." I turned on the lamp.

Maura was sitting up, blinking, her eyes wide. Black beetles crawled on the sheet and on the floor. A thick, glistening mass of them came in under the loose window screens, across the sills, and down the walls. I put on my sandals and crossed the room to close the windows, and the bodies of the beetles crunched underfoot. I picked up Maura, who had wrapped herself tightly in her old shred of baby blanket, and we lay down on my bed. The whole house was filled with the rustling of hard wings. I heard the cats moving around, their claws sometimes catching with a snapping sound on the carpet loops. "This sometimes happens," I said softly. "When I was a little girl, the bugs would come like this. They come all of a sudden out of nowhere, and then they disappear."

After a while, Maura calmed down and fell asleep, her face red and wet. I tried to read the Bhagavad-Gita, but the lamp only attracted the beetles. I sat in the dark listening to the traffic noises from the freeway and fanned Maura with the book.

After a while, I got up and went into the backyard. It was a little cooler outside and there weren't any beetles on the patio. Above the saw-toothed silhouette of the peaks, the Milky Way was low and close. I entered the workroom, warding off the Ping-Pong table with an upraised arm, and stepped over the pieces of the broken jar and turned on a light next to the trestle table. Tom's tools and paints and brushes were arranged in tidy patterns. There were rows of cans and tubes and jars, a stack of folded brush rags, colored with fans of violet, green, rose, and yellow. The canvases were still hidden behind the shelves, dust in the creases of their black plastic wrapping.

I pulled them out and uncovered them and looked at them for a long time, until I felt very sleepy. I thought about him in his uniform standing all day out on the mesa, the sun moving across the sky. I put everything back except the painting of the nude with her mysterious, staring eye. I prized out the staples attaching it to the wooden frame and rolled it up and put it under my arm.

Outside, I watched the three-quarters moon rise over the peaks. A breeze came up. When I returned to the bedroom, I hid the painting under some clothes in my suitcase, shook out the sheets of Maura's bed, swept up the beetles and washed away the cat vomit on the carpet, and then lay down and fell peacefully asleep listening to the hum of the Interstate in the distance and breathing the baby-shampoo smell of Maura's pillow. I slept better than I had in a very long time.

Tom Senior was present in the room. Not particularly in one place. He urgently wanted me to know something. He wanted to prove he was really there. It was like invisible charades. This something he wanted me to know was represented by the color yellow, some yellow article. He couldn't communicate through words but only through making certain images known. He asked

me about Effie. It was done in this way: I'd see an image of her
and then experience a feeling of Tom's presence and a question-
ing sensation. I replied by making images of her talking, studying, driving, moving through the house on her high heels. Effie
happy and in good health. I wanted him to know that she loved
him. I asked him where he was now, and then I saw a tube that
was brightly colored on the inside, like a rolled-up, painted canvas. It floated in a void. He showed me that everything known
was inside the colored tube—time, space, all that had ever existed.
Then I sensed his presence outside the tube, in nothingness.
But it wasn't ordinary nothingness. What is it like? I asked. I
felt a surge of powerful joy in every cell of my body, an electric
shock.

I awoke. I was in bed in a little bedroom in Cibola, in the
moonlight, and Cibola was set among the mountains, on a high
plateau, just a tiny dot on the immense curve of the world.

I lay on my side in a groove of red dirt on the flank of a hill
overlooking a sagebrush plain and a high mountain range. I could
see an enormous distance. I could see the curvature of the earth.
The bathroom door slammed. "Today we do substance," I heard
Effie say.

I opened my eyes. She stood in a square of sunlight in the hall.
"We're also having a test," she told the bathroom door. Her
golden hair was tousled, her face was shiny with cold cream, her
shoulders were rounded and smooth and freckled, and there was
a mottled red triangle at her throat and cleavage. I could see why
Tom had stayed with her, why he had been happy enough to sit
across from her at picnic tables and in bars. She wore her pink
slip and held an open notebook. "God is a universal category."
She raised her voice above the noise of running water. "What is
the aspectical theory of thinghood? A thing *is* as a thing *does*.
Knowing objects. Hurry up, Nancy, we have to go in five minutes. Knowing objects. Husserl. *Evidenz* with a z. *Reell:* capital
R-e-e-l-l." Her suffering was obvious—how could I have missed
it all this time? And it was also obvious that her doings were not

connected to me in any way: she was alone, surrounded by emptiness, pushed along by unseen forces.

The bathroom door opened. "Were you talking to me, Mom?"

Maura stood in her underpants at the foot of my bed drinking a glass of chocolate milk and moving her stuffed animals around on the sheet in a dance. They wore their tissue veils and trains. "My poppa used to carry me a lot," she sang softly. Her legs had grown lanky and brown, and her torso was no longer rounded but straight, with delicate indentations where the ribs were. I sat up and put my hands on her warm back and gave her a kiss. "Mommy, this is a *nice* wedding," she said. "The prince kissed the princess and everybody woke up. Even the *flies* woke up." She smiled at me with unhindered, complete love, her eyes soft and dark and peaceful. I felt a clutching in my chest, as if I might faint. Had she smiled at me like that every morning? "Drink some milk," she said, handing me the glass. "It's good."

"We've got to get cracking, Nancy," Effie said, going into the bathroom.

I took a sip. It was cool and sweet. "It *is* good, Maura," I said, jumping up. "Effie!" I called out. "Wait."

But the door closed and the shower started.

"Hi, Judy," Nancy said. She drew back from me, startled. Her face was fresh and pink, and in the sunlight in the hallway, the fine golden down on the side of her jaw shone. She had put blue eye shadow on her lids all the way up to her eyebrows and was wearing a white skirt rolled up at the waistband and a green tank top. Her waist was narrow and her breasts were high and round. "What are *you* doing up?"

"Nancy, I had this dream." I pounded on the bathroom door. "Effie, listen," I said. "I have something important to tell you." But she couldn't hear me.

I followed Nancy into the kitchen. "I dreamed about your father—" I began as she poured herself some chocolate milk. "It was very strange. I went into the workroom yesterday, I don't know why, and then last night it was too hot to sleep and these beetles came in—"

Nancy ate some potato chips and watched me talk. She looked

uneasy. I didn't mention Tom Senior's paintings. Before I got to the dream, I heard the bathroom door open. Effie came rushing out pulling a pink sheath dress on over her head. "Let's go, Nancy. Where did you put my mascara?"

"Effie," I said. "This amazing thing happened."

"Why, Judy, hon, up so early! How are you today?"

"Great," I said. "I feel absolutely great."

"Well, I am so happy to hear that, darlin'," she said absently. She zipped up her dress as she went into her room and then bent over and started digging around in a heap of shoes in the bottom of her closet. "I never should have gone to the movie last night." She picked out a pair of white open-toed pumps. "I have this gigantic test—"

"I want to tell you—" I couldn't stop smiling.

"What, hon?" She picked up her big white wicker bag, got out her sunglasses, and, her shoes slapping her heels, hurried to the front door. "Nancy, I swear—wipe that milk mustache off your face and let's get going."

"Effie," I said. I followed her out the door and raised my voice. "Stop. *Stop.* I have something really important that you have to know."

"What, hon? Not outside in your nightie. We're so dad-gummed late—"

She was already halfway across the cinders to the driveway and about to disappear around the trailer when I yelled, "Hold it! You have to listen to me. It's about Tom Senior."

She stopped. She turned and faced me, her eyebrows rising above the rims of her sunglasses. Her red mouth was puckered as if it contained something she didn't want to swallow.

I couldn't walk on the cinders with my hurt foot, so I waited while she came back to the porch. There were dead beetles everywhere. "It's important, and I mean it," I said. I told her the whole experience I'd had in the night, but I left out the part about the universe being like a rolled-up, painted canvas. She took off her sunglasses and stood there without moving, her mouth half open, her eyes fixed and bright. Nancy was at my elbow. I could hear her breathing hard.

"Something yellow," Effie said, concentrating.

"It was like a proof that he really was with me," I said.

Effie went inside, to her bedroom. Nancy and I looked at each other. She was wearing her hair up, the way I had shown her, and brushed back from her forehead. Her neck was long and graceful.

Effie returned with a yellow batiste nightgown trimmed with wide bands of yellow lace. "It was my Christmas present. The last thing he gave me."

"That must be it," I said. I wasn't so sure, but it seemed important to act certain, and just looking at the nightgown made me very happy. I don't know why. "He did convey that it was something yellow connected with you." That wasn't quite right, either, but I didn't know how else to put it.

Effie laid her hand on my arm and gave it a squeeze. "Judy, Judy, darlin'—I want you to understand that I accept totally what you-all are telling me. I'm working hard on the mind-body paper, and this fits right in." She folded up the nightie, her mouth turned abruptly down just like Maura's did when she was surprised by a shot at the pediatrician's, and she blinked rapidly.

I put my hands on her shoulders. "Listen, are you all right? Because the feeling I got from him was this incredible joy and freedom—"

"We had such love, Tom and me. Oh, I cried when he went away to the service. I just pined."

"You must miss him a lot," I said.

I felt her shoulders contract. "Well. We got to run. Come on, Nancy. We'll stop at Taco Bell on the way home and bring you a burrito, Judy, hon. And I want to thank you with all my heart."

19

It couldn't have happened at a worse time. Fresh makeup on,
running behind schedule, a big test that morning. And it was so
hot—every day the thunderheads would build up over the peaks
and then blow over or dry up—that I was wringing wet. It was
after I dropped off Nancy. I checked in the rearview mirror and
sure enough, tears were streaking the powder on my cheeks, and
even though I was already really late, I took the first exit that
came up and drove along Frontage Boulevard and parked under
a billboard and just gave up. I mean surrendered totally. I sobbed
from my feet on up, in waves and waves, and this just went on
forever, until I was so weak I keeled over, my head on the steering
wheel, and my heart caught on fire. All along I knew better than
to do this, I knew if I ever started crying I wouldn't be able to
stop. It had just about killed me at the bus station when we said
goodbye to Bud, because he looked about thirteen years old, and
his hair was down over his collar and he still had the fuzzy beard
—we knew all the hair would go first thing—and his face was
white under his freckles, and if I had not given him a real solid
pep talk, which was certainly the last thing I felt like doing at that
moment, he never would have climbed on that bus. If he had seen
one tear, that would have been it for him. But I smiled like a
million dollars, and I had gotten my hair done up, and I wore the
yellow fiesta dress, and I gathered all my strength together and
worked like a Trojan to give that boy a hero's send-off while the
girls stood there like fence posts. If you just cried whenever you

felt like it, you would probably cry nearly all the time, because someone is always going away, and so I think a joke and a smile are better. I have never had much patience for the Gloomy Guses of the world, I tell you. I was right not to cry. I was right at the hospital and at the funeral and all this time. Someone had to be in charge. And anyway, crying just makes you go completely out of control, and people say that thing about how you think you're flying apart, well, that was how I felt, or maybe melted is more like it, and if anyone had seen me like this they would have been destroyed. I thought I'd never leave that spot under the billboard, that the crying was going to be permanent. And it was all without words, I didn't have any words, it was just my body, crying.

In the campus parking lot, I dried my face with some tissues, wiped away the mascara smears and powdered my nose, and dadgummed if I didn't cry all the way to class, walking as fast as I could and thinking: Look how I am suffering. I ran into the back of the classroom, a bunch of tissues in my hand, and thanked the dear Lord that the test hadn't started yet. Dr. Desai was still giving the lecture. I got out my notebook and pen.

Dr. Desai read aloud from a book. He was this dear little dark man from Bombay, and he always wore a black suit, no matter how hot it was, and the first few weeks I could not understand one word he said. I didn't even know at first that he was speaking English. At the beginning of the course I went to his office to introduce myself—I thought he ought to know who I was—and he had a sign on his office door that said "The answer is in the looking" or something to that effect. I asked the boy next to me what Dr. Desai was reading.

The boy said, "Wittgenstein," and I wrote that down.

Dr. Desai read: " 'It is not *how* things are in the world that is mystical, but *that* it exists.' "

I wrote that down. I whispered to the boy, "Is this about Substance? Are we on Substance? I thought we were doing Substance today." But he just shrugged.

Dr. Desai read some more. " 'Proposition 6.522: There are, indeed, things that cannot be put into words. They make themselves manifest. They are what is mystical.' " I could not believe what I was hearing. It was a miracle. It had to be proof of everything Judy said. I started crying again, but I kept it quiet. I blew my nose and said to the boy next to me, "Please excuse me. I have hay fever."

All during the test I had trouble concentrating. I was thinking about how it was going to be the Fourth of July and how it was the first year we wouldn't be going up to the dam, and that was what I had wanted to do so badly and had secretly hoped Bud wouldn't have to report as soon as he did so that we could take the boat out just once before he went away, and then I thought about how Nancy and I could clean up the yard and throw a big barbecue—hamburgers, hot dogs, corn on the cob—and she could invite some kids from summer school, and maybe I would ask the boys Bud went around with, and maybe the Roybals, and we would just have a bang-up time. I never did do right by Nancy's birthday and this would make up for it. When I handed in my exam, I went up to Dr. Desai and I said, "My husband passed away six months ago, and I am so grateful to you for reading what you did, what Wittgenstein said and all, and I want to ask you if you would like to come to a barbecue I am having at my house for the Fourth of July." He gave me this very serious look, and he thought for a while, and he said, sweet as pie, "I thank you very much, but I never attend local festivals."

My aching neck woke me up at sunrise. I put on a white ruffled scoop-necked blouse and a yellow skirt with a ruffled hem that Tom had liked, and I made a thermos of coffee and drove up along Foothill Drive. The sky was all red and pink and the shadows of the peaks still covered Cibola. I parked at an overlook above La Golondrina Park, which is a ritzy neighborhood I wouldn't have minded moving to if I had not already decided to become an apartment person. I sat there looking at the swimming pools in the Cambridge Heights backyards, round, square, rectangular. Their water bills were something I hated to think about. Actually I hated to think about any bills and that was just about all I'd been forced to do for the past six months.

I poured some coffee into the thermos cup. The old-grounds-and-plastic smell made me think of Tom. He and I used to come up here on Sunday mornings when Nancy and Bud were little. I'd set them in front of TV cartoons with a quart of ice cream, and Tom and I would drive to the overlook with iced sweet rolls and the newspaper, but we usually never got around to reading. We'd watch the colors shift on the mesa—that was before the new housing tracts and the freeway and the Monte Vista Shopping Plaza—and we'd watch the sunlight sparkle on the river, and we'd talk about what had happened that week, or make plans for the next week or for our vacations, or figure out what we were going to do when we retired. Maybe some of his ashes were here on this very spot—if Tommy had done the job right.

"That really is the awful part," I said aloud. I put the cup on the dashboard. "That you're nowhere, like Judy said. Not one place where we can sit and talk." I hadn't wanted to think too closely about whether he was near or far away, or whether he *was* at all. But Judy had had the sign from him. No getting around that. We had absolute proof. And of course he must have been trying before to get through, like those people with short-wave radios behind the Iron Curtain. People talk about their dreams and I always wonder if they're fibbing—how can they remember all that stuff? I certainly don't; in fact, I dream about once every ten years, and then it's just a jumble. Well, I can tell you this much—Judy probably wasn't paying much attention, but I know for sure that something happened to her in the night because she was certainly a different person afterward. And whenever I thought of how she put her little hands on my shoulders and said so very gently, "You have had a very hard time," or whatever it was like that—I forget the words, I only remember the clear, steady, kind way she looked at me—I cried all over again.

The wind made a soft sound around the car, like air blowing over the mouth of a bottle, and I said, "The yellow nightie! You *would* think of that." Because the night he gave it to me was the last night we ever made love on this earth. It was important to him, even though he hadn't felt like it in a long time, and he had a lot of trouble, but he wanted that—for us to be together. Frankly, ninety-nine percent of the things people say about sex must be made up. The last year or so, he was hardly in bed when I was anyway. He just couldn't sleep. When I got up in the morning, I'd find him at the kitchen table, ready to go to the Labs.

I said, feeling pretty silly, "Tom, if there is any way on God's earth for you to communicate with me, or just listen while I talk, I surely would appreciate it." I paid attention to the air in the car. When I was a kid, I heard a certain amount of talk about ghosts, and what everyone always said was that there were two sure signs that it really was a ghost: You didn't feel afraid and also, a cold wind or a shiver went through the air. I didn't feel afraid now, mainly because I didn't believe in ghosts, but I did believe in Tom's soul. "What I have seen!" he'd said, and he was radiant, so there was some kind of Other Side. There had to be. The air in the car didn't seem any different, but, yes, there was a little of the feeling of Tom. It was like when I'd come home and know immediately whether he was in the house or not.

On our first date, we went to the Cochise movie theater and saw *High, Wide, and Handsome* with Randolph Scott, and then started to walk to my house. We stopped in the schoolyard and sat in the swings side by side, and he kissed me. We necked for a while, and I thought I might just die. For two years in high school I'd longed for him to look at me and speak to me and kiss me. Really, I only ever wanted the pure love, the kissing, not the rest, but he had ideas of his own, and I had to lift his hands off of me. And then he pulled away and started swinging. The swings creaked. He came toward me and then went away, toward me and away, and he leaned backward and pumped his legs hard, and he went higher and higher and I had to hold my breath. I was afraid he'd go right over the bar. Finally I couldn't help it, and I screamed, "Don't do that!"

I put my forehead on the steering wheel and I said, "Tom, darlin', I know that if you could speak to me, you surely would, and thanks for getting in touch through Judy, although you could have contacted me directly. Remember how you said I shouldn't buy a trailer? Well, I want to tell you that that's exactly what I

went and did, and maybe that's why you didn't contact me.
Anyway, you were so right that I shouldn't have done that. I am
so very sorry, Tom. You must have known—maybe you know
what's going to happen in the future now. Maybe you already are
aware of this, but I was taking the girls to California and the car
went out—well, it didn't exactly go out of control, it's just that
the damned old power steering on this Olds here that I bought
in May made the trailer slide all over the place, and nobody knows
this except the insurance man, but there was a *six-car accident* on
account of the trailer getting jackknifed across two lanes and all
the cars behind it following too closely, and a car ran into the
trailer, into the back, which I did not even see, I swear it—and
then a bunch of cars ran into the ones behind *him,* and it is such
a mess I hate to tell you. And I didn't even know about any of
it and just drove away. I haven't told a soul. And also I haven't
told a soul that the police took my license away after I ran into
the back of that pickup at Lincoln and North Main a few weeks
ago, three strikes and you're out, you know—that business when
the Lincoln got creamed after TGIF all those years ago, that was
on my record—and so now I have to drive without a license. Like
those heart attacks you had at home and we didn't tell anybody,
not even the doctor? Well, it's like that—and anyway, who could
I tell? Who could possibly help me out, and I *have* to drive. I have
to get to the campus to take the philosophy so that I don't just
give up. But that doesn't help the fact that I just feel awful about
it, and one man in the big accident had to go to the hospital, and
I swear to you I was totally unaware of any of this, and we just
went on our way, hoping to get to California that night and save
on a motel. Well, anyway, we didn't go, and it's a good thing
because maybe you would have tried to contact Judy and she
would have been in California, and all you would have gotten
were the cats, because that little cat of yours has four other cats
now, and nobody has the heart to get rid of them and they are
into everything. And Bud is in boot camp at Fort Polk and is
definitely going to qualify for helicopter-pilot warrant officer
training, and you would be so proud of him. Before graduation,
he went and enlisted, just like you did. I know you wanted him

to have his college first, but when the envelope disappeared and I thought he'd have to get a job instead, we figured the safest plan was for him to enlist so he wouldn't get drafted. It's all going to work out because he'll learn to pilot helicopters and then after active duty, he can apply to the college program. But we miss him so much, and I don't know exactly where he's going to be sent after helicopter school. Tom, I am telling you, sometimes I feel like I could just die and go where you are, wherever that is."

I stopped. The feeling of Tom seemed to be fading. I just sat there quietly for a while. "I'll come back soon and tell you more," I said. "I don't know why I didn't think of this sooner. Love you, hon."

The coffee was cold and bitter now, and I dumped it out in the dust. The sun was up high now, and everything had become plain old brown. Dust devils were springing up on the mesa. On the way home, I started to sing "My Adobe Hacienda." I was tired. Something had been taken out of me. But I also felt great. There were so many things I'd never gotten around to telling him, and now I could. There had been a feeling of him being there. There really had.

20

On Saturday morning my mother went to the library to finish her big paper and I lay down in the den and did twenty sit-ups to make my stomach flat. I tried not to think about what was going to happen to me that night because it made my entire insides go insane. Judy came in and put a stack of Dad's classical records on the turntable and started picking up Maura's toys and throwing away all the newspapers and magazines that had been piling up since the last big housecleaning in January. At first I just watched her. After a while, I began to stack all the papers my mother had pulled out of the desk when she was looking for the envelope back in March. I put the stacks back in the desk drawers. By then, Judy was vacuuming, so I decided to scrub the bathroom.

Then I really got involved. She mopped the kitchen and I waxed. We washed the windows together. Even Maura helped. It was another hot day, but the music was like a cool wind. Each time a new piece of music came on, Judy would tell me about it. There was a piano piece by Somebody Schumann that he wrote about his wife, Clara, and there was a frantic part where he goes crazy, and then a part where you could almost hear the piano calling "Clara, Clara!" She said a friend in New York who she thought was now in South America taught her about classical music. Before, when Dad used to listen to it, I never could make any sense out of it. Now it seemed to me like the arrangements of the stars in the sky, endless space, another level of my mind. Cleaning the cat box was no problem.

By the middle of the afternoon, the house was in complete

order and smelled of furniture polish and floor wax. It seemed like
someone else's house, and I was sorry Reuben wouldn't be able
to come inside and see it. I was so jumpy I didn't think I could
eat anything, but Judy found a carton of eggs in the refrigerator
and showed me how to make ghost-horses' necks, which are eggs
on toast with the whites beaten up fluffy and baked, and they
were delicious. After we ate, we took showers and shampooed.
Judy put mayonnaise on my hair to condition it and we gave
ourselves and Maura egg-white facials.

While the masks dried on our skin, we sat in the den and did
each other's nails and drank iced tea and listened to the Branden-
burg Concertos by Bach and watched the thunderheads pile up
over the peaks. Curtains of rain moved down the foothills. The
air became solid and dark blue. We could smell the rain. Lightning cut the sky in half and made a loud hissing, like fireworks,
before the thunder exploded. Big drops smelling of dust started
streaking all the clean windows and then the hard rain hit. We
rushed around closing windows and then Judy picked up Maura
and said, "This is what it's like!" and ran out on the patio, and
I followed her. We all stood with our faces up until the egg white
was washed off and we were completely soaked.

Judy had made a braided corona around the top of my head and
left the rest of my hair hanging loose down my back. I was
wearing her yellow minidress. She laced it up closely, whispering
to me that after I left the house, I could undo the top to make it
sexy, and that made us both laugh.

My mother came to the doorway of the bathroom. "What are
you girls giggling about?" she said.

"Nothing, Mom," I said.

The story was that Teddy Roybal and I were walking over to
the Monte Vista Shopping Plaza to see *Easy Rider.* Judy figured
it was the best thing to say in case my mother grilled me when
I got home. I knew that if she laid eyes on Reuben and saw his
cowboy boots and heard him say "ain't" just once, I'd never be
allowed to see him again.

"Isn't that something how you and Teddy have been neighbor

kids since first grade and now you're going on a real date?" my mother said.

"Oh, Mom, it's not a date. He's bored and I'm bored."

"Bored! I'd dearly love to go to the movies myself. You don't have to go with Teddy if you don't want. You and I could go. But that *Easy Rider*. I fail to see why anyone would want to go twice. I'm telling you, girls, this bathroom just sparkles. You-all really knocked yourselves out. The whole house is like brand-new. This is truly gracious living."

Judy said I'd look better without eyeshadow. She outlined my eyes with her black pencil. "I'd loan you this great stuff—kohl, it's called—but I can't find it," she said.

"I'd go light on the makeup," my mother said. "You don't want to look cheap."

After my mother left, Judy said, "You look so pretty—you're just glowing."

I felt the power welling up inside me again. "I'm pretty nervously excited," I said. "In fact, I could pass out. But I'm going to act very mature."

"If you're in love, you have to not be scared," Judy said. "Even if you are. But don't go getting obsessed about it. I mean, if you get obsessed, then it's a mess."

"Obsessed?" I said. I didn't know what she meant. "Obsessed *qua* obsessed?"

"God, your whole life ahead of you, and you are gorgeous," she said. "I was okay-looking when I was your age, but I didn't even know it. When I think of the fun I could have had, and now I'm an old hag—"

"Judy!" I said. "I mean, I don't believe you." I'd always figured Judy was aware that she was beautiful the way people are aware that they're breathing. "Judy, you are *beautiful*," I said. "I don't know anyone more beautiful than you. Tommy must tell you that all the time. Excuse me for saying this, but sometimes I think so-called legal adults don't know a thing." It bothered me: if Judy didn't know that one simple thing about herself, what else didn't she know? Maybe some very important things. I'd always thought you automatically got all the important things by, say, twenty-one.

"I wish—well, anyway, here's some sandalwood oil. Very erotic. It will drive Reuben insane."

When I felt her finger touch the back of my ear, I said, "Let's always be friends, okay?"

"We will be, no matter what," Judy said. "I mean, we'll really try. But you can't ever be sure about one single thing on this earth, you know. We're just bubbles on a stream. Or something like that. I'm not sure." She lifted the back of my hair and let it drop. "It looks great," she said. "Do that mayonnaise treatment every week. I'll tell you a secret."

I thought she was going to tell me something about hair, but she said, "You're right—what do grown-ups know? Don't think men are everything. It's no good dedicating every moment of your life to them, thinking every second: Will he like this? I'll have to tell him about that—and thinking that you at least have security, because you don't even have that, it's all in the mind, because most of the time they're not even there, and what do you have? Nothing." She got excited. I don't know what she was saying exactly. "You can't just go along, like daytime TV, and use up your life that way. You have to do something daring. At least once in a while. I mean, you could die and never do what you really wanted."

"Okay," I said. "I think everyone should be daring all the time."

I was almost out the front door with Teddy when my mother made me go back in the bedroom and change into a skirt that went all the way to the knees and a blouse with a Peter Pan collar.

The air smelled wet and fresh. There were puddles all over the Monte Vista parking lot reflecting the pink and purple and red sky. At one end of the lot, there was a lit-up stage and a crowd of heads bobbing up and down to the boom and twang of a Fender bass. Teddy and I found Reuben leaning against the motor scooter smoking a cigarette. Some Mormon. And then he handed me one of three miniatures he had of Old Mr. Boston Chocolate Vodka. I acted like I drank several of these a day, had for years. He offered me a cigarette, and I started to take it, too, but then I thought of my father.

After a few swigs, Reuben and Teddy began to pretend they were in a football game, the Rose Bowl. "And a high overhead pass to Swapp!" Reuben said through his nose like a sports announcer as he crouched and ran around the cars.

Oh God, I thought. Here I am, on a date with Reuben L. Swapp. I had to be very careful not to sound like a Brain. I drank some more of the chocolate vodka. The game got funnier and funnier. I started laughing. Reuben leaped up on the hood of a car and back down to the ground, Teddy after him. "Swapp nears the goal line, and—oh, my God, I *don't* believe it—he's running the wrong way!" Reuben said. I laughed so hard that all the muscles in my stomach pulled tight. I hugged myself and bent over. The laughs came up from deep inside and left a sweet taste in my throat. It was the first time I'd laughed, truly laughed, in I don't know how long.

We walked over to the dance, and I felt clear and clean and very tall. When I closed my eyes, I could see the whole parking lot and the entire shopping plaza as if I were looking down from a great height. I felt my hair moving against my back, and I felt Reuben next to me, bony and short. A guy who looked a lot like my guitar teacher, with long hair in a ponytail and a little beard on his chin, asked me to dance. I turned to Reuben, he raised a miniature to me, and I started leaping around with the guy. He was probably from the college. That topped LaDonna's famous senior. All she wrote about now was him, and his class ring, which she figured would be hers by the end of the summer. The music was loud and I couldn't understand the words of the singer. After a few dances, I started to feel dizzy. I was afraid I was going to throw up. I waved goodbye to my partner and searched for Reuben and Teddy in the crowd. I couldn't find them and got scared. Out of nowhere came the strong feeling that I ought to be nicer to my mother. I ought to study harder. *Of ages glide away, the sons of men.* I went up to the bandstand and watched the musicians. The singer, two guitarists, and a saxophone player in pink suits and shoulder-length black hair swayed and stepped in unison. The bearded guy found me and asked me to dance again, but I just shook my head.

"Nancy, you ain't *straight*," said a voice behind me. "I can tell 'cause your hair is movin'." Reuben took my hand. The skin on his palm was hardened and rough. He smelled of oil and metal. I wanted to remember all I could about him to think about later. I couldn't control my smiling. Reuben didn't dance, and so we just stood and watched the band. He stared at the lead guitarist. "Every time he does that one riff, he turns away, so I can't see how he done it," Reuben said.

"You play?" I asked.

He shrugged. "Some."

At the end, fireworks were set off in the parking lot, and red and blue and green streaks oozed down the black sky. Teddy headed for home on foot, and I rode on the motor scooter, my arms around Reuben's waist. He took the corners so fast that at times I had to lean with him almost parallel to the pavement. Suddenly, fear rose up in my chest, and I clutched at him. He was a stranger. What was I doing? What in the world was I doing? "Stop!" I screamed. "Stop!"

"Ow, not in my ear," he said. He slowed down, dragging his boot heel, its metal tap making sparks off the stones in the asphalt. "What's the problem?"

I started to laugh again. "I don't know."

"She doesn't know," he said.

We walked, Reuben pushing the scooter. Dogs barked as we passed front yards, and in each dim house was the blue square of a TV screen. There was the smell of wet lawns, and also of burning meat coming from barbecues. Above was the black outline of the peaks, as if they had been cut out and removed, and the stars. I wanted to talk about the stars, but I was afraid of how I would sound. My mother always said men like to answer questions—it makes them feel smart.

"How does a motor scooter keep from falling over when you ride?" I asked.

"You're always falling when you ride. You fall a little thisaway and then a little thataway, and that's how you balance."

I didn't think Reuben would know things like that. "Same as on a bike?"

"It's physics—something about the earth being one big curve. My brother told me about it."

I stopped when we got to the corner of Lincoln and Cagua. "I'm supposed to be with Teddy, according to my mom," I said.

"Teddy, he's a nice kid."

"Yeah," I said. "A good guy. Well, thanks. This was really nice and all."

"Well." Reuben let the motor scooter lean against his hip and he put his hands on my upper arms. His touch was warm. He was just another kid like me, walking around on the planet Earth. "I'll wait here for Teddy." He grinned and gave his shoulders a quick shake, and squeezed my arms. "Good night and all that stuff."

"Okay!" I said. "Good night." I hurried toward my house, praying that my mother wouldn't be up. I wondered if Reuben was watching me but I didn't dare turn around. The houses were dark and quiet cubes set down in a row, like mysterious temples of an ancient civilization. My street, I said to myself. I put a stick of gum in my mouth and straightened my skirt and tucked some loose strands back into my braid.

Tonight my mother had put a yellow light bulb in the porch light, so the bugs wouldn't gather there. She was waiting inside the screen door. "I thought I heard you coming," she said. "Where's Teddy?"

"Oh—at his house," I said. I'd already forgotten I was supposed to be with him.

"Did you-all have just a wonderful time, hon?"

"Oh, yes, it was nice." I tried to sound bored.

"And did you enjoy that movie again?"

"The movie." It took me a while to form a thought. Here was my house, the living room with the clawed beige tweed sofa with three black cats asleep on it, the wall by the front door that still had pencil marks where my father used to record my heights, the TV on in the den. There was a newspaper on the carpet and a plate with a half-eaten piece of fried chicken on my mother's desk. This is where I grew up, I told myself. "The movie. It was okay. It was okay."

"That ending, ugh," my mother said. She squinted and stuck out her tongue.

Judy came out of her room. She was in her nightie and her face was sad. We'd had such a nice day together, but the happiness had already worn off. "Oh, Nance," she said hoarsely. "How was it?"

I reached for her hand and gave it a squeeze. "It was great. Truly, great." I wanted her to be all right.

"I wouldn't spend all my time with that Teddy Roybal," my mother said, going into the den. "I don't think he's going to amount to a whole lot."

"Oh, Mom, he's just a friend."

I went into my mother's room. Energy came up through my feet and shook my spine and flew out of my fingertips. It was partly the vibrations from the motor scooter and partly what I had been feeling for a few years now, but I hadn't been particularly aware of it before. I wanted to be alone. But there was no place in the house where I could count on that. I should have written LaDonna a long time ago and told her the truth, even if she didn't care about Reuben anymore. Since I'd crossed the street that night to talk to him, I'd been bad about answering her letters. The latest one began: "Have you gone and died?" But how many boys did she need? I lay on the bed, and it started to whirl. I got up. In a minute maybe I would go talk to Judy, and think of a way to tell her I understood all about "Dearest Vik."

But first I stood in front of the bureau and held on to the two knobs of the top drawer, turning the loose one and swaying a little. *So live that when Thy summons comes to join the innumerable caravan.* My mother was watching Johnny Carson, and television laughter drifted in. I looked at the picture of my parents on their wedding day. My father in his uniform, standing behind my mother, his hands on her upper arms. My mother, pretty in dark lipstick and slender in an old-fashioned suit, had a pouf of little curls over her forehead. Just after the nurse had told my mother and me that he was gone, we went in and kissed him. I had never seen my mother cry. I picked up the picture and gave my handsome father's face a big kiss.

21

Tom had always been a morning person, and his presence was still stronger then. And I got to like leaving the house very early in the morning before anyone else was awake, as if I had a secret life, something that was all mine, and I loved going out into the cool summer morning, because it always filled me with hope. On the way up to the overlook I'd think about what I wanted to say, and by the time I got there, I was ready for a communion of half an hour or so.

It helped get things going if I thought about the swings. How we had sat and necked, and then he'd started swinging. I thought about the creaking noise and how he went higher and higher, came toward me and went away, toward me and away.

I said, "Don't do that." Then I said, "When you went away after Nancy was born, and then you called and I said, Just come home, and you did, you know I never said a word, did I? We just went on. I could have made a bunch of trouble about that woman —she was cheap and fat, for instance—but I kept my mouth shut. Didn't you think that was good? Wasn't I being real good? You never said, and I always wondered, but not once did you ever tell me that I was doing the right thing." And then I started to cry. It was all right, because these days I put on my makeup later, while I was driving to class.

And I said, "Listen, I'm sorry I brought that up, but there's something I have to tell you. I don't think this marriage of Tommy's is going to last, although the Good Lord knows that this time I'll do everything I can to keep them together. I know you always say Judy is a very nice, sensitive girl, and it *is* true that she has some fine qualities, but she is just not the same person now. I mean, at least she isn't lying in bed in the dark all the time, and she seems to have more pep, and we had a nice time going to the bookstore the other day, and she was very appreciative when I bought her a book, but when I talk about Tommy, his future and all, she barely seems to care. Doesn't say a word. She told Nancy she didn't want to go to Mexico *or* Africa, she wanted to get a job and save her money so she could finish her schooling. But does that mean she's just going to drop Tommy, who's so completely devoted to her? I don't see how he can manage. He has his faults, but I have prayed that he uses all his gifts to do good and make something of himself, and now I'm worried that we'll have him back sleeping on the couch again and I don't believe I could take another one of his divorces. I've tried my very best to give her a number of booster talks about what's important in marriage and all, and what our marriage was like. See, I kind of think that what Tommy needs is a lot of love and *forgiveness*. She ought to just be able to forgive him about things. I don't know what exactly he did or she did, but he's done a lot for her, and she ought to be more appreciative. I mean, remember her family at the wedding? How they came in pickup trucks? But he's certainly no picnic to live with, and he does have this little tendency to manipulate, and I freely admit that even though I am his own mother. But if she loves him—and there's Maura, don't forget—then she should just forgive him and go on. Don't you think, Tom, darlin'? Couldn't you speak to her? After all, I forgave you what you did, even though I was hurt clean to the bone. What you did to me just killed me, and I never said a word, and there I was, totally worn out, Nancy a bawling newborn and Bud into everything, and Tommy nervously upset, and I was stuck with those kids and you didn't come home. You didn't come home, and you didn't come home, and you didn't come home, and then I found the note and the check in the mailbox! Now, I ask you, was that any way to treat your loving wife after years and years of service? I am just asking you. And I didn't even have

typing or shorthand or any college then—just how was I supposed to support a family? I know you said you'd send money,
but I didn't even know where to find you. I would have just
collapsed if it hadn't been for Tommy. I told him everything, and
he *understood*. He was very mature for a boy of thirteen. You
tended to put him down, but he has always tried very hard. You
never really appreciated him. But that woman! How could you
do that? A divorcée who was nothing but a clerk-typist. And
overweight!"

I had to catch my breath. All those words filled up the space
between my head and the windshield. I said, "And furthermore,
I begged you, and you came back and never said what you'd been
up to, where, why, nothing. And wasn't I good about that? Didn't
I keep my mouth shut? You never saw me cry or carry on for one
second. You know something, Tom Hammond, I don't think you
cared about me or the kids at all. Or you never would have done
that to us. And when you came back, you were just going
through the motions. It was all an act. And all those years after
I went to college and slaved away and got my degrees and landed
a job, I still came home and cleaned and put dinner on the table
every night for you and starched and ironed all your shirts. And
I want you to know that being in bed with you was really work
for me. Hard work. Sometimes it was even painful. I was only
pretending, Tom! To make *you* feel good. So that we would have
a happy marriage! So all of those years that I was a perfect wife,
you never said how good I had been about everything. And really
I was alone a lot of the time. I had to go to Europe by myself.
And you wouldn't talk to me. It was just the *idea* of having a
husband. You know something? I could just kill you!"

I turned on the ignition and tore out of the parking area and
down the hill and onto Foothills Drive. Then I pulled over to the
shoulder and stopped. I sat there, breathing hard. I sat for a long
time. I cried. After a while, I drove back up to the overlook. All
of a sudden I was absolutely calm. I said, "Tom, darlin', I am
sorry I said all that, but the fact is, you are dead. I hate to say it,
but there it is."

. . .

The next time I went to the overlook, I began by thinking of us in the swings together, and when I could feel that Tom was present, I discussed the best way of getting Bud transferred to the Coast Guard. I was going to make that my project. So much had been on my mind that until now I hadn't really thought through what Bud was doing, and talking to Tom had made me see things a little more clearly. I don't know why I let Bud get away with enlisting when somehow I could have gotten him into college and kept him there. And then this business about helicopter-pilot school. I had believed that the service would be good for him, that it would organize him, give him motivation, make a man out of him, since he didn't have his father around anymore. But actually, when Tommy went in the Army, he didn't really change; that LuAnn and all her money went with him, so he was living in places much finer than the officers' housing, and then all he did was public relations work. His manhood was never tested. Maybe the Army would really help Bud, but not if he got killed by Communists in some jungle we didn't even want. On TV you saw what they were doing to our boys, and it was a crying shame, but you had to wonder if it was right for us to be interfering so much in that little country. Tom always glorified *his* war to the boys, but he never left the U.S.A., and we had the best time you ever saw—the most terrific friends, and it was one party after another . . .

And then I said, "After the war was when everything changed for you, Tom. When we moved into the little adobe hacienda. I see that now. I see why you had to do things the way you did. You had to keep yourself going the best way you could. It was tough on you. I know that now. You never were a family-type person, you never should have settled down after the war. You should have had a horse and a coffeepot and a bedroll and you'd have been happy. But we made the best of it, and we had some fun. It wasn't so bad, was it? I think you loved me. I know you did."

22

Strands of cloud materialized in the raw blue. The car mounted a ridge banded with verdigris and ocher, and the sagebrush plateau opened up ahead. A cool wind poured in the wing vents.

Effie passed a battered pickup truck with six Indians jammed in the cab. On its rear windshield was a decal of an American flag and the words "America—Love It or Leave It."

"Sun," Maura said. She and Nancy were playing a naming game.

They were heading north, and the sun, rising above the Cibola Peaks, overlay the interior of the car with geometric fragments. "Have you ever noticed?" Nancy said. "No matter how fast we go, the sunlight in the car stays the same?"

"It's just always there, no matter what you do," Judy said. She lay in the back seat reading.

"Mmm," Effie said. As the blocky outline of Cibola sank into a lake of brown haze in the rearview, she sighed and leaned back. Her shoulders dropped, and her neck relaxed. She had no wish to talk; she was meditating on how to contact Tom when they got to the dam. The ideal place was out in the middle of the lake, but she had decided against bringing the boat—she couldn't figure out how to hook the boat trailer up to the car. His fishing spot on the shore, near where they used to camp, would have to do. She tapped a fingernail on the steering wheel for each piece of news she wanted to give him. One: Tommy was reassessing the Africa plan. It was surely only a matter of time before he was back in the bosom of the family, and she would have to have the Life Talk with him. Now that she really knew what philosophy was, she just couldn't see him as another Dr. Desai, humbly wearing the same old suit day in and day out and lecturing on Being when the government was desperate for people of Tommy's caliber. But when she considered willing all her energy into Tommy so that he could rise to the challenge—law school, for instance—she felt a little tired. Maybe she would have the Life Talk so he'd know she cared, and then he could just do whatever he wanted to do. Two: Bud's unit had scored the highest in physical training and rifle, and his last letter about how the military didn't keep its promises to recruits was just your typical Army grumbling. Besides, the Coast Guard would certainly want a dedicated, upstanding, honorable young man like him, and she had used her best stationery to write Congressman Valdez about this. Three: The life insurance and Social Security payments were finally coming through, and she wanted to thank Tom for arranging for her to be well taken care of the rest of her life. If he was the one who had hidden the envelope for a while, then he must have meant well, because now she could really appreciate what he had done for her.

"Mountain," Nancy said to Maura. "Paradiso Baldy."

Maura saw some red cattle grazing on rabbit bush in a dry, sandy riverbed. "Cows."

"Flowers," Nancy said, pointing at the purple plumes on the sagebrush.

When the speedometer happened to go above seventy, Effie slowed down. Her intention was to drive with unusual care. The thought for the day was "God shows me the way to perfect serenity." As she listened to the girls murmuring, it occurred to her that she was happy. According to *The Dictionary of Philosophy*, what happiness boiled down to was deciding what you wanted to do and doing it, meanwhile putting goodness into your life. Dr. Desai had written on her paper that she possessed excellence of understanding, and he was especially impressed by the phrases in real Sanskrit Judy had added, and the quotes from some of those books of hers. The house was still fairly clean. Sonia had persuaded Effie to try a new hairdo—shorter, looser, curlier. The curve of her foot in its sandal on the accelerator was still pretty. The car was running smoothly. The radio was playing a song she actually knew the words to: "*Vaya con dios,* my darling, *vaya con dios,* my love." Pal Al Zamora's theme song. In the ice chest in the trunk was a cast-iron pot of lima beans and ham hocks she had made and a shoe box full of her fried chicken wrapped in waxed paper. The girls had baked some biscuits. She had never before cooked a meal like this when there were no men around to appreciate it. "It was definitely not my plan to be a liberated woman, girls," she said. "But I must say, it's really nice to pick up and go when you want. You don't ask permission, you don't have to talk anybody into it. You just do the thing. Talk about freedom."

"Isn't that the truth?" Judy said, looking up from her new book, *Sisterhood Is Powerful.* "Men always think that if we do what we want, they're going to get hurt. Did you know that in the history of the world, women were originally the rulers? But they were so powerful the men had to—"

"I don't think that's right, hon—"

"Nope. It says here—"

"Did you bring any of those nice books on Oriental philosophy?" Effie asked. "So sweet and gentle and all, those ideas about acceptance and calm lotus pools and the body is a garment you put on and take off. I believe I would like to go to one of those ashram places and just meditate and get my mind all organized."

Maura waved at a solitary turquoise-colored building. "House," she said.

"That's Freddie's Bar, hon," Effie said. "We always stop there on the way back from the dam. You're too little to remember last year."

"I'm *not* little," Maura said.

"It's closed!" Nancy said. There was a sign in a window: "Exclusive Real Estate Oppty." "What happened? Mom?"

"I don't know, darlin'. That sure is too bad. Maybe Freddie retired. Or maybe he's moved and we'll have to go find him. Don't worry about it."

Isolated volcanic cones began to appear, their black-tongued lava flows splaying outward for miles across the plain. Near Mesita, where the train tracks crossed the highway, the Paradisos, by some trick of the altitude and the clear, dry air, seemed suddenly to rear up and expand. "There's the thunderhead over Paradiso Baldy, right on schedule," Nancy said.

"Where's the schedule?" Maura asked. "What's a schedule?"

"Do you always have to know everything, Maura?" Nancy asked, grabbing Maura and tickling her.

"And there's a roadblock," Effie said. "And police. What on earth? Did something happen in Mesita?"

"If it did, it'll be the first time in human history," Nancy said.

"Mesita?" Judy said.

"This is certainly strange," Effie said. "Maybe someone escaped from the penitentiary—"

"The Fourth, Mom," Nancy said. "You know—Independence Day? They check your license and your car inspection. It's been on the radio all morning."

Effie swerved over to the gravel shoulder and turned off the ignition. She put on the emergency brake and closed her eyes.

Judy sat up. "Are we in Mesita?" she asked. A large trailer court sprawled on both sides of the highway. The wheels of many of the trailers had been replaced with cinder blocks. Rock gardens and brightly painted ceramic donkeys and urns spilling over with prickly pear decorated the yards, which were bordered by truck tires painted white. "Was this here last year?"

"We have a serious situation here," Effie said. "If we want to get to the dam, we're going to have to do something, girls. I just don't happen to have my license."

"I'll check your purse, Mom," Nancy said.

"Don't bother about that," Effie said. "Judy, hon, I do believe that you'd better drive."

"Me? Drive? I—"

"You still have a license, right?"

"I guess," Judy said. "If I brought it." She turned her purse upside down and shook it. Out fell a plastic barrette, a small plush raccoon, an apple, hairpins, a rubber band, cough drops that were stuck together and coated with lint, six dollars and some change, and a plastic wallet. "Here it is. It's expired, though."

"That's good enough."

"I don't know if I—"

"Of course you can do it," Effie said. "You just say to yourself: I know I can do this, the Lord is helping me to do this, I have always been a good driver, and I can just drive no matter what, and I am the best dadgummed driver in the world and could be in the *Indianapolis 500* if I wanted and nothing can stop me. And you do it because you want to get to the dam, and Maura does, and Nancy, and me. You do it for you, but you do it for everyone else, too. Because if there's one thing on earth I have learned, it's that you have to do the thing while the people are alive." She got out of the car and sat in the back, and Judy climbed into the driver's seat.

"It's automatic," Effie said. "You just step on it and go and you don't have to think about a thing, and Nancy will help you, and I'm going to sit back here as quiet as a mouse and serenely read my brochures and catalogues."

Judy tasted acid on her palate. Dust particles streamed in the sunlight as she adjusted the rearview mirror. In her arms and chest and back she could feel the collisions. Cars coming out of nowhere and blindsiding them. Cars ramming them from behind. Cars coming toward them head-on and smashing through the windshield. Cars veering out of the opposite lane and sideswiping them. She could feel herself trapped and suffocating, along with the others, in the wreckage. She braced herself against the seat. "I can't," she tried to say, but she had no voice.

"All you do is visualize where you want to go, you put your mind on that, darlin'," Effie said. "And then step on it."

Judy made herself think about the creek where she used to lie down after working hard on the excavation. Her hot, dusty skin, the cold water rushing over her face. The creek was part of the watershed of the San Ysidro and flowed into the dam. Tom

Senior had given her the wheel of the boat. "I trust you," he said, and made her guess what the illusion was. Putting her hands on the steering wheel, she looked at the traffic moving along the highway. The cars shimmered in the heat, and water seemed to ripple under their tires as they approached the roadblock. The sharp fragrance of sage came in the window. Somewhere out there, Tom Senior had stood alone all day. There had been nothing but sagebrush and sand stretching all the way to the gathered and crumpled folds of the foothills and the cobalt-blue upthrust of the mountains. He had watched the sun change the shadows around him. The clouds, now solidified and shiny, with flat bottoms and high domes, cast moving pools of violet on the gray-green plain.

"You can do it," Nancy said.

Judy stepped on the gas, and the car chugged laboriously back onto the highway. The sun flashed, making her squint and see everything through little colored bubbles.

"The emergency, hon," Effie said softly.

Judy released the brake and a pulsing alertness flared up behind her eyes. She drove uncertainly, sensing the delicate lives around her.

Ahead, moving at twenty miles an hour, was a highly polished black van with a painting on its rear doors of the Virgin of Guadalupe. Judy fixed her gaze on the ethereal face. Her hands were sweating. The car seemed about to slip out of control. When the highway patrolman examined her license, she would say: I was away in the East, things happened, I forgot to renew, now I'm back, I'm very sorry. I'll renew immediately. At the roadblock, she was waved directly through.

"Yay!" Nancy said.

"Yay!" Maura said.

"Now just keep going," Effie said.

"Dear Reuben," Nancy wrote with a new real-ink pen in a tidy hand that slanted to the right, blue-green scallops of ink coming to fine points at the top of each line.

How are you? I am fine? How is your cow? I will not
be able to go to the street dance this week because we are
at San Ysidro dam. Actually right now we are on the
way there, I hope we make it. Is Tiny Tornado or the
Midnight Auto Supply playing next week?

Supraluminally yours,
Sincerely yours,
Nancy H.

*"Maybe it is yourself now ushering me to the true songs (who
knows?),"* she whispered to herself. Two more lines and she was
finished with "Goodbye, My Fancy." Absently making a kissing
sound with her lips, she copied the letter, using only the second
complimentary close. She wasn't sure whether she would mail it.
The letter went into the wooden cigar box beside a piece of
stationery with something she had copied the other day out of one
of her father's college textbooks, a poem called "The Force That
Through the Green Fuse Drives the Flower." She didn't exactly
understand what it was getting at, but it had a mountain spring,
streams, a pool, the blowing wind, blood, and a heaven round the
stars. When she read it aloud to herself it was like talking in a
dream: You didn't know what you were saying, but you had the
feeling it was important. She had cleaned out the cigar box last
night and found all kinds of silly things. "Integer Vitae," copied
from her ninth-grade Latin book, all the A's made like deltas.
Some crazy letters she never got around to sending to LaDonna.
Notes from LaDonna folded into triangular packets like you fold
the flag. A poem about a forest pool with a redheaded boy about
to dive in. Horrible. It was so stupid it made her shudder. Was
she thinking about Reuben in those days? No, he was someone
LaDonna had latched on to. He had not yet come into existence
as far as Nancy was concerned.
"Dear LaDonna," she wrote.

How are you? I am fine. How is Mr. Wonderful the
Senior treating you? Do you have his ring yet. I was at
the street dance the other night and you will never guess

who was there, Reuben and Teddy but I suppose
you aren't interested in any of that. It was kind of
comatose altho I did dance with this nice boy from the
college. How is the weather in Uvalde? It rained here.
We're going to the dam for a few days. I might dye
my hair red, what do you think?

She tore the letter up. "Judy," she said, looking over the seat back
to make sure her mother wasn't listening. Effie was making notes
in the margins of a college catalogue. "Judy, what am I going to
do about LaDonna? I mean, I have to tell her *some*thing."

"Why?" Judy gave her a quick glance, her eyes unblinking and
focused. "Who knows what's going to happen to you and—you
and whoever—by the time she comes home? And who knows
about her and that boy in Uvalde? I mean, we don't even know
what's going to happen five minutes from now. Everybody is
always planning things, and what's the point? In *The City and the
Stars*, remember how the computer controlled reality and people
had been living according to its plan for a billion years? And
nothing new ever happened?"

"And nobody was born and nobody got old," Nancy said. "But
then the boy could see there was another reality—he escaped and
changed everything. I absolutely love that book. I wish I'd
brought it with me. You won't believe this, but all week I was
planning to wear my last year's bathing suit, the old green one.
I tried it on last night and it didn't have a waist and it was so short
it was embarrassing. I'll just swim in my cutoffs and tank top. I
bet I looked like a box last summer."

"You don't now," Judy said.

"You, too—you look really different."

"I feel different," she said.

Judy's words echoed inside Nancy's head: I . . . FEEL . . .
DIFFERENT. For a second, she felt what it was like to be Judy,
her brown oval hands wrapped around the steering wheel, her
head thrust forward, her mouth slightly open, her dark eyes like
a sharp-sighted bird's. A little sad and frightened. Other people
had things going on inside, then—thoughts and feelings and

pictures that they might never say anything about. People were walking around with incredible things going on inside their heads, all of the time. She had known that, of course, but she never really felt it until this moment. "Like how different?"

"Well . . . like all the cities have been bombed, and we're just escaping, setting out on our own, heading for the mountains, and we're strong and we know we're going to survive."

"We certainly have enough food," Nancy said.

The radio played "Born to Be Wild," Steppenwolf. Nancy turned up the volume. "Come on, Maura," she said. "You can sing it: 'Like a true nature's child, I was born, born to be wild.' " Nancy thought of it as her and Reuben's song, although she would never dare to tell Reuben that, and although, now that she knew him, she was not sure if she was in love with him. She had to keep seeing him at least until he kissed her. Maura clapped her hands and sang, "True child!"

"Here's a program I don't think you can beat," Effie said. "The History of Western Thought. A whole summer. You go two weeks to this university in Heidelberg, West Germany, two weeks to one in Perugia, Italy, and two weeks to Oxford, England. If I took a million courses all winter, I could probably understand what they were talking about by next June. And if I signed up for that program, I'd know everything in the world and I'd meet people who are interested in the great ideas. 'Do the thing and you will have the power,' Emerson says. My dream is to be in Plato's Academy and have discourse with intelligent men. But the thing is, even selling the trailer, I still can't afford that program *and* get Nancy started in college if that's what she genuinely wants to do—"

"She'd damn well better," Judy said.

"—*and* do the Marina del Mar," Effie went on. "So maybe we'll stay in the adobe hacienda a bit longer. What do you think, Judy, hon? Maybe I should ask Tommy—"

"Oh, just go do it," Judy said. "You're young-looking and pretty. You go to one of those programs and something is bound to happen." She saw Effie married to an important intellectual. Around-the-world trips to be planned. Seminars to be organized.

Drinks to be made. And then, eventually, Effie would forgive Judy for what she was going to do.

Nancy turned down the radio.

"Interesting that you mention that, because that's exactly what I was thinking," Effie said. "Everyone in my family is so long-lived—Mama outlived three husbands—and all this time I've been thinking, Oh no, the next thirty years alone—because I could never feature any other man but Tom Senior, and it's hard, you know, because sometimes I'll be driving along and I'll see some-one in the car ahead that looks a little bit like him at first, the ears sticking out, or the Stetson, or even some man in a pickup with a teardrop camper, and it puts me in a tizzy, and there will never be another Tom. But the fact is, he's no longer on this earth."

Judy stayed behind the painted van. No one seemed to mind that they were going so slow. She carefully wiped one palm and then the other on her shorts and pulled at her tank top to keep it from sticking to her skin. When a car came toward her in the opposite lane, she crept toward the shoulder. The plain became a darker green and began to slant upward.

"This is *your* pal, Al Zamora, with esoteric euphony all day long," the radio said. "On this beautaceous Fourth of July affair, nineteen hundred and seventy."

"Isn't it good of Judy to be driving so well, Nancy?" Effie said. "I swear, I don't know what we would have done."

"Judy to the rescue," Nancy said. "Where do you suppose all your stuff is, Judy? It has to be somewhere—it didn't just sink into the Atlantic Ocean."

"Maybe it did," Judy said. There was nothing in those cartons she wanted. When Tommy had called to say all their household goods had disappeared en route to Africa, he spoke in a broken and confusing way. She thought it was going to be his last call before he left for Liberia. At first she didn't understand what was lost, what he was talking about. And then Effie spoke to him, and he asked her to mail him his saxophone.

"Nancy, did you give Judy that letter with the fancy stamps?"

"I got it," Judy said. Vik had sent a photograph of a Peruvian Indian woman in a derby, and on the back, the inscription "She reminded me of you." No address. "My girlfriend who went to South America," she said. She was not going to think about him. She tightened her hands on the steering wheel. The lives around her were like fragrances evaporating constantly into the air; she had to take care of them; she had to get everyone safely to the dam. It didn't matter if she was afraid.

Clouds dissolved and formed again above the mountains. A desert hawk hung in the air. No one spoke but Pal Al Zamora. "And now Jim Morrison," he said. "And 'American Woman.' I dedicate this song to all you American women out there. Too *much!* Woo!"

Judy followed the van until the Callosa turnoff. "I'll go the back route," she said. "And stay off the highway."

"You just do whatever you like, darlin'," Effie said.

The road, paved since last year, rose up into the foothills and into a canyon with a stream and then narrowed, climbing a series of steep switchbacks. Now, off the highway, Judy's fear vanished. "I'm doing fine," she said. "This is fun."

The road passed a cluster of dusty cottonwoods and adobe houses. Cars sat on their axles in the hard-packed, neatly swept yards. Chickens roamed in the shade of an apple orchard. "Okay, this is the Indian village," Judy said. "The dig was a little further up." She felt a burst of happiness. It surprised her; it spread through her chest and made her grin, as if she were falling in love.

"Where you went that summer in college?" Nancy asked.

"That's right. Except I don't remember this billboard." It was yellow with crossed red arrows and said SKI CALLOSA. The road wound higher and higher up into the canyon. "I'm sure it's just one or two more turns," Judy said. "You'll see. It's so beautiful. We can stop and have a picnic and wade in the creek and cool off."

In the wide meadow next to the stream was a Swiss chalet, the Callosa Ski Lodge. A ski lift ran up the side of the canyon. "This can't be right," Judy said.

"I seem to remember something about the Indians developing a resort up here," Effie said. "I forget the details."

"But this is exactly where the excavation was. I found the skeleton of a woman. Where the tennis court is."

"What happened to the skeleton?" Nancy asked.

"It's in the museum at the college now. In the basement, probably. It was right where that second net is. How could they do this?"

"I'm truly sorry, hon," Effie said. "I truly am. You know how poor these Indians are. They need the revenue. But when you go back to school, maybe you'll get to find another skeleton."

Judy glanced at Effie and at Nancy and felt a great warmth for them, as if she had already said goodbye.

"Nancy, hon, are you sure you want to do such a big hike by yourself?" Effie called from her deck chair. Nancy wore lime-green shorts and a white tank top and round-lensed sunglasses. Her hair was in a chignon. Had she gotten taller? Slimmer? She looked like someone else's daughter, home from some college in another state.

"Yes, Mom." Nancy hung the binoculars around her neck and placed the straw Stetson on her head. It smelled of Wildroot Cream Oil.

"Alone?"

"I'm a big girl now, Mom, and furthermore, I hiked on the trail two summers ago with Dad." She took a breath and tensed her back, ready for a long struggle. "You really don't have to take care of me anymore, you know."

"Well, darlin'," Effie said after a moment. In the old days, girls Nancy's age already had three kids and were ruling Aquitaine or some place like that. "You have yourself a nice time up there."

Nancy followed the old Indian trail, with steps and toeholds carved into the sandstone, up the side of the canyon. Gnarled piñon trees grew around boulders and gray-leafed scrub oak spread out of crevices. She was climbing a little faster than the afternoon shadow was filling the narrow part of the canyon. Dust rose in puffs under her sandals, the air smelled of hot stone and pine needles, and her breath came in short, even strokes. She heard someone behind her and turned, but it was only the rustling of the leaves in the wind. Her father used to stop and grab her hand to pull her up when she had to take a high step. He had always just been there, like the walls of her room. It never occurred to her that he might vanish. She couldn't remember anything he had said on their hike.

Near the rim, she sat on a boulder. White cloud reflections moved on the dark surface of the lake. The air was thin and chilly, and the late-afternoon shadows were weak, the sunlight abrasive and bluish. She could see the car, the tent, the card table, Effie and Maura side by side in deck chairs, Maura swinging her legs. Judy was on top of the earthen dam, striding in a determined fashion toward the opposite wall of the canyon.

The forest came to the rim on the far side. The forest of spruce, fir, and ponderosa pine that Nancy considered her own. But something was wrong. She stood up to get a better look. There was nothing but black spikes in a waste of black for as far as she could see: burned trunks, and bare branches reaching erratically up into the empty blue.

She found that she was crying. She sobbed for a long time, until her eyes smarted and her ribs were sore. Once, there had not even been a forest here. When this was all under an ocean. That was it, that was what her father had talked about that day. He explained that the sandstone was from the sand and shells that had been at the bottom of the ocean, and he told her about how Paradiso Baldy was an extinct volcano. The energy from the time when everything was molten rock was locked up under the surface of the earth; the energy of the universe from the explosion that began time was the energy that kept everything going right up until this second. And everything would keep going until one day the sun expanded, vaporizing the earth and the solar system. After a while, even the universe would burn itself out. She had not paid very much attention to him. She had been imagining the journey they would take together through the forest. But now she remembered. Before the explosion, there was nothing. Maybe not even space.

She felt a falling sensation in the pit of her abdomen. There was a time when her father had not existed, and when she had not existed. And then somehow she was alive, she was a human being. Like the others. It was so obvious. You had to do things—wear clothes, eat food, go to school. . . . She would live in Paris, France, and wear a trench coat and walk in the rain and write poetry about loneliness. Or maybe just marry Reuben and live in a yellow house. Something vibrated against the field of black. She dried her eyes and peered through the binoculars at the dead forest. Here and there, tufts of new green shimmered along the scorched trunks and branches.

A big boat buzzed past and, planing, shot deeper into the canyon, leaving a white, trapezoidal wake that thinned out for miles. An odor of piñon woodsmoke rose from the embers of the campfire. Maura played on a sandbar with the thermos cup and sang to herself. All Effie could catch was "Thank you, lake." Shiny ripples struck spines of driftwood jutting out of the shallows. Blue flies flashed over the water.

"This is scrambled eggs, Effie," Maura said, bringing her a cup of mud.

"Why, I'm so grateful," Effie said. Her deck chair was in a cleared circle amid yucca and sage. She sat with a towel over her legs and, wrapped around her shoulders, a scarf Judy had given her, yellow with red Sanskrit designs. She smacked her lips, pretending to eat the mud. "How you talk! All of a sudden, you can just talk. Nobody was paying attention and you became a linguistic genius. You are getting to be a big girl, darlin'."

"Did you see the picture?" Maura asked.

"What picture?"

"Of the beautiful lady. My mommy has it." Maura took the cup away and came back with it full of sand. "This is ice cream."

"Mmm-mmm, don't I wish," Effie said, pretending to eat the sand. Strange how kids just went along in their own sweet way, the world happening to them second after second. "That is some sandbar—first scrambled eggs, then ice cream."

"Hold out your hand, Effie," Maura said with authority. She placed a wad of green moss in Effie's palm. "This is liberty."

"Liberty? Liberty?" Effie examined the wet, spongy shreds. "That's really nice." The sun was going down, flooding the west with a transparent gold. The Paradisos abruptly turned a dark plum. She put the moss on a rock next to her chair, stood up, and took Maura by the hand, and they walked along the shore. Maura could only take short steps, and so Effie had to slow down. Maura waved a crow feather she had found. "This is my magic wand," she said.

"Darlin', I'm going to tell you a story," Effie said. "When I was in England, I saw the *queen*. She was going to a movie, and there was this gigantic crowd in the street, and bobbies—those are English policemen—and her husband, who is not a king, you call him a duke, and he followed her with his hands behind his back, and she got out of this fancy black car that had a flagpole on the roof. It was so wonderful."

"And the queen and the king woke up," Maura said. "And the princess woke up, and the whole castle woke up. Even the *flies* woke up. And then they had the wedding."

"That's right," Effie said. From a pipe rising out of a ridge of red rock near the embankment came the jetlike roar of the flames of a natural-gas outlet. To the north, lightning forked through a cavern of gray enclosing Paradiso Baldy. The sky here was so big that it could hold several kinds of weather and light at the same time. A year ago, it was just about this hour when she and Tom had gone out in the boat alone for the last time. The water and the sky were the same. He said, "For God's sake, what are you smiling about?" He was her heart's desire, and how many people ever got their heart's desire? It seemed like she had a lot to tell him today, but now she couldn't think of a thing. He had taken her to the Randolph Scott movie and then they swung side by side, and then he started swinging higher and higher, going away and coming back. "Don't do that," she called. He brushed past her and then away, past her and then away, and he flew up higher and higher and disappeared into the glowing sky.

Judy walked along the embankment. The wall of rock at the mouth of the canyon resembled a crumbling monument, its facade long since slipped off to reveal huge blocks casually piled on one another. Little waves licked the edge of the dam, eroding the earthwork. Miniature branching ravines cut into the soft soil.

She kept her eye on the side of the canyon, on the oval indentation: her concrete observation for today, as it had been exactly a year ago, when she had decided to pay attention to the world. The indentation deepened as she approached. Her breath quickened. I was right last year, she said to herself—it *is* a cave. It was set back under a stone outcropping that seemed to have been wrenched away, raked, twisted, and then jammed back into place, so that the colors of the rock, purple streaked with red and violet, swirled out of the dark, empty center. She followed a narrow path upward. From under the overhang came a cool exhalation. The shadows there were a vibrant mingling of gray, blue, and black. The floor was red earth, smooth and glossy, and littered with finely ground white cornmeal.

With the crow quill, Maura made circles in the mud. It smelled like rain. The water trembled with light. She heard her name being called. Her mother was standing on a high rock. Maura waved the feather at her, and at the lake, and the mountains, and the sky.

A NOTE ON THE TYPE

This book was set in a digitized version of Janson, a redrawing of type cast from matrices long thought to have been made by the Dutchman Anton Janson, who was a practicing type founder in Leipzig during the years 1668–87. However, it has been con-clusively demonstrated that these types are actually the work of Nicholas Kis (1650–1702), a Hungarian, who most probably learned his trade from the master Dutch type founder Dirk Voskens. The type is an excellent example of the influential and sturdy Dutch types that prevailed in England up to the time William Caslon developed his own incomparable designs from them.

Composed, printed and bound by
The Haddon Craftsmen, Inc., Scranton, Pennsylvania

Typography and binding design
by Dorothy Schmiderer